By Nalini Singh from Gollancz:

Praise for the novels of Nalini Singh

'Intense, vivid, and sexually charged'
Publishers Weekly (starred review)

'Singh is one of those rare storytellers who literally never disappoints'
Romantic Times

'Intense, astonishing and radiant'
Kirkus

'I devour Guild Hunter novels. I can't get enough of this epic world. Full of danger, intrigue, and heady seduction, the Guild Hunter series is perfect!'
Sylvia Day

'This is without a doubt one of my all-time favourite series, from the minute I pick up one of the books until the very last page I'm completely and utterly absorbed in the world and the characters and I never want the journey to end'
Feeling Fictional

'Graceful strength, wild beauty, predatory intelligence . . . These things are at the heart of every Nalini Singh Guild Hunter story'
Grave Tells

'Sexy, violent, amusing, and gritty storytelling'
All About Romance

'[A] heart-pounding, action-packed storyline of love and loss; death and destruction; family and friends; intrigue and suspense'
The Reading Cafe

'Nalini Singh continues to show her gift at compelling worlding-building and characterization' *Romance Junkies*

Archangel's
Lineage

NALINI SINGH

First published in Great Britain in 2024 by Gollancz
an imprint of The Orion Publishing Group Ltd
Carmelite House, 50 Victoria Embankment
London EC4Y 0DZ

An Hachette UK Company

1 3 5 7 9 10 8 6 4 2

A CIP catalogue record for this book is
available from the British Library.

ISBN (Mass Market Paperback) 978 1 399 62596 8
ISBN (eBook) 978 1 399 62597 5

Printed and bound in Great Britain by Clays Ltd, Elcograf S.p.A.

www.nalinisingh.com
www.gollancz.co.uk

1

Oh, you must not.

Your tears wound me, but there is no choice. I cannot go on. I have tried until I have no more breath in the shell of my body and no heart in the core of my self.

The river—

—is eternal. What falls will always rise. One civilization or another, what does it matter to me?

My love, you were never this heartless. You ever cared for your people. I saw you cradle newborn mortals in your arms and kiss their soft cheeks.

You see why I must do this, beloved. Do I not, I turn slowly into a monster cold and without sympathy for those who are smaller, weaker, my shell all that remains.

Ah, my heart. Come to me. We will lie inside my fire this day and the next and the next until eternity ends.

And in the heartbeats between lifetimes, I will look into your eyes and I will be whole.

2

Elena kicked out a booted foot to check the give in her opulent ball gown and grinned when the falls of fabric around her legs parted like they weren't there. "Montgomery strikes again," she said, then busied herself slipping her throwing knives into the decorative sheaths at her forearms.

At some point during her roughly two decades as Raphael's consort, she'd said to hell with it and decided to give herself a new trademark: arm sheaths. These days, no one blinked an eye at her preference for weapons as jewelry; it definitely took the edge off, not having to find places to secrete weapons.

Not that she didn't also always have hidden weapons.

Elena was never not going to have a concealed garrote or a dart that blew drug-laced needles somewhere on her person. The latter had been a joke birthday gift from her hunter friends, but she'd realized the real thing could pass as a decorative pendant in situations where other weapons might be seen as a sign of aggression.

Setting her personal style as including arm sheaths had ameliorated the latter threat. Who cared if the snooty old angels called it a "mortal affectation" with their condescending noses so far up in the air that it was a wonder they didn't unbalance and fall over backward. The idiots thought they were insulting her. Hah. Having a mortal heart, a mortal soul, was a gift she cherished in this world where so many frittered away entire centuries because they always had one more day.

What had taken her aback was when a cohort of "edgy" young courtiers began to copy her with jewel-encrusted monstrosities they dared call blades. Those insults of weapons couldn't fly a single foot in a straight line, much less actually hit a target, but per Illium, that's what she got for being a fashion "icon."

Their pretty Bluebell was going to get his feathers plucked one of these days.

The unbound near-white of her waist-length hair being brushed aside, a kiss pressed to the back of her neck that made a shiver ripple over her body as wings of white-gold opened in her peripheral vision.

Her stomach tumbled, as if this was the first time Raphael had ever touched her.

Leaning back into his warm and muscled form, his upper body yet bare, she groaned. "Does that mean you're agreeing to my idea of blowing off this deal and getting naked?"

Oceans ice-blue and windswept crashed into her mind, his laughter filling her world. "Alas, *hbeebti*, I must do my duty today. As must you." Another kiss, this one to the curve of her throat, as he placed one hand on her abdomen. "After it is done, however . . . I know a place where we can tangle wings far from the rest of the world."

Her thighs clenched, the need she had for him a potent addiction; knowing him, *growing* with him had made her fall ever deeper for the Archangel of New York.

Lifting her hand to slide it over the back of his neck without fully turning, she stroked the heat of his skin. "You have a deal and I'm holding you to it." Tired of the pageantry and politics, she needed what only he could give her.

"I like this dress," he murmured, their eyes meeting in the mirror.

His were twin blue flames, the color piercing and impossible in its violent purity, a punch to the heart every single time. The midnight of his hair was tumbled and damp from his quick shower, the planes of his face dangerously striking under skin kissed by the sun.

The Legion mark on his right temple—the shape a stylized dragon—flickered with light that was diamonds tumbling in the ocean. The renewed energy of the mark was a recent development. It had gone flat and lifeless after the Legion gave up their lives, and in time, like a tattoo held too long in the skin, had begun to fade.

It had hurt her to watch, and she knew it had hurt Raphael, too. They both honored the Legion for their sacrifice, but they also missed the otherworldly beings who'd emerged from the silent deep and become an integral part of New York.

The fade had, however, reversed itself over the past few months, until the two of them had begun to hope that the Legion would return. Or at the least, that the Legion still *existed* in some form in the cold embrace of the water from which they'd come.

"You look a goddess risen, Guild Hunter." Another kiss pressed to the curve of her neck.

Goose bumps over her skin, her nipples tight points. "You're the pretty one in this relationship," she teased, though pretty was definitely the wrong word for Raphael. His face, for all its beauty, held an innate hardness, a sense of the martial.

Her lover was a warrior before he was an archangel.

His lips curving, he plucked at the fabric of her gown. "What is this? It feels almost as good as your skin."

"I have no idea, but I love it." Unlike the current rage in the Refuge, the gown was no frou-frou cloth marshmallow. Instead, it flowed over her in a slide of liquid silver-blue, sinuous and cool. The shoulders were narrow, the neckline plunging before it cut away to reveal her abdomen—but that entire top part was also so securely fitted that she was in no danger of revealing more than she wanted to reveal.

From the waist, it fell in what Montgomery told her was an A-line.

Elena hadn't been sure about that—the sketch he'd shown her had looked far too prom gown—but as usual, the butler and his favorite tailor had been right. Constructed of seven separate panels, the skirt was higher in the front, the cut a sharp diagonal from the middle of her left thigh down to the calf of her right leg.

The design made movement easier—she could literally high-kick in this thing if required. They'd even worked with her penchant for wearing boots by giving her ones that matched the dress . . . while building hidden blade sheaths in both, then adding decorative touches in a deeper silver. Not only did the boots look badass striding out of the shorter front part of the dress, they were stable, wouldn't throw her off in a fight.

Her arm sheaths were a glittering black against the dark gold of skin that was a testament to the Moroccan part of her heritage. Not as good as her usual sheaths, but they worked fine. On her upper arm sat the jeweled dagger that Raphael had given her—jeweled but more than functional if she needed to stab a snobby angel in the eye, as she so often dreamed of doing at these events.

But tonight, the dagger wasn't the showpiece. Because from her neck down to her cleavage lived a black "tattoo" that Aodhan had painted onto her skin before she left New

York. Again, it was a thing in vogue with angelkind and she had to admit it was more her style than the rest of current angelic fashion—especially since Aodhan had designed her ink to echo the mark on Raphael's temple.

Hers was more elongated, with lines that seemed to hint at a powerful creature in flight, but that the two markings were a pair was indisputable.

"It'll last a month," Aodhan had told her after the work was complete, the dragon's neck curving around her nape so that the creature lay with its head on her collarbone.

It was the closest she'd ever been to the angel whose entire body seemed to be composed of light, his breath brushing her skin as he leaned in to work. She'd wondered if it would feel odd even though they were friends. Then he'd started the piece and she'd realized that at that instant, she was nothing but a canvas to Aodhan.

"Canvases don't talk back," he'd muttered when she'd dared have an opinion, but his lips had quirked up.

Now, Raphael ran one finger down the lines of the tattoo, coming to a stop at the curve of her breast where it was exposed by the dress. "I do so enjoy how this looks when you are unclothed and wrapped around me."

His wings rose above his shoulders, hers pressed to his body so only the black arches were visible, and it was them in the mirror. Two people whose loyalty was set in stone, and whose love was a slumbering inferno, hot and languid, until they wanted it to burn.

She and her archangel, they'd weathered a psychotic archangel, then a megalomaniacal one, a Cascade of fucking Death, and oh, just for fun, a vampiric uprising in the aftermath of a war that had devastated the world.

All of it side by side.

Raphael traced the line of the tattoo in the opposite direction, then slid his finger back down with luxurious intent, his eyes heavy-lidded as he caressed her.

"I'll stab you if you don't stop that." She glared. "I have

to put on my stupid be-polite-to-the-grand-poobahs face. Stop distracting me with thoughts of nakedness if you're not going to pay up."

His grin was wicked and young and one very few people ever saw. "I'll remind you that I am one of the grand poobahs."

Shifting her wing out of the way, she elbowed him in that rock-hard stomach, then pressed in with a blade without breaking the skin. "Right now, Mr. Grand Poobah Raphael, you're barely dressed. We'll be late if you don't get a move on—and I *will* absolutely stab you if we have to stay later to make up the time."

His grin didn't alter as he drew back, his mood making her entire body tighten. The urge to jump onto him, lock her legs around that delicious body, and put his hand properly on her breast while she kissed the life out of him made her mouth water and her pulse race.

"So bloodthirsty." Hot blue, his eyes made her a promise dark and decadent even as he kept his words light. "Truly, a woman I adore."

She watched him move to the wardrobe where the staff who ran their Refuge stronghold had hung up the formal leathers he planned to wear tonight. He'd already put on the black pants, now pulled on the sleeveless black top that showcased his toned biceps and those forearms that made her want to bite him.

Down, Elena, she told herself. *Save that for when you have lots of time.*

Collarless, his fitted top sealed to the left side with a black zip.

Clean, powerful, sexy enough to make her swallow her tongue.

Raphael's boots were the same shade, and, as she watched, he strapped on the pair of bracers she'd given him as a gift. Made of what appeared to be a single piece of black iron each, with intricate detailing carved into the metal, the bracers covered his wrists and forearms and were designed to ward off sword blows in battle.

Turning away before she attacked him in pure lust, she decided to pull her hair back into a high ponytail.

It revealed the handcrafted amber studs in her ears—one a miniature crossbow, the other the bolt. Created for her alone, and a quiet but clear sign that she was very much entangled with the Archangel of New York.

Having already done her makeup, she was ready when Raphael slid a sword into the sheath on his back. With her dress being backless, she hadn't needed anything to accommodate her wings, but his top had wing slits that he'd sealed using his power. The sheath was built into the top, his sword a ceremonial item given to him by his Seven approximately fifty years earlier for his one thousandth five hundredth birthday.

It bore a carved hilt embedded with seven polished black diamonds set in a vertical row to represent the seven men who called Raphael their liege and who would lay down their lives for him without hesitation.

"Consort." Hair brushed off his face in crisp lines, and expression set in what she called his "Archangel" look, he held out his hand.

"Consort." Grinning, she slid her hand into his.

And had to admit she felt beautiful and strong as she strode out of their suite. That their hand-holding would cause certain angels to have the vapors just made it better.

Why are you smiling that way, Elena-mine? His voice was a sword blade slicing through salt-laced water in her mind.

When she told him, he shot her a laughing look. Then lifted her hand to his mouth and kissed the back. Her heart, it stuttered. Always did. Always would. Because this deadly man she'd once feared and whose violent power had now become a familiar caress was it for her.

However long their eternity lasted, they'd walk through it hand in hand.

The ground rumbled as they continued on down the hallway of the stronghold Raphael kept in the Refuge. Built of dark gray stone, it was too solid to move in a minor tremor, but the vibration was obvious.

His smile faded. "That's the third one today."

"How many does that make over the three days since we've been here? Ten?"

"Around that." Raphael's hair glinted in the light of the old-fashioned gas lamps that bracketed the front door, an echo of a past time left in place for its elaborate metal beauty.

"We've always had the odd rumble or earth shake in the Refuge," he added, "but nothing this sustained as far as I know—but I can't say for certain. I'm young in comparison to many others. I'm sure we'll find out tonight."

Because tonight, they were to mingle with the rest of the Cadre, the first time since the war that all nine archangels were to be present in one place. The reason for the gathering was a meeting of the Cadre, but of course, immortals couldn't keep it simple.

No, there had to be a grand ball to "usher in the new post-war age."

Elena couldn't remember exactly who'd said that, but it had been one of the grande dames of the angelic world—and by "dames" she meant interfering old busybodies of any gender.

As if they hadn't been living in the post-war world for over ten years at this point. Though, she supposed begrudgingly, she could see the rationale behind it—this was the first year of *actual* calm. Every single one of the vampiric uprisings had been dealt with, no one had found any remnants of Lijuan's reborn or Charisemnon's poison for over twelve months, and repairs—or reconstruction—had been completed on the last of the major structures that had been damaged or destroyed.

It felt like they could breathe at last.

Yeah, she could see why people wanted to throw a blow-off-the-roof party. So this might not be too bad once they got past the stuffy polite conversation part; she wouldn't mind dancing the night away with Raphael and their friends. Because pretty much the entire adult population of the Refuge would be there tonight.

Of Raphael's senior people, Galen and Naasir, as well as Trace, would be joining them for the initial entrance. Archangels couldn't just show up to this kind of thing; they had to bring an entourage. It just so happened that Raphael's entourage was ruthless and lethal and as amused by the pomp as him.

Galen's mate, Jessamy, would separate from them prior to the official entrance. Elena had only yesterday learned that as the angelic Librarian and Historian, Jessamy belonged to no court—and to all of them. Of course everyone knew she was closest to Raphael, but to walk in with him would be a grave insult to the rest of the Cadre.

Junior angelic Librarian, Andromeda—Naasir's mate—would also peel away with Jessamy. Not for the same reason, however. It was because Andi technically belonged to a different court.

All five proved to be waiting in the courtyard of the stronghold. "Are we late?" Elena glanced at her wrist before remembering she wasn't wearing a watch. As of the past six months, something in the Refuge had changed, making the devices act wonky. Analog or digital, clocks were a bust.

The scientists were working on figuring out why, but in the interim, Elena'd had to learn to read a sundial—to the great amusement of young Sam, who'd mastered that skill when he was "only a baby!" Never had Elena thought she'd be getting sundial lessons from a grumpy scholar with a giant white mustache while angelic children fluttered around offering encouragement.

Jessamy, her chestnut-brown hair woven into a complicated crown, and her lovely eyes as kind as always, smiled. "No, we are early. It's been many years since the Refuge hosted a major social event and we're as excited as the children."

"Then let us go and horrify the elders." Raphael's pronouncement was met with raised fists from Galen, Trace, and Naasir, and outright laughter from Jessamy and Andromeda.

Elena grinned.

3

"Trace," Raphael added, "I commend you for the pink hair."

"Magenta. Not pink." The suave vampire flowed into a bow as slick as the black suit he'd paired with a shirt and tie a bare shade or two lighter. "I lost a bet to Illium." He sighed as he rose back up to his full height. "You'd think I'd have learned by now, but it was too tempting."

Andromeda, her freckles dancing across her nose and cheeks, and her own hair a halo of glossy brown curls streaked with bronze for the night, tilted her head toward Trace. "What did he have to do if he lost?"

"Dress in monochrome outfits for a week."

"That doesn't sound so bad." Elena gestured to the man with hair of true silver against skin of rich brown who stood with his hand on Andromeda's lower back. "I mean Naasir's rocking monochrome tonight."

Naasir's charcoal gray suit was the same shade as the

pattern on the brocade-style bronze fabric of Andromeda's gown. It could've been a disaster, that fabric, but Andi had chosen a sleek gown that made a statement bold and frankly stunning on her small and curvaceous form.

"Ah, I forgot to mention that I would've chosen the color palette," Trace clarified. "Violent purple was to be the first day, putrid yellow the next. I was looking forward to screaming neon green."

Andi's responding giggle was infectious and they were all laughing as they began to stroll in the direction of the huge open square in the center of the Refuge that had been created by doing away with the usual border walls. For to-night, it was neutral territory akin to places such as the Medica, the Library, and the School.

"The children couldn't stop talking about this after-noon's event," Jessamy told Elena as the two of them fell into step side by side, while Raphael chatted to Galen and Trace.

Naasir and Andi led the way.

In contrast to Andi's figure-hugging gown and Elena's liquid fall, tall and slender Jessamy wore a dress that was an airiness of dusty rose. Cinched at the waist with a golden rope, it was also gathered at the high neck and rippled around her ankles like living fog.

Her wings, those gorgeous wings of vivid magenta that flowed into blush and rich cream, couldn't take her to the air . . . yet. Because in the years since Raphael had used his Cascade-fueled ability to heal her, her malformed left wing had straightened out to the extent that it appeared near-identical to the right.

Only her closest family and friends knew the pain Jes-samy had suffered to reach this stage. The physiotherapy had been brutal enough to leave Galen white-lipped—and Raphael's weapons-master was nicknamed the Barbarian for a reason. But Jessamy was determined to reach the sky on the wing, and Galen was determined to support her every wish. Right now, even though she couldn't sustain true flight, she could maintain a controlled glide if she took off from a high point.

Her joy in being in the sky ... incandescent might be the right word.

"Thank you for coming by," the other woman added. "The children adore you."

"As if I'd miss the event of the year." Elena bumped her shoulder to Jessamy's, the two of them both on the tall end for women. "I'd have been insulted not to be invited to their party." It had been a joyous extravaganza of games and food and music. Now, as the adults partied, the older children would babysit the younger, with adults on rotation to keep an eye on them throughout the night.

The youths on the verge of adulthood, however, had been given dispensation to attend the first hour of the ball. "I can't imagine attending something like this when I was a teenager," she said to Jessamy as they stepped onto a stone bridge lit up by colorful hanging lanterns.

Further lanterns glowed in the trees and along the pathways that wove through the gardens of the Refuge, while large enclosed torches created both warmth and light this cold spring night. The pathways were filled with angels and senior vampires dressed with immortal grandeur.

The sumptuous beauty of it was undeniable.

More than one person shot a glance their way, but no one approached them. "Naasir, are you glaring at people?"

A silver-eyed look over his shoulder, his expression so austere you'd never know that beneath his skin lurked a playfulness feral and unique. "I'm just looking extremely serious."

Andi, her arm tucked into his, glanced back at them. "He's being his most grim-faced self." A whisper. "I am terrified."

Leaning down, Naasir nipped at the tip of her ear with sharp tiger-creature teeth. Andi yelped, then hit him on the chest with no force at all before leaning into him, her hand curled around his biceps. The two were ridiculously adorable, even if Naasir *still* refused to tell Elena his exact species. Oh, and everyone else thought it was just *hilarious* that she didn't know. Ha!

"Ellie! Ellie! Up here!" The hail came from one of the houses that lined the edge of the gorge, the voice small and bright. "Teacher Jessamy! You look pretty!"

When Elena glanced up to the second floor, she saw a boy with wings of brown tipped with black and hair that was all tumbled black curls beaming down at her from an open window. His small body was leaning so far out of it that only his older cousin's grip on his jerkin kept him from falling.

Elena waved back as Jessamy did the same by her side. "Behave tonight and I'll take you flying tomorrow!" Sam remained one of her most favorite people in the Refuge.

Even after all this time, her brain had trouble processing the slow rate of angelic growth, and she was still sometimes surprised that Sam remained such a small boy, but one thing she knew: she'd love him all her life. Kid just had that kind of heart and sweetness.

"Promise?" Sam yelled out.

"Promise!" She blew him a kiss, then waved at his cousin. "And you as well, Tarielle!"

The gangly girl, who was about fifteen in human terms, beamed. "I can't wait!"

"Rafa! Rafa!" Sam waved at Raphael, a tiny metronome on speed. "I'm gonna go flying with Ellie tomorrow! Tari's gonna fly, too!"

Raphael's childhood nickname had had a resurgence among the children after one of them heard an older adult mention it. And since her archangel had always had a soft spot for children, they had free reign to address him thus.

"Perhaps I will join you. If, of course, I'm invited," he said to the children.

Who all but exploded with excitement.

Leaving their small friends, they'd just turned the corner onto another gentle bridge when the ground *shook*.

No tremor this, no mere tremble. The quake was a vicious jerk that lifted up the path and sent Elena crashing down hard on one knee. Pain shot through her. Ignoring it, she grabbed Jessamy before the other woman could be thrown off the path and into the pond beside it. Ahead of them, Naasir did one of those quicksilver movements Elena couldn't follow with the naked eye and lifted both himself and Andi off the ground as it bucked under them. He landed on feet as sure as a cat's.

Sam! Elena yelled at Raphael, even though she couldn't see him. *He was hanging out the window. And Tari was holding on to him!*

I caught both, Raphael assured her, and she knew he was talking about his archangelic power, not his arms. That power was no longer fueled by the Cascade, but it was *power* nonetheless.

I'm holding them until the movement stops. Can you get airborne?

No, I can't even get to my feet.

The shaking didn't stop for what felt like an hour. A house collapsed next to them, dust exploding outward in a gray burst that lined her tongue with grit; Elena hoped to hell the angels inside had managed to dive out into the gorge.

When she looked up, she saw flights of angels in the sky, many with children in their arms. Good. Down here, the air was turning to dust-choked mist, and the fucking water in the pond was *boiling*. "Jess?"

"I see it, Ellie." Jessamy gripped Elena's thigh with her

hand, while Elena continued to keep a death grip on her arm. "I can feel the heat. It's not just motion. It's actual heat."

"Fuck." Elena transmitted the information to Raphael, who was now in the air, from which high vantage point he could help those who needed it. Galen was with him, an indication of trust in Elena that he wouldn't have shown in the first years after she'd become Raphael's consort— because Jessamy was Galen's heart.

"Trace!" she called out, unable to spot the final member of their group.

"Behind you!" the vampire called back. "I'm on the path off the bridge! If this doesn't stop soon, start crawling back toward me!"

Then it did stop. With a massive jerk and resounding crack that made Elena's eyes widen. Hauling Jessamy to her, she rose into the air with a tearing of muscle, just as the bridge collapsed into the boiling water.

Elena wasn't strong enough to carry another angel, but it helped that her friend was so thin and light.

She still barely made it to the area near Trace.

He caught Jessamy as Elena fell more than landed. Once upright, the three of them looked at the steaming water hot enough to scald even from a distance. Just because immortals could heal from what would be a killing injury for a mortal didn't mean that it didn't hurt.

The cauldron would've melted off Jessamy's wings had she fallen into it.

A single second of shock was all they allowed themselves before they began to move. Jessamy broke into a run to take charge of Sam and Tarielle and any other children in the vicinity, while Trace entered a collapsed building to see if anyone was trapped inside.

Elena did the same.

Her left wing dragged and she knew she'd torn a tendon or ligament. Nothing to complain about in the aftermath of a catastrophic quake. She got on with the job.

* * *

It wasn't until an hour later that they had a true idea of the overall damage. Three angels were dead, their bodies crushed so badly even their healing abilities couldn't repair the damage. Five vampires had suffered a similar fate. Elena hadn't known that severe crush injuries could kill both, and wished she didn't know now. Because the crushing had to be *severe*.

People smeared into paste.

Others an inch away from that had survived—but their recovery would be horrific. Thankfully, no children numbered among the dead or badly wounded. The little ones had been saved by the curiosity and excitement that had seen them near windows or on balconies. Easy places from which to take flight or be rescued.

The fatal crush injuries weren't the only ones. Broken bones, less severe compression damage, collapsed wings, the list was long—and included several residents who'd been burned by eruptions of heated natural gas or boiling water.

"What about the mortal villages closest to the Refuge?" she asked when she stopped for a breath. "Has anyone checked on them?"

Raphael, his face streaked with dirt from assisting the trapped—including rescuing a vampire who'd ended up gripping a rock partially down the gorge after he was thrown off the edge by the quake—nodded. "I sent a wing."

Because she, his consort, had once been mortal and still had a mortal heart; where other archangels might disregard mortal lives as not worth saving, Raphael wouldn't.

"No damage," he told her. "No sign of a quake at all. It appears to have been localized to the Refuge."

Shit. "That can't be good."

Raphael's expression mirrored her worry. Because the last time the world had started blowing up, they'd ended up in a devastating Cascade. One from which they had only now recovered.

The world was too fragile to take another pounding. They needed this to be a natural event, not one linked to the power that ran through the veins of the archangels—a power so brutal that it could shatter the earth into a million pieces.

4

Interlude
Fall of an Archangel

Laric was going to be in trouble.

Again.

It wasn't as if he tried to be late. It just happened. Like today, he'd been distracted by the honey cakes his mother had made and now he was going to be late to his lessons at the Medica. But oh, those honey cakes had been pure decadence on the tongue.

Smiling, he angled left and caught a glint in the sky.

He assumed it was another angel, probably one of the warriors wearing gauntlets or other armor . . . until he got closer. The glint had been no armor, but a bolt of angelic power.

Laric rolled his eyes. "Typical."

Every time one of the recent crop of newly strong angels got into a temper, they started to throw around bolts. It was aggravating; if he wasn't a trainee healer who'd taken certain oaths, he'd be tempted to drop a little "calm-balm" into their mead. Put the whole annoying lot of muscle-bound bumbles to sleep.

Another bolt, this one thunderous enough that his bones vibrated even though he was still some distance out from them.

His flesh chilled.

Squinting, he looked more carefully. And gulped. Those weren't two angels acting tough. No, what he was looking at was a serious battle between two *archangels*.

He couldn't see their faces from this distance.

White wings, long black hair, a woman.

Wings of pale gold, dark hair, a man.

Caliane and Nadiel.

Battling with a lethal ferocity that was no lovers' quarrel.

Panic stabbing into him, he dropped. He didn't care how late it made him—he did not want to be in the sky while two archangels fought.

He was so intent on getting to the ground that he didn't see the fatal strike, just felt the flames sear his feathers, melt his skin as the sky turned molten—a cataclysmic burn born of the inferno of an archangel's violent death.

Laric screamed and fell.

5

The Cadre met in the empty square at dawn the next morning, after they'd done all they could to assist the injured and stabilize damaged areas. Aside from the Cadre, the only other people in the square were Elena, Hannah, and Lady Sharine.

Consorts didn't usually attend meetings of the Cadre, but with all three of them in the Refuge, it had seemed the natural choice. That Lady Sharine wasn't officially Titus's consort wasn't something anyone cared about, either; she'd earned her voice at this meeting on her own.

Unexpectedly, however, the quake wasn't the top item on the agenda.

"Where is Qin?" Caliane hadn't bothered to change out of the sophisticated white leathers she'd chosen to wear for the ball, and they were now blood-smeared and dusty, the knees black from where she'd knelt in the dirt to lift literal houses off people. The crisp white of her feathers hadn't fared any better.

"I noticed he wasn't here yesterday morning." Zanaya scowled, the violet-tinged silver of her hair pulled severely off her face and her body clad in a simple linen tunic that ended midthigh.

White plaster dust coated her thighs and streaked her shoulders, dulling the vibrant ebony of her skin. "I wasn't surprised in the least. We all know how much our Qin loves parties."

Elena had come to appreciate the dry humor of the Queen of the Nile, but snark aside, Zanaya wasn't wrong. Elena had spotted Qin's absence, even joked about it with Raphael. "Ten bucks says he arrives at exactly eleven a.m. on the dot tomorrow." The Ancient might've stuck around after being forced awake by the Cascade, but a man who less wanted to be present in the world, Elena couldn't imagine.

"He insults us!" Aegaeon thumped a fisted mallet of a hand on the dark brown leather of his pants, his upper half bare but for a top of metallic mesh that overlay the silver swirl on his chest.

The latter was no temporary tattoo or artwork but as much a part of him as Raphael's Legion mark was his.

"This is a declaration of war!"

"Calm down, Aggie," Zanaya muttered, adding fuel to the fire as only she could.

Elena battled the urge to snort out a laugh; she knew the Queen of the Nile wasn't helping matters, but she loved how much Zanaya couldn't stand Illium's asswipe of a sperm donor and how she made zero effort to hide it.

"I agree with Zanaya." Caliane rubbed at her forehead as Aegaeon's face turned a mottled red and white, his wings starting to glow. "Qin was likely just avoiding the social aspect of things and is still in the air, unaware of the disaster. Questions only arise if he is absent at eleven."

"This quake is the worst in my memory. Worse even than the shakes that turned what was once a mere crack in the landscape into what is now the gorge." Alexander's words wrenched them back to the right topic. "Those shakes were concentrated along the line of the gorge and did not cause major damage to the Refuge."

"My memory aligns with yours," Caliane added, then turned to Sharine. "My friend? Do you remember a time I have forgotten?"

But Illium's mother shook her head, the pale champagne gold of her eyes a delicate brilliance in the dawnlight. "I have no remembrance of such a shake—or of art I created to memorialize those lost in the tragedy. I don't believe we have ever suffered this type of a loss in the Refuge, but we should consult with our Historian."

"Jessamy was able to check on that an hour ago," Raphael said, his once-pristine black leathers now torn and scratched and his hair full of grit and tiny flecks of debris. "The Library and the Archives are mostly standing."

"And what does she say?" Titus boomed in what Elena knew was his inside voice.

"No written record of a quake of this strength in the Refuge. She's also been keeping track of the recent swarm of minor shakes and says that, so far, she's found no earlier reports of similar swarms, either. She did state that she and Andromeda haven't searched everything."

"But she is diligent in her duties and would've already been aware of an event so significant if it was part of our known history," Elijah said, to a round of nods.

"The problem," Suyin murmured, as quiet as Titus was loud, "is that it doesn't appear to be over." She rubbed at her face, grazing the small beauty mark at the corner of her left eye. "We cannot say that it was a buildup of pressure that has now been released."

"Suyin's right." Elijah's golden hair was sweat-damp, dirt streaking the pale brown of his tunic. "The waters that began to boil during the destruction show no signs of cooling, and the toxic heated gasses continue to pump out of the earth."

"My mother could've given us answers did she not Sleep," Alexander said, his voice gentle in a way Elena had never before heard it. "She was an expert scholar in matters to do with the earth."

"Yes." Caliane's smile was soft, a thing of memory and time. "Gzrel was brilliant in her field."

"Do we have a current expert?" Zanaya brushed her wing over Alexander's as she spoke, a silent caress of comfort between lovers and consorts.

There was some discussion before two names were put forward—one a senior vampiric scholar based in Japan, the other an angelic researcher in Elijah's territory. No mortals could be considered. Not for the Refuge, the most secret— and sacred—heart of angelic territory, the place that cradled their children and hid their vulnerable bodies and hearts from the world.

It was also the place that protected every single mortal in the world by never putting temptation in their path. Because if a mortal killed an angelic child? It would be game over for every single mortal in the world, all rational thought wiped out in the face of blinding angelic fury.

Innocent or guilty, it *would not matter.*

Raphael's ability to see mortals as more than disposable fireflies wouldn't matter.

Not in the face of the keening grief of the child's parents.

Not when angelic births were so rare that centuries could pass between each.

Her archangel would do what he could, and he had friends who'd stand with him . . . but over time, archangels fell in battle or went into Sleep, new archangels rose or ascended . . . and immortals had long memories.

Eventually, the extremists among angelkind—the ones who saw humans as cattle to be farmed—would win. A single match to light the kindling laid of arrogance and eons of unchecked power.

Humanity would never again be permitted a voice.

A shiver rippled up Elena's spine.

No, the Refuge *could not* be permitted to fall.

By the time the Cadre had worked out the next steps, Elena was exhausted, but she didn't even think of sleep. Having, after the first emergency response, taken a couple of minutes to change into clothing more suitable for the work to be done, she got stuck back in.

Raphael did the same, the two of them touching base when they could. In general there were no more major discoveries, just the backbreaking labor of clearing debris and—for those skilled at it—undertaking emergency repairs or putting up barriers against the water that continued to boil at lethal temperatures.

As Elena was no builder, she helped with cleanup, and by hauling material for anyone who needed it. Her injured wing meant she was grounded, but she hadn't bothered to see a healer. She'd torn that same tendon multiple times when she was first learning to fly and knew the only remedy was time—and the healers were dealing with injuries of infinitely worse magnitudes.

She was grabbing food for those healers when she saw Suyin rise up out of the gorge, a creature beautiful and inhuman with her flowing white hair, her face without flaw but for the single beauty mark below the far edge of her left eye that was no flaw at all, her wings as white as snow but for the bronze primaries.

Across her arms lay the limp body of an angel whose back was broken, her wings sheared off and her pretty yellow gown smeared with blood and dirt. But her head was still attached to her neck.

Then Suyin met Elena's eyes, silent tears streaking her cheeks.

The angel hadn't made it. Either her spinal cord had been severed at the neck despite the appearance of connection . . . or she'd been crushed until even her angelic cells couldn't keep up.

Elena swallowed the thickness in her throat, and made herself continue with her task, even as Suyin continued with hers.

Time rolled on.

An hour. Two.

Still no sign of Qin.

The clock ticked over to eleven a.m.

Raphael had always had sympathy for Qin. He understood what it was to love until the idea of being without the woman who was his heart tore him to pieces. That Qin loved an angel who couldn't stay in the world because her terrible gift drove her to madness was a hell he wouldn't wish on anyone.

But the other man was still an *archangel*. That level of power came with a burden of responsibility. And while Raphael disliked Aegaeon for many reasons, the other man was right: not turning up to this prearranged meeting of the Cadre *was* a declaration of war.

That, however, wasn't the worst of it.

"After our earlier discussion," Titus said, his expression murderous, "I made contact with my spymaster. Ozias has been in Qin's territory this past week."

No one blinked at that. They all spied on each other.

"She was in the midst of preparing a missive for me. Qin hasn't been sighted for a week, his absence pointed enough that she is certain of the intelligence."

Curses turned the air blue.

Even Suyin, quiet by nature, muttered under her breath, a tic in the fine line of her jaw.

Zanaya's next words were far louder, her rounded cheekbones smudged by a layer of grime; the Queen of the Nile had helped Suyin rescue multiple people from collapsed homes on the inner surface of the gorge.

Beneath the grime, however, her skin was aglow with anger. "He has gone into Sleep, leaving us with only eight archangels in a world that has only *just* recovered from a calamitous war followed by a vampiric uprising?"

Aegaeon threw back his head in a roar that shook what little glass remained in the windows of the houses closest to the square.

Elijah was calmer, but his shoulders bunched hard with muscle as he shoved a hand through the dust-coated golden strands of his hair. "Have you spoken to his second?" A question directed at Titus.

"No. I only managed to speak with Ozias shortly before this meeting. But I think Zanaya has it right—the bastard has gone into Sleep."

"Agreed." Caliane's cold, clear voice. "So, now we are eight."

Raphael clenched his jaw, fighting the urge to yell into the void.

Ten was the optimum number of archangels to have in the world—it allowed enough space between territories that their overlapping powers didn't breed aggression, while also having the right number of apex predators to control the vampires.

The post-war uprising had led to a carpet of blood.

His consort still dreamed about it at times, the nightmares streamers of red across her vision.

Eight archangels . . .

In this time?

Fuck.

He forced his fist to unclench. Quite aside from the logistics, it also meant that every single archangel in this square was now locked in time. They *could not* Sleep no matter what. Neither could they go into *anshara* to recover from even injuries so horrific no one would wish for them to suffer the agony. They had to stay conscious and available.

No room for exhaustion. No time to breathe at last.

"What are the chances we'll get a replacement soon?" Suyin asked even as the thought passed through Raphael's mind. "It hasn't been so very long after the end of the Cascade. We could yet be in a period of flux."

"There's no way to know." Caliane shook her head. "Alexander and I have seen that through the ages. At one time, we ruled with seven for two hundred years, and, in the end, had to compress the world and herd the populations into tighter areas. The only other option would've been a mass slaughter of vampires to ensure no bloodlust."

Which would, Raphael realized, have led to a forced Sleep for a large percentage of angels. Because angels needed vampires, a secret symbiotic relationship that had been born in the aftermath of another war so far back in time that it had been erased from their history. He only knew because his Legion had told him so.

Our people, infected with the deadly toxin . . . made the decision to Sleep eons in the hope the poison would fade. When they woke, it was to find a new people had been born from the ashes of the old, and the toxin had bonded permanently to the blood of the survivors.

Madness and death reigned, until the desperation of a single individual made angelkind understand the fragile new people were their salvation, a gift from their healed world.

Angels were only sane because they could purge the toxin into mortals—thus creating vampires. Remove one element or make it a limited resource and the entire system would collapse. In murdering vampires, angelkind would murder itself—for what mortal would wish to become a vampire once they realized the promise of near-immortal life was a false one that could be wiped out in a single angelic rampage?

Yes, angelkind could force the conversions, but as a whole, they weren't an evil people. Corrupt with power at times, and arrogant far too often, but they loved and protected children immortal and mortal, and—but for the odd extremist—they did not seek to crush mortal innovations, did not stamp out their glories.

Each Making done without consent would be a bead of poison dropped into the blood of all angelkind, until their entire civilization rotted under the weight of it.

6

"Caliane's right." Alexander pinched the top of his nose between thumb and forefinger, squeezing his eyes shut for a second before opening them to reveal irises of the same piercing silver as Naasir's. "There's no guarantee we'll get a replacement." The pragmatic grit of a man who had been a general long before he'd ever become an archangel.

"As for the numbers," he continued, "seven is far beyond brutal. Long-term, it can be terminal. Eight . . . eight can be done. It'll wear us to the bone, but it can be done even with a battered and bruised world." The Archangel of Persia looked around at the rest of them. "We must be as of one mind on this. We *cannot Sleep*. No matter what the wound, or how tired we get."

Each and every archangel in the circle agreed without hesitation.

That was the thing about the Cadre that many didn't understand. Raphael's kind could be capricious and cruel, and often started petty fights with one another—but when it came to the reason for their existence, they did their job. Checked-out archangels like Qin—and power-crazed megalomaniacs like Lijuan—were outliers when placed against the eternity of angelic history.

"At least two of us need to go to Qin's territory to confirm the situation." Alexander placed both hands on his hips. "Then we need to carve up the territories again." For a man who loved land, he didn't seem the least bit enthusiastic about having more to watch over.

Because they were *done*. All of them.

The war might've ended some eleven years ago, but it had left them with a destroyed world. Not to mention sporadic clusters of reborn that crawled out of the woodwork without warning. Lijuan had scattered droplets of her venom like confetti across the various territories, one last bitter laugh at their expense.

The entire reason the Refuge ball had come together with seamless ease—and why many people had been talking about further parties—was that everyone *just wanted a fucking break*. Elena had spoken those words not long ago when they'd been standing on their Tower, looking out over their city.

Manhattan sparkled again, but it carried a scar. A dead patch scorched by Raphael's angelfire where nothing would grow and no life thrived. He'd been forced to wound his own city to protect it against the infestation of Lijuan's diseased insects, harbingers of a plague of putrefaction and death.

The land itself was no longer poisonous, but mortals, angels, and vampires all avoided it, as did the animals. Raphael had once stood on the edge of the scorch zone and seen a ground spider reverse its course just as it was about to put one of its eight feet on the devouring blackness.

Their city was far from the only one that carried such scars. Not all were visible, either, many lingering as murky shadows in minds and souls in damage that would echo down through the generations.

How's the meeting going?

His consort's voice was a shining blade in his mind, the clarity of it an indication of her growing strength. *We are in agreement that Qin has gone into Sleep.*

Elena cursed.

Exactly so, Elena-mine. How goes the cleanup?

Steady, she said. *Reason I interrupted is that Galen and several of the other commanders from around the various strongholds want to move the vulnerable to what seems the most stable part of the Refuge. It's in Suyin's territory.*

Wait, Raphael said, and though he was certain of Suyin's answer, he interrupted the discussion of the Cadre with the request.

The Archangel of China agreed at once. "Of course. Our vulnerable come first. We must also consider whether we want people in the clifftop homes at all."

"I would say the same for the aeries on the inside of the gorge walls." Zanaya rubbed at her face. "The intensity of the damage there makes me believe the gorge may exist because it lies directly above an area where the foundations of the world crash against each other."

"A fault line?" Titus said, startling Raphael with his knowledge of the modern term. "Yes, perhaps you are right."

As Elijah weighed in on that point, Raphael passed on Suyin's acquiescence to Elena.

Thanks, Archangel. A kiss sent to him through their minds. *Also, FYI—people are muttering that the Ancestors are waking—they're saying that's the reason for the shakes. I love that even angels have their bogeymen.*

Let us hope they remain imagined beings, Raphael said in response. Because the so-called Ancestors said to Sleep below the Refuge were reportedly from the dawn of angel-kind. Beings so old that even the oldest of the angels—their very Ancients—had not even an inkling of who or *what* they might be.

As Elena's presence slipped from his mind with the fluid ease of a consort against whom he had no walls and never would, Raphael considered the discussion at hand—which had moved on to who was best placed to confirm Qin's dereliction of his duties.

Aegaeon was right that it must be at least two. Not a rule, but a good tradition, one that was intended to safeguard against any jealousies or accusations of lying when it came to confirmation of the details in this type of a situation.

That the entire Cadre couldn't go wasn't about the damage to the Refuge—there was nothing they could do here now that others couldn't handle as well. It was about a continuous archangelic presence in the world. A fact even more important now that they knew Qin had been absent from his lands for at least a week—the vampires there would've noticed.

Soon, so would vampires outside Qin's territory.

The Cadre couldn't afford to appear distracted.

"I can go," Raphael said. "My territory is stable for the moment." More than that, Dmitri, Aodhan, Illium, Jason, and Venom were all either in the area or nearby. As were Janvier, Ashwini, and Vivek, the senior members of Elena's fledgling Guard.

Young as they were, the latter three weren't well-known to the Cadre, but together, they were a cunning and intelligent team, with a way of ferreting out information that sometimes surprised even Jason.

"I'll join you," Aegaeon muttered, his earlier anger now focused on the absent Archangel of the Pacific Isles. "So I can curse Qin's name and insult his forebears where he most likely Sleeps."

Decision made, Raphael took a bare quarter of an hour to shower and dress in leathers more suitable for a long

flight. His consort met him on the very edge of the gorge—
where a squadron of scholars with furrowed brows and
weary eyes were taking readings using modern equipment;
for now, the inner aeries would stay vacant as Zanaya had
suggested, the risk too high.

"Fly safe, Archangel." Elena, her eyelashes flecked with
dust and her leathers gone a muddy shade from the same,
slid her hand around to his nape. "And don't kill Aegaeon."

"I can't," Raphael said, spreading out his wings in a
show of white gold that glittered in the mountain sunshine.
"Unfortunately, we need all eight of us." He made a face.
"At least we do not fly together. He didn't make that suggestion and neither did I. We simply agreed to leave at this
time. If we see each other during the journey, no doubt
we'll pretend we didn't and continue on."

He kissed her and it was fire in her blood and an eternity
of need and passion and love.

"*Knhebek, hbeebti*," he said when their lips parted, her
warrior archangel with eyes as blue as crushed sapphires
and determination stamped onto his bones.

Stepping back, a sudden devil-may-care grin on his
face . . . he dropped backward off the cliff into the gorge.
Sleep soon, Guild Hunter. You are tired. His voice was the
sea crashing into her mind, a familiar wildness, before he
turned and began to rise high into the sky in readiness for
his long flight.

Elena didn't like the thinner air on the edge of the sky,
but Raphael's lungs weren't like hers. She might be immortal, but she was no archangel. *I will*, she promised, but it
was a promise she was destined to break because ten minutes after Raphael vanished over the horizon, a breathless
angelic youth landed next to her with a message.

The fair-haired boy with red cheeks was around sixteen
in human terms, which made him old enough to have been
permitted to help in the aftermath of the quake. "Consort."
His chest heaved as he gulped in air, but the boy somehow

managed to keep his wings from drooping. "There is a message from your home. The sire's second has marked it as urgent."

Face chilling, Elena took the folded piece of paper he held out. The message must've come through the network used *only* for the Refuge. It had taken Elena time to work out that the Refuge network was a "ghost" system that lay below the interconnected one used by the vast majority of people around the world.

Any wires or other devices were buried underground or placed in locations angelkind alone could reach. The system was also constantly monitored by a small and dedicated team to ensure any accidental incursions were nudged away or otherwise dealt with in ways that roused no suspicions.

"Incursions are rare," Illium had told her when he'd explained the system he'd helped put in place when the technology first became viable, and which he still helped upgrade as needed. "The technical stuff will bore you, but think of our network as a shadow so deep and dark that it becomes invisible."

There was talk of upgrading the system to a satellite-based one, but obviously people could *see* satellites, so it'd need to be attached to some other more obvious purpose. And none of that mattered as Elena undid the seal that told her the message had been taken by their senior steward, Yana, then handed to the young courier.

It was short and to the point: *Elena, your father has suffered a serious heart attack. He's in critical condition in the ICU. Your stepmother has requested you return home. The jet will be ready for you as soon as you can make it to the airfield.*

Elena's mind buzzed with silence, an echoing void that gave her the distance to make rapid-fire decisions. "Thank you," she said to the boy who'd brought the message. "No return message yet." She'd send it directly herself.

The boy nodded and stepped back to take off. Even so young, vertical flight was effortless for him; it was a wonder she'd never take for granted. But even as her panicked mind wanted to snag on the sight of an angel in flight, she was moving, her own throbbing wing thrust to the back of her awareness.

The first thing she did was find one of their senior people—it happened to be Naasir. His shaggy silver hair tied back, he was shirtless, his skin slick with sweat as he helped cart dangerous debris off to an area where it wouldn't be a threat to the residents of the Refuge.

When she told him what had happened, he said, "Go. I'll tell the others."

Numb, she looked around at the devastation. "There's so much to do here."

"He is your father, Ellie. I would do the same if it were Dmitri or Honor hurt." He tilted his chin at the sky. "We're awash in strong angels who came for the ball. The physical work will be done in a matter of days and you're puny anyway."

She knew from the way he cupped her face with one big hand on that last that he was attempting to lighten her guilt. It worked. Because he was right. In the overall scheme of things, she *was* puny. "Will you say goodbye to Sam and the other children? I won't have time." She knew the children adored Naasir—even if he did growl at them when he caught them doing mischief.

They saw and loved the primal creature inside him in a way many adults didn't.

"Yes," he promised before wrapping her in his arms and rubbing the side of his face against hers. "You are your father's cub. Go. He will want you by his side."

Her numbness threatened to crack, her eyes burning. Jerking away on a nod, she headed to their stronghold, which had survived unscathed for the most part. Normally, she'd fly to the airfield, but with her wing injured, she asked

Yana—small and fast and dazzlingly smart—to arrange other transport.

It ended up being a truck with an enclosed cab designed for angelic comfort, her driver a five-hundred-year-old vampire who'd grown up in the region in which the Refuge was based.

He drove like he was part mountain goat.

At any other time, she would've bantered with him about his lack of fear and insane reflexes, but this trip passed in silence.

He got her to the airfield in half the time it would've taken anyone else.

"Thank you," she managed.

Thick beard gleaming in the early evening light, he bowed from the waist. "It is my honor, Consort."

She was in her seat in the jet soon afterward when she realized she had a faint signal. Deciding to take advantage of it before they got in the air, she messaged Dmitri: *Any change in his condition?*

The response was so long in coming that her blood seized, her heart cold.

Dmitri's belated reply told her she'd been right to worry: *He stopped breathing during emergency surgery. They've got him back, but no one will know his full status until he comes out of the operating room.*

Her fingers clenched on her phone.

A crack of sound, the damage a faint spiderweb across the screen.

7

Elena didn't know how she made it through the flight.

Exhaustion alone should've put her under, but the throbbing pain in her shoulder paired with the nausea in her gut kept her up. She knew she shouldn't further stress Raphael, but he was the only one to whom she wanted to speak.

Picking up her phone with its fractured screen, she made the call. But the connection failed over and over again, until at last they were at points on their separate journeys where they both had reception.

She almost broke down at hearing his voice.

After managing to tell him what had happened, she said, "I just thought he'd go on forever." Her voice came out rough, her throat scraped raw. "I never thought about a time when he might be gone." Jeffrey had *always* been there—and some part of her wanted to believe he always would be. "We're still so broken—and now I might never get the chance to fix us."

"No, *hbeebti*, do not walk that road in your thoughts."

Raphael's voice brooked no argument. "You and your father are in a far different place than when we first met. A large part of that has to do with you. You have no reason to dance with regret."

She talked to him until the connection began to stutter. And as much as she wanted him with her, she didn't ask him to come to New York. Because he was an archangel and that meant a duty heavy and demanding. The reason he was on this journey was because another archangel had put his personal needs before that duty—she would never put Raphael in the position to make a choice between it and her.

Whichever decision he made, it would hurt him.

"Elena." A wrench in his voice as they got ready to say goodbye.

"You need to go, find out about Qin." She made her voice strong even if it rasped. "I know you'll be with me as soon as you can. Love you, Archangel."

The connection failed before he could respond. But it was all right. She knew she was loved—loved in a way she'd never experienced before she stepped onto a Tower roof with her stomach clenched against a fear bone-chilling . . . and walked into her destiny.

The susurration of wings, the kiss of a power that was the turbulent ocean in her mind, the way he laughed until those eyes of impossible blue glowed, it was home to her now.

Today, she clutched that feeling close, and tried to pretend she was falling asleep on Raphael's chest, his wings wrapped around her. But her mind couldn't stop going in circles, couldn't stop imagining a homecoming where she stepped off the plane to the news that Jeffrey was dead.

The hours passed with excruciating slowness amid mere snatches of sleep, and her eyes were gritty and dry by the time she walked into the hospital in the very early morning hours, the world outside pitch black. Crossed time zones on top of her lack of sleep after the disaster meant she'd been going for far too long—but adrenaline powered by fear continued to pump through her system.

She saw Gwendolyn first.

The other woman was just walking out of an ICU room, her face worn and her rich black hair pulled haphazardly off her face into a bun at her nape. But even now, with her shoulders bowed and the fine bones of her face stark against the cream of her skin, there remained an ineffable elegance to Gwendolyn Deveraux, a sense of grace that went beyond flesh and bone.

"Gwendolyn."

Glancing up, Gwendolyn stared for a minute before she jolted forward into Elena's arms. Jeffrey's second wife had never before made such intimate contact with Elena, but Elena wrapped her arms around Gwendolyn without hesitation, held her as she sobbed. Gwendolyn had always been slender, but today she felt fragile, a bird with bones delicate.

"Shh," Elena murmured as she rocked the other woman, her chest tight with tears she couldn't shed and her muscles locked into knots. "It's okay. I'm here now. We'll handle this."

8

Drawing back on a gulping sob several minutes later, Gwendolyn wiped at her tears with the tissues she'd stuffed into the pockets of her navy blue dress with a wide skirt and fitted bodice. It was belted in the middle with a fabric belt, the waist-length cardigan Gwendolyn wore over it a crisp white.

Elena didn't take anything from Gwendolyn's smart clothing except that this was her normal. As Elena's knives were hers. She had at least ten on her even though she knew that was overkill for a hospital in her own city. The comfort of the familiar to fight back the panic—Gwendolyn wore her clothing with the same too-precise attention to detail.

The true story was in her reddened eyes and how she'd lost her elegant composure to cling to Elena.

"I'm so sorry." The woman who was technically Elena's stepmother scrunched up the tissues into a ball in her hand. "I've been trying to hold it together for the girls, but you were never a child to me." Her pupils bloomed the instant the words were out, her face falling. "Oh, that's—"

"I understand." Elena squeezed her fisted hand. "We met as adults." Not only that, but at two decades Jeffrey's junior, Gwendolyn had always been too young for any other relationship between them.

"Same way I never saw you as a mother figure," Elena added, "you never saw me as a kid." There'd only ever been one maternal figure in Elena's life, and Marguerite was long dead and buried.

Gwendolyn hadn't once said or done anything to challenge that state of being; she'd even tried to help mend Elena and Jeffrey's fractured relationship, never knowing how deep their wounds, how thick the scars.

But he was still Elena's father.

A piece of a small family that had ended in a river of blood so slick under Elena's hands and feet, the screams of her sisters and of her mother a nightmare that haunted her to this day.

Drip.

Drip.

Drip.

Her chest compressed at the sound she'd forever associate with that night, and with her sisters' mutilated and defiled bodies. Blood dripping off a broken finger to fall onto the floor. Over and over again, on the night a monster had walked into their home, called there by Elena's hunter-born blood.

Pretty, pretty hunter. I've come to play with you.

When the monster had left, he'd taken all their happiness with them.

Belle and Ari dead. Marguerite so brutalized in the soul that, though she'd tried, she hadn't been able to go on.

Elena and Beth and Jeffery might've survived, but they'd never been the same again. Jeffrey heartbroken and Elena full of terror, Beth silent and scared and so small and confused. The only mercy was that Beth hadn't been there that day, hadn't slipped on the blood, hadn't run in terror, hadn't been one more body in the carnage.

Elena had hugged her tight, so tight, when Beth crawled into her bed in the hotel to which Jeffrey had taken them in the immediate aftermath. She'd just wanted to feel her sister's warmth, listen to her breathe, hear her heartbeat. "You're squishing me, Ellie," Beth would complain—but she never wriggled away.

Both of them hanging on to each other with grief-stricken desperation.

Elena's anger, that had come later. With Marguerite's choice to leave them—but they'd already been damaged inside by then. Jeffrey most of all.

"How is he?" she forced herself to ask Gwendolyn.

"It's still touch and go." The other woman put a hand on Elena's forearm. "He asked for you before he lost consciousness." Her gaze, that lovely and ordinarily peaceful dark blue, pleaded with Elena. "'Ellie, get my Ellie,' he said."

Her father hadn't used her nickname for a long, long time. He was the sole person in her life who insisted on addressing her as the long and formal-sounding Elieanora. That he'd changed the habit of her adult lifetime . . .

Her breath caught, her own heart in a painful rhythm. "Can I go in?"

Gwendolyn nodded. "They only allow one visitor at a time. I've sent the girls home for the night. None of the three would leave until I used what Eve calls my 'mom voice.'"

That Gwendolyn so naturally included Beth in her definition of the "girls" said a lot about her heart.

"The archangel's second has been very kind," Gwendolyn added. "When I called the Tower, I thought the receptionist would take a message, but she put me straight through to him after I gave my name. Said I was on a list?"

"Of course you are, Gwendolyn. You're my father's wife. Beth, Amy, Eve, they're all on the same list."

Gwendolyn's smile was shaky, the way she gripped Elena's hand a silent thank-you for including the two daughters she'd borne Jeffrey. "I thought Dmitri would be intimidating, but he was gentle. He called to tell me he'd managed to get in touch with you, and later to say when you'd be landing. I knew you'd come here straight after."

Gentle wasn't a word Elena had ever associated with Dmitri, but then again, he was married to generous and warm-hearted Honor, and even Sam liked him, so maybe it was only to Elena that he was an ass. She was glad he'd pulled out the hidden side of himself for Gwendolyn.

"I'll stay with Jeffrey now," she said. "You go home, get some rest."

Gwendolyn rubbed at her closed eyes. "I know he hasn't been the best father to you," she whispered when she opened eyes that were wet again, the capillaries red against the white, "but he does love you. Please remember that."

Elena nodded because she couldn't bear to hurt this woman who'd done nothing but fall in love with a man whose heart had been given to another a long time ago, then smashed into so many pieces that what he had to offer Gwendolyn was a cobbled-together imitation of the real thing.

The worst of it was that Gwendolyn knew. She was too smart not to know. But love, Elena understood, wasn't always sensible. She, after all, had fallen in love with an archangel who'd made her close her own hand over the blade of a knife, her blood a scarlet warning.

"Is someone at home?" she asked Gwendolyn. "You won't be alone?"

"All the girls," Gwendolyn reassured her. "Harrison and

Maynard are looking after the kids and the Guild's given Eve compassionate leave."

Harrison was Beth's husband, Maynard Amy's. "Good."

"You won't leave him?" Gwendolyn twisted toward the ICU room, the shadows under her eyes purplish bruises.

"I promise."

After finally convincing the other woman to return home and get some sleep, Elena took a deep breath. It didn't calm her. If anything, the medicinal air, sharp and acrid, just made things worse, tightening the knots in her gut until they threatened to strangle her.

"Ellie?" A hesitant question.

Careful to keep her wings flush to her back, Elena turned to find herself facing a small woman with skin of pale brown and eyes of tawny hazel in a rounded face, her curly black hair cut in a neat bob that she'd pinned to the sides. She wore dark blue scrubs, had a stethoscope around her neck.

Elena frowned. "I'm sorry," she said, her brain stuttering on the knowledge that she *knew* this young doctor but coming up blank on the name. "I feel like I should recognize you, but—"

"Oh, don't worry." The woman waved a hand, her nervous expression easing into one so warm that it lit up the bleak chill that was the ICU. "The last time you saw me, I was maybe fifteen, had the worst case of acne, and was padded all over with what Mom called my cuddle layer. Med school took care of that—I barely have time to sleep, much less eat."

A neuron fired. "*Lola?*" Elena's mouth fell open. "You're a *doctor* now?" Last she remembered, her friend Hector Santiago's daughter had been a shy schoolgirl who barely said a word.

A dimpled smile. "Resident anyway."

"How's your father?" Elena asked. "I haven't spoken to him much since he and your mom moved away." The truth was that while Santiago had tried, their relationship had never quite been the same once Elena became entangled with immortals. Neither one of them at fault, their lives just occupying different spaces.

"He's great. He's the chief in a tiny seaside town in Virginia now—I was worried he'd get bored, but he's pretty much a local these days. Has fishing buddies and knows everyone. Says it makes it easier to keep the miscreants in line."

"I'm glad," Elena said, even as her heart thudded and her mouth dried up. Because she couldn't keep delaying.

"I just . . ." Lola Santiago glanced at the door to Jeffrey's room. "I saw the name on the chart and I thought it might be your dad."

"Is there anything you can tell me about his condition?"

"Major myocardial infarction—a big heart attack, in other words. Complication in surgery, but they got him back quickly. Right now, he's unconscious and that's not out of the ordinary, but we'll start to worry if he doesn't come out of it by morning."

"I'll buzz the staff as soon as he wakes." Elena's hands threatened to sweat, her pulse in her throat. "Tell your dad I said hi and that he still owes me ten bucks on our bet over the feather. He'll know what I mean."

"I will. He talks about you all the time, tells us stories of the cases you worked on together. Keeps saying he should invite you fishing, share a beer with you over old times."

Elena wanted to smile, couldn't quite manage it. "A woman with wings fishing. Now that'll be something to see," she got out before her throat closed completely.

Lola's smile was understanding. "I'm around at night all the time, so if you need anything . . ."

Elena nodded, then forced herself to start walking to her father's room. As the door loomed ever larger in her vision, she thought about Detective Hector Santiago and about how they'd worked together what felt like a lifetime ago. Death wasn't the only way to lose people; sometimes, they simply drifted away. But unlike with death, there remained a chance to reach out, come together again.

What's broken between us can't be fixed.

Words she'd spoken herself to her best friend, about her relationship with her father. Now she hoped she'd been wrong, that the last words she and Jeffrey ever said to each other wouldn't be ones scored by the vicious wounds of the past.

Her heart thundered as she put her hand to the cool hospital door . . . and pushed it open.

9

Raphael pushed his archangelic body to the limit in an effort to get his task over and done with so he could return home to Elena. He'd *never* before heard such a tone in her voice: the pain, the fear, the grief, all twined around her complicated emotions for Jeffrey Deveraux.

He'd been wrong to assume he understood all of what she felt toward her father. So many layers she had to her, his guild hunter. He'd be discovering her until they were Ancients ready to lie down in an endless Sleep. Today, however, all that mattered was that he was far from her at the moment when she needed him most.

Like most warriors, his Elena was rarely so openly vulnerable. That she trusted and loved him didn't change the core of her nature, a nature formed on a foundation of fierce independence. Some of the biggest fights early on in their relationship had been a result of her need to be free coming up against his need to protect her.

For her to sound as broken as she had on the call . . .

His entire body fought his mind to turn, head homeward.

"You're an archangel," she'd said to him when he'd struggled against the harsh reality that he couldn't change direction, go to her. "Millions of lives rest on what you find today and the consequences of that discovery. Your responsibility to uncover the truth about Qin comes first."

He knew those hadn't been just words; his consort had walked with him since they came together, understood the silent contract by which he'd been bound since the day of his ascension.

As a result of the urgency of his flight, he was drenched in sweat when he landed outside what had once been Astaad's elegant home in the tropics. Built on a single level, it flowed with the landscape and was awash in tropical blooms. Palms waved against the sky across the estate while the cerulean blue ocean rolled to shore on gentle waves, separated from the house only by a short stretch of white sand beach.

Inside, Raphael knew it was cool tiled floors and huge windows that could be opened to the sea breezes. But where Astaad's beloved harem had once filled its rooms with laughter and color, in Qin's reign, it was a residence quiet and somehow . . . uninhabited.

It was Jason who'd said the latter, for Qin had never held a gathering of archangels in his territory. Neither had he invited any one of them to whom he was especially close. Because Qin wasn't close to anyone in the Cadre. Raphael knew his mother had tried, but the Ancient had remained inexorably remote.

"He is always well-mannered, even gracious," Caliane had said as she braided her hair while Raphael sat across from her in her private garden in Amanat.

They had come a long way since her waking that he could have such a familial moment with her, but that day, they had also been two archangels talking Cadre business.

"But," she'd added, "I get the feeling it is because, at the heart of it, Qin doesn't care about anything in this world. It doesn't anger him or make him happy. All his emotions lie buried with Cassandra. He is akin to a ghost in our world."

Raphael agreed with his mother, but any sympathy he'd had for the other man had died under the scalding burn of the tears in Elena's voice. His hunter so strong, who'd fought at his side with the promise of near-certain death on the horizon and never flinched. His consort who'd never broken under any of the pressures that came with the position. His lover, who hated to cry.

Together.

That was their promise to each other. She'd upheld her end. It enraged him that Qin's selfishness meant he couldn't uphold his. Instead, he had to be here, dealing with a mess that needn't exist.

"Archangel." A familiar vampire, his skin the warm brown shade oft seen in this region and his face bearing a partial tattoo dissimilar to Jason's in detail but similar in how it had been done, emerged from the house.

General Atu had the hardened visage of a warrior, and though he wore modern combat pants and a sleeveless tunic in a tough but breathable fabric suited to the humidity and heat of this region, his weapon of choice was a spear that he held point-down on the crushed white shells of the path.

An act of ceremony, to show he had no aggressive intent.

The vampire bowed. "I welcome you in my role as second to Archangel Qin."

Atu had also been a senior member of Astaad's court, was well respected in this territory. Per Jason, the vampire had done a lot of heavy lifting to ensure Qin didn't become lost in his memories and that he did what was necessary of an archangel.

Raphael gave the other man the same kind of nod of greeting that he would to one of his own Seven. "General."

Rising, Atu met his gaze. "Is the rest of the Cadre on its way?"

"Only Aegaeon at this point in time."

"I offer you a bathing chamber and fresh clothing while we wait."

Raphael nodded and followed the general inside. Better to take a few minutes now when he had to wait regardless. Because that Atu had offered such niceties rather than immediately alerting his archangel of Raphael's presence gave Raphael the answer to his question.

But they must have confirmation.

"We also have a communications center should you have need to contact your Tower." Atu led Raphael to the guest wing of a home that echoed in silence, devoid of the voices of the harem and of Astaad's intelligent and strong-willed senior team.

The departure of the latter was no commentary on Qin; such shifts occurred when one archangel took over the territory of another. But the silence did speak to Qin doing nothing to recruit others to his team—enticing people to join an archangel's court was child's play, but enticing *good* people took effort and intelligence.

The lack told Raphael a great deal about Atu and the load the general had carried since Qin took over the territory. For a second could only do so much in this particular circumstance—Atu wouldn't have had much success in gaining the loyalty of others of his caliber if his archangel made no effort to back his plays.

"Thank you for the offer," Raphael said, though he had no intention of using the communication system when he had the phone on which he'd spoken to Elena. "The house is quiet."

Atu's face didn't so much as flicker. "Archangels are all very different individuals," was his politic answer.

Raphael didn't push him for more, not when he was impatient for privacy. Once in the guest suite—a sprawling expanse that looked out over a mass of hibiscus blooms beyond which lay the sun-sparkle of the ocean waves—the first thing he did was send a message to Elena. He'd have called at any other time, but he had an idea that she might be with her father.

The phone rang in his hand moments later. "*Hbeebti*," he said, pressing one hand against the glass that looked out on all that lush tropical beauty.

"It's so good to hear your voice."

"I hear pain in yours." It stabbed bloody spikes into his heart. "Have you reached your father?"

"Yes, you called just as I was about to walk into his room." She took a shuddering inhale. "I heard the machines beeping as I began to push open the door and backed off. I thought I was going to throw up. I feel like such a coward."

"Elena, you battled not one but two archangels and lived to tell the tale. You will never be a coward." Her courage scared him at times, for how little she thought of her own skin.

But this, he understood, had nothing to do with her brave heart and too much to do with her history. "Your mother was in the hospital for a long time after the attack on your family." His palm pressed so hard on the glass that he had to pull back lest he shatter the window with the power aglow in his wings. "It's not a place you associate with good things."

"I should be over that by now." Furious words whispered low and private. "I shouldn't be haunted by something that happened when I was a *child*."

He struggled against the urge to smash the glass, take to the sky, fly home. "No, *hbeebti*, that isn't how it works. I will fall wounded and helpless from the sky over and over again in my memories until the day my end comes. Some memories become mental scars—they fade but never vanish."

It would've been easy to tell her otherwise, promise her

that her memories of the massacre of her family would vanish with time, but Raphael didn't lie to his consort. "And as a very wise hunter once told me, our memories are what make us."

"Ha." A rasping breath. "What if I have no more time?" This time her whisper was softer, shakier. "What if he dies this way, with anger and pain and recrimination between us?"

Raphael had seen death many times through the centuries, and if he knew one thing, it was that it followed no single path. "Until his heart beats no more," he said to her, "hope exists."

"I'm going to hold on to that, Archangel."

Jeffrey Deveraux, Raphael thought, was a lucky man to have a wife and children so loyal—even when the object of their affections didn't deserve it. But he didn't say the latter. He, more than anyone, understood that some relationships were complicated.

His mother had committed mass murder while lost in madness, then left him bloody and broken in a lonely field far from civilization.

Caliane had shattered his bones and splintered his heart.

Yet, today, he accepted her as his mother and had even begun to trust that her sanity would not once more slip away.

Love was no mathematical equation with absolute answers.

It could be volatile and hard and it could make you bleed.

"And you, Archangel?" asked the woman whose love was fierce and loyal and the most precious element of Raphael's life. "You must be exhausted."

"Yes, I'm going to shower and change." He thrust a hand through his hair, the strands sweat-damp. "Aegaeon won't be far behind me." While Raphael had retained a percentage of his Cascade-given speed, he'd also landed during the flight to talk to Elena, and he'd hit winds that Aegaeon might've avoided on his flight path. "Rest will need to wait until our task is complete."

"If Qin *is* gone, there's going to be no resting for you or any other archangel."

He dropped his forehead against the glass, arm braced over his head. "Let me have my delusions, *hbeebti*."

Soft laughter. "*Knhebek*, Archangel. Take care of yourself or you'll answer to me."

Holding his consort's words of love and care to his heart, he stripped, then used the shower rather than the readied bath. No doubt he'd been spotted by sentries. He'd made no effort to hide his approach, for this wasn't about war.

"Small mercies," he muttered to himself as he dried off his body after shaking any lingering droplets off his wings. Designed to sleek off wet, his feathers didn't require much more when it came to water.

The provided clothing—dark brown pants and a sleeveless cream tunic in the same material as Atu's clothing—were new and fit well enough. Guest items, he guessed, having the vague awareness that his Tower, too, kept a store of clothing for visiting angels who, for whatever reason, might arrive without spare items of their own.

It tended to be utilized by couriers for the most part, since they flew so light. Though regular couriers must have lockers in the Tower for long-term storage, he thought with a frown; he'd had the like during his own youthful stint as a courier. Wooden trunks, the top of each burned with the name of the court to which the courier belonged.

After dressing, he ran a hand through his now-clean hair. The light that poured in from the outside—a thick and rich yellow—caught on the amber of his ring as he lowered his hand. He raised it to his mouth, pressed his lips to it. A kiss for his consort, held in trust inside the symbol of his commitment to her until he could see her again.

He walked out of the room without delay, intending to talk to the general . . . and heard the sound of Aegaeon's loud voice. Following it brought him to the main chamber of the residence.

10

Unlike most angelic homes, this one had no central core for upward or downward flight—because Astaad had built his residence to the local conditions. The glass-paneled central roof could be opened up in the mornings, then closed before the afternoon rains, to be opened up again later to the night stars and the balmy evening air.

Memory flickered.

"If it rains in the night?" Laughter in Astaad's dark eyes, his goatee pristine and perfect as he raised a glass. "Well, then it is fate and it is as well this entire section is a haven for Mele's plants."

The plants, abundant in their richness of green, were gone now, along with the woman who'd tended them.

Raphael had been close to Astaad. Not as he was close to Elijah, but they had been, if not friends, at least friendly allies—and that relationship had grown when Elena formed a friendship with Mele, Astaad's most favored and loved concubine—and a woman intelligent and kind.

As a result, Raphael had been invited to this home a handful of times over the years, as he had welcomed the Archangel of the Pacific Isles to his own home in the Enclave.

He'd seen Mele with her plants once during a visit, up on a stepladder with a long-necked watering can as she took care of a vine that waterfalled from a hanging pot. She'd been wearing a cotton wrap in a complicated sarong that appeared a strapless dress, the print yellow frangipani blooms against a black background.

What he remembered most of that moment, however, was Astaad standing at the bottom of the ladder, scolding her for climbing so high in bare feet, with such a heavy can of water. She'd been laughing, her usually composed expression open and mischievous.

Raphael had melted away, loath to interrupt that moment. He would never understand how Astaad could love Mele so but keep a harem, or how Mele could be so generous with her own heart, but the relationship had worked for them.

Now Astaad Slept in the hope of recovering from a wound grievous, and Mele and her sisters of the harem had left. All that remained was cold tile and seating areas grouped in corners no rain would reach even should the roof be open during a downpour.

Raphael missed his fellow archangel more than he would've predicted. Astaad had always been one of the calmer heads in the Cadre, a man content in his skin and with his life and loves.

Fingers curling into his palm at his side, he looked up as the first drops of the afternoon shower hit the glass of the roof.

"No, I do not wish to freshen up!" Aegaeon bellowed, his hair damp either from sweat or from a quick dunk in the sea. "If Raphael's already here, then let's get on with it!"

"In that we are in agreement." Raphael strode into the chamber proper.

"Rafe," he said, and Raphael knew it was meant to irritate.

"Ah, age is catching up with you, old one," he murmured. "That you forget my preferred name once again."

Aegaeon's face mottled, his fists clenching into mallets at his sides.

Before the Archangel of the Deep could descend into the rage that was his natural state around the man on whom he blamed his son's refusal to join his court, Raphael turned to General Atu. "Qin must have left instructions."

Atu nodded. "I last saw the archangel ten days past. On that night, he told me others of the Cadre would come here, perhaps even all, and that when they did, I was to take them to a locked chamber inside his suite."

Jaw tight and body held with warrior precision, Atu stepped forward. "If you will follow me, archangels."

Aegaeon was scowling when Raphael looked up, but he'd moved on from his continued anger at Raphael. An anger all the more ridiculous because of the truth behind Illium's lack of allegiance to his father. Aegaeon had abandoned his son and the extraordinary woman who'd borne Aegaeon his only child, damaged both in ways unique and terrible.

How had the man expected any other outcome?

Arrogance truly did lead to idiocy.

"Qin planned this," Aegaeon muttered. "It was no spur-of-the-moment decision driven by emotion. That makes it worse."

"Yes." The archangel who'd taken over rule of the Pacific Isles, but never the name, hadn't given in to depression, hadn't been driven to this drastic act by his knowledge that he could never walk in the world with Cassandra by his side.

Such a wrenching call, a part of Raphael would've forgiven. People broke. Even immortals broke. And Qin had been thrust out of Sleep by the Cascade, then forced into the Cadre when Astaad fell during the war.

But for Qin to do what he'd done with conscious intent, while aware of the fragile stability of the world? No. That could not be forgiven. "It remains very much Astaad's home, doesn't it?" he commented as they followed Atu through wide hallways lit by natural light from skylights awash in fat droplets that Raphael knew would be warm to the skin.

He nodded at the wall to his right. "I remember that tapa cloth hanging from my last visit to him, and one of Mele's sisters of the harem did that painting of the children jumping in the waves."

"I was never at this residence before Astaad's Sleep," Aegaeon reminded him. "We met over a different island, then spent most of our time dealing with the various messes of the Cascade.

"I also do not believe he would've invited me here on a short acquaintance. With what you say of the art, the design of this place, and from what I saw of the gardens during my approach, this feels like a home and not a court."

If Raphael had a blind spot with Aegaeon, it was that he tended to focus on the other man's ugly choices and forget his intelligence and capacity for subtle understanding. Such blind spots got archangels killed. He had to put aside his prejudices and treat Aegaeon as both a fellow archangel—and a possible threat.

"Yes," he said, "you're right. I wasn't invited here until two hundred years into my reign, when we'd come to know each other well enough to understand we thought the same on many matters of the Cadre. It was not a place for casual acquaintances."

"Given your words about the house still feeling like Astaad's"—a muscle twitched in Aegaeon's jaw—"Qin never intended to remain here long-term. He put down no roots."

"No, that much he made clear from the first—but I thought his short term would give us a century at the least." Enough to stabilize the world, banish the final lingering shadows of a war built on a foundation of disease and death.

"I don't want to be awake, either," Aegaeon muttered, because of course this must be about him. "But here I am."

Raphael made a noncommittal noise in response. While the turbulent energies of the Cascade may have hauled Aegaeon out of Sleep, the Archangel of the Deep was enjoying being back in power. What he wasn't enjoying was that his son had disavowed him.

Illium hadn't said a single public word on the matter.

He hadn't needed to; that the blue-winged angel chose to stand at Raphael's side rather than his father's was statement enough. The entire angelic world understood Illium's unspoken denunciation.

His stance was an unbearable insult to a man like Aegaeon.

"Archangels." General Atu stopped in front of a pair of closed doors of glossy black. They had slats to allow for airflow, but those slats were at an acute downward angle so that no one could look at what lay beyond. "We are at my sire's quarters."

Pushing open the doors, he revealed a spacious living room that looked warm and comforting—and that bore Mele's imprint. Bright cushions on white rattan furniture, woven rugs that broke up the cool of the golden-gray tiles, it was a place warm and with an innate sense of home.

But the vases the harem would've filled with color were barren.

Raphael looked and found not a single sign of Qin's more than decade-long residence. It didn't matter that his fellow archangel had come out of Sleep with nothing—he was a member of the Cadre, with access to resources end-less. All of Astaad's wealth would've passed to him, for one. Archangel to archangel, that was how succession func-tioned when it came to the Cadre.

He should've acquired *something* to place inside his pri-vate quarters.

Aegaeon picked up a conch shell, held it to his ear. The peace that softened his expression was a thing startling. "This land calls to me always, but I will not take it, not even now." Putting down the shell with care, he met Raphael's eyes with those of an intense blue-green. "It would be dis-honorable to my short association with Astaad."

"I think we're going to have a problem getting anyone to take it," Raphael said. "His was the most spread out of the territories, and not one easily accessible to an archangel already handling another territory." Raphael had no idea how they'd divide matters, but it'd involve significant move-ment. "Several of us may have to take pieces."

"Not ideal"—shoving a hand through shoulder-length hair the same shade as his eyes, Aegaeon blew out a breath—"but yes, that might be the only viable solution if we're to stop any further disruption."

The general stopped again before Raphael could reply, this time in front of a simple white door wide enough for a single angel to pass through. "No one has been inside since I last saw the sire."

Stepping forward, Raphael put his hand on the door.

A sigil—waves that glowed unexpectedly in the hues of the aurora—lit up the center of the door, confirming the general's statement.

Sucking in a breath at the sight, that loyal man went to one knee. "Sire," he said, his voice choked up.

That this hardened general who'd known Qin such a short while would mourn him told Raphael that Qin had been a good leader. But, in the end, he hadn't been a good archangel.

"You may leave us now," Aegaeon said to Atu. Then, in another unforeseen burst of complexity, he gave the general the respect of an explanation. "He was your archangel, but this is Cadre business."

Rising, the general nodded. He sent one last long look at the spot where the sigil had glowed before leaving the suite.

Raphael waited to open the door until after his departure.

He and Aegaeon stepped through, one after the other.

Within was a small study with only a lone narrow window to let in light. And though Raphael had never before been inside Astaad's private quarters, he knew instinctively that *this* space was Qin's. No books on the walls, and only an envelope addressed to the Cadre and a piece of art on the desk—minimalism painful in its clarity.

Yes, that was Qin.

The desk was of glass modern and clear, its legs silvery metal. Behind it sat a chair of an equally modern style. Modern but not severe. The lines of the furniture flowed like the water from which Qin had risen.

That single—striking—piece of art was a sculpture made of an opalescent stone that glowed with the colors of the aurora. A mere handsbreadth in height, it was of a woman laughing, her hair flowing back and her hand outstretched as if to a lover. "It is Cassandra." The beauty of her captured in jeweled tones.

"I'm surprised he left it here," Aegaeon murmured, not touching the object, either. "Such is the kind of treasure I would've expected him to take into Sleep."

"Perhaps we will find an answer in this." Picking up the creamy envelope that sat in the center of the desk, Raphael removed the single sheet of heavy paper within.

The words written across it glowed with the colors of Qin.

Aegaeon sucked in a breath. "I did not know he could do this."

"Neither did I." He filed away the memory to share with Elena, even as the colors faded to reveal a letter penned in a script as fine and as otherworldly as Qin himself.

My fellow members of the Cadre, if you are reading this, then I have made the decision I have struggled with since the moment I woke into this world wondrous and new and made of steel and glass. I have gone into Sleep.

I know you will rail against me, and you have that right. I make no excuses save one: I am only half a being without my Cassandra. I do not exist in truth in this world when she does not. My mind is an organ split in two, while my heart lies beneath the earth.

The vampires who I am tasked with controlling have begun to sense that. They know my will is not in this existence. I have done my duty. I have kept them in check. But I fear for the years to come, as I become less and less without her. I foresee a time when I will not care to keep a hand on them at all . . . and a time where I, too, will become a mad being.

This is a piece of my history that you do not know, for you are all too young. I tried to live without her once before. I made it two centuries, but by then I was so mad that the only reason I survived is because my two closest archangelic friends cut me up into tiny, tiny pieces and buried me in a cavern deep in the ocean.

They knew even an archangel would take time to recover from such an annihilation.

Time enough to regain my sanity perhaps.

They were right.

I did not rise after I was whole.

I chose to Sleep as my beloved Sleeps.

I do so again, in the knowledge that the madness

whispers to me every step I take alone in this new world she finds so alluring and full of wonder.

I leave with you a treasure from the deep where I once lay. I carved it over millennia, in the heartbeats when I woke. I would the world never forget her. I would they remember her as I remember her: as the joyous wild beauty who was ever my closest friend and only lover.

I ask that this carving be placed in Lumia, in lieu of a portrait that does not exist.

I beg no forgiveness or grace, only that you treat Astaad's people with gentleness, for they are yet his people. He was their true archangel, I only a caretaker for a pulse in time.

—Qin, once Archangel of the Midnight Sky

11

Interlude
Graves

Raphael fell to his knees in the dirt, sobs shaking his body and his wings crumpled. His hand clenched on the wood of the implement he was using to dig a grave so small it should've never been needed.

"Rafe." Keir put his hand on Raphael's shoulder, but even the healer's warmth couldn't penetrate the cold at Raphael's core. "You don't have to continue doing this. You've more than done your part, son."

But Raphael shook his head and, after using the back of one hand to roughly wipe off his tears, rose to his feet. He towered over the diminutive healer, but that said nothing of Keir's power.

It blazed kindness and compassion.

"No, Keir," Raphael said, "my blood is responsible for this. I must be here."

"You had nothing to do with your mother's madness," the healer argued, the silky black of his hair wind-tangled against his dusky skin. "Listen to me, Rafe. You're a young man who should've never been put in this position." An uptilted brown, his eyes held compassion endless.

But Raphael *couldn't* listen, his eyes taking in the field that went on forever. Grave after small grave. Mortal children who'd curled up and died of grief after his mother turned her voice into a weapon and sang their parents into the ocean.

He had watched over the children, had tried to make them want to live.

He had failed.

Shoulders set, he turned away from Keir's empathy and heart. The healer was a better man than Raphael, had told Raphael that his mother was sick, her decision made in the tangle of insanity.

Raphael didn't care.

She'd seen what madness did to his father, to her lover . . . and still she'd stayed awake as the phantoms began to howl. He wanted to shake her, scream at her, beg her to make this right.

But she couldn't.

Mortals didn't rise once broken.

Even as Keir tried to speak to him, he bent, began to dig again.

12

Elena's muscles locked in a reflexive act at her first glimpse of Jeffrey.

Only now did she realize that she'd been scared he'd appear diminished, appear small. She wasn't sure she'd have been able to bear seeing the man who had always been a force of nature, who'd once been her beloved and loving Papa, turned fragile and weak.

But somehow, though he lay in a hospital bed hooked up to multiple machines, Jeffrey Deveraux remained himself down to the tension in his face.

Not much, but enough.

Even the cool white of his hair was neatly brushed, the cut as aristocratically elegant as always.

Able to breathe again at this sign that she hadn't lost the father she'd always known, Elena walked fully into the room. She was grateful for the wide door built to accommodate hospital equipment—it made it easier for her to enter without having to crush her already hurt wing.

The chair beside her father's bed wasn't designed for wings. Because angels didn't usually walk into hospital rooms. Her favored method with normal chairs was to flip them around then straddle the seat, but that didn't seem right here. She'd resigned herself to a night on her feet when someone knocked on the door before opening it partially.

A familiar face appeared in the gap. "I suddenly thought about your wings and the chair," Lola whispered before shooting Elena a conspiratorial grin. "I stole this from the admin station." Nudging the door a little wider, she held up a stool.

The thoughtful kindness made her throat thicken. "Thank you." Words run past the sandpaper that lined her throat. "That's perfect."

Mere seconds later and Lola was gone, Elena seated beside this man who'd once been her papa and was now just Jeffrey. Though linked by bonds of blood dark and colored in agony, they'd long ago lost that first innocent bond of father and daughter.

Misty memories on her mind, of a sunlit kitchen that smelled of vanilla and chocolate and gardenias. The latter from her mother's scent of choice, a scent that came in a gorgeous crystal bottle that Ari collected once they were empty. Elena had been around seven when she'd caught her father replacing a near-empty bottle with a full one.

"Papa," she'd whispered. "What are you doing?"

He'd lifted a finger to his lips, his gray eyes sparkling behind the clear lenses of his spectacles. "Let's see if she notices."

Elena had giggled, too young at the time to understand that of course Marguerite would notice, and that the gift was a private game between lovers, Jeffrey making it his mission to never allow her to run out of her signature perfume.

"Papa." The word spilled past Elena's lips for the first

time since Jeffrey had told her about the murder of his own mother, the sound broken and torn. "What happened to us?" She took his hand, that strong hand that had held hers as he walked her down the cold corridors of the morgue so she could see Belle and Ari one last time.

She'd been waking with screaming night terrors, convinced that the monster had made Belle and Ari like him, and that they were trapped forever in a house full of blood. Nothing anyone said would convince her otherwise, so Jeffrey had fought them all to give her a chance to say goodbye.

He'd cried that day, her papa. His broken heart had no doubt shattered impossibly further. But still he'd held the hand of his eldest surviving daughter as he took her to see the bodies of his two murdered daughters. She could still remember the strength and warmth of his grip, and of how he'd zipped up her puffer jacket and put a woolen hat on her head because he knew the morgue would be cold.

"Thank you," she said, even though he couldn't read her mind or her memories, even though he lay insensible. "For holding it together after we lost Belle and Ari, and Mama was so wounded." Not just in the body but in the mind.

Jeffrey, she thought, might've made it out of his own black grief if Marguerite hadn't committed suicide. He'd changed after the murders, of course he had, but Marguerite had been his air and his breath. He'd have done anything for her—even once more become the man he'd been in that sun-drenched kitchen where he'd thrown a giggling baby Beth into the air while Elena laughed uproariously, and Belle and Ari helped their mother with the baking.

"Were our days really that perfect?" Elena said, her throat raw. "Or do I only remember them that way because of what came after?"

Jeffrey's hand clenched on hers just as raindrops began to hit the window. Not much, but it was definite movement.

"Papa, it's Ellie." She squeezed his hand with both of hers. "I'm right here. You're in the hospital."

A rasped breath, flickering lashes, a dull gray gaze.

Elena knew she should call the doctors, but they could wait. If he was waking, that was good, no need for alarm. He'd hate them coming in while he was like this, groggy and with his mind dulled, his eyes fogged with sleep.

Either Gwendolyn or a nurse had left a glass of ice chips on the bedside table. The chips were half-melted by now, but she picked out a relatively whole one and put it to his lips. He accepted it, allowed it to melt, then took another, his gaze growing sharper with each second that passed . . . until she knew he saw her.

Her father's eyes were striking. A crystalline gray with fine striations of a darker black. Normally remote and cool behind the lenses of his spectacles, today they were framed only by the white of his lashes and eyebrows. "Ellie." His voice was gritty, his hand clenching again on hers. "My Ellie-belly."

A sob caught in Elena's throat.

Jeffrey hadn't called her that since before the massacre in their home. At almost ten years of age, she'd begun to be embarrassed by it, that name he'd given her when she'd been a baby with a rounded tummy, and so he'd stopped. It wasn't until this instant that she realized how much she'd missed hearing her papa say it.

"Yes." She swallowed the lump lodged in her throat, so heavy and hot. "It's me. You had a heart attack—that's why you're in the hospital." No point sugarcoating things when that'd just annoy him.

He winced. "I remember that part." Patting at his chest with a hand that held a line, a white strip of plaster sticking down the cannula, he said, "They cut me up?"

"Emergency surgery. Shall I get a doctor to—"

"No." He tightened his grip on her hand. "No, Ellie."

They just looked at each other, two people who'd been on opposite sides of an invisible border for over half of Elena's lifetime.

"I dreamed about Marguerite," he said at last. "She was in my arms and we were dancing in our kitchen. I could hear you girls playing outside and that yappy neighbor dog running around after you."

Elena sniffed. "Romeo." A miniature gray schnauzer, he'd belonged to an older couple and had too much energy to burn. Their home, with four energetic children who loved to play with him, had been his idea of heaven, and he'd often jumped the low fence to join them.

"Marguerite was laughing because I was joking about Romeo trying to find his Juliet, except that he was chasing the wrong species," Jeffrey said. "I think it was half a dream and half a memory. I didn't want to wake up."

Face haunted by his love for a woman long dead, he said, "Do you think the afterlife exists, Ellie? Now that you're an immortal?"

"Yes," she answered without hesitation. "Angels can die, too—you saw that in the war. It just takes a lot more to make it happen. And I refuse to believe that we just end. I refuse to believe that Belle and Ari and *Maman* aren't having the time of their lives beyond the veil we can't pierce in life."

Jeffrey looked away, staring fixedly at the window now blurred by water.

Elena didn't rush him, well aware he was fighting to control his emotions. That was the thing with her father—he'd always had a hard time with emotion, even before everything went wrong. Marguerite had balanced him then, teaching him how to be soft, how to show his intense and protective love for his daughters without crushing their wild spirits.

"I put her in the ground," Jeffrey said, still staring at the window lashed by the cold morning rain, the world outside yet night-dark. "She always said she wanted to be cremated, her ashes scattered, but I put her in the ground because I couldn't let her go." He turned then, met her eyes full on. "You hate me for that."

So I can fly, chérie.

Elena took a shuddering breath on the echo of her mother's long-ago words. "Hate isn't the right word. I'm so *angry* with you for breaking that promise. You know what she was like better than anyone—she was a butterfly, a will-o'-the-wisp. She was meant to fly and you buried her in the earth. It haunts me, the idea of her trapped there."

Jeffrey's hand spasmed on hers. "You're the only one other than me who remembers Marguerite, Belle, and Ari." Rasping voice, his grip increasing in strength. "Beth was too young, has only faded echoes. To their friends, they're a tragedy long in the past. Do you ever think about that?"

"Yes." It hurt her heart to realize that one day she alone in all the world would remember a laughing dancer named Mirabelle, a kindhearted budding photographer named Ariel, and a woman of air and delight named Marguerite.

"Even though only we remember," she said, "we don't talk about them. *You* refuse to talk about them." Anger threaded her voice, and she couldn't stop it even though he was sick and in a hospital bed.

Her father didn't rebuke her. "I was the first person to hold my Mirabelle when she decided to arrive in this world on her own timetable, and I was the first person to give my Ariel a bath. I was their father. *I* was meant to protect them. But I wasn't there when it counted. I don't *deserve* to speak their names."

"Papa." Elena let the tears fall now, her head bent over their clasped hands.

Fingers brushing her hair as Jeffrey raised his free hand to caress her downbent head. "I'm sorry." Rough words. "For so much, Ellie. But most of all, for making you believe you didn't have a father when you'd already lost everything."

Never, in all her adult life, had she believed that Jeffrey would apologize to her, much less with such heartfelt grief and sorrow. Maybe it was the medication. Maybe he'd return to being an asshole tomorrow, but at this moment, she felt something toxic that had been clawing at her heart for too long break away, setting her free.

"Slater was attracted to the house because of me," she said, raising her tearstained face to look him in the eye. "I know you blamed me for it."

"I blamed myself. Because your blood is mine." He clenched his jaw. "My mother was hunter-born. That's where you get it from. I *always* knew the fault was mine. I saw my mother be murdered and still I went ahead and married and had babies, creating more vulnerable people for the vampires to brutalize."

When he met her gaze this time, it was with the face of the hard-eyed father she'd come to know. "I never blamed you, Ellie. Do you know what I see when I look at you? A living indictment of my failure. *I'm* the reason you exist in this world, *I'm* the reason you live a life surrounded by vampires and blood, and *I'm* the reason you had to watch your sisters die. It all comes from my bloodline."

Elena was no longer so sure this was post-surgery meds talking. That had sounded very much like her father. "You know about Mama's parentage now. One of her parents was a vampire. If your bloodline is to blame, then so is hers." She shook her head when he would've parted his lips to reply. "I know you don't blame Mama for any of it, but it doesn't work that way. I'm made of both of you."

"You're wrong, Ellie." Harsh words. "I do blame her. For leaving me. For leaving us. We could've made it but she never gave us the chance." His jaw worked. "We *could've made it*." The anger in his voice wasn't the coldness she'd heard so often over the years—this was red-hot and raw and passionate.

He squeezed her hand with more power than he should've

had. "I hate her a little bit for that. And I love her end-lessly." A moment of searing eye contact. "You're like me that way, do you know that? You love with as much devo-tion, and that kind of love? It'll destroy you if it's in any way betrayed. She killed me when she killed herself. All that remained was a shell."

"No," Elena gritted out, their hands still linked.

Father and daughter.

Survivor to survivor.

Anger against anger.

"You don't get to cop out like that." She refused to break eye contact. "You made choices along the way, including the choice to let me think that there was something wrong with me, that my papa had stopped loving me."

Jeffrey flinched, but his color stayed high, his eyes bright—as if his anger had brought him to life. "You're right. It's easier to be angry with Marguerite than to con-front how badly I screwed up."

His chest rose and fell in quick, fast breaths. "I'm *so proud* of you, Ellie. For always being your own person, for fighting for Eve when she was too small to fight me herself, and for standing up for what you believe in—even if that meant telling me I was an ass."

Elena's chest compressed and compressed, until she couldn't breathe. "How medicated are you?" she managed to get out.

Her father's laugh was ragged, without humor. "I don't blame you for not trusting me, but facing death up close and personal has made one thing clear to me: I don't want to die with us broken. With my Ellie so far from me that Margue-rite would be ashamed of me both as a man and as a father."

A sigh, his eyes fluttering. "Damn," he said, and then his eyes closed.

Elena's heart jolted, but the machines stayed stable, didn't send out any alarms. She got the closest doctor any-way, told him what had happened. After checking over her father, the gray-haired man said, "He's more stable than he was a few hours ago. Excellent news."

He patted her on the shoulder, accidentally grazing the inner curve of her wing. An extremely sensitive part of an angel's anatomy, any touch there was normally limited to lovers and other intimates—and healers. This healer, she thought, had meant only to give comfort. "The way he fell asleep?"

"You have to remember that his body has suffered a massive insult." The doctor made a notation on Jeffrey's chart. "When he wakes, he might not even remember that you two spoke."

But I will, Elena thought after the doctor left the room. *I'll remember every word.* Words exchanged while her father was stripped of his inhibitions and his walls.

Perhaps she should've been angry at being denied those words when he was fully himself, but Elena had lost too many people that she loved. She wasn't going to throw one away when there was a chance to salvage a relationship from the wreckage.

Taking a seat on the stool, she took her father's hand again. "I'm here, Papa." She kept her word through the rainy hours that followed . . . all the way to two hours after dawn, when the machines went haywire and what felt like a hundred people rushed into the room.

13

Elena moved with hunter speed to get herself and her wings out of the way, glad the medics were focused enough not to be put off by her presence. The numbness that had protected her earlier was gone, her heart pounding so hard that it hurt, as if it was beating itself to a pulp against her rib cage.

The doctors and nurses were saying medical words in shorthand bursts but she couldn't process them, didn't understand. All she knew was that they were injecting drugs into her father's IV line and a thin doctor with fine black braids was yelling, "Shut those damn alarms off!" and a nurse whose skin bore evidence of a recent sunburn was racing in with a cart and her father was motionless, and she couldn't tell if his heart was beating any longer.

So when everyone went silent, her ears yet rung and she didn't hear what the doctor was saying when she spoke to Elena. The name badge clipped to the pocket of her lab coat said *Dr. Sharice Gupta*. A nice name, Elena found herself thinking, the world a chamber of silent echoes.

Dr. Gupta's mouth stopped moving. She reached out, placed a hand on Elena's arm, her wedding ring a bright gold against the deep brown of her skin. "Ms. Deveraux?"

Elena looked up. "I'm sorry," she said, sounding so normal that she wondered if she was having an out-of-body experience. "Is my father all right?"

Is my father dead?

The real question. The one she couldn't ask, couldn't even shape in her mouth.

"We've stabilized him." Dr. Gupta shoved her hands into the large lower pockets of the lab coat. "The acute downward spiral is concerning, but this type of thing *does* sometimes occur post-surgery."

Tiny lines flared out from the corners of her eyes as she frowned. "His stats are what they were before the incident, and we've switched to another post-operative drug on the off chance that he had a reaction to his current meds. We'll be monitoring him intensively over the next few hours to see how he responds."

Elena's mind flashed to the image of her father as a small boy who'd had to watch his mother be murdered, helpless and scared and unable to stop the monsters. Jeffrey *hated* being out of control. "Can I stay with him?"

"Yes, but you'll have staff walking in and out throughout."

"That's fine."

Nodding, the doctor cleared the room, but paused to say, "I guess I feel like I can say this because you were one of us once. Human. Able to die. And because I know hunters are tough—I've had more than one of you under my care."

When Elena didn't interrupt, Dr. Gupta nodded in Jeffrey's direction. "Make the most of the time you have with him. There are no guarantees in life or in death. He could make a complete recovery, or he could slip away. If you have anything to say, say it now. There's a lot of literature to support the idea that people in states like his can hear what's spoken to them."

"I will," was all Elena said, and after the doctor left, she went and sat with her father, her hand over his for a long time. But she didn't talk about the past—because she and Jeffrey, they'd already spoken the most critical words. "You won't be alone while you're here. If I'm not here, then Gwendolyn, Beth, Amy, or Eve will be with you. Your family. All of us."

Jeffrey might've buried the majority of his heart with Marguerite, but he hadn't been a bad father to her half sisters, and he hadn't been an awful husband to Gwendolyn. Oh, he'd had his moments, as when—driven by protective fear—he'd tried to forbid Eve from becoming a hunter, but he'd also bought Eve a motorcycle as a graduation present when she finished her training at Guild Academy.

That motorcycle was the precise color and model Eve had been salivating over.

Jeffrey was a complicated man, but he paid attention to his children and treated his wife with respect. He'd loved Eve and Amy, even Beth, as much as he could—and it had been enough for them to love him back. Because that was the only Jeffrey they'd ever known.

The rest? Marguerite? The mistress he'd once kept who'd been a faded copy of Elena's mother? The man Jeffrey had been with his first wife and daughters?

That would stay forever between Elena and her father. There was no need to force generous, loving Gwendolyn to face the depth of Jeffrey's devotion to Marguerite. Elena had not a single doubt that she knew all of it already—Gwendolyn was too bright for it to be otherwise—but there was a big difference between knowing and being told the confronting truth by Jeffrey's eldest living daughter.

It would just hurt her.

Enough people in their family had already been hurt. Elena wasn't going to inflict more wounds—especially when she knew that no matter what, Gwendolyn would stand by Jeffrey.

Because as Marguerite had been the center of Jeffrey's world, Jeffrey was the center of Gwendolyn's.

What a mess.

"But it's our mess, isn't it?" she murmured to Jeffrey as the rain faded away to leave the world quiet. "Our complicated, bruised, and damaged family."

Her father slept on, his expression so at peace that it terrified her.

14

Deep in the earth, Cassandra stirred, her wing brushing Qin's. His choice had brought her consciousness to the surface, and neither he nor she had yet fallen all the way into true Sleep.

"We can't do this for long," she reminded him.

"Long enough." His fingers touched hers, and for this moment in time, they were together in a world without grief.

It was the only way they'd found to be together over the eons since her "gift" stole her future by showing her too much of it. "We are greedy," she found herself saying to him. "We had more than a single mortal lifetime together."

"But we are not mortal, beloved. We should've had millennia." His lips brushing over her knuckles, a phantom kiss in her dreams.

Her eyes burned and she turned, looked at him, her Qin so beautiful and so haunted. Her ability to see the future hadn't claimed just her own life and sanity. "How long can you stay with me?" Unlike the others over whom she kept watch, Qin wasn't wounded. Qin had chosen his Sleep.

"As long as they'll permit me."

They.

Qin had always believed that the Cascade and other matters of angelic power were controlled by the Ancestors. He didn't think any of it was random. Especially the unknown factor that always, *always* tore them apart in the midst of Sleep. They'd go to the earth in each other's arms, and awaken oceans apart.

But not straightaway.

"You look so tired, my heart." She ran her fingers over his cheekbones, sharp and fine, the angle of them as acute as that of his eyes.

Her owls fluttered around them, enchanted by him. Of all the people in the world, Qin alone was the only other being with whom they would not just manifest but play. Once, in another life, she'd found him in a forest clearing. His hair had been an obsidian fall to his shoulders, his wings in all their watercolor glory tucked close to his back so as not to get in the way of her owls.

He'd been laughing as owl after golden-eyed owl landed on his shoulders and outstretched arms.

Oh, but her Qin was poetry itself when he laughed.

He turned in to her touch today, his eyelashes shadowing his cheeks. "I could Sleep for eons, but I rest only when I am with you."

A tear trickled down her cheek as within her the forces of foresight began to howl.

Cupping the side of her face with one long-fingered hand, his eyes a hypnotic black with glowing striations the hue of his sea aurora, he said, "No, not yet."

"No." She closed her hand over his. "I can fight it yet." Whatever the future that bloomed in the slipstreams of time, it wasn't powerful enough to wrench away her senses and her sanity.

Wasn't powerful enough to make her lose her Qin all over again.

But it was growing in strength with every hour that passed, until one day soon, it would be a tide hauling her resisting mind out into the slipstream . . . and away from the man who had been made for her by time itself.

15

A sea of grim faces met Raphael's and Aegaeon's as they stood in Qin's communications room. There was no reason not to use it now that they knew Qin was gone. Any spies of his court would now be in limbo—and to spy on a meeting of the Cadre was an act no spymaster would countenance regardless.

Located underneath his home, the room was paneled in black, with a far cooler ambient temperature than the tropical heat that lapped against the external part of the building.

"There's more bad news." Zanaya's words were unwelcome boulders rolling atop them. "I've just had word that two lost mortal villagers blundered into the far edge of the protected zone around the Refuge."

The entire group but for her sucked in a breath.

"The only reason the two wandered away rather than carrying on further was that they decided they weren't dressed for the inclement weather," the Queen of the Nile added. "Meher is assisting at the Refuge and was on a supply run at the time—and thus close enough to overhear. While his first instinct was to execute them, my third is old enough that he understood they aren't the problem. He made the decision to allow them to walk away."

Aegaeon spit out a curse in a language that had died when Caliane murdered the inhabitants of two thriving cities. Raphael's mother didn't seem to notice, her gaze locked with Zanaya's as she said, "The Mantle is failing," while Alexander nodded.

Raphael was unused to not understanding simple words in a meeting of the Cadre, but his mother's statement made no sense to him.

Titus, Elijah, and Suyin wore looks of confusion akin to his.

"What is the Mantle?" Raphael interrupted when it appeared Alexander was about to continue the discussion.

Zanaya, Alexander, Aegaeon, and his own mother stared at him.

"This is no time for jests," Alexander said with a scowl at the same time that Aegaeon rolled his eyes. "Have you forgotten the lessons passed on to you on your ascension, young Rafe?"

"Raphael isn't the only one who doesn't know what you're all talking about." Elijah's clipped voice. A blunt rebuke of Alexander's condescending irritation.

"I don't, either," Suyin said and was echoed by Titus.

The Archangel of Southern Africa followed that up with: "So the old ones know and the young ones don't. Lost knowledge."

Succinct and to the point, it had the four Ancients going quiet.

It was Caliane who broke the shocked silence. "This knowledge is of our very foundations—it should *never* be lost." Her songbird's voice rose in pitch. "There were safeguards put in place to ensure that."

The eyes that met Raphael's were dark and turbulent, her expression that of the woman who'd kissed his childhood bruises and not an archangel doing her duty. "My son, do you say the archangels in power at the time of your ascension didn't tell you of the Mantle?"

Raphael—his temper stirring—turned to Alexander. "*You* were on the Cadre when I ascended. Why didn't you tell me?"

The Archangel of Persia, his leathers a golden brown suited to his desert territory, the silver of his wing arches brilliant against them, frowned. "I assumed the duty had been done by the two archangels whose territory bordered yours. That is how it has always been done."

"I was one of those two," Elijah muttered, and raised a single golden eyebrow at Caliane. "My lady, you never shared this knowledge with me and you were my dearest friend on the Cadre."

Caliane's face went white. "How could I not?" She looked at the others, then slumped back in her chair and seemed to speak to herself. "I wasn't mad then, and though Elijah was not my neighbor, we were great allies. I should have told him."

"Don't blame yourself, Caliane." Aegaeon's tone held a hesitant edge Raphael had never before heard from the egotistical male.

"You were awake a long time—and the more time we spend in the world, the more our memories tangle. To be frank, I don't remember the last time *I* passed on the information." The confession of a man with honor—when it came to being an archangel at least. "I think I just . . . forgot it? The Mantle has always been there and so I no longer thought about it?"

A mortal wouldn't have understood Aegaeon's confusion, but mortals didn't exist for eons upon eons. Memories became an infinitely less linear and more complex thing once there were layers upon layers upon layers of them.

"The last time I passed on knowledge of the Mantle was about a thousand years before my Sleep." Zanaya winced, the silvery flecks in the midnight of her eyes seeming to glow with an archangel's fire. "Excluding today, I haven't given a flying thought to the Mantle since."

Raphael knew they had no time for anger or recriminations—especially when some of those who hadn't passed on the knowledge were either dead, had gone insane, or were lost to an endless Sleep. "I'm gathering that this Mantle protects the Refuge from incursions?"

"Yes." His mother pushed a stray tendril of hair off her face and behind her ear, her cheeks flushed and her skin tight as she leaned forward in her chair. "I wasn't told from whence it came, only that the Refuge never had to worry about intrusion from the uninvited. That those who didn't already know of the Refuge would simply *not see* anything worth exploring."

"The Mantle doesn't create a total blank in their memories," Zanaya elaborated, her arms angled in a way that said she had her hands on her hips; from the fabric visible on her shoulders, she was dressed in a plain linen tunic suitable for work or sparring. "Rather, it creates the memory of an unremarkable area they couldn't be bothered to explore."

"The archangel who told me of the Mantle," Aegaeon added, "was of the belief that the effect multiplied according to the number of contacts with the barrier.

"This is why the closest villagers never have any interest in the area *even though they see angels flying overhead on a near-daily basis.* I think he was right. Otherwise some young buck or curious child would've long ago attempted to breach our borders."

Extraordinary.

Raphael couldn't believe he'd never considered the point. Because Aegaeon was right—why had no local villager ever followed the flight path of an angel on the ground, tracked them to home soil?

Further, the Refuge, while located in a remote mountainous region most mortals could never scale, *was* still a part of their world. Mortals should've found it by now, especially given the technological advances to date.

It couldn't simply be put down to fear of the archangels. Mortals were stupid in their curiosity at times. Chance alone said that some idiot or adrenaline junkie would've tried by now . . . unless there existed an invisible variable altering choice and chance: the Mantle.

"Wait." Suyin's quiet voice, the sleek white of her hair flowing unbound over shoulders clad in what appeared to be handwoven cloth of deepest brown. "It seems far too coincidental a thing to me, that all four younger archangels should not know."

Lines formed in the smooth white skin of her face, a vee between her eyebrows. "Is it possible the Mantle has been malfunctioning for a longer period of time? That *we* have been affected so that we don't remember it?"

"I believe it's a case of eternity and memory," Caliane argued. "An unusual confluence of events—and in the end some of the Cadre *do* know. We have not forgotten."

"No," Alexander agreed, as Zanaya and Aegaeon nodded. "But let us put that aside. The more immediate problem is that for the first time in memory, we must consider the security of the Refuge."

Zanaya picked up the thread from her consort and neighboring archangel. "It's located in an area high and remote enough that it'd be a deadly climb for most mortals, one that'd require multiple days camping in the snow and the crossing of vast ice crevasses."

Raphael agreed with her. The landscape that offered a breathtaking view on the wing, complete with glaciers formed of preternatural blue ice, and rock formations that glittered in the sunlight, was brutal territory on the ground.

"From what Meher's been able to determine," she added, "it's only the edges of the Mantle that have failed, so even those who breach that section will soon lose interest and leave. We have time to find a solution."

"Is there any way to test that?" Elijah asked. "That it's only retreating from the edges?"

Raphael frowned. "I can ask one of my Seven to show several mortal members of my Tower a satellite image of the Refuge with zero contextual clues, and have those staff members note any points of interest."

No doubt Illium—the one most likely to take on the task—would come up with a believable reason for the test. "If the Mantle has failed higher up, they will see signs of the Refuge, and we'll know."

"Will you then execute the mortals?"

Raphael knew it was hypocritical to be angered by Aegaeon's question when not so long ago, he'd thought along those same lines, mortal lives firefly bursts that could be snuffed out without any real thought.

But he *was* angry—because he wasn't that man any longer, his heart forever altered by his love for Elena. So it took effort to offer a polite reply devoid of even a drop of fury. Emotion wouldn't work here.

"There'd be no point." He folded his arms. "Because if those mortals see it, so will countless others. Many make a habit out of scanning satellite images for fun."

Aegaeon's expression soured. "You should've crushed the knowledge when it first began to rise."

"Aegaeon's right." Alexander's statement held the censure of the general he'd once been. "Mortals shouldn't have access to technology so invasive."

"A world that doesn't grow stagnates and dies, my old friend," Titus countered.

"Stop." Suyin raised a hand, palm out.

Unused to such a firm voice from the Archangel of China, they all turned toward her image.

"None of that matters." Calm and tempered words that held an undertone of steel developed over a decade of rebuilding a territory with nothing but grit and endurance. "We need to work out how to fix this."

"To do that, we must know the origin of the Mantle," Zanaya pointed out. "The one who passed on the knowledge to me said it was a gift of the Ancestors, but that is a meaningless ghost story. Does anyone have concrete information?"

The answer was a firm negative.

"Great." Titus threw up his hands, his shoulders bunching under his simple black tunic. "The Refuge is shaking hard enough to fall apart, the Mantle that protects it is failing, and Qin has decided to Sleep!" Turning, he punched a wall.

Cracks spiderwebbed from that point outward.

Raphael wasn't feeling much more in control, his wings aglow as power aggressive and without direction surged through his veins. Aegaeon's chest glowed, the light coming from the silver swirl embedded in his skin. Onscreen, the others were in no better condition.

Another minute and the entire Cadre would be out of control.

"We start with the Librarian," he said, because it was the only answer he had that might defuse the tension. "We must also make plans to relocate our vulnerable to our beta location should the Mantle continue to deteriorate."

That beta location was underground, beneath an island. A good hiding place and one they could play off as a fun adventure for a short period, but it was no home for children with wings. But angelic children also couldn't live in a homeland accessible to mortals and ordinary vampires.

If angels had a vulnerability, it was their children—angelic young could be wounded, could be easily killed. The reprisal for any such act would, of course, devastate entire civilizations—but there were mortals who wouldn't care, driven by a vicious fury toward angelkind.

Raphael understood that fury better since he'd fallen in

love with his hunter. She'd made him face the cruelty with which many immortals treated mortals and vampires—but that knowledge didn't change the undeniable fact that if it came to a war, angelkind would win.

That had been proven through time.

It was impossible to defeat a race of beings that had archangels at their core. As evidenced by the story Qin had written of his dismemberment, a mortal could blow Raphael into a million pieces . . . and he'd still rise.

Again and again and again.

Better, then, to never give mortals even the faintest hope of easy angelic prey. So it was that angelic children were never visible except in highly constrained circumstances that made them effectively untouchable.

16

Elena decided to walk home; her wing hurt enough that she didn't want to risk taking flight, and it wasn't as if New York's streets would ever be unfamiliar to her. Steam rose out of the grates that lined the street, the sidewalks were clean from the night's rain, the air spring-crisp, and while traffic was flowing smooth enough for morning, the horns and shouts had already begun.

She'd wanted to stay longer with her father, but after Jeffrey's sudden decline, a newly distraught Gwendolyn had clearly needed private time with her husband. Elena had left her stepmother holding on to Jeffrey's hand as she murmured words loving and gentle to her father.

The poor woman couldn't have slept more than three or four hours before Elena rang to tell her what had happened. Despite Gwendolyn's obvious exhaustion, Elena hadn't even considered not informing her straightaway; it would've devastated her stepmother if Elena had made that choice and Jeffrey slipped away before Gwendolyn could see him again.

"Hunter angel! Try my coffee!"

Normally, that moniker made her groan and threaten to murder people. Today, however, she didn't have the heart or the will. She took the coffee the smiling cart operator held out, even managed enough of a return smile that he beamed. "Thanks," she said. "How much do I owe you?"

"On the house!" Short and shiny-faced, with a mop of light brown curls against freckled skin, his accent was less New York and more something on the other side of the Atlantic.

"I'm paying," Elena insisted, uncomfortable with the power dynamic. "If it's good, I'll still tell everyone."

They haggled a bit, with the vendor finally throwing up his hands with a scowl. "Bloody New Yorker!" His accent thickened. "Try to do her a favor and whaddya get!"

Elena was startled into a laugh. "I'll be a bloody New Yorker even if I live to be ten thousand years old."

He scowled, but it was for show, his grin peeking out at the corners of his mouth.

Her own smile faded with every step she took, the hot coffee doing nothing to thaw the chill within. Deep inside, she'd always known that Jeffrey would one day die. Today she'd learned that she'd never be ready for it. Because Jeffrey was the parent who'd *stayed*.

Even during their worst moments, she hadn't forgotten that.

Part of her remained the little girl who'd been so, *so* angry at her mother for choosing to end her terrible pain at the cost of her grieving younger children. That swaying shadow on the wall, the tumbled high-heeled shoe on the checkboard tile, the way Elena had rushed to scoop Beth up and out of the house before her baby sister saw, none of the memories of discovering her mother's body would ever leave Elena.

In the same way, the wounded child within her had apparently believed that her father would be endless, too—except in life, not death.

A wash of wind, an angel landing beside her.

She wasn't the least surprised when Illium threw an arm over her shoulders, their wings companionably crushed against each other. "He called you, didn't he?" she said.

"Yup," answered the angel with wings of dazzling blue and black hair dipped in the same shade, his scent a fresh and tart lime intermingled with an exotic element more luxurious. "The sire didn't want you to be alone. And I *am* your favorite."

She elbowed his tautly muscled gut. "Don't let that head get so big it explodes." But she was glad for his presence as they walked. Because Illium, playful and vulnerable in ways that echoed her own wounds, *was* her favorite of the Seven.

More than anything else, she felt loved by her archangel. Though he couldn't be with her, he'd made sure she wouldn't be alone. "Did he tell you what happened?" she asked after chucking her empty coffee cup into a trash can.

"No. Just that you might need a friend." He squeezed her closer. "I don't need to know, Ellie. I'm just here to astound you with my wit and genius."

"I can literally see your head expanding." Despite her dry words, Elena told him the basics. The rest, she'd talk about only to Raphael. "It's a shock—coming face-to-face with his mortality." Her chest ached all over again.

"He's still young in mortal terms." Illium turned her down a street that led in the wrong direction for the Tower, and, more than happy to meander, she didn't protest. "I'd have been shocked, too, were he my friend."

The streets were busier now and Elena managed faint smiles for the people who walked past and said hello or waved. No one but the odd slack-jawed tourist paid any mind to the fact Elena and Illium were walking together, wing over wing. The people of their city had long ago cottoned on to their friendship and that they were both very much entangled with their chosen lovers.

"How's Aodhan?" she asked, no longer wanting to talk about Jeffrey. The shock was too new, the memory of his sudden decline too bright. Nausea lurched in her gut at the smallest remembrance of it. "He still shut up in his art studio?"

Illium's lover, best friend, and fellow member of the Seven had built that studio five years ago, in a part of the Enclave not visible from the water but that received plenty of natural light.

"I threatened to hide his paintbrushes if he didn't allow me to feed him at least one proper meal a day," Illium muttered darkly. "Someone should've warned me about creative types."

The two of them emerged onto one of the main avenues, the sky above busy with angelic traffic, their wings lit by the pale glow of the morning sun. Below, mortals and vampires, half in New Yorker black, the other half in corporate suits, strode to their jobs or into the luxury boutiques that lined this stretch.

A lunatic messenger on a fold-up scooter zipped down the street, zigzagging through the traffic as if he was on a damn motorcycle. At least he was wearing a helmet. Even the pigeons seemed to be giving him the side-eye.

"Sparkle is lucky I'm such a ball of sunshine." Illium's voice was the embodiment of a scowl. "He growls like a feral wolf half the time at this stage of a project."

Elena chuckled at that most unexpected description of quiet, contained Aodhan. Because if anyone knew Aodhan, it was Illium. The two were each other's forever and had been for a long time, even if it'd taken them a while to realize it. "How's the project going?"

"Breathtaking." Smug pride. "He's almost ready to show everyone."

"I can't wait."

They walked on, content to listen to the city wake up and get ready for business. A blue-haired man in a top of glittery gold mesh and skintight black jeans asked Illium for a selfie "since we're so coordinated, honey," and Illium obliged with a grin, spreading his wings out in a show behind the two of them. He'd never lost his heart, no matter how potent his power. She couldn't imagine him as an archangel ruthless, but the signs of his intensifying strength were obvious.

No. She wouldn't think about that. Not today. Not when her nerves were already close to shattered.

A couple of minutes later, she said, "What's happening at the Refuge?" It wasn't only a question meant to distract her from her circling thoughts about Jeffrey. Keeping on top of a situation like this, especially in Raphael's absence, was part of her duties as consort. "Any updates?"

"The sire asked me to recruit mortals to see if they can spot the Refuge in a satellite image."

As she listened, the blue-winged angel told her the rest of it—including about the Mantle. Once, she might've bristled that Raphael had spoken to one of his Seven rather than to her about such a momentous matter, seeing it as a comment on her capability. And Raphael might've done so because he wanted to protect her.

But she'd matured and so had he.

These days, he treated her as an equal, and she didn't see insult in what were pragmatic decisions that came with being one of the Cadre. Or with the gentle choices made to protect an already emotionally bruised lover. "Did you set up the test before you came to meet me?"

Illium waited to answer until they'd crossed the street, entering a quieter residential area full of spring-green trees that nudged at her memories. "Yes. Played it off as a test of their observation skills, with the aim to spot a concealed building, and hid the Refuge feed in a group of five—one of which does feature a building that's difficult to spot.

"I gave the task to the junior security team—the five of

them do low-stakes computer work for us. First one to spot the building gets an extra paid day off."

Elena's throat burned at the idea of Sam and other angelic children being exposed to the world. As with mortal children, they were so damn helpless. But unlike the vast majority of mortal children, they'd also draw hate virulent and vicious from those who wanted to strike at their elders. "How long did you give the searchers?"

"Three hours." He came to a halt after turning the corner onto a street with lovingly maintained brownstones. "This is where I leave you."

Only then did Elena realize why the other street had looked so familiar. She'd just become used to seeing it from the air rather than from this perspective. "You brought me to Sara." Her throat grew thick.

"I'll meet you back at the Tower." Illium pressed his cheek to her temple just as Elena's best friend opened her door to run down the steps. She was dressed in jeans that hugged her legs, along with a simple sweater of aqua green that made her brown skin glow. Her black hair was pulled back into a knot, her bangs as thick and flawless as ever.

"Ellie!"

Elena let her best friend enclose her in an embrace tight. She couldn't cry, the tears locked up inside like hard little stones, but oh, it felt good to be held by the woman who'd been a part of her life for so long that she might as well be her sister.

A strong gust, Illium a streak of blue in the sky when they glanced up.

It was only after they were inside, with Elena crouched down to pet a big black dog who now moved with slow deliberation and had white in his whiskers, that Sara told her the reason why Bluebell had walked her over.

"I was on the other side of the city helping one of the younger hunters when Raphael called," she said as she bustled about making coffee. "I was going to head straight to you, but he said you'd feel better in my home, asked me to wait here for you."

Elena bit down hard on her lower lip, overwhelmed by the love that surrounded her. "Thank you."

Slayer rose under her touch to pad out, probably to go find his favorite human in all the world. He moved like the very senior citizen he was; in human terms, he'd passed the century mark. Melancholy hit her hard as she stood. She remembered when he'd been a puppy, rambunctious and with so much energy in his body that he'd needed three long walks a day.

"Shut up," Sara said in response to her thanks, the words spoken with the ease of a friendship set in stone. "As if I'd be anywhere but with you at this time." She put an empty mug down on the breakfast counter, in readiness for the dark brew that already scented the air. "You want eggs or pancakes or both? I'll throw in bacon for sure."

"I don't think I can eat."

Sara put both hands on her hips. "You're eating if I have to hand-feed you. I haven't forgotten the whole burning-energy-at-crazy-speed-while-flying thing."

"My wing is injured," Elena grumbled. "Also, you're using your mom voice."

"Good. It works." Sara winked. "Speaking of being a mom, the demon child will be happy with the unexpected goodies for breakfast."

Elena took a seat on one of the stools at the counter. "Pancakes, and don't call my goddaughter a demon child. Zoe Elena is the epitome of an elegant and refined young lady."

Sara snorted as she began to whip up the pancakes. "She's an only child, that's what she is. Expects restaurant service when she comes to visit." A lift of her eyebrows. "So?"

"Bad." Her hand clenched on the mug Sara had just

filled. "ICU." She wanted to tell Sara about her conversation with Jeffrey, couldn't quite get it out. It was too soon, her mind and heart unable to process it. "Shit, Sara. I thought he'd live forever."

"Bastards usually do, so I'd say he has a good shot."

17

Elena almost spit out her single careful sip of hot coffee. Then she began to laugh, and it was a little hysterical. Sara came around to hold her through it, small but strong and capable of love intense and unswerving.

Afterward, Elena said, "Really?" She dared another sip. "That's your idea of a bedside manner?"

"It worked, didn't it?" Her best friend and the respected director of the Hunters Guild was unrepentant. "I'll never forgive him for how he treated you"—she returned to the stove—"but I also know he's your father, so I hope he puts that bastard stubbornness to good use and gets better soon."

Elena grinned, Sara's blunt honesty far more effective than coddling. "I love you."

"As you should." Sara flipped out the first pancake. "Talk to me, babe."

So Elena did. Because this was Sara, who'd been there for her after Jeffrey threw her out, who'd talked through the night with her when they were roommates and Elena was too afraid to close her eyes, who'd been there from the first day of her relationship with Raphael. Their life paths might've diverged, but never had they diverged from their friendship.

"He's the last one other than me who really remembers my mom." Her words came out a whisper.

"Oh, honey." Sara's face looked like it was about to crumple.

"Don't you cry or I'll lose it."

Sniffing, Sara focused on using chocolate chips to make a smiley face on a pancake. "No tears. I'm tough. I'm the director of the fucking Hunters Guild. I just spent two hours helping a greenhorn hunter bag a dumbass vampire even though my knees hurt and I'm sure I have arthritis in my joints. Still got the shot right into his ass."

Elena's shoulders shook. "You're in your forties, not seventy," she said. "And his ass?"

"Dumbass deserved it." Sara flipped the smiley pancake out, poured in the next batch. "You know where he tried to hide after running out on his Contract? In his brother's warehouse."

She slid a plate of pancakes in front of Elena while she made more, and put on the bacon in a separate pan. "Even his brother slapped him upside the head and called him a numbskull who deserved to get caught."

Elena laughed and it was needed, so needed. Then, as she drank coffee and ate, she spoke to her best friend about the other jumbled thoughts in her head, about the panic and the pain and the confusion. The one thing she still didn't mention was that conversation. She couldn't. Not even to Sara. It was too huge, threatened to change the very fulcrum of her world.

A thumping sound above their heads.

"Hear that?" Sara's voice was affectionate. "My gazelle of a child has smelled the bacon if she's up of her own accord."

Zoe, lanky and long-legged and an explosion of wild curls atop a body clad in shortie baby pink pajamas with swords on them, ran down the stairs, a devoted Slayer at her heels. "Auntie Ellie!" For a moment, as she jumped into Elena's arms, she was a little girl again instead of an independent young woman on the precipice of her twenty-first birthday.

Squeezing her close, Elena shook her from side to side, causing her goddaughter to giggle. "What's my Zoe bean doing up so early? Also, when did you grow cheekbones that could cut glass? Where are the chubby cheeks I kissed last week?"

Zoe grinned and struck a pose after they broke the hug. "I have a good sense of smell." She sniffed ostentatiously in the air before filching a piece of bacon off the plate Sara had put on the counter. "And you should see my cheekbones with contouring," she said after disappearing it into her mouth. "*Fi-re*."

Elena fought not to grin.

Zoe, however, wasn't finished. "Did Mom tell you about my decision to get a belly piercing? Guild Director Sara Haziz is *not* in support."

Elena's eyebrows rose into her hair. "You want to poke a hole in your belly button?"

"Yeah. Look!" She pulled up her top to expose said belly button. "Imagine it with a sparkle. I know it's eighties chic, but my college friends say retro is back." She dropped the top. "I just like the look."

"Well . . ." Elena rubbed her chin, aware of an amused Sara plating up food for Zoe. "I mean, I see your point. I guess you could use the hole to carry a tiny weapon. A ring you could rip out in desperate circumstances that turns into a garrote?"

"Not funny!" But she was laughing.

Elena grinned. "How's college going?"

"It's going." Wandering over to slump in the couch on

the other end of the kitchen, she helped Slayer up beside her. "I mean, it's more fun than I expected, so I guess Mom and Dad were right that I should do it for the experience."

Elena all but saw Sara bite back her grin. "Your major itself?"

"Okay, okay, I love metallurgy. Even though I already learned most of it with Dad." Zoe bounced up to her feet, but instead of coming over for food, she ran down the stairs from the kitchen that led to her father's basement workshop.

This time, Slayer stayed put, snoozing in the morning light.

"Is Deacon down there?" Elena hadn't heard any sign of Sara's husband.

Pulling up a stool next to Elena, her plate of pancakes already doused with syrup, Sara shook her head. "Gone for a couple of days to hand deliver a custom order. You know he doesn't trust even angelic couriers with that kind of thing."

"I wouldn't, either, if I was him." Deacon's weapons were works of art. She wondered if he had any idea that angelic warriors got flat-out tearful at the thought of his life span being a mortal one.

A single request and he'd be fast-tracked on his way to becoming a vampire. And because Deacon was so valued, angelkind would also authorize Sara's Making, with Zoe given the choice once she reached the minimum age threshold.

But Deacon had no desire to live forever; neither did Sara.

Elena had learned to accept her friend's choice as Sara had always supported hers. That didn't mean it didn't terrify her, the idea of living on for eons after her best friend was gone from this world; she knew this friendship was one of a kind. No one else would ever be Sara to her.

They'd become hunters together. Become women together.

Footsteps bounced up the stairs and over to them, until

Zoe stood next to her, her happiness vibrant and unfettered. "Sorry your birthday present is late, Auntie Ellie," she said with the sweetness of the child she'd once been, "but I wanted it to be just right."

Bringing her hand around from behind her back, she showed Elena a small throwing blade cradled inside a leather sheath. "The sheath is a standard protective one since I know you have your own, but I made the knife," she said in a rush.

Elena's eyes went hot. "*Zoe*." She took the blade with care. "You *made* this?" Zoe had grown up in Deacon's workshop and was a talented apprentice, but this felt next-level. No toy or practice sword but a functional weapon.

"Yeah." She rocked back and forth on her heels. "I gave my first dagger to Mom, but it was under the cone of secrecy—I wanted to surprise you with one, too."

Elena slid the blade out of the sheath, then laid the metal of it against her palm as she examined the workmanship. No breaks, the lines clean and continuous, even a fine decorative carving along the handle that wasn't indicative of Deacon's way of doing things. Zoe, developing her own style.

"This is good enough to sell, you know that, right?" It wasn't perfect by Deacon standards, but it blew most other makers out of the water.

And for being given in love? It was a treasure Elena would protect forever.

Zoe glowed as Sara said, "See, baby, I told you I wasn't just saying that because I'm your mom. You also know your dad *never* says anything he doesn't mean when it comes to his craft. And he says you're the best apprentice he's ever had—he gets grumpy every time you go back to campus."

Zoe ran over into her mother's arms, the two of them hugging as Sara laughed at being tickled by Zoe's curls. Sara hadn't inherited those curls from her own mother, but the dormant genes had come through loud and clear in her daughter, with stunning results.

Sara and Deacon's daughter was a knockout.

As for Zoe's temperament, she had pieces of both her calm and focused father as well as her intense and driven mother, but the rest was pure, unique Zoe.

"I love it." Elena slid the knife not back into the sheath, but into one of the spare slots in her forearm brace. "Perfect fit."

Zoe's eyes widened. "You're gonna carry it. Eee!" She jumped up and down, drawing Slayer over to her.

Crouching to pet and cuddle him with the tender affection of a young woman who knew her loyal friend was in the final twilight of his life, she said, "I can't wait to tell Dad!"

When she looked up at Sara, Sara glanced at the wall clock. "He'll be awake. But come right back down to eat after, before your food goes cold."

"*Mom*, I'm not seven anymore," Zoe said with a laugh, hugging Sara again.

"Listen to your mother," Elena ordered. "You hate cold pancakes, so if you come back too late, we'll have to listen to you moan the entire time."

Grinning, Zoe shot them both a salute before running off to call her father—who also happened to be a craftsman Zoe respected beyond all others.

"My God, Sara," Elena said when they were alone, "she's better than most people I know who've set themselves up as full-time professionals. That includes immortals."

"She's brilliant." Sara's pride was a fire in her eyes. "I've known since she was about five that she was going to become a weapons-maker like her father."

Elena understood why Sara and Deacon had pushed Zoe to attend college despite that, when Zoe would've preferred to go straight into a full-time apprenticeship with Deacon.

They'd worried what Deacon's solitary way of working, which perfectly suited his nature, would do to their social butterfly of a daughter.

So they'd offered Zoe a deal—try college for a year, and if she hated it, they wouldn't ask her to go back. "She still friends with the same group?" Elena asked Sara today.

Sara nodded. "She chose her major well—a lot of these kids are going to work in fields adjacent to hers." Elena's best friend sighed. "Not that any of them are kids anymore. When did my baby start not being a baby, Ellie?"

Elena patted her shoulder. "She'll always be your baby."

Her mind flared, rippled, rolled backward.

"You'll always be my bébé, Ellie." A kiss pressed to her temple, a laughing smile at a toddling Beth. "And you, too, chérie."

Her accent was familiar and missed, the scent of her a heaven of gardenias. "Now, where are my big babies? Belle! Ari!" she called out. "Come, help your maman set the table."

A crash of feet, two more girls tumbling into the room— who were immediately snatched up into a hug by Marguerite, while Ellie and Beth laughed and ran to attack their sisters' legs.

"Mama!" Belle protested, but she was laughing.

"Something's biting my leg!" Ari looked down, her oval-shaped face warm with delight. "Oh, it's a Beth crab! I'm gonna catch you, Beth crab!"

As a squealing Beth ran off, Ellie pretended to pounce on Belle.

"Ellie." Sara's hand on her arm.

Shaking off the ghostly laughter of her mother and sisters, Elena turned to her best friend. "Sorry. Got lost in my own head."

"I know that look." Sara's voice was quiet, potent. "It's been a while since I've seen it, but I remember. Did you have a flash of memory?"

"A moment I've never before remembered," Elena admitted. "I was younger than I usually am in the dreams, maybe seven or eight. It was a good one," she told her friend. "Happy."

What she didn't say was that it had nonetheless cut her until she bled from a thousand stinging wounds.

Elena walked Zoe to the subway stop where she was meeting up with some friends from college who were also in the city for the week. "We plan to shop and eat," Zoe told her, a glint in her eye. "I might find the perfect belly button decoration."

"Stop messing with your mother." Elena chuckled. "You serious about the piercing?"

"I think so. But I'm also considering doing my left eyebrow—I gotta look tough as a weapons-maker."

"I hear and know nothing."

Zoe snorted, a mischievous child. One who morphed into a nonchalant and sophisticated young woman in front of her friends outside the entrance to the subway. "Oh, this is just my Aunt Ellie," she said to her bug-eyed friends. "Remember, I told you she and my mom have been best friends since forever? Murder enemies and disappear the bodies for each other kind of friends."

Biting the inside of her cheek at that not inaccurate representation of her friendship with Sara, Elena posed for selfies with the excited group before waving them off on their day's adventures.

As a result of the interaction, she was feeling far better than she'd expected to feel this day when she arrived at the Tower. She'd called Illium from the subway stop to check on the status of the satellite image test, and he'd told her he'd hold off on reviewing the results until she got back.

"We had to restart due to a technical glitch, so the team's just finished going over the scans."

Making it back with ten minutes to spare until their meeting, she went to her and Raphael's suite and jumped into the shower for a quick cleanup. Before that, however, she placed Zoe's blade on her knife shelf, next to the jeweled dagger Raphael had given her.

Her archangel was possessive about who gave her blades, but she had the feeling he wouldn't mind this one; Raphael had a soft spot when it came to children, and he had a *specific* soft spot for Zoe. Elena's godchild had spent a lot of time at their Enclave home—both the original and the one rebuilt after the war. She'd played cards with Raphael, attempted to chase him across the lawn, and gone flying in his arms.

It had begun one fateful weekend when Zoe was a toddler.

Sara and Deacon had both needed to head out of town on urgent business that had sprung up without warning in a perfect storm of circumstances. Aware of the importance of their tasks, and knowing that their trusted nanny was on her annual vacation, Elena had volunteered to babysit.

She'd had no idea how to take care of a toddler, but she'd had Sivya and Montgomery as backup . . . and she'd had Raphael. It turned out that an archangel who'd once stood guard in the angelic nursery knew exactly how to deal with a curious little girl who could toddle-run at startling speed—and who loved playing hide-and-seek with her hapless guardians.

The rest was sweet, funny, wonderful history.

As Montgomery had stiffly said, "Why should Zoe Elena stay with another when she is loved here?"

Their butler adored her goddaughter.

Zoe absolutely loved him in turn; when she visited, she could often be found trailing around behind him, helping him "butler"—with breaks to go steal fresh-baked treats from an indulgent Sivya.

Elena's wasn't the only heart that would break the day Zoe stepped through the veil most immortals would never pierce.

"Not today," Elena reminded herself. "Today, Zoe is young and wild and dazzling."

She reminded Elena of Belle.

Gasping, she pressed one palm against the wall and blinked hard and fast. It was the first time she'd allowed herself to think that, make that connection.

Dance with me, Ellie! Look at your feet go! Wow, what a move! Go! Go! Go!

She shoved a fist against her mouth, holding back the dry, hot sobs that wanted to escape.

18

Interlude
War

Raphael and Dmitri stopped mid-spar to look up at the noon sky that had gone a vivid and empty black on a thunderous boom of sound.

"One of them is dead," Raphael said, shoving a frustrated hand through his hair. "The stupidity of it."

Dmitri didn't ask him to explain who he was talking about—his second knew. "By my count, that's three archangel-to-archangel wars since your ascension, and you've only been on the Cadre for a hundred years."

"I'm learning that my kind can't seem to embrace peace for longer than a few decades."

Dmitri rolled back and forth on the balls of his bare feet. "Don't worry, my friend, I'll pin you down and talk sense into you if you try to start a war for no reason but that you're bored."

Needing to work off his anger at the needless death, Raphael took a sparring position once more. The only reason he could even see Dmitri was because of the glow coming off his own wings—a glow born of his simmering rage at the avoidable.

"I'd be most grateful," he said to the vampire who was his closest friend. "I would not want to go down in history as the archangel who ruled for a hundred years before he picked a fight and got himself dead by angelfire."

Laughing, his friend came at him, a blur in the darkness.

It was only later, long after the sky cleared, that a courier landed on top of his Tower with the news.

The Cadre hadn't lost one archangel in a pointless fight today.

It had lost two.

19

Despite the memories crushing her heart today, Elena had herself under control when she walked out of the suite dressed in jeans and an old T-shirt with the "Hunter Angel" logo on it. Her smartass friends had given it to her so long ago that the once glitter-filled logo was all but indistinguishable from the black of the tee, the material soft against her skin.

She found Illium with Vivek, the two of them ensconced in the private room that Vivek used to work on things so confidential they were unknown even to his senior team in the Tower's tech command center.

"*Guten morgen*, Ellie," he said when she walked in, and from the look on his handsome but too-thin face, he already knew about Jeffrey. No surprise. Information was Vivek's job.

"*Āyubōwan*, Vivek," she said, continuing the game they'd been playing forever. "You yearning for sauerkraut today?"

"As much as you are for a cup of tea from Sri Lanka's

green fields." He bumped fists with her from where he sat in his wheelchair.

Despite all predictions to the contrary, her fellow hunter's transition to vampirism had come with more than one hiccup. Initial estimates had said that it would take decades after his Making for vampirism to heal the childhood spinal damage that had left him a tetraplegic.

The healers had been wrong—and right. Vivek could walk already. Only it caused him excruciating pain due to factors unknown. To further the complications, his left leg hadn't matched the recovery schedule set by the rest of his body. It was much weaker than the right and went numb on him at times, forcing him to drag it along behind him.

But the man was as stubborn as any hunter in the Guild, and he did walk often with the help of a cane—but when it came to serious work, he preferred to do it from his wheelchair.

"After a lifetime in this, Ellie," he'd said to her just last month, patting the side of his chair with an affectionate hand, "it's an extension of my body. My speed in the chair and with all the various accessible interfaces is miles ahead of what I can do with my hands and legs."

"It's always been your choice, V," Elena had said after making a Scrabble move that earned her triple points—to his curses. "Chair or legs, all I care about is that you're happy."

She was the one who'd asked him to consider vampirism in the first place; yes, the final call had been his and his alone, with no pressure from her, but guilt still sat heavy in her gut. "I hate that you're in pain. It's not what I promised you."

"I dunno, maybe it's to make up for years of feeling pretty much nothing and complaining about it. Fate decided to bitch-slap me."

To say that Vivek's sense of humor was dark was a major understatement.

Illium, who'd been leaning over one of the multiple screens on which Vivek had queued up satellite images, gave her a careful look, the aged gold of his eyes weighing up her state.

To this day, it gave her a little start each time she noticed his eyelashes were black dipped in blue. Add to this his wicked smile and his willingness to meet mortals on their own playing field and it was no wonder Bluebell had the most vocal fans out of the Seven.

"I got snacks." He nodded at the tray set to one side.

"Sara made me bacon, and chocolate chip pancakes."

"Stop bragging." Vivek scowled, but that was his normal state of being. "Last time she had me over, she offered me black coffee thick enough to be tar, and bitter chocolate— to go with my sunny personality, she said."

Muscles loosening at the normality, she grinned. "What did you do to provoke her?"

"Nothing," was the suspiciously quick response.

Illium's shoulders shook.

"So," she said, biting back a laugh of her own, "any of the team spot the Refuge?"

"Nope." Vivek wheeled himself to in front of the first screen. "Now, I'm going to test if I can see it."

"Because you know where it is"—she nodded slowly—"know the precise spot where to look."

Illium leaned his hip against the worktable. "Exactly."

In strict terms, Vivek was too young a vampire to have any data on the Refuge, but he was different from the usual vampire in two important ways. The first was that because he'd been paralyzed when he was Made, he'd stayed immobile for a considerable period of time.

Vampirism healed by altering a person's cells; it wasn't a magic pill.

In Vivek's case, that meant he'd gone through the initial "out-of-control" or "proto-bloodlust" phase without any physical outlet. The healers had worried he'd go insane, and she knew he'd had intensive sessions with them prior to his Making where they'd stressed the importance of developing iron-clad mental control.

Vivek had succeeded at such speed that the most senior of the healers, Keir, had come to check that his transition had actually been successful.

"Never have I heard of a vampire so composed at this stage of the process," the worried healer had said, the deceptively youthful lines of his face heavy with concern.

Elena hadn't stopped Keir, wanting Vivek to have the best possible care, but she'd known the reason for his control.

"I learned to swallow my screams quickly, Ellie," he'd told her one quiet day in his former subterranean domain of the Cellars. "A kid who can't move, one whose parents have dumped him at an institution where he has no one to advocate for him . . . well, no one cares if he screams—or they care only to shut him up."

Throw in that he was hunter-born but had never been able to exercise those furious instincts, and stifling his emotions and needs wasn't a problem for Vivek—which of course was a whole different issue. But his control paired with the fact he'd entered the Tower as the genius head of the Guild's surveillance operations meant no one in Raphael's team had ever considered him "young."

It would've been stupid not to utilize V's skills, especially when Elena knew his word, once given, was unbreakable—and he'd vowed loyalty to Raphael. He also had a man crush on Raphael's spymaster, Jason. The black-winged angel, in turn, treated Vivek as his right hand. Vivek pretended to be normal about that, but Elena was sure he did a secret happy dance when no one was looking.

Now, there was no laughter. She and Illium watched in unforgiving silence as Vivek went through the relevant images, having already discarded the ones Illium had added so the techs wouldn't get suspicious about his focus on one particular region.

"No," Vivek said at last. "Can't see it."

Elena exhaled, stomach muscles unclenching.

"Only problem I can see is here." Vivek tapped the lower left corner of the screen. "It's an echo. Can you see it? An image on an image."

Frowning, Elena stared, but he had to zoom in and point out the exact parameters before she could make out the shape of it. "What does that mean?"

It was Illium who answered. "That whatever is hiding the Refuge is beginning to disintegrate exactly as the Cadre suspected." His cheekbones cut against the gold of his skin. "Right now, all anyone on the ground will see is rocks and mountain blooms, but the farther the Mantle withdraws, the higher the chance of a mortal or vampire spotting an element that could lead to dangerous curiosity."

"Shit." Elena put her hands on her hips. "Is there anything we or the Cadre can do?" If she'd learned one thing over the years, it was that archangels were a *power*. Raphael had once caught a freaking plane!

"The sire told me the Cadre has no idea of the origins of the Mantle." Illium folded his arms, the arches of his wings vivid against the dark of the screens. "It's so old it's beyond any of their memories."

Her mouth fell open. "But Caliane and Alexander and Zanaya are—"

"—*old*," Vivek finished, rubbing at his temples. "My brain hurts at how old. How can they not know?"

Illium shrugged. "I'm barely past five hundred. I know nothing in comparison." He tugged on a strand of Elena's damp hair, playing with it as his pampered pet cat did her toys; Smoke might be getting on in years, but that hadn't stopped her playfulness.

"Truth is," he added, "the information probably just

faded out of immortal consciousness bit by bit over millennia. Angelkind has a far longer history than any angel awake in the world at the current time."

The idea of that span of time . . . Elena's mind refused to give shape to it. "If they don't know how it works, they can't fix it."

"I'll start hunting," Vivek said at once, and she could almost see the sparks as his mind fired up. She sometimes wondered what it was like inside Vivek's complicated and brilliant brain—the man could handle more incoming data than anyone else she'd ever seen, without losing track of any of it.

"Jessamy reaches out to me every so often with the more esoteric research stuff she isn't able to track down through other methods," he told them. "Even old material ends up online, sometimes as an image or a reference in another object."

Elena'd had no idea that Vivek was in touch with the angelic Librarian and Historian, but it made sense now that she considered it—both were in the business of information.

"I'll hook up with her on this—I mean I've always assumed her security clearance is at the pointy end?" At Elena's nod, he continued. "It'd help if angels digitized anything, but even Jessamy's fighting me on that."

"It's hard to keep secrets when they become electronic," Illium pointed out. "The Library and Lumia, in contrast, have stood for eons—and held our secrets safe."

"But physical media fades." The thin lines of Vivek's face were flushed with passion. "At least this way, angelkind wouldn't lose data."

Illium considered that. "Maybe, V, we *should* lose information. In a race of immortals, history can become a crushing weight." A slight glow around his wings.

Elena's gut twisted. They all knew Illium would one day ascend—he was too strong at too young an age for it to be otherwise—but his growing power had flatlined after the tumult of the Cascade. That meant nothing except that he was back on a normal trajectory, the growth slow enough that ascension wouldn't tear him apart . . . or so they were hoping. Because that glow to the wings? That was an act meant to be limited to the Cadre—except Illium had been doing it for a while.

As for the words that had fallen from his lips . . . yes, their Bluebell had depths most people who saw only the surface flash would never know. He was far more than beauty and a quicksilver wit, far more than wicked speed in flight and laughter untrammeled. He was exactly the kind of person who should be an archangel . . . but she worried the power of it would ruin him.

The Cadre was no place for an angel gentle enough to rescue a stray kitten, and bighearted enough to keep up a friendship with mortals who inevitably died and broke his heart.

"No philosophy today, Bluebell." Vivek hunched over the keyboard, beginning to call up various data networks. "Not when the loss of this piece of information could doom the entire world."

Doom was a strong word.

Unfortunately, it was also the right one.

20

Deep in the earth below the Refuge, a being of age incalculable stirred, their rest disturbed. But that rest was so profound and so long held that the disturbance was shrugged off after a moment. They settled again. But . . . they were no longer quite as asleep as they'd been before the disturbance . . . and neither were their brethren.

21

The situation with the Mantle and the quakes didn't negate the immediate problem of Qin's territory having no direct archangelic oversight. The Cadre had to deal with that or they'd find themselves having to handle vampiric unrest on top of the shakes that threatened the fall of the angelic homeland.

Aegaeon and Raphael had split up to do the flyover across Qin's scattered territory. Raphael knew it'd take them at least one and possibly two weeks, because this wasn't simply a flight. Both of them would be landing in multiple areas, because the aim was to be *seen*. He and the other archangel would also be deploying a firm hand where trouble had begun to foment.

General Atu had lived up to his reputation as a man on whom an archangel could depend; he'd curated an up-to-date list of possible insurgents and hot spots. It included a city held by a powerful vampire who hadn't been raised to that leadership role by either Astaad or Qin.

As evidenced by Raphael's own second, vampires could hold the most senior positions. Angelkind had never stopped strong vampires from reaching their full potential—that would be an idiotic waste of resources when intelligent and strong vampires were far more useful than vacuous court angels with not an original thought in their well-coiffured heads.

But vampires couldn't simply *annex* a position of power, for that betrayed a disregard for authority that could lead to wider unrest. More to the point, it showed a dangerous lack of critical thinking, because angels—specifically *archangels*—were the apex predators.

The vampire named Minjarra had apparently forgotten that.

Having been briefed on Minjarra by General Atu, Raphael wasn't in the mood to play games when he hit the glittering cosmopolitan city on Australia's eastern seaboard. The sprawling island continent comprised the largest single piece of Qin's territory.

Astaad had kept three residences here. Though none of those residences had been as favored as his homes on remote islands in the tropics, he'd made regular appearances at them throughout the year, often staying up to a month—he'd also done flyovers in between those stays.

Qin, per the general, hadn't left the island for the past two years.

Two years was a long time when it came to vampires and bloodlust.

After flying into the city awash in the pale sunset hues of early evening, Raphael didn't bother with subtlety. He didn't have time for it. Still in the air, and only a short distance from Minjarra's grand estate—an estate right next to one of Astaad's former residences—Raphael blasted out a message using his violent mental power: *Minjarra, I summon you to a meeting! You have ten minutes.*

He said nothing else.

The man would know where to go—and who had summoned him. Raphael had come in on a flight path that'd had people on lower floors of high-rises rushing to their windows and cars screeching to a stop in the street as drivers shoved their heads out the window to stare up, alongside wide-eyed pedestrians.

Fear had pulsed off the city, its citizens' terror a single heartbeat.

Because archangels didn't fly that low unless they wanted to make a point.

When he landed on the flat roof of Astaad's residence, it was to be met by an angelic squadron Atu had contacted in advance. "Archangel." The squadron leader went down on one knee, her squadron moving as one with her.

"The stronghold is secure, but Minjarra has continued his encroachment into Archangel Ast—Archangel Qin's lands." The correction was fast, the error telling. "He makes no threats and his people carry no weapons, but we have found him and his teams in various remote parts of the estate."

"What does he say when you confront him?"

"That he made a promise to care for the animals that live on the estate. I was assigned here by General Atu after the war. Neither he nor I know of any promises or agreements."

"What is your judgment of him?"

A hesitation before the squadron leader squared her shoulders. "He is blatant in crossing into the territory despite multiple warnings, but he and his people *do* seem to be focused on the welfare of the animals, and have never acted with aggression. I don't believe he wishes to grasp at power. In this, I am in disagreement with my commander, General Atu."

"Report acknowledged." The squadron leader's take on Minjarra intrigued him. It was certainly a more nuanced report than that offered by Atu. "Take to the skies above his estate."

"Archangel."

He stayed on the roof after they took off in the martial glide of a trained wing. He could glimpse the whitecaps of the ocean on the horizon, though it was some distance away on foot. Far closer—on the left edge of the roof—sat a loud bird. It scolded him with all the mannerisms of an old biddy vampire. He must tell Elena about the white crested thing that he knew was unique to this continent.

"Archangel." The squeaky voice had him turning to face a tall and curvaceous vampire who held a tray in trembling hands. Her skin was golden brown, but her face bleached white with fear. "Cold drinks. Food."

"My thanks." He drank the entire glass of ice-cold juice that held little black seeds, but waved off the food after placing the glass back on the tray. "I will eat later."

Nodding, the vampire began to back away. Her pulse skittered in her throat.

To this woman, he wasn't the angel Sam called Rafa, or the lover Elena tangled wings with in the skies. He was nothing but a blinding voice that had exploded inside her head. He'd done that on purpose. Now everyone in the area knew that an archangel was in residence—and that he *was not pleased*.

His anger was no facsimile. It was born of his desire to be with his consort. He wouldn't get to do that for however long it took to sort out Qin's mess. In the meantime, the rest of the Cadre were turning their territories inside out in an effort to locate any historical references that might relate to the Mantle.

Given the latter, it made sense that Raphael was one of the two archangels set this task. His territory was young, had no buried archives of which he was aware. Aegaeon, in contrast, was based in a land ancient and was chomping at the bit to return there.

"But I'm already here," he'd snarled. "It'll go faster if I just do what's needed than if we ask one of the others to travel to this territory." A curt nod. "Fly hard. Fly fast."

They'd parted on those words.

This Minjarra just had the bad luck to attract Cadre attention when every archangel in the world was stretched to the limit. Patience wasn't in short supply; it simply didn't exist.

Especially not for those who might attempt to steal power.

"A promise to care for animals," Raphael murmured, staring at the horizon. "An odd excuse if not true. But it does give him plausible reason to be in areas he shouldn't be in." Simply because the squadron leader hadn't caught him in insurgent activities didn't mean they weren't taking place.

Movement on the steps leading up to the roof.

The vampire who appeared on the rooftop seconds later—just under the deadline—his dark, dark skin flushed with heat and shining with sweat, and his body clad in a chocolate brown suit paired with a white shirt, his hair thick and dark, was a surprise. He didn't meet Raphael's eyes with the arrogance of a man who thought himself better than an archangel.

Instead, he went down on one knee with every appearance of sincerity. "Sire," he said. "Is it true? Do you lead us now?"

Raphael blinked—for that had been hope in Minjarra's voice. "Rise." He kept his voice cold as he tried to work out if he was dealing with a clever predator—or if Atu had made an uncharacteristic error, while the squadron leader saw true. "Why ask such a question when you know it is Qin who rules this land?"

Getting to his feet, the vampire finally met Raphael's gaze, managing to hold it long enough to say, "Archangel Qin has abandoned us." His jaw worked, his gaze dropping. "I know it is an act traitorous to say that, but how can I not?"

Fisted hands, new heat under his skin. "He hasn't been

in these lands for two long years. The only reason we are holding together is because of the experienced and re-spected senior angels once under Archangel Astaad's command—but we don't have the full complement. Many died in the war."

Once more, he met Raphael's eyes, his own holding a plea. "I've done my best to maintain stability, but I'm not meant to do so on my own. General Liyanage was the angel I called Commander, but he fell in the war. I've been wait-ing these many years for a replacement." The words poured out in a passionate, angry rush.

As if they'd been building and building to explosion point.

"Have you been in touch with General Atu?"

"Until he stopped responding to me," was the brusque reply. "He told me to know my place and not question my archangel." He shoved his hand over his hair. "Atu is smart, but he was too loyal to his archangel, didn't care to see flaws. We—all of us in this land—have learned to rely only on each other."

Raphael considered the devotion in Atu's expression at the door to Qin's private study, the way the general's voice had shaken. "I hear of your encroachment on this estate—an archangel's estate."

A hard swallow, the vampire glancing down. "Yes, I am guilty on that charge. But Lady Mele nurtured many old or injured or orphaned animals on this land, animals she en-sured were looked after with love—but the majority of her keepers lost their lives to reborn, and Lady Mele couldn't return here after Archangel Astaad's fall.

"The animals began to die or attack each other in des-peration, for the squadrons have no idea what to do with them but kill. I put together a team to care for them—and yes, the team and I do encroach into lands we shouldn't to do our tasks. To be fair, the squadrons watch us, but haven't acted against either me or my keepers with violence."

Raphael now had two competing narratives on the situation, with his instincts telling him Atu had steered him wrong. Whatever the truth, he'd find it—a stronghold had many eyes; it was just a case of asking the right person the right questions. "Gather the angels and vampires with whom you say you've been working," he ordered Minjarra. "We meet tomorrow night at your residence."

"Sire." The vampire bent in a deep bow before retreating from the roof.

Frowning, Raphael was about to move on to another matter when it struck him that he was leaving a valuable resource on the table. He took out his phone and initiated a visual call.

The woman who answered had a lovely oval face with skin of rich brown framed with hair of soft black. She'd lost weight in her grief, her eyes dark pools of sorrow. "Archangel Raphael." Mele's voice was quiet but welcoming. "Is all well?"

22

"Yes, Mele," he said to this woman who had been a huge part of Astaad's life. "How are your sisters of the heart?" he asked, using the term Elena had told him Mele used for her fellow members of the harem.

His tough, independent, and possessive lover had refused to surrender her unexpected friendship with Astaad's favorite concubine, even after the entire harem left Astaad's home for a small island Qin had signed over to them.

No one could say that Qin had been unkind to the harem; fact was, he couldn't have them inside his territory. Any member of the Cadre would've done the same, for they were a physical reminder of another archangel, and past loyalties.

"My sisters yet mourn," Mele said, her voice soft. "We watch the horizon for our archangel each day as we wake, and each night before we sleep. He was the center around which we spun, the love which warmed us." A sad smile.

"What do you need of me, Archangel Raphael? I will do all I can."

"I want only information." Then he asked her about Minjarra.

"He speaks the truth," she said at once, her eyes flaring. "I broke the rules that say the intimates of a past archangel shouldn't interfere in the affairs of the new archangel, but I was so worried for my animals."

"I'm not here to castigate you," Raphael reassured her. "The time after the war was chaotic. It would've been easy for things to be overlooked."

"Yes, I worried no one would remember my beasts, and I couldn't bring them here, for the journey would be arduous, and they wouldn't thrive in this climate. So I asked Minjarra—a good neighbor and a loyal part of my archangel's wider court—to care for them for the short term.

"I believed new keepers would be assigned once matters settled down, as did he. They never were, so Minjarra has kept up with the task all this time though it was dangerous for him. Please, do not punish him. The fault is mine."

The only one at fault, Raphael thought, was Qin. But he couldn't say that to Mele—for Qin had still been an archangel. "Minjarra isn't in trouble." Mele's testimony confirmed what he'd already believed, which meant he could now put Minjarra where Qin should've put him: in a position of trust where he had the public backing of an archangel. "I do, however, need further details on the current situation in this territory. What can you tell me?"

Mele hesitated.

"I know you, Mele," he said, his voice gentle because this wasn't his hunter, who could stand toe to toe with him.

Mele's strength was a quieter thing, but her gifts were no less valuable for that.

It was Elena who'd pointed that out. "You all ignore her like she's beautiful but dumb arm candy." A knife playing over and in between her nimble fingers. "You never look, never see that she watches and listens and learns. Mele's never going to be flashy or in your face—but neither is Aodhan. And he's one of your most valuable assets. She's the same for Astaad."

The comparison with Aodhan had been startling—and accurate. It had also made him pay careful attention to this member of Astaad's harem, and what he'd learned had only added to his confusion about why Astaad didn't simply call Mele his consort. It was clear the archangel relied on her for advice, that he discussed matters with her—and that he loved her.

"You would watch over this land for Astaad," he added. "You wouldn't be able to help it."

A sigh, a swallow, before she gave him a concise breakdown.

Toward the end, she said, "I am not a consort, do not have the right to speak so, but Archangel Qin didn't care for his people. My archangel cared. Archangel Qin did only his duty, no more."

It was the harshest statement he'd ever heard out of Mele's mouth.

She continued before he could reply. "But let us end on a happier note. How is Ellie? I have been a bad friend in not accepting her offer to host me and my sisters in New York, but that she cares to love us even in our unending grief . . . she is a friend I treasure."

Yes, he thought, his hunter knew how to love—and how to hold her people close. "She holds the fort for me while I deal with the situation here." It was a deliberate choice not to mention the situation with Jeffrey—Elena would share that when she was ready. "I'll tell her we spoke."

"I would appreciate that, Archangel Raphael." There was a hitch in her voice when she next spoke. "You have my eternal gratitude for looking out for the lands my own beloved archangel so cherished."

Call ended, Raphael attempted to track down Aegaeon.

The older archangel refused to carry a phone, so it took three hours. When they spoke at last, it was on a phone that belonged to the wingleader who'd located the Archangel of the Deep.

"I'm discovering the situation is worse than we were led to believe," Raphael told the other archangel, having spent the ensuing time checking into multiple other situations. "Atu may well have allowed his loyalty to blind him to harsh reality."

Loyalty that unquestioning was a negative asset, not a positive. Any being in power needed someone at their side who'd speak the blunt truth. Dmitri had done so with Raphael even when Raphael was at his coldest and worst—his second had called him out, made him confront his arrogance.

"I'm finding the same," Aegaeon said in what was a mutter for him. "Qin seems to have faded away from active governance two years prior. Astaad's network of senior vampires and angels have managed to hold things together, but their numbers were cratered by the war and without archangelic assistance . . ."

"Yes, we have a problem." The fact of the matter was that there were just fewer strong and trained people to go around.

Lijuan's megalomania had cost countless lives.

It'd take *at least* two centuries before the numbers stabilized, as younger angels and vampires turned into seasoned warriors who could help hold a territory. "Do you have anyone who can be seconded from your territory?"

Aegaeon hissed out a breath. "No, but I'll have to find someone. As will you. If all eight of us do, we can patch up the holes in the interim."

"What a fucking mess." He rubbed his forehead, what sympathy he had for Qin having long since drained away.

"What about my son?" Aegaeon demanded. "When will he ascend?"

Raphael didn't talk about Illium to Aegaeon. So he left it at, "You know there is no answer to that." Had Raphael his own way, Illium wouldn't ascend for at least another millennium.

Raphael had ascended at a thousand years of age and he'd barely survived the cataclysmic forces of it. He wouldn't wish that for the young angel. And Illium wasn't ready, even if the world needed him to be ready.

An early ascension would destroy their bright, beautiful Bluebell.

"We'll talk again tomorrow after I've met the most powerful angels and vampires in this part of the territory," he said to Aegaeon.

"I will do the same."

They hung up.

Raphael already knew who he'd second here: Andreas. He'd intended for the warrior angel to take over one of his own cities that had lost its ruling angel, but that part of his land was surrounded by multiple other cities with strong hands at the helm. It'd survive without its own senior lead. Andreas was also the kind of angel this territory needed: intelligent, calm, and not afraid to be hard when needed.

Elena had always thought Andreas's harsh hand a cruelty, but even his hunter had come to understand that for some immortal crimes, cruel punishment was the only kind that left a mark. The promise of eternal life made many immortals and almost-immortals jaded to the point of not caring about pain, imprisonment, or other "normal" rebukes.

Raphael took no pleasure in being cruel—and crucially, neither did Andreas. The warrior wasn't one to find gratification in such actions. To him, they were simply a tool.

Raphael could trust him in this land wounded by neglect.

23

Interlude
Bloodborn

"Bloodborn? You are certain?"

"Yes. Uram is no longer an archangel but a creature out of our worst nightmares."

"No, I do not believe it. I must see for myself."

"There are images . . . from his palace. Of bodies de-fleshed and organs displayed. And worse."

"This should not be."

"Yet it is. Now, we must come to a decision about what to do about it."

24

Elena walked into the ICU four days after her return home, her mind tense with the news of another major quake at the Refuge. No more buildings down, no further casualties, but the instability was close to constant at this point, with the earth trembling more often than not.

She'd also spoken to her archangel, and the news he had was only slightly better.

"The Cadre has agreed to second a number of their own people to Qin's territory to hold it together in the interim," he'd told her, his face drawn and the midnight of his hair tumbled from the winds through which he'd flown. She'd wanted only to hold him, give him a place to rest, a person with whom he could lower his shields.

"In the meantime we'll redraw the territorial boundaries. But with the Mantle failing, the latter can't be our priority. Andreas and the others will be tasked with squelching any unrest while we deal with the far bigger issue at hand."

She hadn't been surprised at his choice of Andreas for

the position. A soft hand wouldn't do, not with a territory already that unstable. But knowing Andreas's way of handling matters, she'd asked the question any consort in her position would've asked. "Do you think he might come in too hard, risk a revolt?"

"You've never seen Andreas lead, Elena-mine. He is very, very good. Never harsh for the sake of it and never wasteful of his people. His wing respects and likes him, as do any others who've worked with him. Even you like him." A smile in the last words.

"Hmm," she'd said, her feelings toward Andreas still complicated—she could understand his way of dealing with issues, but not necessarily agree with them. "You know him better than I ever could, Archangel." Their acquaintance was measured in centuries, hers in years. "If you think he's right for the job, then he's right for the job."

She'd looked at that face of astonishing masculine beauty, taken in the faint hollows that had begun to develop in his cheeks. "And you, my Rafe?" she'd said, using the nickname of his youth as a kiss of affection between consorts. "You look tired. Are you resting at all?"

"That should be my question, *hbeebti.*" Those eyes so blue as to defy the laws of nature had searched her face. "How is your father?"

She'd told him all of it, and now she walked into the ICU once more.

Though the antiseptic smell no longer made her nauseous, her stomach still clenched reflexively when she turned the corner toward Jeffrey's room . . . and came face-to-face with Amy.

Amethyst Gwendolyn Deveraux was her mother's daughter. Eyes of darkest blue, hair of raven black with a natural wave to it, and skin of such a rich cream as to be luxuriant. Not a freckle in sight.

Her eyes flared at seeing Elena, but she didn't nod with stiff politeness and walk away as she'd always before done.

"He still hasn't woken again." Shoulders tense, she glanced up at Elena, the height difference between them significant; Amy and Eve were as petite as Gwendolyn, while Elena carried Jeffrey in her long legs and bones.

"Did you two fight when he woke while you were here?" Amy demanded.

Elena didn't blame her half sister for the suspicion. "No. The opposite." Leaning one shoulder against the wall, her arms loosely folded, she gave Amy a tired smile. "We weren't always like we became, Amy. The night he woke, he was the father who lifted me onto his shoulders and who gave me piggyback rides, the man who read me bedtime stories."

A red flush on her half sister's cheekbones, but her words weren't angry. "He never did any of those things for us," she said quietly.

Elena hadn't meant to cause the other woman any hurt, felt sick that she had. But from what little she knew of Amy, her half sister wouldn't accept apologies or platitudes. "If I had a piece of him that you never saw," she said, "then you've experienced a part of him I never did."

Jeffrey *had* been a different father to Amy and Eve, but that wasn't necessarily a bad thing. "He's been a firm presence through your entire life. I only really had him for ten years of my life."

Amy's shoulders dropped. Lifting a trembling hand to her lips, she whispered, "I can't lose him." Huge, wet eyes. "He's the person I go to whenever I have a problem with no easy resolution, the person who knows the right things to say, the person who never lets me down."

Elena didn't begrudge Amy that connection with their shared father. "It'd destroy me if he goes before we've fixed this fight we've been having for decades."

Their eyes met, Amy's shimmering wet.

Elena hesitated before straightening and reaching out to take Amy's hand. The other woman flinched, but instead of pulling back, she closed her fingers over Elena's. They stood there in silent sympathy for a single long minute that forever changed the relationship between them before Amy took a deep breath and said, "Mom's with him. Eve did the morning shift."

Elena already knew that, having caught up with her youngest half sister earlier that day. She didn't know when she'd stop seeing Eve as the round-cheeked eleven-year-old who—in the most down-to-earth manner—had told her that "I just want to be a bit less fat, but I really like cake," but the truth was that Eve was now the age at which Elena had first met Raphael.

Eve still liked to wear her black hair in twin braids that reached her shoulders, but no one would ever mistake her for anything but a petite powerhouse of a hunter. Her dark gray eyes remained as beautiful, but age had added a maturity and knowledge to them that made Elena both proud of her and nostalgic for the little girl she'd once been.

"How are your babies doing with you here and their grandad sick?" Elena asked Amy after they broke their handclasp. "The twins must be, what, three years old now?"

Amy studied her. "Do you judge me for that? That I'm a homemaker?"

"My mom was a homemaker," Elena said through the roughness of her throat. "She was the center of our world."

Amy blinked rapidly, and then, to Elena's surprise, reached out to squeeze her hand again. "I'm sorry. I can't imagine either one of my girls dealing with what happened to you and Beth. It gives me nightmares if I ever think about it."

She exhaled, broke contact. "And they're doing well. Maynard's such a good dad to them, and his family is lovely. My sister-in-law's stepped in to manage anything he can't—you know he's Father's COO? He can't take time off, given the current situation—Father would strip his hide for that."

"That I can believe." Jeffrey expected total dedication.

A faint smile from Amy before she glanced at her watch. "I better head off. If I hurry, I can get home in time to join the kiddos for dinner."

"See you tomorrow," Elena said, and they moved past each other.

It had been the longest conversation they'd ever had.

Gwendolyn was still with Jeffrey when Elena reached the room, so Elena stayed outside, her back against the wall next to the room's open door. The nurses had proved to be good about overlooking two visitors in the room so long as no one got in their way, but Elena's wings *would* get in the way. So she was in the hallway when her phone buzzed.

Glancing at the screen, she saw the symbol that indicated a news alert.

She frowned; she hadn't signed up for a news alert service.

About to delete it and block the number, she saw a message pop up from Vivek: *Ellie, shit's going down. Dmitri's trying to touch base with Raphael, but he's in flight somewhere over Qin's territory that doesn't have reception.*

A cold shiver rippling along her spine, Elena clicked open the link he'd forwarded her. A major quake had just devastated the southern part of Elijah's territory, one big enough to topple smaller buildings and collapse bridges. Casualties were a given. "Damn it."

Vivek forwarded her another alert before she'd completely processed the first. This one was about a small quake "cluster" in New Zealand. It hadn't caused as much damage as the one in Elijah's territory, but the time proximity of the two had seismologists making ominous references to the "Pacific Ring of Fire."

Another message from Vivek: *This hasn't hit the media yet, but I've intercepted messages from various volcanologists and seismologists about a volcano off the coast of Japan. They're picking up deep sea quakes only detectable by their instruments, are worried it's a sign of a huge underwater volcano about to blow.*

Hearing the scrape of a chair on the tile floor, she glanced into Jeffrey's room to see Gwendolyn rising from her vigil by Jeffrey's bed. Elena slipped the phone into her pocket and turned to face Gwendolyn as she exited the room.

"Ellie." Face far too thin, she accepted Elena's hug, hugging her tight in return. Her perfume was a delicate array of roses with an undertone of bergamot, as elegant a scent as the woman herself.

"No major change, that's what the doctor told me," she said when they drew apart.

"That's good news." It wasn't, not really, not when Jeffrey's current state meant he hovered on the line between life and death. But she wasn't about to douse the flame of Gwendolyn's—and her own—hope.

However, her resolve faltered when she walked into the room after she'd convinced Gwendolyn to go get a few hours of much-needed rest. Jeffrey's cheeks were hollow, his face beginning to lose the stamp of the granite will that had been a hallmark of his personality throughout his life—even back when he'd been her papa.

"It's Ellie," she said, taking a seat on the stool no one had removed from the room. "I thought you'd want current news—but I'm afraid it's not good." Needing to believe that he could hear her, she told him about the surge in quakes and followed it up with updates from the finance pages.

Afterward, she just held his hand and watched the machine that monitored his damaged heart. Her own heart, it hurt. *I ache to talk to you, Raphael.* But her mind wasn't powerful enough to reach him across the world, and it wasn't until hours later, as dawn touched the horizon, that she got the chance.

Beth had arrived earlier and squeezed a chair into the spot next to Elena with the wriggly ease of a baby sister used to getting in between her siblings. Once there, she lay her head on Elena's shoulder and sniffled into a tissue.

Elena hugged her, and in the process, caught the glimmer of a strand of silver in the strawberry blonde of Beth's hair. It punched the breath right out of her, the knowledge that her little sister was now older than her in strict mortal terms. Elena had stopped aging when she became an angel, while the march of time continued on in Beth's fragile mortal body.

Her arms spasmed tighter around Beth, holding on with panicked desperation. "Don't cry, Bethie." She rubbed her chin over her sister's head. "You know he's a tough bastard," she said, channeling Sara.

A sobbing laugh. "Only you would call Dad a bastard while he's right there."

"We have an understanding." Elena tried to infuse humor into her voice. "It's a compliment. He's always stuck around. I don't think he's going to give up now."

"He did stick around, didn't he, Ellie?" Beth snuggled further into her, forever the baby sister to Elena's big sister.

There should've been two older sisters, Elena an aggrieved middle child, but Belle and Ari were gone and Elena was the big sister Beth knew and remembered best. "Yes." She pressed a kiss to Beth's hair. "How's Maggie?"

Elena's niece was now eighteen and a half years old, a blooming young woman with her mother's loving temperament sprinkled with a streak of Ari's steel spine. Memories hidden in the genes, Elena thought as Beth told her of her daughter's dance performances and how the two of them were already planning a trip to a London fashion museum as her graduation gift.

"I love how you are with her." Beth was the kind of mother Marguerite had been: interested in her children and eager to help them flourish. "And with Laurie, too. Did he enjoy that motocross race I couldn't get to?" Her nephew's race had fallen on the same date as the Refuge ball.

Beth's eyes, that stunning turquoise bequeathed her by their maternal grandmother, just glowed. "Won third prize and has been wearing the medal at every opportunity. He's so proud of himself. He told me to make sure I have a copy of his photo from the prize-giving to give to you because you're going to want to put it up on that wall in your home."

Her laughter was affectionate. "And by the way, we have been instructed not to call him Laurie anymore. That's for babies, apparently. He's decided he wants to use his given name."

"Laurent it is, then." Elena could just imagine her thirteen-year-old nephew deciding it was far more sophisticated to be a Laurent than a Laurie.

"Oh, and Maggie's designing you a fancy jacket in her textiles class. Don't tell her I spilled or she'll *Moooom* me."

Elena joined in her sister's laughter. "Your secret's safe with me. I can't wait for the jacket." Maggie was as into fashion as Zoe was into weapons. "And Laurent is right. I definitely want to put that picture on my photo wall." A wall of memories that she was building against the unknown future while trying to live in the present.

You know what I've learned from my baby girl? To enjoy the now. It'll be gone soon enough, and no one knows what the next hour, much less tomorrow, will bring.

Words Sara had spoken to Elena one night as they sat on her rooftop lounge.

Elena knew her best friend was right. That didn't mean it was easy when she was surrounded by symbols of the unavoidable and relentless passage of time. The longer she lived as an immortal, the better she understood the depth of Illium's strength: he was more than five hundred years old . . . and he continued to have mortal friends.

He'd been a pallbearer for a baker in Harlem during her residence in New York, and he still visited the bakery—and the baker's elderly widow. The last time she'd seen him with one of their distinctive blue paper bags, she'd said, "How do you do it? Keep on loving people who die on you?"

A shrug, sorrow deep in those golden eyes. "You can't contain love, Ellie, and you can't predict friendships. Lorenzo was one of the best friends I've ever had, and his wife remains one. I wouldn't give up all the nights I spent laughing with them, no matter the anguish."

Elena wasn't sure she had the same strength, wasn't sure she wouldn't curl up inside at some point, so heartsick at losing person after person that she just couldn't do it anymore.

25

Elena only left her sister when Beth was no longer teary, and the last sounds she heard from the room were of Beth regaling Jeffrey with the tale of Maggie's first proper boyfriend. "Of course Harrison's losing his mind. I had to remind him that she's not Daddy's little girl anymore, and her boyfriend's a good kid. Though I'm sure you'll probably run a background check on him the minute you wake."

Lips curving, Elena decided to return to the Tower on the wing. Her injured tendon had healed, but she didn't risk a vertical takeoff, instead climbing up to the hospital roof. Though emblazoned with a landing circle for a medical chopper, it was empty when she reached it.

Elena took a deep breath.

The cold morning air infused with the chaotic mishmash that was the scent of the city was a welcome change from the medicinal aroma of the hospital, and she inhaled appreciative lungfuls of it as she glided off the roof before winging her way up to a higher elevation.

Her city, soft in the morning light, nonetheless pulsed with life. When she spotted a bunch of kids at a neighborhood basketball court jumping up and down and waving at her, she swept down to dip her wings—close enough that she heard their cheers and raucous joy.

The interaction made her day as much as it made theirs.

Only minutes later, she'd just entered her and Raphael's suite when her phone lit up with an incoming call from her archangel. Emotion roared over her. "Raphael."

"*Hbeebti*, I would see you."

"Wait, let me patch the call onto our big screen. Where are you?" The signal was clearer than it had been during their previous conversation.

"A small communications center on the far western edge of Australia."

Thanks to Vivek's lessons, it took her mere seconds to get the feed up onto the screen. Her archangel wore faded leathers of deep brown, his ceremonial sword visible over one shoulder, against the arches of wings held with warrior control. The two of them raised their hands in unspoken harmony, touching their fingers to their personal screens.

"I miss you," she said, her voice cracking on the words.

The blue flame of his eyes blazed, as did the Legion mark on his temple. So much wildfire in the lines of the dragon that her breath caught in a hope painful. Until this unexplained resurgence, she hadn't seen the luminous white-gold, its edges iridescent with midnight and dawn, since the war . . . where the Legion had laid down their lives to save the world.

You are in our memory, they'd said in some of the last words they had ever spoken. *The* aeclari *of the Death Cascade. The* aeclari *who . . . loved us.*

"I dream of you." Raphael's voice was gritty, his jaw a rigid line. "I sleep but an hour here and there, but when I do, I dream only of you."

Her skin felt too tight, her emotions too big for it to contain. "Did you hear about the quakes?"

"Yes." He thrust a hand through his hair. "Jessamy joined us at a Cadre meeting held an hour ago, as did several other learned scholars, but none of them have discovered anything useful."

A message bubble popped up on the side of the screen. It was from Vivek: *I found a weird thing that might be important.*

Forehead creasing, she told Raphael of the message. "I can put him on the call with us."

Raphael gave a quick nod.

A surprised Vivek was on a split screen with Raphael half a minute later. "Archangel Raphael," he managed to get out, coughing to clear his throat.

"What did you find, Vivek?" Raphael said.

"I've been running searches on any literature I can find, even things labeled myths and legends. I figure history gets old enough, it starts turning into story." He carried on when neither one of them interrupted. "This came up in a book of myths said to originate in ancient Egypt. It's about the gods they used to worship."

Elena wasn't startled at the mention of gods. Regardless of the immortals among whom they lived, all human civilizations had gods, the need driven by the belief that there had to be more in this universe than what they could see and experience.

Elena understood that, believed the same. The idea that her mother and sisters were just gone when they stopped breathing wasn't one she was ever going to accept. Her hand fisted, her mind awash in memories of the dreams in which her mother spoke to her; she wanted to believe that was Marguerite's soul, reaching out to her from beyond the veil.

"What does your myth say?" she asked Vivek.

"It talks about a 'great unraveling' due to the actions of a particular god—what little I managed to unearth of this being makes it clear they were considered a dark god."

Vivek's face vanished, to be replaced by a set of Egyptian hieroglyphs. A glowing circle appeared around one: an eye with a red center. It had nothing in common with the protective Eye of Horus except that both depicted the same organ. This eye had a starburst pupil of black within the red of the iris, fine red veins crawling outward from it. No eyebrow, nothing to soften the pulsating stare.

"Dramatic," Elena muttered. "A bloody evil eye."

Vivek's face reappeared. "Exactly. Anyway, the myth states that the evil act or entity—I can't quite tell which—was so terrible that it caused the earth to shake and splinter, until empires fell and civilizations were lost, and the world had to begin again. It ends with a homily about watching for evil so that we don't lose eternity. It isn't much."

"But it has the earth shakes"—Raphael spread his wings, his eyes narrowing—"and we did recently experience a great evil. Keep digging."

"Sire," Vivek said, and logged out, leaving them alone once more.

"Lijuan?" Making a face, Elena folded her arms. "I mean, she was evil, but powerful enough to cause all this? I can't see it, not when we defeated her."

"What if it's not the bigger evil, but the more insidious one?" A glow pulsed off Raphael's wings. "Charisemnon created a disease that could hurt angels. It led to the first ever death of one of our kind from a disease.

"But that"—Raphael shook his head—"isn't as important as the fact that if Vivek's find isn't just a tale, then—"

"—we're talking not only about the fall of the Refuge," Elena completed, feeling sick, "but the destruction of the entire world."

26

Two days after Raphael had ordered him to keep digging, Vivek had exhausted all his usual avenues of research. He knew of only one other way he might be able to get further information on this particular esoteric subject.

What he'd found online had been the scan of a page of a book. No other fragments seemed to exist. But if anyone knew more about or could get their hands on a copy of the lost tome, it would be a certain vampire from the gray heart of the city.

Jessamy herself consulted Katrina when on the hunt for books so rare that even the Refuge had no copy. He couldn't leave that stone unturned. And if his body heated at the thought of finally getting to meet her, well, he'd always been reckless. Vampirism had just made it worse.

But he had to wait until dark, because Katrina didn't do daylight.

His skin was tight with anticipation by the time he pushed away from his desk close to midnight. There were no guarantees that he'd get to see Katrina, but he wasn't above dropping Raphael's name to make sure he did. He felt no guilt about that—because he did need to speak to her. That it'd ease his fascination with the mystery of her was an unexpected bonus.

After changing into clothing suitable for what he planned—a slick suit in a deep brown that echoed his eyes, paired with a black shirt and no tie, the collar open at the throat—he abandoned his wheelchair in his Tower suite and picked up his cane. Of a wood dark and polished to a shine, it had been created for him by former hunter and current weapons-maker Deacon.

"A gift, V," the Guild's former Slayer had said. "For all you did and still do to keep our brethren safe. I owe you more than you'll ever know."

Vivek loved the thing, but its strength and beauty could only assist him so much; it couldn't fix the damage in his body.

Leaning hard on it, safe in the knowledge that Deacon had designed it to handle far more weight and force, he took the elevator down to reception. The vampire on duty smiled at him, her teeth pretty and white, and her bronze-streaked black hair pulled back into a sleek bun, not a stray tendril in sight. "Good evening, Vivek. May I assist you with any-thing tonight?"

He thought about asking her to call him a cab, dismissed the idea almost at once. He hadn't been walking much and needed to make up for that. "No, but thanks, Suhani. Also, I thought I was a workaholic, but you put me to shame. Do you *ever* go home?"

"I keep my coffin under the desk for catnaps."

He rolled his eyes. "Fucking place is full of smartasses. Can't believe I used to think you were a straight arrow."

Soft laughter from behind the glossy wall of her desk. "Have a good night."

He lifted a hand to her, then greeted the vampire on duty

outside the door, before making his way out to the main drag, outside the Tower precinct. Each step was a throb up his spine; faint beads of sweat had broken out along his hairline by the time he reached the place where the cabs sat, waiting for passengers even at this time.

Getting in, he told the driver where he wanted to go.

The skinny Black man whistled between his teeth. "You sure, man?" he said as he pulled out into the night streets. "That area's so dangerous I'm half-afraid some bum's gonna steal my wheels if I stop for a light."

Vivek realized then and there that the man had mistaken him for a mortal. It was an easy mistake to make. Vivek didn't read as a vamp at first glance. Only way to know was to spot his fangs—and he didn't exactly go around flashing those. Right now, he looked human. Painfully, vulnerably human. Because vampires didn't have limps and didn't use canes.

"I know the area," he said, leaving it at that.

"Your funeral," the driver muttered, then sang along to the smooth music pouring out of the speakers.

Vivek stared out the window at the blur of multihued light that was New York passing him by. He'd spent a good percentage of his life inside walls or underground, the former forced onto him, the latter a choice. At times, he didn't understand the outside world at all, didn't know why Ellie thrived in it, or why his other friends kept inviting him out to clubs and parties and expeditions into the wilderness.

The outside was also awash in the scents of vampires he didn't know, and the overload hurt hunter senses he hadn't been able to use for most of his lifetime. He'd shut them down in his youth, suffocating that which made him hunter-born—the same thing that would've been his biggest asset had he not been paralyzed.

Those senses had reawakened with a vengeance during his transition, but Vivek had lived in a body that couldn't hunt for a long time. He knew how to stuff his discomfort into a tiny box that he shoved to the back of his consciousness. That didn't mean he enjoyed the constant assault on his nose.

What a joke he was—a hunter-born who'd never hunted. His fingers clenched on top of the cane.

He was pretty sure something inside him was stunted, a bit of growth that had never taken place. Probably needed therapy for that, but after a lifetime of being watched and touched by others, he'd had his fill of medical personnel of any kind. Didn't matter if they were kind or not; he could barely even grit his teeth through his appointments with the physiotherapists and Tower healers.

"Here you go, boss." The cab driver pulled up in front of a black building with a black door and blacked-out windows. "Look, man, I ain't the type to get into no one's business, but you *really* sure you cool?"

It still surprised Vivek when he realized that some people were just nice. Like Jim and Nellie, the only people he considered family though they shared no blood, were nice. Good thing he had them in his life or he'd have grown up a misanthrope who believed the worst of everyone; but as it was, he only expected the worst of most people.

After paying his bill with a simple scan of the sleek watch he wore under his suit jacket, he shifted to exit the taxi . . . and flashed his fangs at the driver.

The man's jaw literally unhinged. "Holy shit!" A grin wide and dazzling. "Go get your freak on, my man!"

He mimed a high five motion before he pulled away. His words told Vivek he had an excellent idea of what lay behind the walls of the black building. No surprise; cabbies in New York knew everything. Several were informants for Vivek. He'd made a mental note of this cab's medallion number almost automatically. Never knew when it might come in handy.

Turning onto the deserted street that wasn't actually deserted if you looked into the alleyways and shadows, he made his way to the door. The driver needn't have worried. No one approached Vivek. Mortals might not realize who he was, but the angels and vamps all knew him. Word on the street was that he must have "connections"—or a skill so rare as to have been Made despite his physical condition.

No one wanted to mess with a vamp that hooked up.

He wanted to snort. Yes, he had friends despite himself—Ellie was the reason he'd even been considered for Making. He never forgot that, or how she'd set him straight when he'd attempted to turn her offer into some sort of savior deal. Ellie respected him—enough to not pull any punches when he was being an ass.

A man needed friends like that.

But connected or not, here and now *he* was the threat. People who'd lived hundreds of years tended to forget about modern weapons—like the souped-up stunner in his coat pocket. Or the poisoned sword built into his cane. Because *of course* Deacon was going to build a sword into his cane, and Vivek had decided it had to be poisoned, because that might do enough harm to a rampaging angel to give him a shot at escape.

The stunner would definitely down an angel. He'd tested it on a Tower volunteer—and the angel had cursed him for days in the aftermath. It hadn't taken her down for long, though. Five minutes max. But five minutes was plenty of time for a man who knew how to hot-wire almost any vehicle known to man and had plenty of other tricks up his sleeve.

Five minutes could mean a lifetime.

He hadn't brought along his gun, the twin of which had caused a scar on Raphael's wing that had turned into a permanent pattern after his feathers regrew. Good thing the archangel wasn't holding a grudge. That gun meant *serious* business—and had felt too heavy-duty for tonight's task.

Tonight, he wanted to make friends, not enemies.

Reaching the black door, he rang the weathered bell that

hung over it, then waited. The slot in the door slid back a moment later, dark eyes scanning him. The slot shut, then the door opened to reveal a dimly lit interior, black carpet against black walls.

The bouncer shut the door behind him.

Vivek tipped the vampire because that was just good strategy. People talked to those they liked, and Vivek's understanding of that was why he was now number two in the Tower's information network.

Jason was number one, and no, Vivek wasn't jealous. He was in awe. The black-winged angel was Raphael's spymaster for a reason; he seemed to divine data out of thin air at times. He was also generous with his knowledge now he'd seen that Vivek knew what he was doing, too.

Jason was the quietest angel Vivek had ever met, but he didn't think he was flattering himself to believe they were becoming friends. A slow process, Jason on the opposite end of the social spectrum from Illium, but Vivek was more than content with the progression. It was obvious Jason took relationships of any kind seriously—if and when they did turn the corner into true friendship, it'd be the real deal.

The spymaster had already taught him never to disregard a young or weak vampire. "Often, they are the very people whose presence is forgotten in what can be opportune circumstances from a spymaster's point of view."

Tonight, Vivek paused long enough to give the bouncer a chance to speak.

"Thanks." Tip disappearing into a stylishly cut pocket of the navy suit he wore with a black T-shirt, the buff man flashed him a grin, fangs glinting. "You're in luck tonight."

When Vivek raised an eyebrow, the vampire said, "Katrina's here." Breathless voice, his skin flushing. "The mistress in the flesh."

Lightning flashes of exhilaration chased away the heaviness that was a constant in Vivek's blood. "In the public salon?" As far as he knew, the owner of the Boudoir was always on the premises, but he'd never once spotted her in the seven months since he'd first discovered this place.

Katrina was a whisper, an enigma created of people's fantasies.

Vivek knew the reality was apt to be a disappointment, but he couldn't help himself. He was a man who liked to find answers. And come what may, he had to speak to her tonight.

There were no other options left.

27

"I don't know if she's still in the salon," the bouncer said. "She came to speak to me for a moment earlier. She especially came to find me." It was obvious he hadn't expected the consideration from the woman at the head of an empire of carnality and excess. "I'm not sure where she is now."

A minute later, when Vivek walked into the sumptuous space set up with richly upholstered armchairs, sofas, and a gleaming bar, the walls and the floor carpeted in dark ruby velvet, and the furniture antique with gilded accents, it was to find the room quiet.

Raising a hand in welcome, the barkeep turned to pour Vivek his usual. Sutrek was wearing the same type of thing he usually did: black pants and a fitted T-shirt in the same hue that showed off his body while remaining practical.

Jeans were not welcome in the Boudoir.

The thought of his upcoming drink made Vivek's mouth water; he liked to tease Elena about her accidental blood

café empire, but he was secretly addicted to the more decadent options among their offerings—and they now supplied
the Boudoir.

Vivek nodded a hello at the male vampire who lounged
on the chaise longue on the other side of the room, his ruf-
fled white shirt open halfway down his ripped chest and his
features languid. His skin was glossy white, inhuman in its
marbled perfection.

The male didn't respond, just watched Vivek skirt past
a settee that held two stunning vampires dressed in skintight bodysuits. One was Black, the other white, both their
skin tones on the extreme ends of the spectrum. Their
bodysuits echoed their skin color, but their lips glistened
ruby red, their hair scraped pitilessly back into identical
buns at the backs of their heads.

He'd never seen them apart. Everyone called them the
Twins.

The two looked at him with huge round eyes that held
not avarice nor lust nor any other emotion he could name.
What stared back at him from those eyes was age. He had
no idea of the Twins' age, but he had a feeling they were
considerably older than Dmitri, and Raphael's second was
over a thousand years old. But not only were they old, they
were . . . not quite human in any sense.

A whole different species.

Not every old vampire got this way, but the ones who did
were damn fucking creepy.

The white twin ran her fingers over his sleeve. "Play
with us, broken one." Her voice was a sibilant whisper, her
irises so pale as to almost merge into the rest of her eyes,
her pupils tiny black pinpricks. "You interest us."

"Not part of the merchandise," Vivek said, and moved on.

He'd learned to be blunt with the Twins. Nothing else
worked. And even that only worked part of the time. They
seemed to have no concept of the word no, and from the
way the majority of people reacted to them, he could see

why. Each twin was striking on her own, but together, they were unearthly.

He was also sure they'd laugh while disemboweling him, were he ever stupid enough to accept their invitation to "play."

He made sure the stool he took at the bar was against the plinth at the corner; it protected his back while giving him a view of the entire space. Violence wasn't welcome at the Boudoir, and those who indulged in it got summarily thrown out and banned for a decade. Harsh, but he'd never seen what would happen should vampires as powerful as the Twins try something.

Better to be prepared.

The two continued to watch him, small smiles on their perfect faces. On any other person, he would've called that type of smile smug, but on the Twins, it was just disturbing. Especially when he knew why he interested them. They'd told him.

"You are unlike the others. Unique." Unblinking black eyes as inhuman as her white twin's pale gaze. "You were broken, remain partly broken."

"We usually break things," the other one had purred, "but you are broken already. We want to see if your bones hurt, if you cry at new hurts."

Yeah, real sexy talk there.

Fighting off a shiver, he consciously switched his attention to another corner, where a man in a white shirt complete with cravat and snug brown breeches lounged on another old-fashioned settee. His skin was a shade or two paler than Vivek's, his compact body flawless.

He looked almost normal—until he stared at you and you realized one eye was ice-blue, the other a brown cracked outward with black. It wasn't the heterochromia that was disturbing, it was the way those eyes didn't blink except for once every ten minutes.

Vivek had timed it one night.

A woman who Vivek had discovered had been born a long fucking time ago in what was now Cambodia lay with her head in the man's lap, her black hair silken strands and her gown all air and lightness around her. Her feet were bare where she pushed them against the edge of the settee, her toenails painted a virginal baby pink.

She was . . . doing nothing, just staring vacantly at the ceiling while her companion ran his fingers through her hair. Look without knowing the context and you'd assume she was the merchandise, he the buyer.

The truth was that they were both the merchandise.

That was the thing with the Boudoir—the merchandise was all old vampires who chose this life. No one who worked the private rooms needed to work here. Every single one was ridiculously rich.

Vivek had done the research, and the numbers made his head spin. Turned out if you lived long enough and made a few smart decisions along the way, you could literally burn money every night and still be filthy rich.

That group didn't, of course, include ordinary staff like Sutrek and the bouncer, both of whom weren't yet two hundred years old. All patrons of the Boudoir knew that Katrina's staff was off-limits. No touching. No flirting. Nothing but business.

"Quiet night," he said to the barkeep after thanking him for the drink. "No other customers?" He'd never been sure about the Twins, but he was fairly certain they were buyers, not sellers.

"Party on an upper floor," Sutrek murmured, leaning in to chat. The hint of red on the olive brown of his cheeks said he'd fed recently. Probably right before his shift. "Most everyone's up there. Wild, I hear. Open invite if you want to head on up."

Vivek shook his head. This was as far as he went in the Boudoir. He was never a customer except when it came to the drinks. What brought him here was . . . he didn't know. A sense of recklessness? More likely a need to show himself where he could end up if he didn't get a handle on the part of him that had gone numb a long time ago and that kept whispering ever darker promises to him.

There were no rules here. No one would break down the door to stop consensual violence or bloodletting. Even if it got out of hand. Because the people who worked here were so bored of immortality that risk was the only thing left.

"You're the strangest customer I have." The barkeep polished his already spotless bar while giving Vivek a sidelong look out of eyes long and narrow in shape beneath delicate epicanthic folds. "No offense."

"When have I ever taken offense, Sutrek?" Vivek made a humming sound of contentment at his first sip of the blood. Before his transition, he'd thought drinking blood would be a necessary but nauseating act, but to be a vampire was to be a creature of blood. It was second nature. The rush when it hit the cells, the powerful pump of his heart . . . as good as any sexual experience he'd ever had.

"Powerful vamps can turn on a dime when it comes to emotional reactions." Leaning muscled arms on the bar, Sutrek nodded subtly at the vampire who was lounging by himself, his long blond hair motionless as it fell to the carpet and his fingers hanging so loosely that he might as well have been dead—except that his eyes were open just a slit. Just enough to watch the Twins.

Who were now licking each other's tongues, putting on a show.

"His Majesty there—literally used to be the king of a tiny country somewhere—puts on like he doesn't care about anything, but two months ago, he almost took off my head because I asked him if he wanted to sample a new variety of blood."

"I could've told you he was unhinged." Vivek took another delicious sip. "Next time just ask me who to watch out for. Two centuries ago, our blond king made a habit out of biting off people's fingers and eating them."

Sutrek blinked and went stiff. "The rumors are right. You're like Jason. You know everything."

Vivek felt his skin heat, was glad his skin tone meant that it probably didn't show except as a slight glow that could be attributed to his fresh intake of blood. "Don't worry," he said to Sutrek. "I know what happened in the Mediterranean and it's no one's business but your own. I've wiped it off all official records as a favor between friends. Live your life—there's nothing hanging over you anymore."

The barkeep's pupils all but took over his irises. "I—" He closed his mouth, swallowed hard, then picked up Vivek's half-drunk blood and threw it back down his own throat. "I'll get you a new glass."

A stir without movement, a sudden silence descending on the room. He caught the scent first, lush and rich and not the least bit girlish. No, the scent was mystery and sensuality and *power*. Then she emerged from the doorway that led deeper into the Boudoir, and Vivek just stopped breathing.

She was tall, at least a couple of inches taller than him, her skin a flawless golden cream that no mortal would ever possess, and her lips plump and pink without any stain or color that he could see. He was half expecting her hair to be a blazing red, but it was instead a midnight so rich that it was obsidian. A dark contrast to her pale green eyes, the tilt of which made her appear sharply feline.

Her breasts plumped over the deep neck of her sleeveless gown of dark green velvet, her exposed left leg long and perfect in the slit of the figure-hugging dress.

The mistress of the Boudoir was more fascinating than anything he'd conjured up in his imagination.

He'd tried to trace her, found nothing except records for this establishment, an establishment that had only popped up three years ago. He wondered if she was one of those near-immortals who shed identities like a lizard shed skin, and hoped this one would stick until he could satisfy his rampant curiosity about the most mysterious woman in New York.

The Twins sighed when she ran her fingers over their shoulders before she went to the couple in the corner and murmured something that made their faces light up. Plastic dolls brought to life by her.

The king who'd once eaten fingers looked at her with a needy gaze, but she ignored him in a cut that made him whimper and curl into himself, his back to the room. Katrina didn't seem to notice, her attention fixed on Vivek. He was aware of Sutrek sliding the glass of fresh blood toward him, then all but disappearing into the woodwork as Katrina came to stand beside Vivek.

Her power kissed his skin, prowling over it like the cat in her eyes. He'd felt this kind of vampiric power before; he lived in the Tower, after all, was around some of the strongest vampires in the city on a daily basis. But hers was a thing all in itself. A thing rich and dark and violently sensual.

Sex was power to Katrina and had been for a long, long time.

28

Those feline eyes glittered at him as she accepted the flute of blood that Sutrek placed in front of her before once again attempting to fade away. But she reached out without looking at him, gripped his wrist.

Turning to his pale face afterward, she said, "You are very good at your job, Sutrek." Her voice was as rich and as sensual as the rest of her, with the slightest undertone of huskiness. "I appreciate you."

When she released his hand, the vampire stumbled away with an expression of mingled fear and devotion on his face.

Vivek was fighting a reaction far more carnal, one he hadn't experienced for a hell of a long time. He'd enjoyed sexual intimacy before his Making, and he'd had no trouble finding partners who liked him exactly as he was. A hunter named Neve Pelletier had been his favorite bedmate for years until she'd fallen madly in love with the man who was now her husband and the father of her children.

Vivek hadn't begrudged her that love, and they remained friends to this day.

Finding sexual partners after being Made hadn't been hard, either. In fact it had become almost too easy. He'd learned to be expert at what he gave lovers to make up for the things he couldn't give them, and it turned out that now he had a fully functioning body, his skills put him head and shoulders above many a man on the street. His problem now was that his one-night stands kept on trying to get back in touch.

But unlike with Neve, Vivek had no emotional involvement with those one-night stands. He and Neve had known they'd never make a good relationship, but they'd been friends long before they got naked together. He'd enjoyed playing poker with her after they were intimate, her sitting wrapped up in the sheet with one leg casually hanging out and a cigarette in her mouth.

She was the only person for whom he'd broken the no-smoking rule in the Cellars. Though he'd complained the entire time about her giving him lung cancer on top of the whole paralysis thing.

She'd cackled like a hyena.

She used to text him while she was on the road, passing on random pieces of data that she thought he'd enjoy having, despite the fact that they had no useful purpose at all. She still sent him the odd haphazard fact. Their friendship would endure—he knew that—even when she retired from being an active hunter.

But not even with Neve had he experienced this kind of reaction. It was physical, yes, but it was also visceral and internal. Katrina's voice raked over him like nails scratching his skin in the most delicate places.

"So," she murmured after a sip of her drink, "you are the vampire who comes into the salon and never goes any further."

"And you," he found himself saying, "are the vampire of

unknown age and unknown origin who has made an empire out of ennui."

A smile that didn't reach her eyes. "Are manners not taught in this century?"

Vivek knew she wasn't talking about his reference to her age. "My job is to spy," he said, holding that feline gaze. "Can't help looking. Especially when a vampire as fascinating as you moves into town."

It might've taken him a while to visit the Boudoir, mostly due to medical issues after his transition, but he'd known of Katrina much sooner—because she'd quickly become a power player in the gray underbelly of the city.

Drugs, sex, darker things—they all flowed through the gray.

The slightest flicker in her expression. "Spies don't usually go about stating their purpose."

"I'm a different kind of spy," he said, well aware she already knew his identity—no one rose to Katrina's level of power without being a dab hand at intelligence gathering themselves. "And tonight, Lady Katrina, I have a request for you."

An arched eyebrow that told him he was getting above himself.

His skin pulsed, his cock threatening to wake. Oh yeah, he was in trouble. "Not personal," he said, because while he could spend all night verbally tangling with her, he had a job to do. "In my facility as part of the Tower team."

A lack of motion in her face as she took him in.

He didn't blame her for thinking him full of shit. He was sure that hundreds of people of all descriptions tried to get close to her, if not for her sensuality, then for her power. Reaching into his jacket pocket, he pulled out one of the gold-on-black cards that Aodhan had hand painted for him.

"A bit flashy for my job description," Vivek had said, even as he held the cards close with covetous pride. Only a hundred cards. Each one worth a ridiculous amount of money because each was a piece of original art by Aodhan.

"These are not everyday cards." Aodhan had given him one of those rare smiles that he gave only friends—and yeah, Vivek felt good that he'd gained that status.

Because he and Aodhan? They had things in common no one else could truly understand. Vivek's whole weirdness about touch? Aodhan got it as no other person he'd met ever had—or could.

"These," the angel formed of pieces of refracted light had said, "are cards you give to the most arrogant and most powerful . . . to make the point that you, too, are very arrogant and even more powerful."

Vivek knew Elena groaned at the political games played by immortals, but he found those complex games enthralling. Like the most intricate and multilayered board game on the planet.

"My credentials," he said, offering the card to her in the way he'd been taught was polite among the old immortals: held flat on the palm of one hand so that the face was visible.

Another long moment of eye contact before she glanced down.

She sucked in the slightest breath before she put her drink on the bar to pick up the card with extreme care, making sure not to touch the surface at all. When she looked up, her eyes held a glint far more dangerous than her sensuality, a glimpse of the predator under the skin of beauty and sex.

"Come, then, Vivek Kapur of the Tower, let us talk." She made his name a purr of sound . . . if that purr was a razor designed to stripe him with bleeding wounds.

It was Vivek's turn to throw back his drink, a shot of liquid courage before he followed his beautiful doom out of the salon and into a long, dark corridor. She glanced back at one point, saw the cane and the way his leg dragged.

She was a predator. He braced himself for a cutting comment.

Instead, she paused so he could catch up, then walked with him. Her scent brushed his senses as they moved, twining around him in bonds luscious and intoxicating. *Fuck.* Why had Elena never warned him that being hunter-born meant they couldn't only track vampires by scent, but that they were more susceptible to those same scents?

Unless this wasn't about his abilities . . . but about his response to Katrina.

"Your pulse is a beacon." She stared at the spot on his neck where his pulse no doubt jumped. "If you are to survive in our world, Vivek Kapur, you need to learn not to turn yourself into a buffet invitation."

Vivek was fairly certain he wouldn't mind being her buffet.

Predator, he reminded himself. Will eat you alive. "Still getting used to the hunter sense of smell."

"Interesting. You simply go around offering information on yourself."

"It's a way to build trust. I read it in a book once."

No smile. No twitch of the lips. No verbal response.

A wall sconce appeared in the distance. Beside it stood a vampire of androgynous appearance with brown skin, huge dark eyes almost too big for their skull, and a shock of daisy-yellow hair that fell to their shoulders. They wore a black suit, paired with a shirt in the same vibrant yellow.

"Mistress," the vampire said, coming forward. "Has this one followed you? Shall I cut off his head?"

Vivek didn't make a joke; he happened to know that the vampire was highly capable of actually cutting off heads. "Met a friend of yours the other day, Xai," he said before Katrina could respond. "Davanh says you still owe him a sword for the one you broke over his 'dumb skull.'"

A long, slow blink before Xai smiled the smile of a cobra. Cold, bright, meaningless. "You are a strange one. I like you." Then they walked on ahead to open the door.

"Do not provoke Xai," Katrina said, a slight amusement to her tone. "My friend has . . . a temper."

"I know. I've heard about their private graveyard." He made himself sound more knowledgeable than he actually was on the subject; the truth was that both Katrina and her closest associate were enigmas without a past.

He wasn't even sure of Xai's full name, that was how little he knew about the vampire with the slim, long body and hair that rotated through the color spectrum. And he'd dug hard. All he'd found out was that Xai was violent if angered, and that the vampire had a low irritation threshold.

In general, however, people had discovered that if they left Xai alone, Xai wouldn't pick a fight. Rather, the vampire might watch you with cold eyes, as if deciding whether to eat you or fuck you.

Not that anyone had. Fucked Xai, that is. If they had, they weren't talking. Too scared, probably.

As for Katrina, Cox was the last name she'd put on her business documents. She didn't frequent the places Xai did—but her name, too, brought up no history. She was also never seen in the social world of the immortals; Vivek's trusted sources of social gossip had passed on that influential vamps and angels both had been trying to entice her to a party or a ball since the day she moved into the city, but she'd turned them all down.

Ahead of them, Xai opened the door. "Welcome to my lady's lair." That same cobra smile.

Katrina walked in, looked over her shoulder. "Come, Vivek Kapur. Make your request."

He stepped inside.

29

The silence of the night beyond the windows heavy today, Elena brushed her father's hair off his forehead. He'd hate how helpless he looked in the hospital bed. *She* hated it.

"Jeffrey," she said, in the hope that the address would get through to him—because he despised that his eldest living daughter called him by his name. "Time to wake up. I've got things to do, and look, I'm sure Amy's husband is great, but you're the engine of the entire operation.

"Also, while we're on the subject, you really need to make Gwendolyn an official part of the business. From what I've picked up during my chats with her, your COO is coming to her for the big calls because he knows she can make them."

Her father's eyes opened. "She doesn't want to be part of it. Wants to focus on being a wife and mother—and now grandmother. Told her years ago she should be my CFO." The words were a rough croak but understandable . . . before his eyes closed right back up.

Elena blinked and was wondering if she'd imagined the entire exchange when one of the machines beeped.

A doctor came in soon afterward, checked on her father, and smiled. "Good news."

Elena had to focus to hear the rest of the doctor's words past the roar in her ears. Soon as the physician was done, she messaged Gwendolyn and her sisters. They arrived en masse over the next couple of hours, and—with the doctor's permission—Jeffrey was surrounded by his entire living family when he opened his eyes again four hours after that sudden burst of words.

His gaze was cloudy for a bare moment before it grew sharp, alert.

His shoulders straightened, tension back in his face. Not the tension of pain or worry, but the tension that made him Jeffrey.

After a sip of water to wet his throat, he looked at them in turn. His eyes lingered on Gwendolyn, who tearfully kissed his cheek, then rested on Beth, Amy, Eve. Elena, who was to his left, came in last for his attention.

She tried to work out if he remembered anything of their first conversation in this room, but saw no indication of strong emotions on his face. Then Amy laugh-sobbed and said something, and the moment moved on.

It wasn't until she rose from his bedside an hour later that his fingers brushed her wing. Thinking she must've not held her wings close enough to her body while turning, she looked back.

Her father made a motion for her to come closer.

Gwendolyn and Beth were at the door chatting to a nurse about Jeffrey's upcoming move out of the ICU. Amy had gone outside to call her husband, while Eve was on a coffee run for the entire group.

No one else would hear what Jeffrey had to say to her.

Bracing herself, she bent close to his lips.

"Do you think we should dig her up, Ellie?" A whispering rasp. "Disturb her peace?"

Her heart slammed into her rib cage. "I don't think *Maman* is at peace," she whispered back. "She never wanted to be in the ground."

Swallowing, Jeffrey stared over at Gwendolyn and said nothing further. But what he had said . . . he remembered.

It changed everything.

Seven days after his meeting with Minjarra, and Raphael stood atop a mountain that offered a three hundred and sixty-degree view over this corner of Qin's territory. Green and lush beneath the glowing rays of the setting sun, it was a far cry from the red sands and desert at the heart of this island continent.

"You'll hold Australia together with Celesta," he said to Andreas.

The experienced and deadly angel crouched on the edge of the cliff, his wings—a dark amber with filaments of gray—pulled back as he took in the territory now under his command.

Lip curling at Raphael's words, he glanced up. The pale green-tinged hazel of his gaze was striking against the dark hue of hair he'd cut back to his nape. "The Knife? You're leaving me alone with Caliane's *Knife*?"

Raphael hadn't had many reasons to smile over the past weeks, but now his lips twitched. "You'll be fine. Celesta doesn't murder most people."

Andreas gave him the finger.

Throwing back his head, Raphael laughed for the first time in what felt like an eon. Many people would have been appalled at Andreas's lack of respect to his liege, but while Raphael was his archangel, Andreas was also a warrior who'd fought tirelessly beside Raphael. They were friends.

"Celesta isn't so bad," he said in the aftermath. "She babysat me once upon a time."

"That explains why you like women with a penchant for knives," Andreas said sourly as he rose to his feet. "Did you ever think about that? That she imprinted you to enjoy bloodthirsty women?"

"No, but you've opened my eyes." Celesta had been his favorite babysitter, even though she was rarely called upon to do the task. She hadn't seemed to realize that small children shouldn't be doing certain things, so had happily tied a rope to his ankle, then tied the rope to a tree when he'd wanted to dive-bomb a waterfall. The rope was so she could pull him back up if he got too tired to fly there on his own.

Andreas sighed. "I suppose she'll stay in the other half of this country. It's a big one. We'll never have to interact in person."

Raphael looked at the other man with a bit more interest. "Do you two have a history of which I'm unaware?"

The barest hint of a flush on Andreas's cheekbones. "Let's just say the Knife has a taste for young angelic flesh and leave it at that."

That particular statement could be taken many ways. Celesta, after all, was a vampire. But while he and Andreas were friends, they weren't close enough friends for him to push it any further. "With the work Aegaeon and I have done to remind the vampiric population that the Cadre is watching, they shouldn't give you too much trouble. If they do, come down hard. We have no time or room for a softer touch."

Andreas gave a curt nod. "I heard the Refuge suffered another significant quake yesterday."

"Worse, it's spreading. I just got word of a volcanic eruption in Indonesia, while another previously dormant volcano in Iceland has begun to spit smoke." The Mantle was also retreating faster with each day that passed; at this rate, it'd fail in a matter of weeks.

"Now that you, Celesta, and the others are here to hold Qin's territory, Aegaeon and I can add our efforts to those of the rest of the Cadre as we try to stop the devastation." It had all begun with the shake at the Refuge, so they'd focused their efforts there, in the hope that any solution would ripple outward to the rest of the world.

"Did Titus have any luck?"

Raphael shook his head. Titus's Cascade gift had been tied to the ability to move the earth. Like all of them, his power was no longer as potent as it had been during the Cascade, but it did still exist.

"He says he can feel movement far beyond even that picked up by modern sensors. Continuous ripples on a constant rhythm. But when he tries to stop the movements using his power, it feels like it just slides off—as if the motion is so strong that his power is nothing but a gnat on a tiger's back."

Hands on his hips, Andreas blew out a breath. "Well, that's only slightly terrifying."

Raphael agreed. "Titus will keep on trying—he's in the Refuge right now." Sharine, the Hummingbird, watched over his lands in the interim, her own deputy taking over her duties as the Guardian of Lumia in the short term.

"I'm sure half of the ingrates in my territory wouldn't notice if I keeled over dead in front of them," Titus had said last time they'd met. "For my Shari, though? Oh, only the best china will do.

"Tea will be made in the middle of the savanna exactly how she likes it, and oh, but we must stay for sweetmeats." He'd beamed with pride. "Even the worst vampires behave better with her in the vicinity."

The latter was the critical point; Sharine's presence, backed up by Titus's warriors, would keep the southern half of Africa stable while he was away for an extended period.

It also helped that Titus was good friends with his neighbor, Zanaya; she'd offered to do regular flights over his territory to remind any troublesome vamps that while Titus might be gone, the land wasn't free from archangelic oversight.

However, trouble was unlikely to arise. Titus had dealt with a huge reborn problem post-war. His people were in rebuilding and nesting mode.

No one had time to waste on bloodlust or uprisings.

"One vampire who recently showed signs of bloodlust was summarily thrown down a well by his friends and told to stay there until he snapped out of it," Titus had shared with a huge laugh. "Otherwise he was welcome to eat his own face."

But even bighearted and genial Titus had stopped laughing these past days of failure after failure to find anything close to an answer to the fracturing of the planet—or the unprecedented retreat of the Mantle. That the two were connected was clear, but how was anyone's guess.

Beside him, Andreas frowned. "I asked my great-grand-many-times-over uncle about the Mantle. I have no idea how old he is, but he was old when Lady Caliane was a child, he tells me. But he had no knowledge of it."

"Jessamy consulted him, too." The grand-sire in question had only woken four years earlier, and had—by his own admission—been enticed to stay awake with stories of a mortal turned angel. "He tried his best, but he cannot tell us what he never knew."

"I'll keep searching. We all will."

Raphael clapped Andreas on the shoulder, and they stood in silence for long minutes, watching the sun rise higher in the sky. "You are ready. It's time for me to fly home."

"Good journey, sire." Andreas went down on one knee, in this moment a warrior to his liege rather than battlemate with battlemate.

Raphael took off in a steep vertical rise, carrying in the pocket of his dusty and worn jerkin a copper-colored rock with veins of shimmering gold that he'd found in one of the vast deserts of this island continent. He'd give it to Elena to put in her greenhouse.

She liked to tuck small natural treasures inside that space.

Afterward, he'd hold her as he hadn't been able to during one of the worst times in her life. His heart hurt in ways he'd never believed it could hurt before he fell bloody and bleeding with a dying mortal in his arms.

30

Beloved, the weight is too great. They will fall. And all beginnings will come to an end. I see this in the river of time.

I cannot rise to help them. I cannot walk again without you. Do not ask this of me. I will go mad, become a monster ravening.

No, my heart. This I do not ask of you. But oh, the child of mortals worries. Her heart aches.

Why do you love her so?

In that one lives an understanding of loss and eternity that is a quiet shadow of our own. She has loved and still loves those who cannot walk into time with her. She has lost sisters. As have we. She will mourn forever, as we mourn.

Your heart ever holds small creatures close.

Not so small this child of mortals. Not so small at all. I would see her grow. I would see her become. And so I will meddle once more.

Always your greatest sin, my love.

Oh, how you make me laugh, even if only in my dreams. Tell me of your meddlesome plans.

No living archangel can wake a Sleeper, that is our law. But . . . there is no law against one Sleeper awakening another . . . What say you to the one of whom I dreamt yesterday?

Him? That one is a breath away from being an Ancestor. He will burn down this world.

I cannot see. I do not know. The river is murky. I just know that it must be him. Let us see what he makes of this world of steel and glass where a once-mortal stands beside an archangel. For this, I think, he has not seen even in his truly immortal lifetime.

His Sleep is deep and not meant to ever be broken. Will he even wake?

I do not know. I can but try.

31

Elena had been watching for Raphael since the instant he told her he was homeward bound. Now, in the post-dawn light, she flew up into the misty air of their city waking to the day, then headed deeper into the territory.

Raphael's route home was an overland one at this point in his journey, and she was through with waiting, even if that meant hours of flight to meet him. She needed him with a desperation that was a clawing pulse within.

The mist lay cool against her skin, the other angels she saw during her flight yawning or powering down after a night shift, no one in the mood to chat.

Good. She wasn't in the mood to talk, either.

It was forty-five minutes into her journey that the sun broke through the clouds . . . and she felt the first whisper of the sea in her mind. *Raphael!*

He wouldn't have heard her, her power a mere fragment of his. But she tried again at five-minute intervals. And succeeded on her seventh attempt.

The sea crashed into her mind with a roar of whitecaps. *Elena-mine, you are far from home.*

No, I'm flying toward my home.

Hbeebti.

The single word enfolded her in his love as he so often enfolded her in his wings when they hugged.

She didn't reply, couldn't speak. And didn't know she was going to break into harsh, wracking sobs when she finally flew into his arms after what felt like eons.

"*Elena.*" Holding the hover for both of them because her wings had crumpled the instant she wrapped her arms around him, he held her tight and she felt the tingle of electricity that told her he'd triggered his ability to create glamour, hiding them from sight. Her ability to sense it had emerged sometime after he'd given her a piece of his heart.

Her archangel had torn his beating heart out of his chest so she would live.

Safe in his arms, protected from any prying eyes, she cried and cried. She'd managed to keep it together this long, be the strong older sister, the tough eldest daughter, but her heart was bruised and battered and she could finally let go, held in the arms of the only man who had ever understood all the pieces of her.

He nuzzled her hair, kissed the side of her face, and, at some point, flew them down to a lush patch of woodland so they could land in a space quiet and private. She sobbed into his chest as the ocean crashed in her mind, as the scent of Raphael embedded itself back into her skin, into her bones.

She couldn't speak to him through her devastation, whether by voice or through using her mind, but she was aware of his murmuring words, conscious of the hand he'd thrust into her hair to cradle the back of her head, of the wings he folded around her.

Aware of being loved.

* * *

Raphael had never seen Elena cry this way. *Never*.

Through all that they'd experienced together, all that they'd survived, all her nightmares, she'd never so completely shattered. It devastated him. He wanted to rage, to rend and destroy, but that would achieve nothing. He just had to bear the scalding burn of her tears on his heart, the agony of her pain tearing him to pieces.

A stirring in his mind, a voice so *old* in his head.

Ah, young Rafe. These . . . these are the tears of the child she once was.

Raphael crushed Elena closer. *Go away, Cassandra*, he said, not caring if he was being rude. *Go to fucking Sleep. We don't need any more problems*. It wasn't Cassandra's fault that she saw the future, but he couldn't deal with portents of doom today. Not when Elena was ripping herself to pieces in his arms.

"*Hbeebti*," he said, kissing her temple, her cheek, any part of her he could reach. He wanted to ask her to stop, but that would be for himself, so he didn't have to see her in this much pain. What she needed was to let it go, pour that old and twisted grief out of her where it couldn't fester. "I have you. I have you, Elena-mine."

I am sorry. Cassandra's crushing age of a voice. *I did not mean to wake. But this twilight is the only time when I can be with my Qin*.

Angry though he was at Qin, a stab of sympathy pierced his heart. How long had Qin been separated from Cassandra? How many eons had he waited for a miracle that would allow them to be together? Raphael had just spent the minutest fraction of that time away from Elena and it had ravaged him.

Qin had spent eternal lifetimes.

Please go, he said again, the words a harsh request. *I want to be with Elena and Elena alone*.

The weight on his mind vanished. But the seer had left behind a sense of the portentous, and he knew she'd be back. He'd deal with that later—though, more likely, Elena would have to deal with it. Cassandra liked her better than him, had probably only spoken to him because Elena was in distress.

I told Cassandra to go to fucking Sleep, he said into Elena's mind out of desperation for the savage roughness of her tears.

He didn't think she'd heard him . . . until several minutes later when her tears slowed to a painful, horrible quietness. "Cassandra?" Her voice was rubbed raw, cracked and wounded.

His own eyes burned.

Cupping her face, he kissed her lips, tasted the salt of her tears.

She, his strong, tough hunter, just stood motionless as he kissed her cheeks next, drinking away her tears, and wishing he could take her pain away as easily. When she made the slightest motion that indicated she didn't want to stand any longer, he took them to the forest floor.

Putting his back to a tree with a solid trunk, he pulled her body between his legs, her head against his chest, and her wings lying to one side. For a long time, he brushed his fingers through her hair, dropped kisses onto the soft strands, and tried not to feel utterly helpless all over again.

Around them, the forest began to come to life once more, the forest creatures they'd disturbed deciding it was safe to go about their business. A doe with round dark eyes walked around the corner, froze when she saw them, but carried on her way when neither one of them moved.

A while later, two birds landed just beside one of Raphael's spread wings and began to peck at the ground. He watched them, his mind wanting to spin backward.

"Does it remind you of when your mother made you

fall?" Husky words, Elena's hand pressed to his heart with a caressing tenderness.

His hunter, so wounded and still caring for his own wounds.

"Yes," he said, because he knew she'd hate for him to brush off her question because her pain was newer, fresher. "They brought me berries, the birds. I think they thought I was a fallen chick." Broken and battered on the grass, he'd become part of the very landscape over the months. Flowers had grown around him, birds had landed on him.

"It's like a children's story," Elena said, as the birds continued to peck away, undisturbed by their conversation. "Except for the whole falling-and-breaking-every-bone-in-your-body part."

He chuckled, more out of relief that she was coming back to him than anything else. "The broken body does make it a bit gruesome." He ran his fingers through her hair again. "Have you been holding your tears inside all this time, *hbeebti*?"

She nodded. "I didn't consciously know I was doing it."

"I sent your Bluebell to take you to Sara so you wouldn't be alone." He hated that she might've felt that way.

"I know. She's been a rock. Illium, too." She rubbed her face against him. "I wasn't alone, Archangel. But falling to pieces with anyone but you is another story."

"You'll be the death of me, Guild Hunter." Tucking her hair behind her ear, he held her as they watched the forest live and breathe around them.

It was several minutes later that she said, "Did I imagine it or did you say you told Cassandra to fuck off?"

"Not quite. I told her to go back to fucking Sleep."

Elena jerked up so she could stare at him. Squawking, the birds flew up—but only to land on the branch above and begin scolding them.

Elena spoke over their chittering. "You what?"

"She was poking her nose in. Again." He scowled, hating the shadows under his consort's eyes, the far-too-visible bones of her cheeks. "Have you been sleeping? Eating properly?"

"No. But neither have you." Her scowl was a dark mirror of his. "You need a haircut, you've lost enough weight to start getting hollows in your cheeks, and I know from the time your messages came in that you haven't been sleeping even as much as you usually do!"

They glared at each other.

Then they were kissing, their arms wrapped fiercely around each other as she drank in his taste, he hers, ravenous in their need to be one. "Is the glamour still on?" A breathless question.

"I've just reinitiated it," he said, aware that her ability to sense the shield remained erratic.

She tore off her jacket to reveal a tank top. His mind blanked. He had no memory later of how they stripped her pants, panties, and boots off or when they undid his pants just enough. All he knew was that he ended up with a wild-haired and sumptuously half-naked hunter riding him while he gritted his teeth and tried to hold off, not come in a hot surge like a callow youth.

He pulled her tank top down so hard he ripped it. Her breast filled his palm, her nipple a rigid point. He squeezed the soft flesh of her lower curves with his other hand, voracious for her. She cried out when he suckled the line of her throat, then hauled her up and off him to suck hard on her breast.

Unwilling to be a quiescent participant, his hunter shoved at his shoulders and shifted her body at the same time to tell him what she wanted. Him. On the ground. "Wait," he said, and pulled away long enough to tug off the top half of his leathers and kick off his boots.

Then he was on his back on the leaves, and she was sliding the tight slickness of her body over his cock once more, her naked thighs pressing against the leather of the pants he still wore.

His back arched, his cock driving so deep into her that their bodies slammed in a passion that was almost violence. Wings spread, she pressed her hands to his chest and ground herself against him. His own wings were glowing— he could see the reflection of it in her eyes. Reaching between them, he pressed the pad of his thumb on her clitoris, so slippery and hard.

"*Raphael!*" She came in shocked pulses around the intrusion of his cock, her wings fluttering in an erratic beat and her eyes aglow.

Gripping her waist with one hand, he rubbed and played with her clitoris with his other, pushing her to the edge and beyond. Her pupils expanded; her breath lost.

Then he touched her where their bodies joined, the intimacy stark and primal.

A gush of slick heat, Elena's body turning liquid for him.

No longer the Archangel of New York but a man who had turned barbarian with his lover, he rose up into a seated position and lowered his mouth to her breast even as her thighs quivered around his hips.

"Archangel." A shaky, husky word whispered against his ear.

"Again, Hunter-mine," he said, wanting to give her pleasure enough to wipe out the pain, erase the agony of her tears.

Her laugh was soft and a little lazy as she played with the ultrasensitive arches of his wings. He ran his fingers up the inner curves of her own wings in vengeance, aware that his hunter had developed an extreme sensitivity in just *that* spot.

She shuddered, her muscles clamping down hard on him. "No fair."

He smiled against her throat . . . right before he pushed up into a vertical takeoff from his seated position, with

Elena's thighs locked around him. She screamed, then laughed. "How did you even *do* that?"

"I'm an archangel," he said, moving her body on his in a way that made sweat break out on his skin and his consort shiver. The truth was that what he'd just done took effort even for an archangel, but for whom else would he attempt such feats?

Only her. Only Elena.

Arms wrapped around his neck, she rubbed her breasts against his chest, kissed and nibbled at his throat. Raphael could feel his control fraying, his need for her a pulse inside his skull. But he wanted to give her more, still more.

So, after kicking off his pants at last, he flew them high, high, *higher*.

Then he dropped in a wild spiral, their bodies locked, naked and sweat-damp and hot. His cock moved in her in erratic motions due to the spiral, creating a vortex of pleasure that had her nails digging into his skin as the wildfire of her hair haloed around them, their lips connected in a kiss that held need stripped of all artifice.

He ate her up, one hand fisted in her hair while he held her safe with his other arm.

"Raphael, Raphael, Raphael." She gasped his name against his lips as they met again for kiss after kiss, no touch ever enough.

His fingers sank into the toned softness of her curves; he told himself to pull back, that he was going to bruise her. But he couldn't. Because this was his hunter, with whom it was impossible to hold back.

Having never lost sight of the earth rushing closer, he twisted them back up into flight moments before they would've crashed, the motion making Elena cry out as her body clenched around him in pleasure raw and untamed.

This time when they fell, he fell atop her, his body thrusting into hers.

She pushed back as the wind roared past them, their

rhythm frenetic and their eyes locked when their lips weren't. She came with her hand gripping the most sensitive part of his wing and her eyes holding his. Grinding deep into her as the earth rushed toward them, he followed her in a violent burst that had pinpricks of light exploding behind his eyes.

32

Interlude
Murder of Potential

Fazani loped up the long path to his friend's home. He grinned, delighted that he'd managed to keep his visit a surprise. When Jari had asked him to come for a stay, he hadn't initially thought he could, and so had sent his regrets to his friend—only for the situation to change a few weeks later.

Amused at the thought of startling Jari by just turning up, Fazani had contacted the other man's majordomo, made all the arrangements, and now the day was here.

He *had* expected to be stopped by a guard or two by now, but perhaps they were staying out of the way since the majordomo had already cleared him. That made sense . . . at least until he got closer to the fort built of local yellow-hued stone and still saw not a single guard, or a single pair of wings in the sky . . . but for those that belonged to vultures.

The scavengers circled overhead in a lazy spiral.

His heart racing, he knew he should stop, turn back to

call for assistance—but he couldn't. Jariel had been his friend for a lifetime, the two of them having grown up together from the time they were babes in the Refuge School.

"Jari is strong," he told himself as he broke out into a full-on run. "Stronger than any other angel in this region."

The smell hit him first.

Of death . . . and of things burned.

Yet he saw no signs of fire.

Skin blazing from the power of his run under the scorching sky, he came to a halt a short distance from the main entranceway after realizing it was open. That was nothing unexpected. An open door was the norm in a fort as big and as active as Jari's. But there should've been a guard or doorkeep by it, Fazani's friend a stickler for correct protocol.

His stomach lurched as he closed the distance to the silent house that should've been alive with the sound of voices and wings, vampires and angels flowing in and out as they went about their business. Jari held this territory for his archangel, and his people always had a thousand things to do.

But they did it with a smile because Jari was no hothead. He never had been. He could be demanding, but he'd also been born with a balance within that rubbed off on others. Even Fazani, whose frenetic energy had almost caused his teacher to tear out her hair.

There were no smiles today.

A teardrop hit his jerkin.

Because he knew. Even before he saw the sight that awaited in the entranceway.

Screaming Jari's name, he fell to his knees on the dirt, his wings crumpled and his hands pressed to his eyes to hide from the sight he would never ever forget. Jari, strong, intelligent, and pragmatic Jari was gone. Burned to ash but for his head . . . which sat atop the ashes, staring at Fazani with eyes filmed over with white.

33

Elena woke with her legs splayed over her archangel's thighs and one of her breasts shoved out of her partially torn tank top, which was designed to control said breast and its mate.

Lifting one heavy arm, she rearranged the top. It pretty much stayed put.

When Raphael made a complaining sound, she slumped back on his chest. "I'll get naked later."

Right now, she was only mostly naked. Raphael's hand was cupping her butt, her clothes strewn across the fallen leaves. "Wow." She took a deep breath, exhaled. Said "wow" again.

Raphael patted her butt. "Yes."

Her laugh bubbled in her chest, making her shoulders shake. "I think this goes in our top ten."

That got her a little spank. Grinning, she kissed the line of his neck, feeling young and happy and as if they were just two people in love. Just Elena and Raphael. No politics, no problems, and no families that had been destroyed a lifetime ago.

"How are we not pancakes after that wild ride?" She kissed his jaw.

He turned his head so she could kiss the other side, too. "I told you, Guild Hunter, I am an archangel. I need to show you more of my skills if you have such little faith in my abilities."

Giving a little laugh at his smug arrogance, she kissed him again and they allowed themselves a few more precious moments in this place out of time. But it couldn't last. Because they weren't just Elena and Raphael.

Sighing, she got her legs back in some sort of order, then looked for the rest of her clothes. But after getting them on—while Raphael set himself to rights, too—which involved flying up to see where his pants had landed first—she went right back to lying against him, in the cradle created by his legs and wings.

Maybe it was selfish to keep him to herself even longer, but her need was endless. She wanted to be in his arms and she wanted to hold him in hers.

"Tell me," he said, his voice a rumble against her.

So she did, going through all of it, even the things she'd already told him. From that night when Jeffrey had first spoken to her, to their most recent conversations when they were alone. "It's not every time," she added. "He's still weak and sleeps a lot. But when he does wake while I'm there by myself, it's usually only Mama he wants to talk about."

Her heart squeezed. "Last night, though, he mentioned Belle and Ari." The big sisters Elena never got to see grow up, become the blazing stars they had always been meant to be.

Belle, a dancer at home in the spotlight.

Ari, Jeffrey's right hand and future CEO.

"He used to speak about them right after they were murdered," she said thickly, "but one day, he stopped. I know that he probably couldn't bear the pain, but to me, it felt like they'd vanished. Especially after he put away all their photos."

Raphael's wings rustled as he curved one over her.

Stroking her fingers along the inner softness, she continued. "But last night, he said he'd seen them in his dreams, and they were angry with him. Belle was shouting and throwing things, while Ari was sitting there, arms crossed, with a disappointed look on her face. Then he laughed."

Elena's throat felt like sandpaper as she continued to speak, her body's ability to heal no match for her grief. "When he stopped laughing, he said that was exactly how the two of them had been.

"Belle was always the hot-tempered one, while he used to tell Ari she'd make a great school principal because she could make anyone behave just by looking at them. It's the first time since I was a child that the two of us laughed together—because he's right. That's what they were like."

Raphael could well imagine both sisters—because Elena had spoken to him often about the two elder sisters, who, according to her, would've interrogated him the instant he and Elena became entangled. "Belle wouldn't have cared that you were an archangel and could turn her to ash, while Ari would've hacked into Tower files to find out dirt. She was like that. Protecting us without the fireworks. Together, my big sisters were a powerhouse."

He ran his hand over the sleek beauty of Elena's wings. His consort carried all the colors of night and day in those wings, the midnight at the arches flowing into indigo and a blue as deep as the dark heart of the ocean, before merging into softest dawn and brilliant white gold. "Did your father reveal or know why they were angry with him?"

"Yes. Because of how he acted after they died." She was silent for a while. "He asked me if we should exhume and cremate them, too."

"*Hbeebti*." No wonder she was so distraught—this wasn't only about her father's heart attack, but about the massacre that had forever altered her childhood.

Elena sat up so she could face him. "It was an easy decision with my mother. She never wanted to be buried. She said that while she was still alive. I've never been able to believe that she's at peace in that grave where he put her."

Angelic burials had their own rituals, but that didn't mean he didn't understand Elena's need for this mortal way of doing things. It wasn't about the actual ritual, but about fulfilling her mother's final wish on this earth. "But your sisters had no chance to make a choice."

She nodded, her throat moving as she swallowed. "I like to imagine that they *are* at peace, their remains only a shell they discarded when they left this world. What right do I have to disturb them? They didn't give me permission like my mother gave me permission."

Raphael bent his leg so that his knee was behind Elena and she could brace herself against him. "A difficult choice." One he couldn't imagine having to make. "Does Jeffrey have a view on it?"

"Not yet. I've never seen him like this—so . . . lost. I'm almost not sure he won't revert back to the Jeffrey I've known for most of my life, but he's definitely all there. Brain acute as ever. He's already begun to give instructions to do with his businesses. It's only on this topic that he seems to rely on me."

Elena remained shaken by that. Her father hadn't relied on her for anything after those first years following Marguerite's death, when he'd asked her to watch over Beth now and then so he could finish up work in his home office. Even that had been rare; she'd never minded, but he'd said he didn't want her becoming a de facto caregiver for her younger sister. He'd hired a babysitter for Beth.

"Most of the time when we talk," she told Raphael, "it's just me and Jeffrey, but Gwendolyn's been in the room a couple of times and she told me that he doesn't talk to any of my sisters like that. Just me."

"Because you were there." Raphael's voice was gentle, the way he'd lifted his wing against her back familiar and needed. "You're the only one of his children who was not only there at the most devastating moment of his life, but you remember. You've said yourself that your younger sister has but a few fleeting recollections."

"Looking back, I think Beth's brain shut down to protect her. She was only six when we lost Ari and Belle, a bit older with our mom." Elena's heart filled with a rush of protective love, Beth forever the small girl with her hand gripping Elena's as they stood at their mother's graveside.

"She should have more memories, but she doesn't. She told me once that all she has are what she calls 'shadow memories'—faded and fuzzy images she can't make out. I'm glad for her." Never would Elena want Beth to suffer as she'd suffered.

All those night terrors.

All the echoing screams.

All the blood she couldn't forget.

That swaying shadow against the wall.

The single high-heeled shoe on the tile.

Red. It had been a shiny poppy red against black and white tile.

A portrait of clean contrasts seared into her mind.

She thumped a fist against her heart, as if that would dislodge the old pain, make it fade away.

Raphael squeezed her nape. "So you see, you are the only person with whom Jeffrey can truly speak of this. I think, unlike you, he has not let anyone else that close."

"While I have you and Sara." Elena nodded in a jagged motion. "I'm pretty sure he's never even really talked to Gwendolyn about the entirety of it. I saw the look on her face one day when we were discussing something—I can't remember exactly what, but it was bad, and I had the sudden thought that she didn't know. He'd never told her."

"Has she ventured any views on the disinterment of your sisters?"

"Only once. Gwendolyn's always been careful not to push her way into the past, into the life of the family we once had. I don't know if that's just how she is, her sense of boundaries, or if it's because she's protecting herself from being hurt."

"Not from you."

"No," she said. "We barely interacted before I became involved in Eve's life. The rare times we did, we were polite to each other—I never had any strong emotional response to her, positive or negative." That had changed; Elena hugged her stepmother often now, seeing in her a new fragility born of the knowledge that Jeffrey had never loved her as he loved Marguerite.

"What did she say on the occasion she weighed in on the topic of your sisters?"

"She said, 'If I were to die, and my children had already passed, I'd want to be with them, Ellie. Whatever the choice made for them, I'd want that to be the choice for me, too.'" Elena pressed her lips together. "My mother *loved* her girls."

"But she also left you," Raphael said, completing the words she couldn't say.

"Most of the time, I think I've forgiven her, but then I get this hot bite of anger and I want to shake her, make her explain herself."

Raphael stroked her wing, strong and warm and a man who'd never leave her of his own volition.

Leaning deeper into him, she said, "I think Gwendolyn's right in what my mama would've wanted. And I think Belle and Ari wouldn't only want the same, but that they'd far rather fly with her than lie in the earth." Theirs had been a family full of freedom and sunshine, the cold dark foreign to them. "I won't have graves to visit, but I barely do that now. I've always hated thinking of them in the ground."

"Does Beth have a view?"

Elena smiled, her entire being awash in tenderness. "She's being the baby sister and saying that she'll follow my lead." Her heart ached. "I saw strands of silver in her hair the other day."

It wasn't only that Elena had stopped aging. All her scars were gone, her skin healthier than it had ever before been. Beth, in contrast, wore the lines of life on her face, had sun-freckles across her nose, and had complained laughingly of her "bad knees" when she rose from her chair.

Raphael enclosed her in his wing. He knew. He understood. He'd been born an immortal, but his best friend had been a mortal. And though Dmitri had become a vampire, his family hadn't. Elena didn't know much about Dmitri's past, but from how little he mentioned it, she could guess that it had been painful. She'd picked up enough over the years to know that he'd had children.

Children who were now gone.

Children Raphael would've known.

As he'd known so many of the people his mother had sung into the sea during her madness.

Yes, her archangel understood what it was to mourn mortal lives.

So they sat here in this quiet forest that was a haven, and he didn't tell her she wouldn't one day have her heart broken to pieces by Beth, and she tried to breathe through that truth . . . until the earth shook.

Hard.

A blue radiance hit the side of Elena's face at the same instant.

Raphael's Legion mark wasn't glowing. It was *blazing*. White lightning crackled along the lines of the stylized dragon, and then . . . a pulse of wildfire. Slow, so slow, but a pulse nonetheless.

"It's as if your mark is echoing the pulse of some great Sleeping creature." She didn't know why she spoke those words; maybe Cassandra had whispered them to her beyond her conscious hearing.

"I can feel it," Raphael said aloud, gritting his teeth as the earth continued to roll around them.

But as fast as it had started, it stopped.

Raphael's mark blinked out at the same time.

They sat in stunned quiet for a second, the sudden extinction of the glittering blue light making the world feel as if it had gone night-dark. The decision to move was silent, the two of them rising to stand far enough apart that they could take off through the canopy without tangling wings.

Elena's took her to the sky with ease, well healed now and far stronger than they'd been when she'd first grown them. Vertical takeoffs had seemed an impossibility then, but today she smoothed out into flight beside Raphael without hesitation.

As they were flying too fast to talk, she reached out with her mind. *Fly ahead.* He could far outpace her. *You need to do a damage assessment on the city.*

The blue fire in his eyes was a thing piercing. *I am not leaving you after I have finally come home. I'll be in range to receive a report from Dmitri in less than an hour.*

Elena's front jacket pocket buzzed. *Or sooner.* She reached for the zipper. *Someone's calling.*

Ah, I did not charge my phone when I left.

"Are you with Raphael?" was Dmitri's curt question when she answered.

"Yes," she shouted over the roaring wind of flight. "Wait!" She held up the phone. Comprehending the silent signal, Raphael flew slightly below her—the span of their wings meant he couldn't come close enough if they flew side by side.

Now.

She dropped the phone into his hand, saw him put it to his ear as he eased up on his speed at the same time to lower the interference from the wind noise. Instead of easing up with him, she kept on going. He'd catch up without trouble, and this way, she could ensure she didn't hold them back any more than necessary.

How bad? she asked when he returned to fly next to her.

No casualties reported so far, and while a few buildings have lost windows, the shake seems to have been worse in uninhabited or sparsely populated areas.

Elena frowned. *That's weird.*

Yes. A sigh in his voice. *I do not want weird,* hbeebti. *I would far rather deal with a major quake than anything weird. Mind-numbing boredom would be far more welcome than the least whisper of weirdness.*

Elena made a face. *Yeah, because it's never just one weird thing, is it? It's always the start of something, and—*"Oh, fuck!"

34

Elena came to a halt in the sky.

So did Raphael.

They both stared down at the swollen creek below. A small enough thing, nothing at all like the vastness of the Hudson. Pretty when it sparkled in the sunlight.

"What *is* that?" she said, her hands on her hips.

"Looks like . . . scales."

The word perfectly fit the iridescent patches that rippled over the water, sinuous and strange and unlike anything Elena had ever before seen. "Did Dmitri—"

"No, he said nothing of this." Raphael pulled out her phone from his pants pocket to make the call. "Dmitri, how does the Hudson look?"

Frowning at Dmitri's answer, he hung up without good-byes, the two men having been friends for so long that such niceties weren't necessary. "He says it appears normal, and that he'd like it very much if I didn't curse it with my questions."

"Should we fly down?"

"Yes, we must."

They soon stood beside the creek that looked like a snake that curved and flowed, its scales gleaming in the sunlight. But the water itself was normal, and when Raphael tested it he felt no shock of power. Neither did Elena.

"Pass me the phone—I'll take a video," Elena said.

They took off the instant she was finished. They couldn't allow this small anomaly to keep them from heading to the city. Except . . . the anomaly followed them. Iridescent scales appeared in every body of water they passed, a stunning and languorous river of inhuman color.

Then they reached the Hudson.

"It's beautiful," Elena said begrudgingly. "Weird but beautiful." The colors were astonishing, jewellike in their clarity. "You said the waters changed on your ascension. Plus I know stuff happens when archangels wake, too."

Raphael's face was no longer as grim as it had been. "This doesn't feel like an ascension—it is too slow. Ascensions are hard, fast, as you saw with Suyin. But yes, it's possible that an archangel is waking." A sudden, unexpected smile. "I don't know these signs, so it may be another old one. It's the one weirdness that would be a good thing right now."

Elena was in firm agreement. Even an old blowhard like Aegaeon would be welcome. "Let's ask Caliane if she knows who it is."

"I am seeing the same phenomenon in my territory," Caliane said when they called her from the Tower; with her hair pulled back, her face was stark in its perfection of bone structure. "The colors are astonishing but I know not to whom they belong. I would remember if I had ever previously seen such a display—it's too striking to forget."

"Time for a meeting of the Cadre?"

"Yes, let us see what the others are experiencing."

The answer was . . . nothing.

Elena, who'd slipped out of shot to stand against the wall, frowned. How was that possible? Every single other awakening had caused signs throughout the world. Several of the Cadre even sent their people out to overfly waterways. Each squadron came back with reports of "all systems normal."

"So it is only mother and son who experience this." Aegaeon folded his arms, his lip curled.

Elijah stepped in even as Aegaeon was parting his lips to deliver his next shot. "Perhaps it has to do with your Legion, Raphael. Your mark is sparking with light again."

Elena's eyes snapped back to the mark. Elijah was right; the stylized dragon had once again come to life. Not with the intensity she'd seen in the forest, but it was far brighter than it had been at any other time since the Legion sacrificed themselves.

"Perhaps," Raphael acknowledged. "We will monitor the situation."

However, in the days that passed, they saw no sign of the otherworldly beings who'd become such an integral part of the city. Their building, a haven of plants next to the Tower that Elena cared for in their absence, appeared as it always did, no odd growth patterns or hues.

Right now, it was clothed in bright spring green with splashes of color from eager new blooms. Her favorites were the short purple freesias that raced to the front of the line every single year.

But while the Legion building carried on as usual, the Hudson and other waterways continued to change into rivers of iridescent scales without warning, and the region experienced another shake that did only minor damage and caused no deaths. Other than that, life kept on as normal.

Except, of course, nothing was normal.

In other parts of the world, two more volcanoes had erupted, causing mass casualties, while a third was showing all the signs of an impending eruption. Angels and archangels had responded to assist as fast as possible, but even an archangel couldn't stop a geothermal event. All they could do was fly survivors out and help in the heartbreaking aftermath. Elena had seen more angels cry over the past couple of weeks than she ever had in her lifetime.

People were scared.

That included angelkind. Because the Refuge continued to suffer severe quake after severe quake, until only half its structures were habitable—and the poisonous pools of boiling water had spread, swallowing up bridges and eating away at literal stone.

Angelic children had now been underground for two and a half weeks.

"It's begun to have a psychological effect on the little ones," Jessamy said to Elena during one of their regular conversations.

Purplish shadows sat under the burnt sienna hue of the other woman's eyes, her naturally thin face now inching dangerously close to unhealthy. "They're meant for air and sky, not for caverns below the earth. The Refuge is too quiet without them, and everyone in a bad temper for the lack. Galen growled at me today and slammed a bowl of oatmeal on my desk, wouldn't leave until I ate it."

Elena could understand the weapons-master's worry. But she knew her job as a friend. "*Men*," she said with a scowl. "As if you can't feed yourself."

Jessamy's cheeks grew pink. "Actually, I keep forgetting to eat." With that, she grabbed nuts out of a bowl and shoved them into her mouth. "Galen left these, too, plus dried fruits," she muttered after she'd chewed and swallowed the mouthful.

Elena couldn't laugh at what both of them would've found funny at any other time. "How is the structural situation?"

Jessamy's headshake was dejected, her lips pursed tight. "We've had to take down two more large buildings. Many of the pathways are cracked, bridges deemed too hazardous to cross. A new sinkhole filled with toxic hot water appeared only hours ago—right next to the School building."

"Shit." Elena had kept up with the official reports Trace sent on behalf of the Refuge team, but this must've happened after his latest missive.

"Yes, exactly that." Jessamy tucked a loose strand of hair impatiently behind her ear. "I did get a bit of good news earlier, though. Vivek tells me Katrina might've had some luck in tracking down a longer record of the myth Vivek first discovered."

Elena wasn't sure what she thought of the owner of the Boudoir. Katrina was a law-abiding citizen on the surface, but Elena was well aware of the dark threads that ran through the vampire's entire operation. She had the feeling that the world only ever saw a part of Katrina—the palatable part.

The rest was kept under lock and key.

But Elena was also no longer the hunter who'd seen the world in strictly black-and-white terms. She'd matured, learned that neither mortals nor immortals could be so cleanly divided. People were complicated. Katrina could be both a threat—and a woman with a conscience.

"You think it'll be useful?" she said to Jessamy.

Jessamy's slim shoulders rose and fell in a tired shrug. "Immortals are old enough that it might be an important piece of our history turned into myth. Or it could be nothing but fantasy. We won't know until Vivek retrieves Katrina's find."

35

The full moon was high in the sky when Vivek got out of his favorite taxi in front of one of the gates into Central Park. This time Hakim just shook his head. "You gonna gimme your next of kin, boss? So I can inform those good folks that your foolish skinny ass walked into your death, never to be seen again?"

Vivek grinned. "I'm one of the monsters, remember?"

But Hakim was having none of it. "Naw. You one of the soft bellies. Well, your funeral, boss. Make sure I get an invite."

Vivek was still scowling at being called a soft belly when, leaning hard on his cane, he entered the lush green alleyway that would lead him to the spot Katrina had chosen as the location of their meeting. The murmuring void that was the night was full of eyes that watched him. Because Hakim was right in one sense—at midnight, Central Park was full of predators, mortal and not.

None of those predators, however, prowled up to him

with nefarious intent. Neither did anyone slither out to make an indecent proposal. Because vampires got off on illicit nighttime assignations just like mortals. He figured angels, too. They just had the advantage of being able to meet in the sky or on rooftops far from prying eyes.

As for why no one approached him with sexual intent, a large number were probably wondering what the hell a Tower vamp was doing here—and worried he was about to bust them for something. The rest were likely turned off by his visible disability. A certain class of vampires bought into the whole "vampirism leads to physical perfection" spiel, and he was a walking slap in their conceited faces.

Vivek could've raged about that, but he'd lived too long in this body to be bothered by random assholes. Vamp or not, they all sang the same pathetic and unoriginal tune. Not worth the waste of energy. The pettiness in him did find it funny that his mere existence messed with their worldview. Factor in his attachment to the Tower, and wowee, he'd probably caused more than one rage stroke.

He smiled.

A stir in the night ahead of him, a woman in darkest red stepping out of the shadows. Her gown featured a wide, flowing skirt but was fitted to emphasize her tiny waist and curving hips, the creamy flesh of her breasts plumping up over the curve of the neckline. The hat that sat jauntily on her head was the same hue but festooned with black ribbon and a spray of black blooms on one side.

A small black fan hung from one wrist. Diamonds twinkled in her ears.

Pushing up the strap of the messenger bag he carried on one shoulder, Vivek spoke past his thudding heart. "Lady Katrina. We do meet in the most interesting places."

She waited until he was next to her before turning so that they walked side by side. He could almost hear the watchers skittering away.

"I've always enjoyed this park in the night hours." Katrina's husky voice stroked over him with near-tactile intent. "It is both active and secretive."

Having not spotted Xai, he raised an eyebrow. "You're not worried about being attacked?"

Her laughter entangled him in a sensuous trap. "No one touches Lady Katrina."

He realized he still had no idea of her age or her power. But the fact that she could walk here at this time without being molested? Yes, this woman was dangerous, a predator among predators.

Now, she glanced at his cane then up at his eyes. "It causes you pain to walk."

Vivek shrugged. "My choice."

"But it is not my choice to have to deal with you should you collapse from overexertion." A regal tone. "We will take a seat on that bench over there." She flicked her fan at one of the ironwork seats tucked into a small green corner.

Vivek gritted his teeth. "I'm not a child to be ordered about."

An unblinking look that was in no way human, the creature that prowled behind Katrina's eyes a thing cold and of *age*. "If you wish to stand here until your leg buckles, go ahead. I will walk over your helpless body and return to my business."

His face hot, Vivek bit back his anger. This wasn't about him. It wasn't even about the Cadre. No, it was about the dead and dying. About the countless children trapped in rubble or underground as the world went to hell—as he'd once been trapped in a hospital bed.

He took a seat.

When she followed, her skirts brushed his legs.

Shrugging the bag off his shoulder after he took several breaths to calm his temper, he opened it, reached inside. Rage would get him nowhere, not with a vampire of Katrina's age and power. She'd have seen that uncontrolled reaction over and over through time. He had to be smarter, more cunning.

"Why are you carrying champagne flutes?" Her tone was arch.

"So we can drink this." He pulled out a black bottle marked with a distinctive label of embossed black on black. "From the premier blood café in town. In honor of your find."

"We did not have such things in my time. Blood from the vein was considered good enough."

Unable to control the reckless edge within, Vivek flipped his hand to expose his wrist. "Anytime, Lady Katrina."

A total stillness that told him he invited death. "I have very high standards for my blood."

The hairs had risen on his arms when she went motionless, but why be a little reckless when he could go all the way? "Then," he said, "I hope this vintage lives up to your expectations."

Eyes yet frosty, she accepted the flute he offered her, but didn't take a sip until he had his own in hand. He raised it in a toast. "To the text you managed to find out of thin air."

The first sip was rich and luscious, his reaction to it a silent confirmation that he was no longer human in anything but his heart and thoughts. It was fire in his veins, a pump of energy visceral and rich. "Wow." He turned to find her watching him with eyes that no longer seemed so frigid. "It's good, admit it." Yes, his mood was clearly for death.

"It's passable," was the cool response—but he knew he was safe. When she brought the flute to her lips again, she was no longer an inhuman ice sculpture but a woman powerful.

"When I first considered becoming a vampire," Vivek said, savoring the lingering taste on his tongue, "I wondered how long it'd take me to get used to the taste of blood."

"Only to wake up and realize that blood was the most delicious thing in the world to you," Katrina completed. "Yes, it's quite a shock, is it not, that first taste?"

"It still took me a while to get used to it," he admitted. "My body wanted it, but my brain kept telling me it was blood I was drinking."

"And now?" Katrina's murmured question, the way her eyes lingered on him, made him feel like a teenager whose crush had finally deigned to notice him.

"Pure pleasure in my throat, ambrosia on my tongue." He leaned forward, his forearms braced on his thighs. "I could keep on talking to you this way forever"—why pretend when it was obvious he had it bad for her—"but the situation is becoming worse by the hour."

"Yes." No more softness, but no ice, either; this was Katrina in business mode, focused and determined. "I have friends with children. They are beyond terrified for their babes." The sound of glass against metal as she placed her flute carefully on the bench between them, then reached into a pocket of her dress.

He hadn't realized it had pockets until that moment, but of course Katrina would demand clothing both stunning and practical. When she withdrew her hand, it was with a copy of a handbound but *extremely* thin book that appeared brand-new.

"The original was located in deep storage in the home of an angel of whom you need not know—he prefers to be left alone," Katrina said. "I talked him through how to create a scan using a device that I had shipped to him."

Vivek didn't ask *how* the book had been located; that would be like asking a magician for their tricks. "Did you do the binding?" he asked instead. "It's excellent work."

"No. That was Xai."

"Well, I didn't see that coming."

"Even a spy cannot know all the world's secrets."

Leaning back with a grin, he put his flute beside hers, then accepted the book. The image on the cover made his breath catch.

36

Vivek had seen the mark before—on Raphael's temple.

Jessamy had also sent him images of the same symbol in old places in the Refuge. No one knew why the carvings had been done, or when.

Vivek had always thought they might be remnants of the last time the Legion had risen.

"That is a true copy of the book," Katrina said as he traced the lines of the image. "I watched my acquaintance every step of the way. He didn't attempt to skip or hide anything. For him, there was no reason to do so. He was far more interested in the scanner."

Nodding, Vivek opened the book to the first page of text, but the moonlight wasn't strong enough for him to read the words. He took out his phone, shone the light on a language that meant nothing to him.

"I can't read it," Katrina said before he could ask. "Even my acquaintance—who is very, *very* old—couldn't read it. He did say it appears somewhat similar to the old angelic tongue—the one that is passed down from generation to generation unchanged."

Vivek's instinctive reaction was to argue that language always changed, but then he consciously considered what she'd said. And realized he'd missed a specific bit of angelic culture. "So that any angel who wakes after a long Sleep can still talk to other angels?"

An incline of her head, the diamonds glinting in the moonlight. "Old angels pick up languages at rapid speed, but even they can't absorb it the minute they wake."

"Smart." Vivek continued to flip through the pages, hoping for another image, but there were none. "Is your acquaintance older than Lady Caliane?"

A pause. "No," she said at last. "I'm fairly certain she is the elder. You should also send a copy of the text to the Librarian. The angelic Library holds exemplars of dead tongues."

He hadn't known that, either; it irritated him. Vivek hated being out of the loop. "If you can't read it, and your friend couldn't, either—"

"—acquaintance," she corrected, ice creeping over her tone once more.

Wondering at their history, Vivek said, "If your acquaintance couldn't read it, either, then—"

"—why do I believe this may be linked to the myth with which you first came to me?" Katrina completed, then turned the book over in his hands until he was staring at the back cover . . . and an image of that unusual evil eye.

Staring, pulsating red.

"During my search for further information on your odd little myth," she said, "I found another myth connected to it. The available text, too, bore the image of the evil eye." She once again reached into her pocket, this time to retrieve a piece of paper folded in four.

When Vivek opened it, he saw it was a photocopy of what looked like an ancient book. The evil eye sat at the very top of the page. "Ancient Greek?" he said, after running his eye over the lines. "I can't read it, but I recognize it."

"Yes. It states: 'Watch, it was said in the Book of Marduk. Watch for evil. When it rises, come together in defense against it. Only together will the world hold. Apart, civilizations will splinter and empires will fall. This was said. The'—and there's a word there with no translation that I can find, but it is similar to Psyche."

"Like the mythical goddess?"

"Yes, but I am using it only as a placeholder, remember that. It is not *quite* Psyche, but it is no other known word, either. I checked with a scholar whose native tongue was Ancient Greek."

Even as Vivek digested the information that Katrina knew someone who'd lived in the time the language was spoken, she went back to her translation. "His suggestion was that for translation purposes, I translate it as the 'soul.' If I do that, the line reads: 'The soul has been broken and must be melded together again for the body to hold. Else there is but death and rebirth from the ashes.'"

"Cheery."

"Indeed." Katrina pointed once again at the untranslatable word. "That word shows up again in references to what is termed the Book of Marduk."

"I know that name," Vivek murmured, frowning. "God related to Babylon? Few thousand years ago?"

"Yes. He was an angel," Katrina said offhandedly. "Mortals made gods of angelkind once—still do in some quarters."

"But then it can't be related to the myth. That history hasn't been lost."

"That's what I would think, except for this." She ran her finger over a line of text in the paper that he'd missed because it was so faded. "I had to put it under a strong lamp to read it."

It took him serious concentration to see it. But when he did—"Shit." It came out an exhale. "It's in the same language as the book."

He looked from the piece of paper to the book. "This is the Book of Marduk."

"That was my conclusion."

Vivek rubbed his face, trying to put it all together. "How did you even know either of these texts might exist?"

"I didn't. First I sent out an inquiry with the image of the evil eye and got this." She tapped the piece of paper. "Then, I put out the word that I was looking for anything written in this tongue." She ran her finger over the near-invisible line. "The book was the result. My acquaintance had forgotten about it, but his son remembered seeing it as a child in his father's archives."

Vivek put both the book and the piece of paper into the messenger bag with care, then picked up his drink and threw it back. Another shock of energy, another pleasurable buzz. "No ambiguity in that prophecy or warning or whatever it is."

"Fight against great evil together or fall," Katrina said. "We know that firsthand. We watched the Cadre work as one to defeat she who would've ruled the world in death."

Vivek was liking this quiet trend of never mentioning Lijuan by name. Immortals, it seemed, had a way of erasing someone out of existence by refusing to acknowledge they had ever walked the earth. It might take them a millennium or seven, but they had the time. "Can I ask something, my lady Katrina?"

A cool glance as she handed over her empty flute. "Ask."

"You weren't in New York during the war. Were you part of it elsewhere?"

A slight curve of her lips. "You are ever the spymaster's apprentice, searching for information."

"My fatal flaw."

Katrina's gaze took in his face. "I am not a warrior," she

said at last. "Like you, I deal in information. And I know and am known by many old and . . . not necessarily 'good' people who will not talk to others. Let us say I was in charge of recruitment for the forces of a senior angel, and that those forces helped defeat multiple waves of reborn."

She flicked open her fan, waved it to create the slightest breeze. "After the recruitment phase, I was in the business of arming our troops."

"You're an immortal arms dealer?" He put no judgment in his tone; he'd always known she walked in the gray. And when the time came, she'd chosen to arm their troops, not those of the enemy.

"I was once, in another lifetime," she said. "I dusted off the skills to help ensure she who was evil wouldn't achieve her objectives. My friends in that world were happy to join me in my quest. Even arms dealers have standards, and in using her own people with such callous disregard, she who was evil incarnate turned even the least moral of us against her."

Friends, Vivek noted, rather than acquaintances. And decided he had a new goal in life. To be described as Katrina's friend, rather than a useful acquaintance. "Will you come to the Tower if asked, in order to authenticate the provenance of this book?"

"Only at the request of the archangel," she said. "But the provenance will not assist you. My acquaintance is what is called a hoarder in modern parlance. He collects not only books, but many types of objects.

"His huge estate is nothing but an endless warehouse. He does not keep records. He only wants and takes and holds. Remember it was his son who recalled seeing the book during an exploration of the hoard many years ago, and he knows not from where it came."

Vivek figured a hoarder of this extent was likely to be known to a number of older immortals; Vivek could track him if needed. "Huh. I never figured that angels and vampires could become hoarders, too. But it makes sense. With that much time, even collecting a little here and there would end up in a hoard."

"No." Snapping her fan shut, Katrina allowed it to fall off her wrist once more. "As with mortals, immortals keep their homes manageable. Items are traded, sold, given away, or discarded, only those most precious to the owner kept.

"My acquaintance does not—cannot—do any of that. Once he has something, he *must* hold on to it." A thread in her tone that Vivek was certain was empathy. "It is an illness, I have heard it said by both angelic healers and mortal physicians. Having witnessed the way he lives, inside a home stuffed to the gills and dank with the smell of rot, I must agree."

When she rose, he rose with her, his bag on the side away from her and his hand braced atop his cane.

"That is all the knowledge I have been able to unearth," she said as they began to stroll in the direction from which he'd come.

Vivek nodded, his nostrils flaring as he breathed her in, the cold night air no match for the scent of her. "If I can, I'll tell you what comes of the hunt for the language." Because if this ended up Cadre business, then Vivek's mouth would be sealed shut.

Katrina stopped without warning, turned to face him. "Why are you breathing so hard?" An unreadable glint in her eye. "Is it your leg?"

He ground his teeth against the flash of annoyance. "No, the infusion of blood will stave off the degenerative effects for the short term." That was another reason he'd bought the blood. He was far more mobile after a drink, at least for the next hour or two. "I'm breathing this way because I'm drunk on your scent." If she could be blunt, then so could he.

They stood in the silvery light of the moon, close enough

that he saw her pupils expand. "And what"—a purr—"do I smell like to one of the hunter-born?"

He'd had time to think about it, unravel the layers of complexity. "An indulgence of dark orchids twined with shards of musk, and beneath it all, a delicate whisper of flowers I can't name, but that might be poison hidden within the most beautiful blooms. You smell of dangerous intoxication."

Her lips parted, lush and pink. Her breath caught in her throat. And her eyes . . . the pupils expanded until they almost took over her irises. When she spoke, her voice was husky with an edge that told him he talked with the predator beneath the sophisticated skin. "You are either a very brave or very reckless man, Vivek Kapur."

Unable to predict her next move, his shoulders rigid and his hand tight on the head of his cane, he didn't so much as take a breath.

Katrina leaned toward him, her breath against his throat as she said, "Be careful how far you push me, young one." She'd turned and walked away into the darkness before he could snap back a response, a woman who was at home in the night, and who had no fear of the shadows that lingered within it.

37

He stirs but does not wake.

It will take him time. He has Slept longer than eternity itself.

You were ever fascinated with him.

Do you blame me? I was a child, and he was . . . a monster, beautiful. The last one of his kind to walk the earth.

My memories of him are not as clear as yours. I was but a babe when he declared he was done with life and that the time for his final Sleep had come.

Ah, my love. I forget that you are the younger. My fresh-faced lover whom I seduced.

Will you forever remind me that I am the younger? We are so old that they call us Ancients of Ancients in the waking world.

But to me, you are simply my Qin.

The earth shakes again.

Yes, he stirs again. Each stir brings him closer to breaching the veil of Sleep.

I pity those who walk the earth.

You are just jealous because he was the first man to make my heart skip a beat.

He is not a man.

No . . . no, he is not. He is something quite apart.

38

"I found it!" Jessamy's cheeks were flushed pink on the screen as she waved a piece of paper in the air, her braid fuzzy and strands of hair around her face.

Unused to such exuberance from the serene and composed mate of his weapons-master, Raphael hesitated. But Elena took it in stride. "What, Jess?"

His consort's face was no longer as worn—she'd had several nights of restful sleep now that her father was out of the ICU, with the doctors cautiously talking about a full recovery rather than possible complications.

In hunter-black today, her hair in a practical braid, she looked both alert and strong.

"The language!" Jessamy beamed. "In the book!" She waved the piece of paper again. "It's a tongue marked as Old Angelic in our records."

"That can't be correct." Raphael frowned, crossing his arms over his worn-in brown leathers. "We all learn Old Angelic and it's not the tongue in the Book of Marduk."

"The Book of the *First* Marduk," Jessamy corrected. "That's what we're calling it for the time being, because it can't belong to the Marduk we know. And yes, I agree about the confusion with Old Angelic.

"The label on the exemplar wasn't in the same tongue, but in one a little in between. Andromeda is cleverer than me at such work." A proud smile. "She's the one who managed to bridge the gap and translate the meaning. But she took me through her method and I agree with her that it says Old Angelic."

Raphael tightened his wings to his back, while Elena said, "A language older than the one taught to all angelkind—and that I'm studying right now? Isn't that meant to be the oldest tongue in angelic history?"

"It's been a shock, believe me." Jessamy's eyes were as bright as a child's, her historian's heart awash in excitement. "The other odd thing is that we only found this record because we were actively hunting. It wasn't in the same place as the rest of the language records. If I were the type of person to create theories of conspiracy, I would say it had been hidden on purpose."

Sparks in Raphael's Legion mark, energy he could now feel . . . like a limb stretching awake with pinpricks of pain and pleasure entwined. "Was anything else hidden with it?"

But Jessamy shook her head. "The only reason the record survived is that it was cut into near-impermeable stone. I'm assuming by archangelic power. But even that stone has worn down, the writing faded."

"That kind of time . . ." Elena blew out a breath. "I wonder if Cassandra could've read it? The language? She's the oldest angel we've ever spoken to, right?"

"Cassandra's age is unknown," Raphael murmured, "but yes, she comes from another time. The sole occasion on which Qin actually spoke to me about her—in the direct aftermath of the war—he said that she had spent millennia of her life alone, and did not deserve to stay that way for all eternity. He said he wished he'd been born when she had, so they could've had those millennia together."

Unspoken had been the reason why: Cassandra's catastrophic gift. A gift so cruel that it made her claw her eyes out over and over again, only for them to grow back in a curse of immortality.

"She's not all the way asleep yet. If we need to ask her to rise, it's possible." Raphael rubbed at his forehead. "Can you translate the book now that you have the exemplar?"

Jessamy frowned. "Usually, we could. It's passed down from Librarian to Librarian that when we make an exemplar of a dying language, we're to leave a translation guide with that exemplar. Most Librarians leave many, *many* such guides. That's why the languages archive sits far from the Library on the very edge of the Refuge—because it's so large."

"But not this time?" Elena said.

"No. The single stone tablet is the only evidence—aside from the book—that this language ever existed." A twist of her face that was naked distress. "I can't make myself believe it, but it's almost as if a Librarian went to great lengths *not* to carry this language forward in any meaningful way."

"Could there have been a disaster that affected the records?" Raphael frowned.

"The Refuge has stood as long as angelkind has existed," Jessamy said. "No disaster that could've affected the archives has ever been noted in the records—as I have already noted our current disaster."

"What if it *was* on purpose?" Elena said, two furrowed lines in her brow. "What if the reason it's called Old Angelic is that it was the precursor to what we now call Old Angelic, but the angels of the time decided to wipe it out of existence in favor of the new version? Could that be done in a world of immortals?"

Jessamy's face fell at the idea of the purposeful destruction of knowledge.

Raphael, however, nodded slowly. "Yes," he said. "If the decision was made at the level of the Cadre, the order pronounced as law. It wouldn't take that long—it could be effected by no longer speaking it, and not teaching the next generation of children the language.

"Some slippage is inevitable, but fluency would fade generation after generation. And at some point, all the old ones who knew it as their main tongue would Sleep." He considered his own words, added, "Our current Cadre is top-heavy with Ancients, and a number of non-archangelic Ancients also walk the world—this is a rare situation brought about by the Cascade. Many angels decide on a permanent Sleep after a certain span of time."

"Taking their language with them." Dropping a knife into her palm, Elena played the blade through her fingers. "Why erase a language, though? Did angelkind decide to simplify their language?" She made a face. "This student says it's not simple at all." She pointed at herself. "But, jeez, maybe the older version was even worse."

"Old Angelic *is* a clunky tongue," Jessamy agreed, her expression still aghast. "That's why it's only used for basic communications with the newly awake." She made a pained face. "Much as it hurts me to say this, it makes sense that a Cadre long past decided to phase out a previous tongue that was even more ornate and difficult."

All three of them considered that for the moment.

Until at last, Jessamy took a deep breath and said, "It's an intellectual curiosity, but it doesn't give us the answer to our most pressing question, does it?" No shine on her face now, the tiredness returning.

"You have done well," Raphael said gently, for he would always have time for this kindest of angels. "The entire Cadre has faith that if there was something else to find, you'd have found it."

"Yeah, Jess, don't beat yourself up about it. If Vivek's right about why the Legion mark is on the cover—that it has to do with when they last rose—then all this happened waaaaaaay back in the past."

"There's a vacuum." A tremble in Jessamy's voice, her eyes unfocused. "I never before truly thought about it, but we don't have the story of our origins. Those records were lost long ago."

Elena looked from Jessamy to Raphael. "Um, we're talking millions of years, right?" A faint smile on her face, she shook her head. "I don't think any sentient species will ever know *exactly* where they came from—it just doesn't work that way. We didn't even know about the whole humanity-rising-after-angelkind-poisoned-itself bit until the Legion told us."

"Angels have always kept excellent records," Jessamy insisted.

"Unless angels appeared out of the ether fully formed, Jess, your"—she winced, corrected herself—"*our* species has origins. It just so happens that the angelic cave-painting period was so long ago that time has erased all signs of it. Either that, or the conspiracy theorists are right and angels are aliens who flew here from outer space."

"We are not aliens," Raphael said firmly. "This is our home—it is in our blood." Every angel born knew that; it was difficult to explain, but there was a resonance in the blood that told them this was home ground. He'd have to ask his Elena if she felt the same. "Flying through space is painful."

"Are you serious?" His consort's mouth fell open. "Have you tried?"

"I was young and stupid once." He shrugged. "A friend and I decided to see if we could fly to the moon."

Jessamy made a squeaking sound. "Can I write a record of this?"

"No. I do not wish my stupidity immortalized. Especially as I was already an archangel at the time." His face tensed. "It was Uram. We decided to attempt the flight together." Never knowing that one day, Raphael would be his friend's executioner.

Elena's wing brushing his, his hunter giving him silent comfort.

He was different then, he said privately to Elena. *A better man. A good friend.*

I know. I've seen that man through your memories of him.

Out loud, he said, "Most angels beyond a certain point in development and age don't really *need* to breathe. But it hurts if we don't. Archangels need even less air than most, so Uram and I thought we should be able to fly in space. After all, we surely had the power to escape the planet's gravitational pull."

Jessamy, her eyes huge, leaned forward. "Did you?" A whisper.

Raphael nodded. "We survived fine in thin air. But in no air? It felt as if our lungs would destroy themselves. The physical pain was the worst I have ever felt—and I say that after having experienced much more since then. We could *technically* have made it to the moon, but we'd have been insane from the agony by then."

Jessamy's look was tortured. She picked up a pen. "Please, Rafe." A rare slip into the name she'd called him as his teacher once upon a time. "Can I just—"

"No. Not even for you, Jessamy."

As Jessamy dropped her face into her hands with a whimper, Elena mimed pushing her own jaw shut. "Just when I thought I knew all the wild things angels could do. Fly into space? Seriously." She shook her head. "So, not aliens, then."

"No, this is our home soil. We grew here."

"And you've been here so long that you've got no origin story at all at this point," Elena said. "No, wait, you have those Ancestors. Is that your origin story?"

"Ancestors are more myth than history." Jessamy raised

her head from her hands. "Trust me, Ellie, I've tried to track down more information about them, but it all circles back to childhood tales. Not a speck of actual history in any of it. I think they're phantoms we created to fill the gap of our distant past."

Raphael couldn't disagree. "Keep searching," he said to the Librarian. "For anything. We'll do the same."

"Wait." Jessamy held up a hand. "Vivek mentioned a language program he could run the text through in the hope the machine will be able to unlock its secrets. I will speak to him if that's acceptable?" This time, her tone was formal, the request of the Librarian to an archangel.

"Yes, he's cleared to the highest levels."

After Jessamy said goodbye, Galen came on to discuss security-related matters. Elena shot him a quick salute before slipping away to go meet her sisters. Raphael's weapons-master and his consort would never be best friends, but they respected each other, which was what mattered.

"How bad?" he asked the man the others in the Seven called the Barbarian.

Shoving back the thick red of his hair, Galen met his gaze with eyes of a pale and striking green. "The disintegration of the Mantle has sped up. Naasir had the idea to nudge a pair of tiger siblings into the area accessible to mortals, and that's worked to keep them away for now."

"How long until Refuge structures become visible?"

"If there's no further escalation in the speed of the disintegration, then eight or nine days at the latest. But the Mantle is now the least of our problems—we've lost the School as of moments ago. The sinkhole beside it expanded at violent speed to swallow it whole."

Galen's muscled shoulders were locked, his biceps bulging against the metal armband that carried Jessamy's amber. "I don't know if anything of the Refuge will be left by the time the Mantle fails completely."

"Wait," Raphael said, as his screen began to light up with red alerts sent through by Vivek and Dmitri.

He scanned the subject lines.

Life-threatening dust storm.
Raging forest fire.
Category 5 hurricane.

The Ancestors help them all.

39

Beth had baked a cake for this gathering of sisters that she'd organized after declaring they needed to spend time together outside of the hospital; she'd set the cake up on a wicker table on her patio. That patio was covered by a clear roof over which grew masses of roses that Elena had helped Beth plant—and that she still dropped by to deadhead with her sister.

Alongside the cake was a pretty floral teapot as well as four matching cups and saucers. "Where're the kiddos?" Elena picked up a cup by its fragile-seeming handle to examine the flower pattern.

"School." Beth's dress—white with red hearts—flared gently around her as she turned; her cardigan was a matching red, as was her headband. "Maggie's staying late today because she's in the play they're putting on. Lead role." Her face glowed. "My baby girl enchants people."

Placing the cup back onto its saucer with care, Elena smiled. "She definitely enchants me." Beth's firstborn was as delightful and as sweet as her mother, with a face lovely with its soft curves and big brown eyes.

"And your favorite nephew is at soccer practice," Beth added. "He got your rebel genes, Ellie. Told me yesterday that he plans on getting a full-sleeve tattoo soon as he's an adult."

"Hey, don't blame me." Elena held up her hands, palms out. "Also, most of the hunters I know have tattoos. I always figured I'd eventually get one—I mean, Jason has a facial tattoo, so there must be a way to get permanent ink even with angelic healing. I might ask him the details."

Beth pretended to glare at her. "Do not say that in Laurent's vicinity. You know he thinks you are the number one most 'fly' person in the family—though I don't think kids use the word fly anymore. Both tell me I embarrass them when I talk to their friends." Good-natured laughter. "I tell them that's a mother's job."

Elena grinned. "You should talk to Sara. Zoe's talking piercings."

"We need a mothers-of-tweens-teens-and-young-adults support group."

Laughing, Elena took her sister's hand. Beth's skin was warm and soft. "You're looking better, Bethie."

"Now that Dad's out of the worst woods," Beth said, "I feel like I can breathe again." She squeezed Elena's hand. "I know he wasn't much of a dad to you, Ellie, but he's the only one I had as a parent for years and years. Even after Gwendolyn came, I looked to him first."

"I know." She touched her sister's perfectly curled and set hair with the gentleness of an elder sibling used to caring for a sister who was smaller, weaker. "I was worried about him, too. It must've been a thousand times worse for you."

Beth gave her one of those suddenly wise looks, unexpected in a sister who tended to float through life on laughter and joy, not paying too much attention to the unpleasant.

"No, Ellie. I think it was the worst for you, because he's always loved you in a different way from the rest of us."

"Beth—"

"Hush." Beth shook her head. "I don't mean that in a favoritism way. I mean you're the one most like him, the most stubborn, the most sure she's right. And because of that, he has a totally different relationship with you than he does with us. For better or worse, you're his equal, while we're his children."

"I'm not sure I like that," Elena murmured. "I needed a father when I was young." She'd long moved past that stage, but that didn't erase the wounds left behind.

"I know." Beth squeezed her hand again, her eyes soft when she looked at Elena. "After I became a mother . . . I began to understand things I never before had because I was the baby of our little family, and even you babied me."

Elena's throat hurt. She hadn't met this Beth before, this older, more mature version of her flighty and soft younger sister. "Bethie," she said, her voice a rasp. "You're not supposed to grow up."

Instead of laughing, Beth said, "Grow old, you mean?" A tenderness to her expression, the fingers of her free hand affectionate on Elena's cheek. "I get that, too, Ellie. The fear you must have inside you—because I see it in my husband's eyes each night when we say good night. He lies awake for hours. I know that because sometimes I wake and he's just there looking at me."

"I told you when you first met that Harry guy that he was creepy," Elena muttered.

"Oh, hush." Beth broke their handclasp to pour them both tea. "You like him now that you've seen how he is as a husband and father."

"Upgraded from zero stars to three. Best I can do as your big sister." It was easier to make jokes than to confront the truth Beth had laid out in front of her.

But her suddenly tough sister wasn't letting go. Not today. "He's *so* afraid, Ellie. Of the day I go. Of the day our children go."

Elena had always blamed Harrison for his own pain; he was the one who hadn't waited for Beth's test results to come back before he'd chosen to be Made. Only to discover that Beth was incompatible with the toxin that Made vampires. Now, however . . .

"I tell myself that most mortals have a single lifetime with their loved ones," Elena said past a too-tight throat, "that there are a ton of messed-up immortals who've had eons to get a relationship right and never managed it because there's always more time. That it's quality, not quantity, that counts . . . but, Beth, the idea of you not being here one day . . ."

Tears burned her irises. She fought back the flood with clenched teeth and another hard swallow.

"I know." Beth's smile was that of her somewhat scatter-brained sister again, bright and cheerful. "Imagine how I felt when you were flying into battle against angels who were throwing literal thunderbolts of power." A nudge with her elbow. "I'm always going to be your *first* baby sister. No matter what happens or how many years pass, I'll always be that part of you. No one can ever take my place."

Elena looked at her. "You sound so smug," she said with a shaky laugh.

"I am." Beth made an even more smug face before taking a sip of her tea. "Also, I expect a monument to your love for me after I'm gone. A giant statue."

"Birds poop on statues."

Beth snorted tea out her nose, and then they were both laughing so hard their stomachs hurt. They didn't even notice that Eve and Amy had arrived until their two half sisters walked through the back gate.

"No one answered the door," Eve said when they looked up; she wore camo-green pants paired with a long-sleeve black tee, over which she'd strapped on the forearm sheaths

Elena had gifted her on her graduation from Guild Academy.

"Evie!" Beth beamed. "Amy!" She hugged each one in turn.

Because this was Beth, Elena thought. She might be smug about always being Ellie's "first" little sister, but she had enough love in her heart not to mind that Elena now had two other little sisters.

Elena hugged Eve, too, squeezing her much shorter sibling tight. Eve hugged her back as hard. Their relationship was different from the one Elena had with Beth, but it was as fierce. Not only was Eve so much younger, her bond with Elena was built on what it was to be driven by the need to hunt.

When it came time to greet Amy, Elena waited for her to take the lead, still not certain where they were in their relationship. Amy, dressed in a stylish navy pantsuit paired with a lacy camisole, black heels on her feet and her hair sleek and straight, came in for a hug. She didn't hold it as long as Eve, but neither was it surface gloss. Elena found herself gently patting Amy's back as they parted.

Amy's smile was lopsided. "It's funny, you know," she murmured, while Beth was chatting to Eve about the cake she'd made—because taut, toned, and in-hunter-shape Eve still loved cake as much as she had as a child.

"I hunt so I can eat cake," she'd said more than once, while scooping up bites of cake with a golden cake fork. Because Eve also loved her cake forks, the fancier the better. Elena had gifted her a vintage enameled set for her last birthday.

"What's funny?" she said to Amy. "Eve's desire to taste every cake in the world?"

Amy's shoulders shook. "She's adorable, isn't she?" A smile thrown at the most petite member of the family. "No, how you did that patting thing. I do that with Eve. I've always thought of myself as the big sister."

If Elena was close with Eve, she felt a dancer with two left feet when it came to Amy. "I'm sorry if I overstepped."

"No, I didn't mean that." Amy's smile faded. "I guess I was just hit by the realization that I could've had a big sister all this time if I hadn't pushed you away."

Elena shook her head. "You were caught up in the emotional undertow of things that happened long before you were born. I always understood why you did what you did. You had to support your mother."

Expression shifting in a subtle but profound way, Amy glanced over to make sure Beth and Eve were still involved in their own discussion before saying, "I've never spoken about this to Eve. I feel like I have to protect her, you know?" A stiff smile. "All my life, I've known that my mother loves my father more than he loves her. So I thought he must love his first children more than us, too."

Elena didn't know what to say to the first part of that— because it was true. Jeffrey had *loved* Marguerite—in a way he'd only been capable of loving one woman. Part of him had died with Marguerite, obliterated beyond any hope of recovery.

But she could respond to the second part of Amy's statement. "He's so proud of you, Amy. He's been telling me what a good mom you are to your kids, and how you've chosen to volunteer with an organization that helps victims of childhood trauma. I can feel the love and pride pumping off him."

Elena nodded in Eve's direction. "It might've taken him a while to get his head screwed on straight when it comes to Eve being a hunter, but part of his reaction at the start was due to fear."

It had taken Elena time to give her father grace for his wounds, but she saw them now. "He lost two daughters to a psychotic vampire. He was petrified of losing a third. My father's problem has never been about loving his children."

Amy's eyes shone wet. Blinking, she looked away for a

moment, but nodded. "Yes." A waterlogged sound. "I did eventually figure that out." She took one deep breath, two. "As I figured out that it was my mom's choice to stay with him even knowing that she could never live up to Marguerite.

"Over the years, I was so angry with Mom, too. How, I thought, could she just accept being second best?" She twisted her lips. "Then I fell in love and understood that sometimes, it isn't a choice. Sometimes you love so much that you'd accept crumbs from your love's table."

This wasn't a conversation Elena had ever thought she'd have with Amy. But oddly enough, it was easier than it would've been with Beth. Because while Beth was older, she had always been Elena's little sister.

Amy, meanwhile . . . she felt more like another elder sister.

"We have a complicated family."

"I think that's the most diplomatic way to put it." Amy's smile was wry.

"Hey!" Eve threw up her hands, her ponytail swinging. "Are you two going to keep lollygagging or are we eating cake?"

"Where did you hear that word?" Amy laughed, the sound reminiscent of Gwendolyn's gentle joy. "It feels like something a grandma would say."

"Or a three-hundred-year-old vampire." Eyes dancing with glee, Eve accepted the huge slice of cake Beth put on a plate for her. "Was behind her in a queue at the grocery store and she was muttering about how the cashier was lollygagging with all the customers and holding up people who had things to do."

Eve made a wicked face. "I was tempted to point out that it was hardly as if she was growing gray hairs standing there, but I behaved myself. Though I did roll my eyes behind her back when I saw the bottled blood she was holding—cheap watered-down crap. She'd get more nutrition in a single glass at one of your cafés, Ellie."

"Hey, don't knock the cheap stuff." Beth served up three more slices. "My favorite 'champagne' is a pink one that costs eight dollars a bottle."

"The horror!" Amy cried, clutching at her heart. "Were you even a young woman in Gwendolyn Deveraux's house? Does she have any idea of your taste in fizzy pink water?"

"We have a 'don't ask, don't tell' policy." Beth winked and passed her a slice of cake. "Strangely enough, though, Mama-Gwen has stopped gifting me five-hundred-dollar bottles on major occasions."

As everyone cracked up and Beth passed Elena a slice of cake, Elena realized that this was the first time in her life that she was surrounded by all of her living sisters in a setting joyous and warm.

But somehow, she didn't feel like a traitor to Belle and Ari.

In fact, after she took her seat on the cushioned wicker chair that Beth had had modified to accommodate her wings, with Beth on one side, Eve on the other, and Amy across from her, she could almost feel Belle leaning over her shoulder, while Ari stood on the other side of the table, one hand on the back of Amy's chair.

Both of them smiling and enjoying this moment where all six of Jeffrey's daughters were together as family for the first time.

40

Interlude
Archangel of Disease

Charisemnon watched the large monitor one of his people skilled in such matters had put up for him. The vampire had called this a "live feed" of the room that held Charisemnon's second crop of subjects, all of whom he'd infected with a slightly different strain of his most promising disease.

He sat alone as he always did here, watching them whimper and crawl and roll into balls. The vampires were interesting . . . but he was far more invested in the angel who sat slumped in a chair in the corner. Five hundred years old and a weak hanger-on of a courtier no one would miss.

He was crying tears of putrid green, his movements weak as he scratched at his arms.

Until a chunk of flesh came away.

Then he began to scream and thrash, falling to the floor in his panic. His wings *collapsed* under him. Not folding in the normal way. Not even as if he'd broken a wing. As if they'd *rotted*.

Charisemnon's heart raced and he leaned closer to the screen.

Had he done it? Created a disease that killed immortals?

He didn't move all night as the angel thrashed and screamed . . . and got quieter and quieter . . .

41

An hour after they'd sat down, and Eve was groaning and patting at her washboard-flat abdomen while saying, "Surely, I can fit in another piece. My stomach is capable of expansion. Also, we—"

The entire table shook so hard that the remaining cake crashed to the floor, followed by the table. The four of them bolted upright at the same time, but the ground was moving too violently for Elena's sisters to make it to the safety of a reinforced doorway, and the table that had gone down was a lightweight one that wouldn't protect them if the trees next to the patio crashed through the roof.

She met Eve's eyes. "Lawn!" It was the closest area with nothing that could fall on them.

Eve—tiny but muscled—grabbed Amy and began to make her way there, while Elena hauled Beth out from under the roof, then picked her up under the arms. She wasn't strong enough to do this, and Beth's feet scraped the ground, but she got her sister to the lawn before coming back to assist Amy.

Eve ran full tilt beside them, and Beth was waiting to grab Amy when Elena all but collapsed onto the earth with her. All four of them went to the ground as one to ride out the waves of rolling earth. Elena opened her wings over her sisters, tucking them close to her.

Elena!

I'm safe, Archangel! But this is going to be bad.

The shaking stopped.

The group lay on the earth for several more seconds, waiting to see if it would start again, but nothing, only an eerie silence.

Even the birds had gone quiet.

Elena got to her feet, with Eve following, then a shaky Amy and Beth. "Everyone okay?" After getting a round of nods, she said, "I have to fly, check on the damage."

"I can walk the neighborhood," Eve said, "see if anyone needs help."

"I'll join in after I check on the kids." Amy held up her phone.

Beth, who was already dialing on her own phone, nodded to show she'd do the same.

Leaving her sisters to it, Elena took off. The houses in the neighborhood looked okay at first glance, though she could see people milling around. A couple of children too young to be at school waved up at her, and she dipped her wings to show she'd seen them; hopefully, that would take their mind off what had just happened.

The first sign of major damage came five minutes later, when she overflew the playing field attached to a local high school. The green had been split in two, a literal small canyon now separating the two jagged halves of the field. There were, however, no players on the field, and she could see no emergency vehicles nearby or en route, so it looked like they'd gotten lucky there.

Her stomach tense, she flew on. And kept seeing damage to the landscape . . . while houses and other buildings stood unbroken. A few bore minor cracks, but that was it. *Raphael, any buildings down in Manhattan?*

No, came the astonishing answer. *Countless cracked windows, but that's the worst of the damage. No casualties found so far. We* have *lost multiple roads, however—you'll see the oddness of it when you fly in.*

I'll be there soon.

It was no surprise to find the Hudson rippling with the jewellike tones that made it appear a huge and glorious snake. The sight was so stunning that it had become a tourist attraction, with a local company offering helicopter flights over the area. Since the sight couldn't be predicted, however, tickets only went on sale when it appeared—and sold out every time.

Today, she saw not a single non-angelic flyer in the air—and all watercraft were powering in to berth if they hadn't already done so. The Tower had to have grounded aircraft and ordered boats back to shore. A good precaution.

Because, while lovely, the water below her was choppy. She'd never seen waves like this on the river. Huge rolling arcs that glittered with the colors of the shimmering scales. Fascinated, she nonetheless flew on, needing to see Manhattan with her own eyes. All those tall buildings, all those people in the streets . . .

The edge of Manhattan brought good news. People had gathered outside, as if they'd evacuated, but the buildings stood tall. A few gaping holes where windows had once been, but that was it. And though she could hear the sirens of emergency vehicles rising up into the air, she couldn't see any ambulances nearby.

She flew on.

And came to a halt in the air. "What the hell?"

Fifth Avenue had a jagged crack running through it, just like the football field. Only . . . not a single cab or car or person appeared to have been caught in the ragged maw. It zigged and zagged all the way along the tarmac in such an erratic line that it was almost as if a sentient mind had gone around the vehicles and people.

A number of cabbies who'd halted in the street stood staring at the crack, gesticulating to each other across the massive gap that now separated the two sides of the avenue. One had his soft cap in hand and was slapping it into his palm as he spoke to another, who was scratching his head while staring down at the strata of earth exposed by the crack.

As Raphael had warned her, it wasn't the only affected roadway. *Archangel, the roads.*

You haven't seen the whole of it. Head to the Tower.

Beyond befuddled, she flew on . . . only to come to a screeching halt above the Tower. Raphael, who must've been keeping an eye out for her, flew up from the roof to join her where she hovered with her mouth open.

Snapping it shut with effort, she said, "Either Beth baked magic mushrooms into her cake, or the grass around the Tower has turned into scales."

When she looked from the landscaping to the Legion building, she saw that the luminous scales were climbing it, turning the leaves and branches into jewels.

"I'm afraid what you're seeing is very real."

At his grim tone, she looked away from the astonishing sight below—and was caught by the electric energy that sparked in the mark on his temple. It took effort to focus. "What am I not seeing?"

"If an Ancient *is* waking—and all indications are that they are," Raphael muttered, "the Tower appears to be the focal point."

Elena's eyes went wide. "Um, would an archangel be able to obliterate the Tower if they woke below it?"

"*I* can obliterate the Tower if I want. So yes."

"Well, shit."

"Yes. Shit." Raphael folded his arms across his chest and glared down at the ripple of iridescent color. "This has never before happened, to my knowledge. The odd angel in Sleep has woken below a house or similar, but no *archangel* has ever made that mistake.

"From what I know of those who have Slept, they seem to have a subconscious awareness of what lies above—a few even talk of sleepily *shifting* within the earth to ensure they come out in open air."

"Like they just, what, tunnel in the earth?"

"No. They say there are never any tunnels around them when they wake, but often, neither are they where they were when they went into their Sleep. Perhaps the ability to shift position without physical movement is a gift of deep Sleep."

"Makes an immortal kind of sense." Because he was right; otherwise, they'd have heard of angels accidentally destroying monuments, warehouses, garden sheds, and who knows what else. Given enough time, a lot of stuff got built over what was once open ground.

She chewed on her lower lip. "Tell me the rest of the Cadre's started to see the signs."

"No. Only I and my mother."

"I need to learn swear words in Old Angelic." Elena rubbed her face. "But look at the bright side of things. At least we won't have to rebuild New York again. Only a few roads. No big deal."

Raphael exhaled, hands on his hips. "You are right. The damage, even the possible loss of the Tower, doesn't matter in the greater scheme of things." His expression turned bleak. "Right before the quake, the Cadre heard from Tasha."

Elena's blood chilled. "Is she still head of security on the island with the children?" A deeply trusted member of Caliane's senior team, the angel had volunteered for the position, her duty to protect angelkind's greatest treasures.

"Yes. A tsunami hit it an hour ago, swamping the entire landscape."

Ice forming in her cells. "The children."

"Safe underground." Raphael shoved a hand through his hair. "But Tasha told us they're trapped until the water recedes, which it's showing no signs of doing."

"What—" She never got to finish her question because the sky exploded.

A literal blast of sound above the Tower that spread outward in a burst of stark white that cleared the sky of blue in a surge that soon obliterated the horizon.

"It's everywhere now!" Raphael called out to her over the ringing in her ears. "Dmitri's just had a call from Tzadiq, asking if we're seeing the same."

Tzadiq, Elena remembered, was Titus's second.

She glanced down on that thought to see Dmitri on the balcony outside his Tower suite, phone to his ear. And it struck her. "We need to evacuate the Tower!" Because the scales were still crawling up over the Legion building . . . though they'd stopped at the base of the Tower. "Oh no! I think the Sleeper's under the Legion building!" She began to turn, more instinct than conscious thought.

"No, Elena!" Raphael put himself in front of her, a wall of immovable power. "If it falls, we can rebuild it." The waves crashed into her mind as his eyes became her world. *The Legion would not want you to put yourself at risk.*

Gritting her teeth, Elena forced herself to stop as emotion lodged in her throat and twisted in her gut.

Her heart would break when that building fell.

I know, Elena-mine, Raphael said as a siren sounded. It was loud enough to reach across Manhattan, and those within a block of the Tower in any direction knew that was their warning to get the hell away from the Tower.

Angels erupted from the Tower, going not skyward but sideways to land on buildings far from the Tower. All strong enough to do so held a non-flyer. Meanwhile, on the ground, cars began to turn, while pedestrians just dropped what they were doing and ran.

Dmitri had put that siren in place during the rebuild after the war. It could pulse out multiple patterns of sound. This one was the simplest—and everyone in the city knew what it meant, and that it was serious. No hesitation, no questions, *run*! That was the order drummed into the entire populace.

Tower inhabitants had different instructions.

Snapping out of her heartbreak, Elena blew her archangel a kiss, then fell—to land on the balcony outside the technological control center. Her assigned task during an evacuation was to clear the techs. Raphael, meanwhile, would be on the roof by now, on standby to fly out anyone who was stuck.

She found Vivek alone inside. He was shutting down systems at rapid speed, while shunting everything to a remote mirror of the center they had in another skyscraper in the city that most people thought was just an apartment building favored by angels. The secondary control station had been Vivek's idea, and after the war and all else the city had survived, it was smart thinking.

"I'm going, I'm going!" he yelled when she ran in. "There, done!" In his wheelchair today, he wheeled himself out while she ran ahead and input an emergency code into a panel beside the elevator.

It came up smoothly. This was part of the plan, too, that code the only one that would work during an emergency override. Non-flyers in the upper floors would've been flown out by now. Those on lower floors would be racing down the emergency stairs; anyone left behind or who couldn't get out was to go to a balcony or make a call for rescue.

Even Vivek had agreed to angelic assistance if the elevators were deemed a risk.

"Go, Ellie! Get out!" he called the second his wheels cleared the entry to the elevator.

She ran as the elevator doors were closing, fighting her instinctive urge to search for others who might need help. Dmitri had been blunt about how that would be the worst possible thing to do.

"If it works as designed," he'd said, that hard, dark-eyed face set in "don't fuck this up" lines, "and everyone does their job, *no one* will be left behind. That's why we have multiple contingencies built in. Anyone who goes back *in* breaks the system."

Tech floor clear! she reported to Raphael as her feet slammed onto the balcony. *I'm out!* She rode the winds away from the Tower at high speed.

Raphael's mind hit all of them a minute later: *Stage 1 complete.*

"Wow," she said to Aodhan, who'd just landed beside her on her assigned building, the intense white light of the sky dancing off him in a brilliance that was painful if looked at directly; he was a violent glow even in her peripheral vision. "I never expected it to go that smoothly. Guess Bluebell was right—Dmitri *is* the Dark Overlord of Planning."

"Yes, Dmitri is the best of us at operations."

"Illium on his way to the Enclave?" She knew the blue-winged angel had been in charge of clearing the infirmary with the wings under his command.

"He and his team completed their task in under a minute." Pride was a quiet underscore to the words. "Picked up the patients in their beds and flew. They're crossing the Hudson, will be at the Enclave shortly."

All wings not assigned to specific tasks would land on rooftops within sight line of the Tower, ready to assist.

Raphael would join her once he completed stage two of the plan: *he* was the final contingency, the one person who could survive being blown up. He'd use his mind to search for anyone trapped, unconscious, or otherwise injured who couldn't call for help, then go in to get those people.

Elena didn't particularly like the idea of her archangel being blown up, even if she knew he would—eventually—come back. He'd still suffer impossible pain and horror. But a bare thirty seconds after his voice had hit her mind, she saw the sunlight glitter off the distinctive white-gold of his wings as he took off from the Tower roof.

Evacuation complete.

A cheer went up around them, but it was muted. Because the reason for the evacuation was obvious now—the scales had crawled up the Legion building until it was all but engulfed.

When she turned to look at the Hudson, she saw sprays of water that drove several meters into the air and hoped the infirmary team was clear. Beside her, Aodhan opened his wings and took off without a word. None were needed. She'd known why he was standing next to her—because she was Raphael's consort, and if this were a war, she'd be a high-value target.

His job was to help her protect herself while Raphael couldn't.

The sky remained a searing white that hurt the eyes, and even as she felt the gust of wind that was her archangel landing next to her, the heavens opened up, though there wasn't a single cloud in that white sky, and rain began to hit them in a hard burst . . . only it wasn't rain.

42

Elena stared at her hands, then looked at Raphael's hair, his wings.

"Raphael, is this . . ."

"I'll kill them," he gritted out, doing something with his power that blasted the iridescent angel dust off him *and* her. Then he created a bubble of power that meant they wouldn't be recoated in the stuff. "Whoever it is, however old they are, I will strangle them with my bare hands."

Elena's lips twitched. She couldn't help it.

Hbeebti, *do not think I didn't see that.*

Sorry. She bit the inside of her cheek to keep from laughing as, around them, others exclaimed at the dusting of a substance that was considered more valuable than diamonds by mortals—but that could also be an intimate act among angelkind.

It's likely one of your Bluebell's ancestors waking up, was the bad-tempered response as Raphael glared at the final disappearing meters of the Legion building. *Dusting another archangel? This one wants war.* His Legion mark burned with wildfire as vivid as it had been when the Legion walked the earth.

Elena patted his arm. *Or they're just old and lost control. Be polite. Don't mention it.*

Another burst from the sky—and this time it *was* rain. Washing away all that precious angel dust. Elena hoped some mortals had been fast enough to scoop up and store a handful. They'd get a pretty penny for it, be able to pay for an entire university education or even buy a house, depending on their haul.

Raphael dropped the bubble. "At least the idiot is polite enough to offer a shower in the aftermath."

Crisp and cold, the rainburst vanished as quickly as it had come, but it left behind a film of shimmering scales across Manhattan. It was beautiful, Elena had to admit, but then she looked again at the Legion building and felt her heart break.

All these years, she'd held it safe, kept it thriving for the day the Legion would return, only for it to be encased by the massive power of an archangel who had never known the astonishing, eerie, and loyal beings who'd won her heart.

Raphael's wing brushed over hers before he wrapped an arm around her shoulders to tug her close to his side. "Plants grow again," he murmured to her. "Your Legion would understand."

"They weren't my Legion."

"In this, they were." A brush of his lips over her wet hair as they stood there watching the colors of this unknown archangel eat up the last green pieces of the Legion building.

Everything stopped. The world hushed.

And then . . .

Elena sucked in a breath.

The Legion building was *morphing.* It was literally twisting into the shape of an enormous snake . . . No. She frowned. Not a snake. Leaning back, she looked at the mark on Raphael's temple, then at the wildness taking place where the Legion building had stood. "That's a freaking dragon."

Raphael reached up to touch his mark. "It's pulsing," he said, staring at the building that was no longer a building but instead a creature out of myth and legend . . . a creature that echoed the mark on Raphael's temple.

A mark similar to that found in various places in the Refuge, hidden and old.

A roar of sound as the "dragon" of multihued light took off . . . leaving the Legion building untouched. It flew high, high, higher, until she had to arch her neck to keep it in sight.

A second later, it turned and dived—straight at Raphael.

Raphael stood his ground, his jaw clenched, was still standing as unmoving as granite when the dragon of light morphed into an angel unlike any Elena had ever seen. He landed hard on the rooftop right in front of Raphael, his landing spawning cracks in every direction along the impermeable surface.

His wings were more like the Legion's than any other angel Elena had ever met. Leathery and thick, though they were black rather than the Legion's gray before the beings began to become more differentiated. And the angel's weren't wholly leathery. She could see a fine coating of black feathers over the leather. But it seemed to her that those were cosmetic more than anything.

No primary feathers that she could see—no secondary ones, either.

What she *could* see were gleaming black claws that thrust out from the two top edges of his wings.

His skin was a burnished brown, his hair thick and dark.

He wore sleeveless leathers of a deep bronze.

But that was where his resemblance to other angels ended. His face . . . She swallowed hard as she took in the right side of his face. Scales iridescent and hypnotic covered that entire side, continuing up into the midnight of hair that reached his nape.

Those scales also ran down his neck to pour across his shoulder and down his right arm, to crawl over the back of his hand and halfway down his fingers before fading off into skin. A single piercing blue eye of fierce paleness looked out from within the scales that should've been monstrous but were instead an eerie fascination.

The eye matched the one on his other side, but his face on that side was sharp lines and skin. The split between his two sides wasn't centered, however. It was more a gradual fading. The scales merged into skin partly along his jaw and across his forehead, blended slightly into his nose.

His lips were just kissed by the scales on one side, softly curved on the other.

He should've looked a nightmare.

He didn't.

He looked a dangerous dragon in angel form.

Without warning, he raised a hand toward Raphael.

Elena tensed.

Just as the angel's blue eyes turned from human to reptilian, a long, slitted black pupil replacing the roundness of his angelic eyes.

Raphael had no idea who—or *what* he was looking at. That this man was a violent power was obvious. He incited the same reaction in Raphael as any other archangel, except for an odd . . . echo. It was the only way he could describe it. Not only was the Legion mark still throbbing, but something within him seemed to be echoing the other archangel's pulse.

Now, the unknown being raised a hand.

Raphael's instinct was to shove it away, make it known that this was *his* territory. But something in the way the angel looked at him held him back—there was no challenge or aggression in those striking eyes that reminded him of Venom's. Rather, they held an odd and almost Naasir-like curiosity. Wild. Open.

He permitted the angel to touch his fingers to the Legion mark.

Wildfire crackled from it and down the scales of the other man's arm.

The new angel—*archangel*—smiled and, dropping his hand, said something to Raphael in a voice so gritty and deep that it nearly hurt the ear. The language was also incomprehensible.

"We no longer use that tongue," he said in the language taught to him as Old Angelic. "This is the one we use now."

The other being cocked his head, listening.

Raphael spoke again, going through a set pattern of words designed to nudge the language awake in Sleepers who had been too long gone from the world.

"Ah," the being said at last. "The new tongue." It came out grating and harsh.

The new *tongue? Is that what he said?*

I believe so, Elena-mine. "We call it Old Angelic."

A sudden smile, those reptilian eyes flashing back to angelic. "Yes, I see now." He raised his hand again, and for some reason, Raphael allowed him to touch the Legion mark once more.

It reacted as before, wildfire sparking between them.

"Blood of my blood," the being grated out, thumping a fisted hand to his heart. "Son of my son."

Raphael's heart crashed against his rib cage. "Who are you?"

"Marduk."

Jessamy was correct, Raphael said to Elena. *The Marduk we know of from Babylon was either a descendant or just carried the same name. This is the Marduk from Vivek's book.*

"I am Raphael," he said aloud. "You stand in my territory."

Marduk's eyes flashed back to their other form, and he looked around with a curious gaze before returning his attention to Raphael. "Why did that impertinent child, Cassandra, wake me?"

He was getting easier to understand now. Either his voice was settling, or Raphael was becoming more used to it. "Lady Cassandra is no child."

Marduk stared at him again. "I cradled her when she was but an infant and I eons old. She will forever be a child to my eyes."

Holy shit, Archangel.

Yes.

"You are not an Ancient," Raphael said with certainty. "Are you one of those we call the Ancestors?"

A quicksilver smile from Marduk that almost made him seem an ordinary angel—but for the rippling scales that shimmered in the sunlight. "No, blood of my line. I am not so old as *that*."

Double holy shit,

As always, hbeebti, *you have a way with words.* Because if this being wasn't an Ancestor, then what the fuck did angelic Ancestors look like?

Yawning, Marduk stretched, then turned with reptilian suddenness.

To stare at Elena.

"My consort, Elena," Raphael said, a warning in his tone. This Marduk might be old, but Raphael would allow no trespass.

Marduk held out his scaled hand, palm up. That palm was half-covered in scales.

After a pause where she held his eyes, Elena placed her palm flat on his, and he closed his fingers around her hand with gentleness conscious. "Different," he said at last. "New. Not blood of my line. Yet . . . marked by my blood."

He's sensing your cells in my body, Elena said.

Raphael wasn't sure what he thought of that, or of Marduk in general, but the angel didn't appear to be threatening or warlike.

"Elena." Marduk rolled out her name as if it was a new sound on his tongue. "Why do my Legion dream of you?"

Elena's hand flexed hard and flat in his. "Are they alive?" she rasped. "Did they make it?"

Marduk tilted his head to the side, as if processing her question. "They are Legion. They are endless. Now, they rest. They heal. They become again."

A single tear rolled down her face at the confirmation. "They sacrificed themselves in a war against a terrible enemy."

"That is their duty and why I made them." His voice was thunder rolled in gravel.

Frowning, he looked at their clasped hands. "They should not feel as angels do . . . and yet, they dream of you." His eyes, no longer angelic, held hers.

She didn't blink, didn't look away. "I love them," she said simply.

He was the one to blink, his eyes shifting back. "I will know you, Elena, Consort of Raphael," he said at last, then dropped her hand. "But first"—his attention back on Raphael—"tell me, young child of Marduk, why has Cassandra meddled where even she, that brazen girl, should never go?"

43

To say the next meeting of the Cadre was interesting was an understatement of magnitudes vast. Marduk hadn't made an appearance onscreen; he insisted on an in-person meeting despite Raphael making it clear that they could use modern systems to communicate far more quickly.

"No," the archangel had said—for he *was* an archangel, if one unlike any other. "It must be a meeting in person."

He wouldn't elaborate on that, but Raphael had the sense that the man who wasn't an Ancestor, but might as well have been, wanted to take everyone's measure. None of the others argued with Raphael's request for an in-person meeting—likely for the same reason. The searing white sky of Marduk's awakening had also blanked any and all cameras in the vicinity, so no one who hadn't physically seen Marduk knew anything of his being.

Even archangels could fall victim to curiosity incurable, and since they were all aware that none of them had the energy for war, there was little to hold them at home. Especially now that the assigned senior angels and vampires had taken Qin's former territory in hand.

To give everyone time to make arrangements, the meeting was set for the third night hence.

Raphael had multiple options for where to hold the meeting of the Cadre, and he was against holding it at his and Elena's Enclave home—their haven—until he got some wise advice from Sivya.

His cook rarely ever raised her head above the parapet, not because she was anything less than courageous and competent, but because she was content in her work in the kitchens, happiest away from the politics of the archangelic world.

That she heard the tail end of his discussion with Elena about the Cadre meeting was an indication of the trust in which he held both her and her mate, his butler Montgomery. He knew both would lay down their lives rather than betray him or Elena.

So when the slender angel with wings of palest gold placed the tray of savories she'd just baked on the study table, but hesitated after they'd thanked her, he glanced over from the armchair in which he sprawled, his tunic unlaced at the throat and wings allowed to fall as they would.

It was the morning after Marduk's awakening.

He and Elena had only then returned home after having spent the night hours helping people in another part of their territory who'd been hit by a windstorm severe enough to topple houses. She'd gone ahead, while he'd joined her after the Cadre meeting, it clear to him that Marduk had no aggressive intentions toward his city.

Hard to explain how he knew, but he *knew*.

Knowledge born of their bond of blood? Perhaps. But it had given him confidence enough to leave Marduk in the city while he went to assist his people. His lands had thus far escaped the major catastrophic events that had hit the others, but only by a matter of degrees.

"Sivya?" he said when the angel remained silent.

A blush of color on her cheeks, she kept her eyes a touch lowered as she said, "Sire, if I may speak?" The delicate coronet in which she'd braided the pale blonde of her hair shimmered in the sunlight that poured through the library windows.

"You do not ever have to ask for permission for that in this home. It is a given." Sivya had come to him from an archaic court, one in which a majordomo drunk on his own power had enforced the hierarchy of the court with vicious intent. Raphael had long ago taught her that he far preferred his residence be a comfortable home, not a stuffy court; but the lessons of youth, he thought, lasted long.

When Sivya shot Elena a quick glance, he nudged his hunter with his mind. *Elena, she needs your permission, too.*

An exhausted Elena, egalitarian in her hunter ways, stared at him for a second from the armchair where she was cleaning her knives—she found the act soothing. When she turned to their cook, it was to say, "Sivvi, if I ever turn into one of those stuffy old angels who wants everyone to bow and scrape, please do stab me with a sharp kitchen implement so I come to my senses."

A snort escaped Sivya's lips, her hand flying to her mouth in the aftermath of the startled response. But her eyes were bright with laughter when they met Elena's, and she smiled at Raphael after dropping her hand. "I would not damage one of my chef's knives by using it in such a way."

Raphael was so surprised by the joke made by the soft-spoken cook that it took him a second to get it—it was Elena who'd gifted Sivya the set of coveted chef's knives handcrafted in Japan. By then Elena was laughing, her hands coming together in an appreciative clap.

Grinning, he raised an eyebrow at their cook. "What is it you wanted to say?"

"Sire, if I have it right, this meeting of the Cadre is not about war or any type of aggression? Rather, it is about introducing Archangel Marduk and—even more so—attempting to find a way to protect the world against the ravages we are all suffering."

"Correct."

"To be welcomed into the home of another and offered sustenance is a gift precious," Sivya said. "A symbol of friendship and trust. It begins the meeting as you wish it to go on."

Raphael considered that with a scowl. He'd never feel friendly toward Aegaeon, but he could see Sivya's point. If the Cadre had ever needed to work as a unit, it was now. War was one thing, cooperation in peacetime quite another.

"The house is built to accommodate larger gatherings," the blonde angel added, "though I know at the time, you thought only of friends, not the Cadre."

"Yes," he murmured with a slow nod, then glanced at Elena.

Who made a face, but said, "Hard to be impolite and hostile when welcomed into someone's private home. Isn't there something in your guesting rules about that?"

"Elena"—he widened his eyes—"is that you, *hbeebti*? I could swear you just referenced the Rules of Guesthood."

While Sivya made a heroic effort to not burst into laughter, Elena pointed her dagger at him. "Ha ha, Your Archangelness. I'll have you know I remember all kinds of things from my politics lessons with Jessamy. She gave me an A+, so there!"

Laughing at this moment of joy stolen from the seriousness of what they were all dealing with at the current time, he thought over Sivya's suggestion all the way through. "It does mean the meeting will begin on a foundation of good behavior."

So it was decided.

The Cadre would be coming to the Enclave and into their home.

44

Come the second night after Marduk's awakening and Raphael could sense him nearby. A single query to Dmitri and he discovered the archangel stood on the Tower roof watching the city.

He did that last night, too, then spent all of today on other high vantage points. Dmitri's mental voice was powerful and clear. *Don't think he's been in his suite except to clean up. I'd be worried he was casing us for a strike, but he reminds me of the Legion. As if we're all animals in a zoo and he's a fascinated bystander.*

Can you blame him? Raphael said. *To wake up after who knows how long—and to Manhattan?*

Man probably thinks he's hallucinating half the time.

Ending the conversation on his second's laughter, Raphael turned to Elena, who also lay awake beside him. "I'm going to go speak with Marduk. You should sleep, Elena-mine." He'd talked her into a nap earlier in the day but knew she needed more hours of rest—she wasn't yet old enough an immortal to keep skipping sleep.

"I am tired, and I want to get up early to visit Jeffrey," she admitted. "I also have the feeling that Marduk will talk more if I'm not there. I'm getting 'protect the woman' vibes from him." A curl of her lip. "Definitely one of your ancestors."

Raphael kissed her scowling lips, his mark sparking as he did so. It had stopped throbbing, however, which was a mercy. "He'll find out who you are soon enough, Guild Hunter."

"Harumph." Despite the dubious-sounding response, Elena kissed him back, her passion and love entwined with an affection so deep and true that it warmed him to his bones. "Go talk to that angel straight out of some people's nightmares—and other people's fantasies."

Raphael raised an eyebrow.

"I'll tell you later," she said. "But let's just say there are folks out there who *really* like scales."

"I may wish to remain uneducated."

Elena's laughter followed him out the door.

He carried that laughter with him as he walked up to the roof. When he exited, it was onto a rooftop lit only by small uplights at the corners that acted as landing beacons. Around him glittered the lights of his city, the sky clear of even the smallest cloud. The wind, soft and cool, tugged at the loose white shirt he'd thrown on over black pants.

"The lights are like stars on the earth," Marduk said to him in a voice that had become less grating and deep in the time since his waking—but not by much. No one would ever mistake his voice for anyone else's.

"I have that same thought at times." He walked to stand next to this being who was his ancestor—there was no way to avoid that, not with the mark on his temple and the echo in his blood anytime they were within a certain proximity to each other.

"The Legion always said they came to me because Elena and I are *aeclari*."

Marduk glanced at him in that slow, deliberate way he had. "Yes, they will only ever go to *aeclari*. Not just to those of my blood."

"Coincidence, then?"

A shrug of those massive shoulders. "I was part of the first *aeclari*."

Raphael felt punched in the gut. "Where is your consort? Why is she not with you?" *Aeclari* were pairs. Always.

"She Sleeps. I'm not going to disturb her simply because Cassandra cannot keep her nose out of the Sleep of her elders."

It made Raphael's head hurt to hear Cassandra referred to as young and feckless. Not when she was the oldest being with whom he'd ever communicated—until now.

Marduk continued. "Perhaps it is coincidence, and perhaps it was time." A glance at Raphael out of eyes gone slitted. "You are of my line. Yet I sense no others of my direct line in this time."

That answered one question. "It must have been my father who was of your line," he said, his thoughts filled with memories of a laughing man with eyes of a vivid green that held a hint of aquamarine. Nadiel had been the best father in all the world—until madness ate him up from the inside out.

"My mother is awake in this time," he told Marduk. "She is Caliane, Archangel of Amanat. She saw your colors in the waters of her territory."

"Because she is your mother, the tie through you." Marduk turned away again, staring out at the glitter of Manhattan, the flow of traffic on the streets its lifeblood.

Raphael tried to see through his eyes. "Do you find this city strange?"

A long pause before Marduk said, "It is vibrant. That is good. Civilizations come and go, but cities must be alive to thrive."

"How many civilizations have you seen come and go?"

"Too many." Marduk's voice held tiredness for the first time. "I should not be awake, young one. There is a reason I Sleep, a reason the Ancestors Sleep. We chose to give this world over to the young and we have all kept our promise through eons uncounted."

Raphael wondered what his mother would say to being called young. "I think you're awake because you need to be awake." When Marduk turned to him with those penetrating eyes, Raphael decided it was time to tell him about the failing Mantle and how it appeared to have triggered the fall of the world itself—but Marduk glanced sharply left without warning, toward the entrance to the roof.

"I was wrong. There is another of my line here. Weaker . . . younger, so I cannot feel them from afar, but present."

The door opened to reveal Venom; the vampire wore a black-on-black suit fitted to his body with flawless tailoring and accented with a tie of the same viper green as his eyes.

"Sire," Venom said with an incline of his head. His gaze was uncovered tonight, the bright green of his irises slitted in the middle. "Do you and Archangel Marduk wish for refreshments?"

Raphael knew why it was one of his Seven who'd come up and not another staff member—because they knew Marduk was lethal. As Naasir might say, he was a tiger who was behaving for the present, but you could never forget that he *was* a tiger—with razor teeth and a liking for flesh.

"Yes, Venom, bring up a tray if you would. But before you go, Marduk wishes to make your acquaintance."

Venom was too experienced to show surprise. Walking across, he politely inclined his head. No bow, because Venom was a senior member of Raphael's court. "Archangel Marduk."

"One of the new creatures," Marduk murmured. "Created after my time. But with droplets of my bloodline in you."

Venom held the gaze of this new member of the Cadre, the nictitating membranes of his eyes sliding across then back at a speed that was difficult to catch with the naked eye. "I was Made by Archangel Neha. She Sleeps now."

"Two archangels at one time." Marduk's smile was of a predator pleased. "My line is strong."

The idea that he might, in some convoluted way, be related to Neha made Raphael's head spin. But if there was a blood connection, it was so far distant as to be lost in the mists of time—except for Marduk's ability to sense it.

"Thank you, Venom," Raphael said after it became clear Marduk had satisfied his curiosity.

"Sire. Archangel Marduk."

"So the Legion spoke true," Raphael said as the vampire left the roof. "There were no vampires in your time."

Marduk shook his head. "I Slept after they were first made. I did see the change, but it had nothing to do with me. I was the last of my kind, a sentinel whose task it was to cede the world to the new generation."

"Are we not the same kind?"

A slight smile. "Yes, Raphael. We are . . . and we are not. One become of the other. As I am become of the ones you call the Ancestors."

Exhaling, Raphael decided to take advantage of Marduk's willingness to talk. "How far back does angelic history go?"

"Into the dawn of time itself," was the answer that told him nothing—and everything.

They stood there in silence, just watching the city. When Venom came up with the food and drinks, he had Janvier with him. The Cajun vampire held a folding table that he set up at speed, before Venom set down the food.

The two left with a stealth that was second nature.

Raphael was sure both would have much to say about Marduk when they were alone, but for now, each kept their silence.

Walking over to the table, Raphael poured two drinks. "Honey mead," he said, handing Marduk a glass of the drink preferred by many older angels.

Marduk held up the amber liquid to the lights of the city, watching it with the patience of one who had all the time in the world. When he finally threw back the drink, it was with a sigh of satisfaction. "It has not changed since my time." Going over to the table, he poured himself another, held up the bottle toward Raphael.

Raphael accepted the refill, then watched Marduk pick up a slice of deli meat.

He ate it with a snap of teeth that made Raphael wonder what Marduk ate, and whether he had more in common with Naasir than with other angels. *Venom, bring up a tray of meats. Like you would for Naasir, but sear it a little.* He didn't want to insult Marduk by giving him raw meat if that wasn't his preference.

Sire.

Marduk was chewing on another piece of sliced cold meat when he returned to stand with Raphael. "I am hungry," he said after swallowing. "I had forgotten what that felt like."

"Venom is bringing up more food," he said. "You haven't eaten since you woke?"

"It's taken this long for my body to catch up to this time." Marduk finished off his mead. "We are not meant to wake from such a long Sleep, Raphael. It is meant to be for eternity."

"Do you not miss living in the world with your consort?" Raphael's question had nothing to do with governance and the Cadre, and everything to do with his love for Elena.

Marduk's smile was a thing alien . . . and yet, Raphael saw that expression in the mirror when he thought of his guild hunter. "We lived an existence glorious. When we chose to Sleep, we did it side by side, her hand in mine."

"Does that work? To keep you together?"

"Not for all—but *aeclari*? Yes." A meeting of eyes. "You will not lose her to the shift of Sleep when it is your time."

Raphael's chest expanded. "Will your consort know you've gone?"

"Yes. In a dreamlike way. But if I do not return to her within the millennia, she *will* wake—and I'm afraid she always wakes in a bad temper, my warrior consort. She is not one for wakings, whether to the dawn or from Sleep. Better I'm back with her sooner rather than later."

Raphael understood now how Elena felt when angels talked about a hundred or so years as nothing. Because Marduk was talking in terms of millennia. "My consort would be most interested to hear about yours. Elena is also a warrior."

"I will speak further with her."

Raphael left it there. Elena wouldn't thank him for fighting her battles—and she'd held her own with archangels long before she became an angel. She'd no doubt deal with Marduk, too. "Do all of the old ones of your time look like you?"

A faint smile. "You are impertinent." He slapped Raphael on the shoulder. "It pleases me."

Raphael wasn't sure he liked being treated like a child—but at the same time, Marduk probably couldn't help it. He decided to let it go for now. All would depend on how Marduk treated the rest of the Cadre—*and* how he treated Raphael in front of others. "That doesn't answer my question."

"Some questions are not meant to be answered." No smile now, his deep, grating voice inflexible. "We Slept for a reason. Our time is past. This is your time. We should be, at most, faint shadows on an even fainter horizon."

Raphael thought of the legends of the Ancestors, not a single true fact known about them. "You succeeded. But I will ask one more question—was it a conscious decision made across all of you of such an age?"

Marduk took his time to respond. "In a sense," he said at last. "And no, son of my son, I will not tell you more. That history is of another time, another people." He spread his arms wide. "This world didn't exist then, not as it does now. The mortals were . . . I would not have expected from them what they are now."

Putting down his glass, he walked to the very edge of the roof, spread those strange, silent wings. "Will you show me your world, Raphael? I would see more of it."

Raphael put his own glass beside Marduk's. "Let us fly."

Having decided to have a cup of soothing tea before she tried to sleep, Elena was passing by their private balcony when Raphael and Marduk swept down from the roof to angle off deeper into the city.

Her thin robe of silvery silk was no proof at all against the night air, but she stepped outside anyway, unable to tear her eyes away from her archangel silhouetted against the electric starlight of their city.

"Magnificent," she murmured, her breath lost as it always was when she saw Raphael in flight.

She almost didn't notice Marduk, and *that* she could've never predicted. But in the night, Marduk's wings made him all but invisible, his scales only shimmering when hit by light.

Though, she thought with a frown, scales wasn't the right word.

When he'd touched her, his skin hadn't been hard or jagged at all. Rather, it had felt like touching the skin of a beautiful snake—smooth, warm, enticing. She could understand why those who'd seen him were fascinated by him.

To her, however, he was a weight of age in her mind, so

old that she couldn't see him as a man, only as a being out of a whole different world.

Cassandra, she said, speaking to the place inside her mind where she'd once heard the Ancient. *What have you done?*

Helped you, child of mortals.

Every hair on Elena's body stood right up. She hadn't heard Cassandra's voice for a long time. Not since she went into her Sleep after the war. *Are you waking?*

No, child. I am . . . in a twilight between Sleep and wakefulness. I am with my Qin.

Pain in Elena's heart now. *Are you all right? Is he?*

Yes. We are together again. Age pressing into Elena's mind, even more potent than Marduk's—because his came from the outside, while Cassandra's voice was deep inside Elena's mind. She'd never heard Marduk's mental voice, and quite frankly, didn't want to; she could barely bear the heaviness of the years in Cassandra's.

An immensity of sorrow in the seer's next words. *I will fade from the twilight soon, child of mortals.*

Wait, Elena said. *Marduk? Can we trust him?*

Marduk is a great warrior, a berserker fighter—and the reason for the great peace that saved our kind from annihilation.

Then Cassandra was gone, her voice whispering from Elena's mind with one last sigh, an Ancient settling into her Sleep once more.

Staring at the night sky into which Raphael and Marduk had vanished, Elena wondered which one of Marduk's avatars this world would see. The warrior, the berserker, or the peacemaker?

45

When Elena went to visit her father in the predawn hours—after a solid six hours of sleep—it was to find him wide awake, the room lights muted but not off. "You're late," he said, sounding more like the father she'd known for so long—except for the edge of worry in his eyes.

"Things have been happening." She put down the bottle of cold water she'd grabbed from the vending machine. She knew he hated the tepid water provided by the hospital. "Have you heard?"

"Gwendolyn refuses to give me back my phone," was the gruff answer. "Says I'll start working all hours again. And the television in this room is broken—I have half a suspicion she did something to make sure I couldn't watch the stock market reports."

Elena would've expected acrimony at Gwendolyn's actions, but her father's voice was calm, even a touch amused. "She knows you."

"Yes, she does." An affection in his tone that she'd never

before heard—but, then, they never spoke about his relationship with Gwendolyn. "So, what is it that's happening?"

Elena told him. And had the satisfaction of watching his
eyes flare behind the clear lenses of his gold-rimmed spectacles. "How can he be an archangel with wings and a face
like that?"

"You wouldn't ask if you stood next to him. The power
that pulses off him is like Raphael's, like Caliane's." Death
barely contained.

"Is he . . ." Jeffrey tapped his head.

Trust her father to ask that question. "Yes, he's fully sentient. He just doesn't look like the angels we're used to
seeing."

She considered whether to share the next bit . . . but
whatever else he'd been to her, Jeffrey had never once betrayed any of her secrets. "The mark on Raphael's temple,
it's linked to Marduk. According to Marduk, they're of the
same bloodline."

Jeffrey took time to think that over. "Ellie, do you ever
find your head struggling with the concept of time as seen
by immortals?"

Elena grabbed the bottle of water and unscrewed the
cap. "Here, have a drink before it gets too warm." She
needed a minute to think.

Jeffrey didn't argue, an infrequent event at the best of
times.

After he'd had enough, she recapped the bottle and put
it aside. "Yes," she said to his question. "But what I struggle
with most is knowing that all the mortal people I love will
be gone while I live on."

The harsh lines of Jeffrey's face softened in a way subtle
but as obvious as a neon light to Elena. "Poor Ellie. We'll
all leave you." There was no sarcasm in the words, only a
genuine sadness. "I'm sorry for that, *azeeztee*."

Azeeztee.

Jeffrey had rarely used that term of endearment even

when their family had been intact. It had been Marguerite who'd used the affectionate term she remembered from her own devastated childhood. But he'd done it often enough that his statement took her back to a past that could never again exist.

She couldn't speak.

Jeffrey closed his hand over hers. "I'm happy you're immortal."

She jerked up her head. "What?"

"One of my babies will live forever," he whispered. "It doesn't make up for losing Mirabelle and Ariel, but it gives me a little peace." He squeezed her hand. "Beth and Amy both have children, pieces of them to be carried into forever in another kind of immortality.

"My wild Eve is like you—I never know which way she'll turn, but she's vivid and stubborn and has so much life yet to live. But you, my Ellie, you'll live into eternity. The comfort I feel . . . you have no idea."

Unable to articulate her thoughts—not even knowing what her thoughts were—Elena just nodded, then nudged the conversation in another direction. "Have you decided what you'll do about succession?" The two of them had already spoken more than once on this subject.

"Amy's Maynard is the best option to succeed me as CEO. He's proven his mettle even further during my illness." Jeffrey sounded cool and clear. "He'll receive compensation at a level commensurate to his position, with performance bonuses built in; but I'll be leaving the company in equal parts to my children. Gwen is in full agreement."

"Dad—"

"No, Ellie." He held her gaze, his own flinty. "I know you don't need it, but you're still my child. I'm not going to cut you out of your inheritance. I might not have given you a lot in life, but I can give you this."

"I really don't need it," Elena insisted. "I have more

money than I know what to do with." Forgetting anything else, the hunt that had brought her into contact with Raphael in the first place had made her rich beyond any mortal's wildest dreams.

"I won't budge, so stop arguing." Jeffrey kept hold of her hand. "I need to give you this."

Seeing on the monitor that his pulse was starting to accelerate, she decided to just nod. When the time came, she could honor his wishes by holding on to the shares he bequeathed her, but using the dividends to set up a trust for the children of the family. Perhaps for education.

The truth was that *this*, having an actual conversation with her father, was far more important to her than any financial inheritance. "I've been thinking about your question about Belle and Ari." Even as she brought up the topic, she was half expecting him to reject the subject, pretend they'd never talked about this.

But, expression solemn, he said, "I should've never put that burden on you. It's my duty as their father to make that decision."

The relief that rushed through her veins was a shock. She'd thought she'd dealt with this, but now that he'd said it, she realized it had been crushing her, the idea of making the wrong call.

"I just need to know one thing," he said. "Will it give you comfort to have their graves there as time passes?"

"I don't go often," she admitted. "I hate thinking of them in the cold earth. It doesn't fit Belle's spirit or Ari's sparkle. I see them more in my memories than I do in the place they're buried."

"Then, Ellie, I think we let them fly with Marguerite." His voice turned gritty. "She'd like that, your *maman*. So would Belle; no matter how rebellious she got, she still asked for Marguerite when she was sick at night, or when that one boy broke her heart. She'd want to be with her."

Elena's throat got thick; she hadn't known about Belle having a relationship with a boy, or that Jeffrey had known and permitted it to go on. She'd always believed he'd have been too strict.

"And Ari, my quiet, smart, Ariel, she was more my baby than Marguerite's, did you know that?" A small smile. "She'd come hide in my office when Mirabelle and Marguerite were being 'extra French'—that's what she'd say when your sister and mother fought in that impassioned way they both had.

"I kept her favorite soda in my little office fridge, and she'd grab one and sit and do her homework or chat to me, and we'd just look at each other when we heard Belle stomp up the stairs."

Another deeper smile. "After a while, I'd go up to talk to Belle, calm her down. Ari would do the same with your mama. Those two were equally hot-tempered, but their temper passed as fast, and one would soon apologize to the other. They never could stay angry with each other.

"My Ari was such an integral part of their life, *our* life. We can't have her, but Belle and Marguerite can. I think Ari would want that. She was always the caretaker, wasn't she?"

Elena nodded jaggedly, not fighting the tears that wanted to fall. "Yes. I think it's the right decision." Jeffrey might've made the tough call, but she could see from the way his shoulders eased at her words that they mattered to him.

"I'll start the planning when Gwen returns my phone. It'll take time to get the necessary permissions."

"Don't push yourself." Elena used her hands to wipe off her face. "We want to do this right—and I need you standing strong beside me for that."

"When I'm released from the hospital, then."

"I'll take that." Able to see that he was tiring, she spoke quietly, telling him what else had been going on in the city. She also snuck him a couple of pieces of interesting stock market news—as per Marcia, the genius behind their shared blood café empire.

Her father's smile was slight but real as he slipped slowly into rest.

Elena wasn't expecting the stir at the door, the whisper of wings. She glanced up already knowing who stood there. Never would she mistake the sound of his wings for anyone else's. "What are you doing here?"

"He is your father, but you are my consort." Raphael put his hand on her shoulder, his fingers curving to cup her neck. "How is he?"

"Better." Leaning her head against his thigh as he stood beside her, she felt the tension leave her body. "Why isn't the entire ward in an uproar?"

"I spoke with the head nurse before my arrival, asked her to arrange it so the corridors were as clear as possible— she let me in via an emergency exit."

He stroked her hair.

"What's Marduk doing?"

"A great impression of a gargoyle above Times Square. He thinks it's the greatest show on earth."

Elena's lips twitched. "He definitely created the Legion."

"No doubt."

The two of them stayed by her father's bedside, talking now and then but otherwise just being until the nurse who'd let Raphael in popped her head inside to whisper that things were going to get busier in the next hour.

The older woman's tone was as competent and as businesslike as the tight black curls she kept cropped close to her skull. Not even a hint of being awestruck by the presence of the Archangel of New York.

Elena wasn't surprised. After spending so much time in the hospital, she'd learned that nurses—especially ones as experienced as this one—were just built differently.

"Thank you, Dionne," she said to the forty-something

woman. "My stepmother should be coming in a couple of hours to have breakfast with Dad."

"We'll look after him until then," Dionne promised with a smile, her accent rich with the rhythms of her birthplace of Ghana. "I've already told him I'm going to tattle to Gwen if he tries to wrangle, bribe, or buy a phone off anyone."

Chuckling, Elena rose from her seat and preceded Raphael through the door. In the corridor, several staff members halted in their tracks. They'd become used to Elena's presence—and she *had* once been mortal, after all—but seeing the *Archangel of freaking New York*? Yeah, no.

Panic, awe, angelstruck devotion, their faces froze.

Dionne, however, was a star. She ordered nurses, doctors, and orderlies alike to "stop catching flies and get back to your actual jobs" in a tone that made it clear she wasn't kidding around. It was a measure of the respect in which she was held that everyone but the angelstruck orderly scuttled away.

"He'll come out of it after we leave," Elena told the scowling nurse. "It's like a trance."

"Huh. Got trained on it at nursing school—never seen it in person before, though."

Leaving the orderly staring after them in utmost devotion, Dionne walked Elena and Raphael to the same emergency exit through which Raphael had entered. "Goes right outside," she told Elena. "One of those old-school metal ladders there, but I suppose you can just fly off the balcony. It's not exactly roomy, though."

"We will have no trouble," Raphael assured her.

After she deactivated the alarm and opened the door, Raphael tugged a feather off his wing, handed it to her. "Shall you ever need a favor from the Archangel of New York, it is yours."

Dionne stared at the feather, then lifted her head, and though she was clearly having difficulty with the cold burn of Raphael's power, she held her ground. "I'm just doing my job, Archangel." She didn't take the feather. "I don't need payment."

"It is not payment," Raphael said with a gentleness he usually reserved for children. "It is a gesture of thanks."

When the nurse hesitated, Elena touched her fingers to the other woman's arm. "Keep the feather as a memory for your grandchildren. That's some story you have to tell, about how you snuck an archangel onto a hospital ward." Because no one would mistake this feather as belonging to anyone but Raphael.

Dionne's face lit up, and she finally accepted the feather that glittered white-gold even in the hospital lighting. "I'll do just that. Thank you, Archangel. And if you ever need another secret entry, just call me."

It was a warm end to the visit, and they were soon in the air. Decisions had to be made. But first, she had a question: *Is Marduk still above Times Square, you think?*

Oh yes. Raphael turned his wings in that direction. *He sends me a comment now and then. His latest was about the naked painted man who believes himself an insect born into a human body.*

Wow, he's getting the full Times Square experience.

Raphael's voice crashed into her mind. *It's very odd to have him in the city, an archangel who I can say with everything in me has no desire for territorial incursion. Neither does he play any other political games.*

Makes sense if he doesn't want to be awake. Elena swept down below Raphael.

He seems to believe his consort will be fine without him by her side for a period.

I suppose after eons in Sleep, a break of a few hundred years is an annoyance that can be shrugged off.

That was when she spotted Marduk.

46

The strange archangel really *was* doing a good impression of being a gargoyle. He'd positioned himself on the corner of a building in such a way that he was swathed in shadows, invisible to anyone who didn't know what to look for. Elena had only spotted him because she always looked for the Legion, even knowing they wouldn't be there.

Though they were too far apart for their eyes to meet, she felt him watching her as she and Raphael flew on. The hairs on her nape rose, her instincts not knowing how to handle this angel who wasn't an angel but a creature far more primal. *I just saw him. To your left, top floor of that new high-rise with the square cube thing at the top.*

I see him. You know, Guild Hunter, he murmured, *in the grand scheme of all the things another archangel could be doing in my territory, emulating a gargoyle is minor.*

Unease or not, Elena almost laughed. *Are you feeling any edginess yet?* Two archangels couldn't be in the same space for a long period without becoming aggressive toward each other. It hadn't seemed to happen as fast during the war, however—perhaps with their energies being burned in the fight, there hadn't been enough left for the aggression effect.

This time around, however, not only would Marduk be in the city, so would the rest of the Cadre—all of them at full strength.

No, Raphael said. *But it's been a short time and we share a bloodline. It may be that I can tolerate him longer than usual—as I can my mother.*

The Cadre meeting tonight?

If it goes for longer than two or three days, it'll get uncomfortable with so many of us in such close proximity and no other outlet for our power—but discomfort isn't madness.

According to my mother, we would need to sustain the contact for about two weeks to risk becoming slaves to our basest instincts. Regardless, I've asked Dmitri to set up firing zones where the others can go blow things up.

Elena turned her face into the cold wind, letting it wipe away her worry. *Good to know. Are we hosting them all in the Tower?*

No, that would be a recipe for disaster. Each has been assigned a home of their own, complete with staff, as far apart as possible while keeping them within equal distance of the meeting location.

Once again, I'm grateful I don't have Dmitri's job.

Venom took charge of this, he said, to her surprise. Not because the vampire wasn't competent, but because he was young and this was Dmitri's domain.

As if sensing her confusion, Raphael said, *He has proven to have a facility with such matters in the past few years. Dmitri thinks he'll eventually get to a point where he can take over fully from Dmitri when needed.*

That's a big deal. Right now, at least two of the Seven had to step in to cover for Raphael's experienced second.

Raphael dipped his wings. *Look,* hbeebti.

She glanced in the direction he'd angled his wings . . . and groaned. An aurora danced over the sea in the distance. The colors were faint to the naked eye, but she understood the display for what it was all the same.

Coming to a halt in the air, as Raphael did the same, she said, "Qin."

"He's not all the way under." Raphael's tone was hard. "What the hell is he doing?"

Elena thought of her conversation with Cassandra. "I don't think it's on purpose. Cassandra said they're in twilight—between Sleep and wakefulness. The only time they can be together."

Raphael's Legion mark blazed. "When were you talking to Cassandra?"

"Last night." Elena folded her arms. "And don't glare at me. I was going to mention it. Why does she always put you in a bad mood?"

"Because she should be Sleeping," Raphael ground out. "What else did she say?"

"She basically confirmed that she did wake Marduk." Elena's head wanted to turn in the direction of the building where the maybe-Ancestor was hanging out. "She says he once ended a great war. I think she sees this as a favor."

Raphael narrowed his eyes, his attention still on the sea aurora. "We'll find out soon enough whether it is or not."

By the time the coming sunset began to streak the sky with orange and red and unexpected pink, everything was ready, the huge central core of their home set up to welcome the Cadre.

While their home only had two levels, those levels were both high, and at the top sat a skylight designed by Aodhan; it sent bright shards of light into the space even on a cloudy day, as if the artist had woven starlight into the glass.

The mezzanine upstairs flowed from their bedroom

suite and the guest rooms. The kitchen, library, and staff lounge were on the ground floor, but on the outside of the core. Maeve, their architect, had designed it that way so that the core could be "locked" for private meetings once any guests had left their rooms.

She could've designed it so the bedrooms exited onto the external ring, but this was Raphael and Elena's home. A meeting such as the one to take place today was rare in the extreme—there was no point in segregating this beauty in the heart of the house. Most days, it was the area through which everyone passed as they moved from one room or level to the next.

Elena had populated the area with an arsenal of greenery, some from the freestanding greenhouse beside the house, a precious few from seedlings of mother plants in the Legion building, still others from her favorite nurseries.

The greenery included a palm that grew halfway to the ceiling, and a big-leafed tree that looked as if it had come out of a rainforest. Ferns lush and curling softened the space, along with many other plants Raphael couldn't name. All the shades of green were striking against the white tiles riven with gold that lined the floor.

That floor wasn't cold, however, for on the central section lay a huge rug that had been a gift from Alexander after their home was rebuilt. A gift unexpected, but well-chosen. Cream and gold, with touches of a vivid blue, the Persian carpet was the perfect accent to the space. Montgomery changed the seating depending on who they were expecting, but that seating configuration was usually either on or around the carpet.

His Seven preferred to sprawl in comfortable sofas and the like.

For the Cadre, it was luxurious single armchairs with firm but comfortable cushions in cerulean blue and curving wooden arms. The set had been hand carved by talented artisans in Amanat and given to him and Elena by his mother as a housewarming gift.

In daylight, the pale honey-colored wood of the arms glowed in the light that fell from Aodhan's glass sky. At night, the light came from a chandelier delicate and lovely, designed by Lady Sharine. Another gift, Illium's mother turning up in person to supervise the installation of the droplets of crystal that looked like falling rain.

Montgomery had placed the odd object d'art in the small nooks in the walls, and Raphael had discreetly ensured that all those pieces of art belonged either to him or to Montgomery. His butler no longer "rescued" as many items as he used to from homes where those items were not being properly appreciated, and, well, it was a small enough peccadillo to accept from such a loyal member of his staff.

"I love this space," Elena said right before the meeting, as she stood beside him, her eyes lifted to the skylight designed with jagged pieces of glass that melded in haunting and lovely harmony with Lady Sharine's rain of crystals. "It's welcoming, even with the formal chairs."

As she spoke, he watched her, this extraordinary woman who was his consort—a fact for which he was ever grateful to fate. She wore a light layer of cosmetics today, in honor of this first major gathering of the Cadre in their home, and her hair was a ripple of near-white down her back.

Thanks to Montgomery, she'd become known for gowns in shades of blue, but today, the butler and the tailor with whom he worked had gone for a gown so deep a blue it was near black. Softer than many of the styles she'd previously worn, it had long sleeves and a V-neck created by overlapping panels of fabric.

Fitted to the waistline, it then flowed to the ground in a grace of air. It bore two slits, one on either side—but those would only become visible should she kick out her legs to access the weapons strapped on them.

Her amber studs glowed in her ears, and on her wrist sat a bracelet of white gold carved with elements taken from the Guild's historic coat of arms. A gift from Beth for a milestone birthday in mortal terms. A gift he knew his hunter would treasure for all eternity—though he'd also seen her touch it with sorrow in every line of her face.

His Elena. A born hunter. An angel Made. A sister tender. And a woman who never gave up, no matter what the obstacle. Her loyalty was unbreakable, her love a fierce caress that he carried with him every second of every day.

"Raphael, are you listening to me?"

"*Knhebek, hbeebti*," he said, reaching up to cup her cheek. "More than eternity itself."

Her eyes shone with a light that shouldn't have been possible in an angel so young. "You stop my heart, Archangel." Elena didn't know what had gotten into Raphael, but the way he was looking at her . . . It stole her breath, destroying her in the best way.

It was tempting to kiss him, fall into him, but they couldn't afford to be distracted with several of their guests already crossing the Hudson. Most had arrived in the city earlier in the day, a couple late the previous night because of the distance involved in their travel, but all were itching to meet Marduk. Enough to leave their seconds in charge of territories all hit by various natural disasters—but none would stay on after the meeting for the same reason.

Because while this might appear a social occasion with everyone in formal dress, it was rather a council of war in peacetime. The Cadre *had* to meet—because all their usual avenues of information and answers had failed, with a distraught Jessamy having informed the Cadre that she had nowhere else to search.

Even Vivek had admitted that he was going around in circles at this point.

Marduk was their last chance.

She saw the same knowledge in Raphael's eyes, and between them passed a silent vow that no matter what, they'd walk into it together.

For now, she turned her head to kiss his palm, then ran her own hand over the black of his formal leathers. Sleeveless, and sealed down one side, the stark color of the jacket was unrelieved but for the golden design on one shoulder: his sigil, which now included a dagger. Included her.

He wore no sword today, in deference to the fact that he was a host welcoming others into his home. His hair remained a touch longer than he usually kept it. Despite the softer look of it, he appeared as ruthless and as dangerous as ever, his eyes a searing hue that burned. Only she knew of the heart within the lethal power of her archangel.

"Where is our guest of honor?" she said past the primal urge to drag him away to a private place, anchor herself against the unknown with the physical.

Raphael seemed to be having the same problem.

Raphael, we can't.

47

A touch of his fingers to her lips—a silent promise—before Raphael took a deep breath and became the Archangel of New York rather than her lover. "Last I knew, Marduk was watching people in Central Park from one of his high vantage points. As we haven't yet seen a single photo in the media articles about him, I assume he's using glamour to conceal his presence."

"Do you think he has any concept of time? I mean, will he show up before the meeting starts?" Elena glanced at the central doors that led into this room, then at the set on the other end. Those doors were inside the house, and most of the time, they were left open.

Today, however, both sets would be closed while the Cadre was in session.

"I'm not certain—I've built in time enough for me to fly out and get him." A raised eyebrow. "But I have a feeling he's planning to make an entrance."

"Why doesn't he freak you out? He's not . . . like other

angels." She frowned. "I like him, but there's something there that's . . . not anything close to human. I used to think that about archangels once, but Marduk blows that out of the water."

Raphael shrugged. "I see him as a wilder variant of our bloodline." He shifted so that he faced the main entrance, held out his arm for her. "Our guests begin to arrive."

Elena caught the scent of green forests overlaid with spice as they walked toward the orange radiance of late afternoon soon to turn into evening. Her angel-scenting ability remained unstable and weak, might never get any stronger, but this scent she knew. "Elijah and Hannah." So far, she hadn't picked up Hannah's scent on its own, but she *had* picked up that Hannah carried a hint of Elijah's scent, a kiss atop the skin.

"Eli." Raphael greeted the other archangel with true warmth, their friendship having become set in stone over the years since Elijah had first reached out a friendly hand. The blond angel with his golden skin and wings of pristine white was older than Raphael, had once been a war general under Caliane.

His consort of over nine hundred years, Hannah—her ebony curls beautifully arranged in an updo dotted with diamond pins and her dark skin glowing, her wings a lush cream with a whisper of peach in the primaries—was one of the most elegant women Elena had ever met. Quite frankly, she'd been intimidated by the angel until she got to know Hannah—and found in her a friend warmhearted and funny.

The artist the world knew as refined and talented also had quite the facility for hilarious caricatures and rude cartoons. The latter of which only her closest friends ever saw.

"I have to keep up *some* appearance of being a proper consort," she'd said with a grin after Elena told her that her wicked wit deserved a wider audience. "Also, secret fun is always better."

Elena greeted her with a tight hug that was returned with equal delight. "How are you?" She knew Hannah had been knee-deep in mud prior to her and Elijah's flight to New York, assisting people affected by a flash flood.

"Not good." Hannah's dark eyes were tired. "I almost didn't come—even dressing up today felt frivolous. But my love made me understand that it's not only about us; the populace will see images of us on the way to and from this meeting, and find comfort in our appearance."

"Caliane told me the same thing."

Hope, Elena, Raphael's mother had said. *It is our duty to offer the people that when we can offer nothing else. We have no answers, but the world will fall apart if we appear ragged and on the edge of desperation—even if that is the truth. We must give every appearance of having the situation in hand. For if the archangels themselves have no answers . . .*

Elena had felt her blood chill at the undoubted result, her mind awash in the dark red of blood as vampires panicked themselves into bloodlust—and mortals became helpless prey.

"She's not bad for a mother-in-law," she added.

Hannah laughed, her small movements making the evening sunlight glitter off her figure-hugging black gown. Though she had a stunning body, she rarely wore form-fitting clothing, her style tending more toward floaty gowns when she wasn't in paint-splattered smocks.

Aegaeon arrived as Hannah's laughter rose into the air.

The sound seemed to put him in a less irate mood than usual. She knew he wouldn't have chosen to have the meeting in New York, but while he might be an ass as a man and as a father, it turned out that as an archangel, he took his duties seriously enough to just deal with it.

He had, of course, gone for his usual exhibitionist getup of bare chest and tight leather pants with boots. The silver swirl on his chest was as much a part of his skin as Ra-

phael's Legion mark, and on another archangel might've
fascinated Elena. As it was, she channeled all the lessons
poor, beleaguered Jessamy had given her and made polite
noises of welcome as they led the three arrivals into the
core.

She couldn't have done this in her initial years as Raphael's consort. It wasn't about becoming less human, less
herself—it was about maturity and knowledge. These days,
she understood the need to put on a polite face, and that she
couldn't simply stab people who annoyed her—though, she
wouldn't lie, the latter remained tempting, especially with
powerful angels. It wasn't as if it would hurt them. Which
just made her more annoyed.

Since she knew it was better that Raphael and Aegaeon
have as little contact as possible, she took charge of showing him to the more casual mingling area Montgomery had
set up away from the circle of chairs. He'd cleverly used a
number of her plants to turn that corner into a "room" separate from the business side of things.

Their besuited butler stood ready to pour drinks, and
Sivya had outdone herself with the array of food.

Elena and Raphael didn't usually have waitstaff, their
household staff limited to the strictly necessary. However,
Montgomery had sourced a slender young vampire to be
his right hand tonight. Luz had been the manager of a five-
star restaurant before being Made and had worked in a senior angel's home for the past decade.

"I hope your lodgings are comfortable?" Elena said to
Aegaeon, reciting one of the rote small-talk sentences Jessamy had taught her.

"Good enough," Aegaeon said, and she knew that even
if they'd handed him everything he'd ever wanted, he'd
have given the same answer. But then he smiled at her.
"Thank you, Consort. I'm sure you had much to do with
ensuring the comfort of the home in which I am a guest."

Elena almost choked on the champagne of which she'd

just taken a sip. It took intense effort to hold back her cough. Good thing Montgomery had the best poker face on earth, or he'd be in hysterics. If Aegaeon didn't know who she was after being aware of her since he woke more than a decade ago, there was no hope for this lump of male chauvinist angel.

"Elena, we must greet our new guest." Raphael took her arm, while he and Aegaeon ignored each other, Hannah and Elijah sliding in to fill the social vacuum.

That was real friendship, right there.

She broke out into a huge smile when she saw the angel coming in to land. Waving, she laughed as Titus dipped his wings in a showy hello before his boots hit the earth.

"Where's Lady Sharine?" she said after allowing herself to be lifted off her feet by the huge power of his hug. The gold of his formal breastplate was hard against her, every other part of him warm and welcoming.

Titus put her down. "I see who is the favorite," he rumbled, before exchanging the clasp of warriors with Raphael, ending with slaps of each other's shoulders.

"I have only one favorite, Titus," she whispered with a wink. "Just don't tell Raphael."

Booming laughter, before Titus said, "My lady follows. She was caught up in sketching the beginnings of a new artwork inspired by your city. I was ordered to go on ahead so I wouldn't be late to the meeting of the Cadre. I do as my lady says." He sounded so smug that it was adorable.

Titus was head over heels for Lady Sharine, the Hummingbird, and he didn't care who knew it. And though she didn't take the title of consort, the entire Cadre seemed to believe it was only a matter of time and treated her like a consort in everything but name.

Elena wasn't so sure the Hummingbird would ever be that predictable. Illium's mother was far from who she'd once been—and she might spend millennia sinking into her new skin before she tied her flag to anyone else's, even to that of the man she adored as much as he did her.

You couldn't be around them and not see that.

Titus didn't care about the formalities, just that she was his. He wore her symbol—a hummingbird made of amber—in his breastplate. She wore his amber as a pendant that she never took off.

More wings overhead, coming from the other direction, and all at once the manicured green of the lawn was filled to the brim with archangels. Alexander, in formal leathers of a tan that echoed the deserts of his homeland, beside him Zanaya in one of those tiny dresses only Zanaya could pull off.

This one was a deep purple halterneck that shimmered with silver, the colors an echo of the luxurious tumble of her hair. On her feet were silver boots that laced up her calves. And on her back, between the starry night of her wings, rode a ceremonial sword studded with amethysts that was formal wear rather than a weapon.

It was grumpy Galen who'd taught her the difference. "Some weapons are displayed for their beauty and the artisan's skill. They carry no aggressive intent—you must learn to recognize the difference if you're to be an asset at Raphael's side when the Cadre play stupid political games."

At least she and the weapons-master had the latter opinion in common.

Tonight the weapons were jewelry, not politics. Caliane, too, wore a ceremonial sword in the same position, but had gone for a gown of crisp white with a rippling skirt, a braided gold belt around her waist. She'd pushed her hair off her face using jeweled gold combs, the jewels the same shade of sapphire as the eyes she'd bequeathed her son.

Suyin, in contrast, had chosen formal leathers of deep bronze with detailing in a rich plum shade. The ice-white of her hair was as straight and glossy as glass, but for a single thin braid on one side that she'd woven through with threads of shimmering plum. Her wings were snow-white, her primaries bronze. A bronze bracelet encircled her wrist, the design distinctive. A gift from Aodhan to Suyin to honor the time he'd spent as her second.

Suyin wore it as a silent symbol of her friendship with Raphael.

See, Elena thought, *I'm getting good at this reading-between-the-lines stuff.*

The gathering glittered with so much power and beauty that it hurt.

It got even worse once they were all inside, such violence of energy hanging in the air that she saw Luz shiver before Montgomery murmured to her, and the other woman took a deep breath, got it together.

The tiny hairs on Elena's nape rose up at that instant, even as Raphael's Legion mark blazed. "He's here," she said, without needing to look outside to confirm.

"Yes." Raphael's wing brushed hers. "I say we let him make his entrance."

Marduk walked into the room wearing the new set of leathers Montgomery had helped organize to Marduk's specifications—sleeveless and of a deep green, the clothing threw the beauty of his scales into stark focus.

Conversation stopped.

Elena could all but see Aegaeon struggling to accept that Marduk was an archangel, while Caliane watched him in a way that gave nothing away. Zanaya made no effort to hide her curiosity, was the first one to speak.

"Archangel Marduk," she said. "I am Zanaya, Queen of the Nile."

Another stir near the doorway before Marduk could reply, and Lady Sharine walked into the room dressed in an ethereal gown of indigo gold that echoed her feathers.

Marduk turned, looked at her.

Sharine, the Hummingbird, no longer a woman with a fragile mind lost in time, held his gaze with the sparkling champagne of her own. No aggression. But no give, either.

Marduk, who'd shown no deference to absolutely anyone until now, offered a small bow. "I have met you before I ever met you." That gritted stone voice. "Your essence is ageless and endless."

Sharine smiled, and in her smile was the agelessness Marduk had seen. "I must paint you. You will sit for me."

Despite his apparent liking for her, however, Marduk shook his head. "No, my consort would not be pleased. She will already be most annoyed I am awake without her when we made a pact to Sleep together—if I tell her I sat for a painting, she will rain down all the fires of eternity on my head, then haunt my Sleep with furious nightmares. Perhaps if she wakes, we will sit for you together."

Sharine's smile grew deeper. "I will hold you to that."

Elena, meanwhile, found herself looking at Marduk with a new eye. He'd mentioned his consort before, but this time—perhaps because she'd become more used to the deep, grating tones of his voice—she'd heard the love that underlay the words. *I'm curious enough about the woman who took Marduk as consort that I'm tempted to poke at Cassandra to see if she'll tell me*, she said to Raphael.

A whispering flutter of wings filled her mind. Not angelic wings. The wings of owls with golden eyes . . . like the one that sat in a large indoor palm in the corner, its feathers as white as snow. *Ah, Archangel? Do you see that owl?*

Yes, unfortunately I do. He downed his drink. *Stop waking her.*

It is too late, child of mortals. Laughter in Cassandra's voice, the ancient weight of her presence tempered by an odd youthfulness. *Tell your consort that I linger in twilight still, unwilling to go into my rest without playing witness to what Marduk will do in this world.*

Rubbing at her temple, Elena conveyed the message to Raphael. "Sorry," she whispered. "I really thought she was asleep."

A gleam in her archangel's eye as he leaned down to murmur in her ear. "You, Guild Hunter, must promise to make it up to me."

Even as passion fire licked over Elena's skin, Zanaya went forward to greet Marduk, and the others followed suit. Marduk gave short nods and thumped a fisted hand over his heart to acknowledge the welcome of each. Until Hannah. With her, he lifted her hand almost to his lips, his smile unexpected.

Wow, he can be charming.

Only to Lady Sharine and Hannah, apparently. Did Cassandra tell you of his consort yet?

Ah, child of mortals, his consort is . . . exactly what Marduk needs.

The owl in the corner that clearly only Elena and Raphael could see blinked sleepily.

Cassandra's voice slowed in cadence. *You would like her.* A sighing murmur. *She once threatened to cut off Marduk's head and feed it to a three-headed . . .*

Elena strained toward the voice, but knew Cassandra was gone even before her owl spread its wings and rose toward the skylight, fading as it flew into Cassandra's dreams.

Marduk snapped up his head without warning to glare at the owl.

When he looked back down, it was straight into Elena's eyes. His gaze had gone slitted, a raptor given human form, the chill blue inhuman in its very essence.

When Raphael stirred beside her, she stopped him with a slight mental touch—and didn't break Marduk's gaze. It was a weight on her mind, a pressure relentless . . . before Marduk threw back his head and laughed. "Blood of my line," he said afterward to Raphael. "You chose as I chose."

Then he turned abruptly to talk to Suyin.

48

Half an hour later, Elena went to check in with Montgomery. "This is the strangest cocktail party in the history of cocktail parties."

The butler was too well-mannered and trained to allow his lips to so much as twitch, but he replied *sotto voce*. "I have always said archangels are predators, but Marduk reminds me of a great beast watching over sheep while twitching its tail, deciding which one he'll eat."

Elena was glad she hadn't been drinking anything at the time because she'd surely have spit it out. "Montgomery, you have a way with words." Because he was absolutely right; Marduk was just . . . different.

Like her Legion had been different.

It made her wonder if Marduk would adapt as they'd adapted. Somehow, she didn't think so—because he was the creator, the template from which the Legion had been cast.

Now, she watched as he listened to Alexander with an attentiveness so intense that some might see it as aggression.

However, as every archangel in this room had already learned, Marduk's reactions were not readable in the same way as those of the rest of the Cadre.

Even Aegaeon, the easiest to rouse to anger, had soon settled. "He's not like us," he'd said to Titus in Elena's hearing, while giving Marduk the side-eye. "Is this what we came from?"

"Magnificent, isn't he?" Titus had slapped his fellow archangel on the shoulder. "I should like to have skin that will ward off sword blows as if they are nothing."

That had made Elena take another look at the scales that rippled up one side of Marduk's body. Titus, she realized, was right. She didn't think a sword would get through that multihued toughness of skin.

"My fellow members of the Cadre." Raphael's voice rang over the conversations in the room.

Everyone stopped, looked at him.

"We needed this time to become acquainted with Archangel Marduk," he said, "but that time must, of necessity, be short. The Cadre must now do its duty."

Solemn faces, no disagreement.

The archangels took their drinks and began to head toward the circle of chairs.

Hannah, after a touch of her hand to Elijah's, came to Elena. "Are you staying?"

Elena shook her head. "You?" Each consort had to make their own decision.

"No." Hannah's eyes lingered on Marduk. "He's . . . distracted by us. You and me and Lady Sharine. Not because we are women, I think, but because he misses his own love."

Elena hadn't seen what Hannah had, but they were two very different women, with different skills—Hannah was no doubt right.

"Lady Sharine." She smiled as Illium's mother came to join them. Sharine had already kissed Elena on the cheek with maternal warmth and told her that she looked lovely. No matter how old she got, Elena didn't think she'd ever not get soft in the heart at seeing approval in those eyes so lovely and kind.

"We are leaving, yes?" Sharine murmured. "Marduk hurts when we are near."

"Yes." Hannah's expression held a kind gentleness.

Their insight and empathy made Elena realize how young she was in comparison to both of them. So much still to learn. "Montgomery's set up the library for us," she said, leading them out of the room that Montgomery and Luz had already departed.

All members of staff would now leave the premises until summoned back by Raphael. None lived in the home—most lived nearby, while Sivya and Montgomery had their own cottage in a private little grove on the far end of the property.

"Or, if you'd both like, we can fly to see Aodhan's mural," she suggested. "I already asked and he said you'd be welcome." It wasn't his top secret project but a large-scale painting that he was working on inside a warehouse, far from prying eyes.

"I would enjoy that very much." Sharine's eyes lit up. "I should not talk of favored protégés, but truly, he is my favorite."

Hannah, who'd tucked her arm through Sharine's, laughed as Elena shut the doors to the core behind them. Montgomery had already shut those on the opposite end.

"I have had no protégé yet," Hannah was saying. "I don't feel old enough—but I think if I had one so brilliant as Aodhan, I, too, would favor him."

Good luck, Archangel, Elena said as she joined the other two women. *I hope Marduk has some answers for us.*

A rush of ocean waves in her mind, the salt-laced sea on her tongue, before Raphael retreated.

The Cadre was now in session.

* * *

Marduk sat directly opposite Raphael, Caliane on one side of him, Alexander on the other. Next to Alexander was Zanaya, beside her Suyin. The Queen of the Nile and the Archangel of China were two very different angels in personality and styles of rule, but at this moment, they had their heads bent together, murmuring to one another.

Titus sat beside Suyin, which put him to Raphael's right. To his left was Elijah, beside him Aegaeon. Raphael had made sure not to end up next to Illium's father, and the other archangel had worked to the same goal. Nonetheless, this Cadre held far more friends to Raphael than enemies.

Elijah had never been an enemy, even if it'd taken Raphael time to understand that. He'd once been Caliane's general, had protected that which was most precious to her. It was a loyalty he'd carried into and beyond ascension.

Caliane, of course, would fight to the death to defend Raphael, a fact with which Raphael still occasionally struggled. To trust her after the horrors of her madness . . . those scars would take a long time to fade.

Titus, too, was a friend, a good-natured archangel who liked Elena far better than he did Raphael. It made Raphael smile.

Suyin was an open ally. Raphael had helped her when she'd been at her weakest, and Suyin had been clear that, come what may, she'd never forget his assistance. Furthermore, one of his people was part of the pair who'd rescued her from Lijuan's clutches. Naasir and Andromeda remained among her favorite people in all the world.

Zanaya was neither ally nor enemy. She had come too recently out of Sleep to be either. What he did know was that she was far more interested in building up her own territory than in making war on others.

Alexander fell in the same boat. He'd been warlike once upon a time, but he was . . . older these days, in ways both good and bad. The loss of his son had broken his heart, and it would never again be the same. But his grandson had tempered that agony, made him focus on family rather than conquest.

And, of course, he was now consort to Zanaya, as she was to him. Whatever had occurred between the two archangels seemed to have brought him a peace that Raphael had never before seen in the Ancient.

That left Aegaeon alone as the one person he would call a true enemy. Raphael was quite content to leave that a forever state of affairs—for he would never forget how Illium, so bright and quick and happy as a boy, had cried after his father's abandonment.

A man who caused such pain to a child who *adored* him was no one Raphael wanted in his corner.

Then there was Marduk.

Blood of my line.

No enemy, then, but his motives remained murky.

"We meet due to the most exigent circumstances." Caliane sat with her hands curled loosely over the ends of the chair arms. "The Mantle falls, and with it, our world. This connection, I think we all agree, holds true."

No one decried her taking charge of the meeting. It had somehow become natural that Caliane would open and close their meetings. Whatever madness had once infected his mother, it had long since passed, leaving her with a wisdom riven with sorrow endless.

Their blood will ever coat my hands.

Words she'd spoken to him as they stood on soil that had once held a thriving city, then later, only the graves of the soul-shattered children of those she'd sung into the sea. Today, it was an open field, the graves long since lost to time—but it remained a place sad and haunted, land on which no one wished to live.

"Marduk," she said now in that flawless voice that could be a weapon terrible. "You are older than any other archangel in this room. Do you know the answer to the question of why the Mantle is failing when it has held for all eternity?"

"Raphael has told me of events that have occurred within his lifetime." Marduk's grating voice filled the room. "The madness of two archangels, the loss of one, and the near loss of the other."

Caliane didn't flinch, but Raphael knew that within, his mother mourned. She always would. She had fallen in love only once in her immortal lifetime, would never fall again.

Some loves could not be redone, could not be found again.

Should Elena die, Raphael would do his duty—and then he would walk beyond the veil in the hope of finding her once more.

"He also," Marduk continued, "told me of a relentless series of minor wars during the first few hundred years of his reign, and of a larger war that brought a disease that touches angelkind."

"Charisemnon, that pus-boil on the earth." Titus fisted his hand on his thigh.

Marduk nodded in firm agreement. "I have also learned of the Archangel of Death, one who turned her own people into shuffling half-dead shells."

That wasn't quite the correct description of the reborn, but no one argued.

"I have heard of Antonicus. And of Astaad, Favashi, and Michaela. Four archangels perhaps forever lost," Marduk continued. "It is also not the first time in the recent past that such a huge loss has occurred."

"I did not even know of Narcisse and Bhumi until of late," Suyin murmured. "So short a time they had as archangels and friends before they turned on each other."

A hundred years. That was how long Narcisse, Archangel of the Sun, had ruled. Bhumi even less. Her reign as Archangel of Persia had spanned a mere seventy-five years. Their deaths had been a foolish waste.

"We lost Jariel, too." Titus's face burned hot with rage, as it had the day he'd told them of Jariel's abomination of a murder. "He was to ascend—and he would've been a good, strong, and calm-of-mind archangel. But he was killed in cold blood, his brain and body turned to ash but his head left untouched."

Marduk's face held as much anger as Titus's, though he hadn't known Jariel. "Never have I heard of this kind of atrocity. Only a rare few ascensions can be predicted, but those angels are protected by the Cadre. We understand what it means, comprehend that there is no promise of another ascension should one fail."

"Don't forget Uram," Elijah said, his voice resonant. "The first archangel gone bloodborn in living memory."

"Yes, he is the worst harbinger of all, worse even than your Archangel of Death. I would say he stands equal to the Archangel of Disease."

Intrigued, Raphael leaned forward. "Why? Lijuan did the most damage."

Marduk's piercing eyes held his, the pupils round at present. "Because Uram and Charisemnon fractured the foundations of our society. Megalomaniacal archangels are to be expected in a race of immortals. But only *once* before have we become diseased. And *never* in all existence has an archangel gone bloodborn. Angels, yes, but never an *archangel*."

Several people sucked in air.

Elijah frowned. "No, that cannot be so. Lijuan said she'd heard of others in the distant past."

"I have also heard of such," Caliane murmured, to a round of nods from the other Ancients. "She did not lie on that."

Marduk's smile was grim. "You carry eons of history among you. Which one of you actually *knows* of a case? Not from gossip, or from tales told around a fire, but true knowledge."

I killed the last one, did you know?

Lijuan had boasted of that to Raphael, but the one she'd referenced had been an angel, not an archangel. Much as Raphael dug through his memories and knowledge of their history, he couldn't find a single concrete example of another member of the Cadre who'd gone bloodborn.

"You're saying they're just stories?" Zanaya's scowl did nothing to mar her intense beauty. "How can that be when we've all heard the same?"

"Being bloodborn is a primal terror we carry in the blood." Marduk's voice itself was a thing primal, guttural. "It is angelkind's greatest fear. And so we tell stories of it as all peoples tell stories of that which terrifies them most."

Raphael's skin chilled, his mind awash in memories of bodies eviscerated and displayed like trophies. "Uram was the only one."

Marduk nodded. "Add that to the rest, and you have had too many destabilizing events within a short period."

Only an immortal of Marduk's age would term a span of over a millennium as short.

"It has ramped up to the extreme in the last quarter century," Marduk continued, "but even that concentration of events would not have been enough to tip the scales if not for the previous incidents involving the deaths of multiple archangels within as short a lifetime as Raphael's."

"Are you saying the Mantle is failing because our kind has suffered shock after shock?" Alexander scowled. "Surely it would've fallen before were that the case. This can't be the most unstable period of all."

"It is," Marduk said bluntly. "If we don't take into account the period that resulted in the eventual birth of the mortals. That was worse. But this . . . this is another lethal wave in the timeline of angelic history."

Raphael sat back, his head spinning. He'd thought this chaos of existence *normal*. The last decade had been one of the most stable he'd ever experienced—and even then, they'd had to deal with lingering reborn and vampiric uprisings. "Are you saying archangels can go entire millennia in peace, without madness, without wars?"

All the Ancients stared at him.

And he knew the answer before Titus said "Shite!" and rubbed his hands over his face. "That the youngest of us can't even comprehend the idea of a time of extended peace is confirmation of Marduk's words."

If they excluded Suyin, who had only ruled since after the war, Titus was the second youngest in the present Cadre in terms of the length of his rule. Yet it was clear from his words that he *had* experienced a time of peace and calm.

"Is there a solution?" Suyin's quiet voice tempered by the steel in her spine.

Raphael knew he wasn't the only one holding his breath.

49

"Yes."

Marduk's response sent a cacophony of questions into the air. But the archangel out of time waited until they'd died down to speak. "This knowledge should be part of your history." His eyes were no longer angelic but of the other part of his nature. "It should *never* have been lost, not when the old ones put processes in place to ensure it would pass from one archangel to the next."

Caliane's brow furrowed. "It has been an eternity since your time, even longer since theirs. The Ancestors are legends to us, ghosts of a past long forgotten."

But Marduk sliced out a hand. "This was set in place *for* eternity. But that is a problem to fix after we fix the Mantle." He leaned forward, both elbows on his thighs. "You must reset the #?**!!"

Raphael winced, while the others hissed out pained breaths or gritted their teeth. Because the word Marduk had spoken had no meaning to them beyond being a string of guttural sounds that hurt the ear.

Marduk looked from one to the other, a scowl on his face. "In the new language, it would translate to . . . the Compass."

"A compass?" Aegaeon threw up his arms. "What use is a compass?"

"It's not an actual compass," Marduk growled with the first hint of temper. "It is merely the closest word in the current tongue. You, it seems, cannot speak its true name."

"What is it?" Alexander asked, and it was the practical question of the general he'd been before his ascension. "An object?"

"The Compass was created by the combined power of the old ones," Marduk answered. "Such power as you cannot imagine. The subcomponents will never wear, no matter how many eons are to pass, and the base, too, is endless and self-regenerating."

The hairs on Raphael's arms rose up at the idea of an object of such age, a thousand questions in his mind.

"The subcomponents are tied to archangelic blood. No one but a member of the Cadre can hold on to one. Another being might pick it up, but they will be overcome within moments with the urge to put it down and walk away."

"How?" Titus demanded, the gold of his breastplate shining under the chandelier his love had created. "You are talking of power that bends time to its own will."

"There is a reason the old ones Sleep forever." Marduk's tone was ominous. "Their world is gone, their time is gone, their power too damaging for this world."

"You're saying even if these subcomponents, these pieces of the Compass, have been misplaced"—Elijah frowned—"they will be misplaced within an archangel's territory?"

"Closer. An archangel's home or other trusted place they frequent." Marduk leaned back in his chair, slapping his hands to his spread thighs. "The tie is absolute. Each piece will always attach itself to one archangel. No archangel can hold two."

"What about in times like now?" Zanaya demanded. "When we no longer have a full Cadre?"

"It doesn't matter. A subcomponent is only 'alive' when it has an archangel with whom to resonate. So for you . . . you must find eight. The dormant pieces aren't part of the equation."

"Don't you mean nine?" Aegaeon snarled. "You're forgetting yourself."

"I don't count." Marduk's voice held no room for argument. "I came into this time when the unraveling had already begun. It must be the eight that existed with the first quake."

"Qin," Alexander said, the single word hard. "We have no idea when exactly he went into Sleep."

"It was before the quake," Raphael said. "Atu last saw him over a week prior, so I think it's safe to assume that."

"Eight pieces," Suyin murmured. "I will have to search Lijuan's most private palace for mine. It is apt to be there."

"It will be near you," Marduk insisted, his scales appearing to alter color in the cascade of light that rained off the chandelier. "The subcomponents are designed to find their way to their archangel. The base, however, can only be found by triangulating all eight other pieces."

"But why?" Zanaya twisted so that she faced Marduk, her temper afire in the glow that pulsed off her wings. "Why this . . . game!"

Marduk watched her with an unblinking gaze. "It is no game. It is a reset, exactly as I stated."

"For the Mantle?"

"For the world." Marduk's smile was cold. "From what I know of this most recent Cascade, it well demonstrated that the power we carry in our bones and blood can flow and ebb, rise and fall.

"Cascades are created of *us* because we are the biggest reservoirs of power in this world. It is *our* energy that fuels the very planet on which we stand. We have within us the ability to annihilate it out of existence, shatter it into dust."

Raphael suddenly saw it, where Marduk was going. That forgotten field. Excruciating pain. The birds. The grass growing around him. Later, having to put himself back together.

Heart and mind and limbs and skin and blood and every tiny cell.

"It's a safety," he said in a beat of silence amid the furious discussion that had broken out. "To prove the Cadre can work together. A key to retune the power that burns through the world, before it destroys that very world. The failure of the Mantle is the initial indicator of the need for the reset."

Marduk's smile was feral. "Blood of my line," he said in open pride. "You see it. When the old ones decided to Sleep, it was after a time of terrible war and loss. Their wisdom came at a grave cost, but with it, they set up the Cadre system. A thing of trial and error, until it became clear that the optimal number was ten. It was also understood that it was critical the Cadre function as a *unit*."

Titus scowled. "You're saying the world is falling apart because the currents of power that run through it—*our* power—have become too unstable."

Marduk brought his fist down on his thigh. "Yes, Titus! This is so!"

"Too many changes." Caliane's face was solemn but tired with it. "Too many ripples in the river of power. Had the Ancestors not set this safety in place that forces a Cadre to work together—"

"—the world would burn as we turned against each other," Suyin completed.

"What is the alternative?" Alexander insisted. "If a Cadre fails to initiate the safety and the Mantle falls?"

"The Cadre dies, the world becomes chaos infinite for a turn around the sun, and then civilization restarts with those few who survive." Flat words that brought with them an eerie silence as every archangel but Marduk stopped so much as breathing.

"In not working together, you prove yourselves unfit to continue," he said into that absolute quiet. "You end the instant the Mantle falls. So do your consorts, seconds, courts, and anyone of your bloodline, regardless of age.

"Any vampires you've created, or who have been created by those of your court, die with you. That combined power returns to the system, and, one year to the day, the system resets itself."

"Our Ancestors didn't play games." Raphael held the gaze of the man who was part of his own lineage, his thoughts a mix of rage and admiration. That anyone would threaten Elena, threaten *children*—it was grounds for annihilation; but he also saw the wisdom in what the Ancestors had done.

Their brutal regime ended in the chance of a restart, as opposed to an archangelic war that might destroy the planet itself, ending their species and every other species on the planet.

Marduk shrugged. "Archangels are arrogant. This gives you sufficient motivation—whether you care for your own skin, or the skins of those you love."

Aegaeon folded his arms across his chest. "We need a description of these objects for which we are to search like jesters stumbling about in the dark. Or is that a secret, too?"

Marduk's eyes went slitted like those of the great winged serpent whispered of by his skin. "None of this is a secret. It is knowledge meant to be passed from archangel to archangel in an unbroken chain. This isn't a *test*. The Compass exists because it needs to exist.

"The olds ones saw that in their own time—with power this violent, there will be periods of fatal echoes, dangerous ripples. Our kind *must* have a way to calm that storm or, at best, our entire civilization will fall . . . as it did once before. At worst, our very world will fall."

It was in the war that unmade our civilization that the Legion came to be . . . by the time we gained victory, angelkind was nearly destroyed, and our home hollow and dead.

The Legion's words. A story of a world so battered, it could no longer sustain life. Caused by war. Caused by *archangels*.

"As for the appearance of the subcomponents." Marduk's voice slammed into his consciousness, pulling him out of the memory. "They take the shape of a blade. This makes it easy to slot each piece into the base to complete the Compass."

"What about the base?" Caliane's features were strained, the blue of her eyes stark against her skin. "What does it look like? Perhaps we have seen it?"

"The base is irrelevant until you have the other parts." Marduk waved away the question. "It *cannot* be seen or known until that point in time. It has no set appearance."

"I know where my piece is," Titus said without warning. "Embedded in my crest—or at least the physical representation of it in my main court." He frowned. "I found it the day after my ascension. It was in a dusty old trunk in the court I was to take over—I was fascinated by it, having never seen metal of its like. I still haven't."

"That is how it works." Marduk's inhuman tone. "It finds its way to the person it's meant for."

"I have a vague memory of Sha-yi talking to me of a dagger that was a relic of utmost importance . . ." Caliane pressed two fingers against her temple. "I—"

A sudden pause.

"Yes, I've seen it. Not in Amanat. It was once, but no longer. I think . . . it lies in Archangel Fort. Part of Neha's golden throne that I had placed in storage . . . and I especially noticed the blade. I meant to go back to it, examine the strange metal from which it is made."

"I have never seen anything of its like to my memory," Suyin said.

"I can't say I have, either," Elijah murmured. "But I have been in my territory for hundreds of years. If what you say is true, Marduk, it'll be close by."

"I will search both my chosen home and my predecessor's favored palace." A scowling Aegaeon kicked out his booted feet, crossing them at the ankles.

"I believe I've seen such a blade." Zanaya looked into the distance. "What I can't recall is if I saw it in my first reign or my current one."

Alexander, who'd been quiet until then, reached down into his boot to pull out a blade, held it out.

The metal was unlike any Raphael had ever before seen. It wasn't multihued or in any way flashy, but it seemed strangely *fluid*. As if it was alive while lying quiescent in Alexander's hand. And . . . "Can you hear the hum?" he asked, raising his hand to push absently at the Legion mark that had begun to throb with renewed fervor.

"What hum?" was the resounding answer—from all but Marduk.

The other man gave him a considering look but kept his silence.

Letting the conversation continue, Raphael listened as Alexander explained why he had the blade—the subcomponent of the Compass. "I found it in the sands near my court soon after I woke.

"Though the blade is nowhere as sharp as my others, I felt it was meant for me as soon as I took hold of it." He closed his fingers over it now, and in that moment, they all saw the eerie blade glow within his fingers, light blue-black escaping through his firm grip.

"So"—Marduk looked around the circle—"all that remains is for the rest of you to find your pieces of the Compass."

"No archangel ruled this land until I took it over," Raphael pointed out. "There wasn't enough mortal or vampiric civilization here for an archangelic base. No other archangel could've left behind a blade for me."

"It will be here," Marduk insisted. "That is its entire purpose—to find an archangel, then stay dormant until needed."

Archangels—even angels—shifted in their Sleep, Raphael remembered. Was it possible these so-called subcomponents had access to the same power?

"Can we set our people on the hunt?" Caliane asked.

"No. To their eyes, it will be nothing but a dull blade. Only an archangel can help another."

After that, no matter how much they spoke, there were no further answers.

"I am not an Ancestor!" Marduk shouted at one point, the bass of his voice filling the chamber and bouncing off the walls in a roar. "I was a *child* to their eyes when they chose to Sleep. I know only that which I learned as an archangel in my time—and you now have that knowledge."

In the end, they—one and all—decided to return to their territories in haste, to search for or retrieve their part of the Compass.

As archangels lifted off into the star-speckled night sky to scatter in all directions, Raphael stood on the cliff edge of his Enclave home with Marduk and watched them fly. "The last time I had so many archangels in my territory was during the war."

Marduk, his head turned skyward, said, "It is a glory to see the skies filled with wings again."

Raphael glanced at the other man, wondering if he was simply talking about waking from Sleep to see the sight . . . or if he was talking of a time when the skies had emptied. But even before Marduk looked away from the sky and to the waters of the Hudson, he knew the old archangel wouldn't answer him.

So he asked a different question. "Why did the Ancestors make the decision to hide our early history?"

50

"Because in a world of immortals, history can become a weight that halts growth. To allow their children to spread their wings without fear, the old ones decided that their mistakes and their world—a world they nearly destroyed—should vanish into the mists of the past."

It was a deeper answer than Raphael had expected to be given.

"How long?" he asked. "How long ago did the old ones walk the earth?"

Marduk's smile gave nothing away, his eyes that of the creature that marked his skin. "The current time, the current history of angelkind? It doesn't even begin to compare to the age of the old ones. They began with the dawn of this world, and they ended with the dawn of yours."

A riddle? Or the absolute truth?

"Where do you consider yourself to fall?" he asked, curious. "In the old world or the new?"

Marduk turned to watch a wing of angels take off from

the Tower. From this distance, they were dots against the sky, but their aerial finesse couldn't be missed—they flew as a disciplined team, one large shadow angel with a single goal.

"That's Illium's wing." Each wing had a different style, and Illium's was as quick, sharp, and innovative as the angel himself. "Aegaeon's and Lady Sharine's son. You've met him—golden eyes, blue wings."

Marduk's smile spread until it was full-out laughter, his face lit with humor. The sound was deep, wild, of a creature too big for this world. "Ah, now I understand why the hot-headed blue-haired one wishes to rip you to shreds. But why is Titus so sanguine?"

"Because Lady Sharine would rather shoot out Aegaeon's eyeballs than ever again touch him." Raphael enjoyed the image; watching Illium's once-broken mother, a woman who'd nurtured Raphael at his most wounded, come further into her power with every year that passed was a privilege.

"For such as her, even my impatient mate will sit still for a portrait." He stared out at the gleaming steel of Manhattan. "I wonder what my consort will think of this world when the time comes. I will dare her wrath and wake her for a few years before we return to our Sleep."

"We'll need you until we get a permanent ninth," Raphael pointed out.

Marduk shrugged. "What will that take? Five or six hundred years at the most? Lady Sharine's child has within him the seeds of ascension. If you say you do not feel it, I will call you a liar, blood of my line."

"We all feel it," Raphael confirmed, his chest tight. "We just hope it's not too soon. The forces of ascension would tear him apart. I barely survived and I was a thousand years old. Illium's only just passed the half-millennium mark."

"Hmm." Marduk continued to stare out at the glittering skyline of his city. "Come, young blood, let us search for the piece of the Compass that belongs to you." With that and no answer as to whether he fell in the old timeline or the new, he snapped out his wings in a leathery silence eerie and alien.

Raphael's own opened with a soft susurration.

They were halfway across the Hudson when he saw Elena heading toward them. She'd changed into her flying leathers, complete with a jacket that covered her arms and sealed around her neck. Wildfire arced over her wings in a silent lightning strike.

Raphael was expecting commentary from Marduk, but he said nothing. Not then, and not when they landed on the Tower roof. Instead, he walked to the edge from which they could see the Legion building. "I sense their hearts within." A murmur made in that voice unlike any other, a roughness of crushed stone touched by emotion. "I would be pleased to see my Legion again."

He moved his head in that characteristic motion he had, slow but intense. Looking past Raphael, he stared at Elena. "You can help search for the blade."

"Me?" Elena frowned. "From what Raphael's just told me, I thought only archangels could recognize it."

"You have some of my cells in your body, *hbeebti.*"

"Enough?"

Marduk shrugged. "We won't know until we make the attempt."

But though they searched nonstop for the next three days, there was no sign of anything even similar. Raphael's territory just wasn't *old enough*. His mother, however, had retrieved hers from Neha's throne, Titus had taken his from his crest, and Elijah had discovered his in Hannah's art studio.

"I was using it as a palette knife," a mortified Hannah had confessed to Elena. "To my eyes, that's all it was. I felt no compulsion to hand it to Elijah."

"Of course not," Marduk said when Elena passed on that piece of information. "She is his consort. The piece knew it could pass into his hand when needed. There was no urgency."

Elena remained uncomfortable with Marduk, the age of him making her teeth ache, but he also reminded her of her beloved Legion. "You speak of these Compass parts as if they're sentient."

No smile, those dragonish eyes looking at her with unblinking focus as he said, "Perhaps the metal is not metal at all. Perhaps it is the blood of the Ancestors frozen in time." Even as that unnerving idea made her shiver, he smiled. "Or perhaps I am amusing myself."

"I'm not sure he wasn't telling the truth the first time around," she grumped to Raphael later that night, after another unsuccessful search through every archive available to them—including in the homes of old angels who lived in the territory.

The latter would've been an unlikely place to find the Compass part anyway, since it was meant to be located close to an archangel, but they'd run out of options. Even as they fought to think of any other place they could search, they got word from Zanaya.

I have it, she wrote in a message sent to the Cadre. *Discovered it in my weapons chest. My second tells me she found it somewhere in the fort and thought it was perfect for me and placed it there—and then she forgot to talk to me about it. She never forgets anything. What are these cursed objects?*

Elena was in sympathy with Zanaya. An item that could always *find* you? "What is that if not straight out of a horror film?" she said to Illium as the two of them stood on a Tower balcony late that afternoon, after another fruitless day of searching.

"It is simply power."

Jolting at the sound of Marduk's voice, she scrambled back—and looked up. There he sat like a gargoyle above the balcony. "Eavesdropping is rude!" she yelled, while her heart fought to slow down.

Marduk dropped down to the balcony. "Yes," he said. "That I find you the most interesting being of all in this world is no excuse. My apologies." He bent low at the waist.

Elena didn't care about the apology—what she was more worried about was that he found her interesting. She didn't want to be found interesting by Marduk. "Even archangels shouldn't have that kind of power," she said, wanting the conversation off her. "The kind that flows through endless time."

"The old ones agreed with you," was Marduk's startling response. "There's a point at which power becomes only destruction."

"Good thing the Ancestors are safely Sleeping, then. Else they'd probably see us as food."

No laughter from Marduk, just that gleaming gaze landing on Illium. "Your energies are unstable. Fine veins of serrated gold."

Elena's mind filled with the image of Illium's body riven with veins of gold, his back arched as light poured out of his mouth, his scream silent and of agony. Before she could ask Marduk more about what he saw—and most importantly, whether he could stabilize Illium more than Raphael had already done—the archangel took off in the eerie silence effected by his wings.

He'd aimed himself at the Legion building.

"He never sleeps in the suite we assigned him," she told Illium as both of them glared after Marduk. "I'm pretty sure he sleeps in the Legion building."

"Well, there's definitely no getting past the resemblance." Illium's wing overlapped hers. "Though, you know, sometimes he reminds me of Naasir."

"Yes, but there's something else there. A cold consciousness buried beneath the beauty of his skin." Because Marduk's skin *was* beautiful, the iridescent scales soft to the touch and carrying colors from darkest green to rich blues to onyx.

She narrowed her eyes as Marduk flew past the Legion building. "Will you tell Raphael I'm going to see my father for an hour? I'll rejoin him in the search afterward." Her archangel had gone inside to take a call from one of the Cadre just before Marduk made his appearance.

Illium brushed his knuckles over her cheek. "Fathers complicate lives, don't they, Ellie?"

Elena hugged him with one arm, his body hard with muscle under his white T-shirt, the warm scent of him familiar. "Yes, they do."

"Helps that mine is one hundred percent asshole." He rubbed his chin over her hair. "No mixed feelings for him on my end. With you . . ."

"Yeah." She didn't say she wished he'd have a chance to build bridges with Aegaeon as she had with Jeffrey. Aegaeon had abandoned his son while Illium was just a little boy; Elena, by contrast, had had a father who cared for her for much of her childhood—and even when Jeffrey turned cold and hard, he'd *stayed*.

Stayed to fight with her. Stayed to be an asshole. Stayed to raise Beth.

He might have let her down in many ways, but he'd never abandoned his family. It was a fragile foundation on which to rebuild their relationship, but it might just be enough.

"Good luck, Ellie." Eyes of aged gold awash in hope for her as she swept off the balcony—into the cold afternoon air barely lit by the sun. When she glanced back, he raised a hand to her in a wave, the funny and smart blue-winged angel who'd become one of her closest friends and who deserved a life lived free of the shadow of murderous power.

Fine veins of serrated gold.

Her hand fisted, her stomach in free fall.

51

Elena tightened her abdomen in readiness for her arrival at the hospital. She hated the antiseptic smell of the place even more now than she had before Jeffrey's stay, but she'd learned to grin and bear it. She also knew her father waited for her to visit.

Conflicting with her desire to continue rebuilding their bond was the relentless urgency of the search for Raphael's part of the Compass, the countdown having narrowed to a matter of days now. But she knew an hour wouldn't make much difference. Not when she and her archangel had already exhausted every possible option and would be retracing their steps.

The rain crashed into her mind moments later, kissed by the salt of the ocean.

Aegaeon has recovered his subcomponent. It was in the palace he currently occupies, set into a display of decorative blades. That leaves Suyin and I alone who have yet to find anything—Suyin has the challenge of a vast territory, while I have the challenge of a territory so new there are no old places to search.

She could hear the frustration and exhaustion in his voice. While no new disasters had hit the wider world, the Refuge had suffered so many quakes over the past twenty-four hours that the senior team there—created of angels and vampires from across the Cadre's people—had made the call to evacuate everyone but those who *needed* to remain.

Included in the latter were people like Keir and Jessamy.

The healer needed to be close to his charges, because a few of the patients in the Medica couldn't be moved without catastrophic risk, and Jessamy because she was doing everything she could to preserve angelic history.

So far at least, the Medica had remained undamaged.

The Library, too, was still standing, but it was showing signs of an unstable foundation, while the Archives had been damaged enough that Jessamy was boxing up precious records and artifacts as fast as she could. Young couriers were then flying the boxes out to a mountain fort high in Caliane's territory that was built *into* the side of a mountain.

Not in use and inaccessible to anyone without wings, with one of Caliane's squadrons on guard duty, the fort would hold the records safe for the time being. Once Jessamy and her small crew finished with the Archives, she planned to begin packing up the Library, too.

Galen, Naasir, and Trace were all also at the Refuge, doing what they could to further shore up the Medica, since that was the one building that would be near-impossible to fully evacuate. One young angel inside had a spinal cord that was half-severed at the neck. Moving him, even with every modern advancement in the world, could end his life.

Elena began to turn, though the hospital was already within sight. *I'll head back.*

No. Go see your father. I, too, am going to stop for the time being—I'll have a sparring session with Dmitri, hope it helps me clear my mind. There's no point in going over ground we've already covered; it'll just be a waste of time.

We'll find it, she said, though she was no longer anywhere near as confident as when they'd begun. It wasn't that Raphael *didn't* have old things in his possession—but he knew where all of those old things were.

A mental kiss against her mind, before Raphael withdrew.

It took effort for her to put their conversation to the side when she reached her father's room. His visitor numbers were no longer severely restricted now that he was out of the ICU, and these days she often found him in the company of either Gwendolyn, Eve, or Amy.

Today, however, his visitor was a handsome Black man in a pin-striped business suit whom she recognized as Amy's husband. Maynard was saying something about share prices when she walked in, while Jeffrey looked at a bound stack of papers and nodded. Both froze when she walked in.

She grinned. "You're safe. I won't rat you out to Gwendolyn."

Maynard's returning grin was quick, wide, and held a warmth that embraced her. Yeah, she could see why her half sister had fallen for him. At first, she'd worried that Amy had gone for a hard-charging type like their father, but from what little she'd learned of Maynard, it seemed that while he *was* driven and ambitious, he had a temperament that was diametrically opposed to the Jeffrey with whom Amy had grown up.

She'd caught this man snuggling Amy in the hospital corridor, seen how he looked at his wife when they were together, witnessed his open affection with his children. It turned out he'd even tried to work from home as much as he could while Amy was at the hospital. He hadn't wanted their young children missing both Mom and Dad.

From all outward appearances, he was a gentler, kinder father than Jeffrey had been to Amy and Eve.

Just because Elena loved her father didn't mean she was willing to gloss over his faults.

"Phew." Maynard wiped his brow. "Gwen threatened to call my mama last time around so *she* could chew me out."

Jeffrey shot his son-in-law a look of wry amusement. "I'd tell you to grow a spine—except I'm relieved that Ellie's not ratting me out, either. So we can be scared of my wife together."

Maynard and Elena both laughed before Maynard picked up his briefcase and took the bound document from Jeffrey. "Getting rid of the evidence," he said with a wink. "No dummies here."

"I knew I liked you for a reason," Jeffrey said.

Elena smiled, amused at both of them. "I didn't mean to interrupt."

"No, we were almost done," her father said. "Making plans for further empire building under Maynard's watch."

Maynard closed up the briefcase. "When don't you want to build further, Jeffrey? But seriously, thank you for the vote of confidence on the deal."

"You earned it."

Walking over after exchanging a quick handshake with Jeffrey, Maynard paused awkwardly. "I usually kiss Beth and Eve on the cheek, but since we're not quite there . . ."

She shook the hand he held out, liking him more with each second that passed. After he left, she closed the door behind him and said, "Is he as good a husband and father as he seems to me?"

"Better." Jeffrey's expression turned somber. "He's like I used to be once."

A heaviness on her chest. She tried to dispel it with humor, not ready to go there yet. "Is he sneaking in every day?"

"No, the nurses snitch to her," Jeffrey muttered. "She

could see I was losing my mind lying here vegetating. Today's visit wasn't planned, but I do have *some* work privileges now."

Outward grumbling, but no actual anger from a man who'd never taken orders from anyone. Elena had the haunting realization that he was more tired than he let on. A fact apparent right then, as he lowered his bed to a full recline. "Do you mind if I rest a bit before we talk, Ellie? This blasted heart attack did a number on me."

"Of course I don't mind." She fluffed up his pillow.

He was asleep by the time she took a seat in the special chair Izak had flown in for her from the Tower. According to Dionne, the youngest member of her Guard had caused quite the stir when he walked into the hospital—all golden curls and square jaw, his eyes a sweetheart blue, Izzy was young and pretty and shy when it came to attention.

"Oh, that boy blushed bright pink when several of the nurses smiled and waved at him. A few even forgot they got men waiting on them at home."

No one had dared ask for his number, but Elena didn't think the distance would last should Izzy become a repeat visitor—poor Izzy despaired of it, but he just didn't give off a scary vibe.

"It'll come," Dmitri had said to him one time, his hand gripping Izak's shoulder. "I wasn't the least bit scary as an infant, either."

"I am *not* an infant." Izzy had scowled.

"Clearly not. I must be mistaken to remember you in diapers."

Dmitri was an asshole, but he could be fucking hilarious. Elena'd had to bite the inside of her cheek to stop from bursting out in laughter at the appalled look on Izak's face. "You do not remember me in diapers!"

"Oh, no? Ask your father sometime who babysat you when they had to fly from the Refuge for two weeks for an emergency family matter."

"Well, it can't have been you!" Izak had protested. "You were Raphael's second back then, too! Seconds don't have time to babysit!"

Dmitri had left him with nothing but an enigmatic smile.

The memory should've made her smile today, but her mind kept going around in circles. Especially after Vivek forwarded her a news update. The calm in the wider world had broken—Caliane's territory had just been hit by a massive quake, as had Alexander's, with an uninhabited section of Suyin's completely devastated.

Time was running out.

But where else was there left to search for Raphael's part of the Compass? Together, the two of them had gone through every level of the Tower, subterranean and surface. They'd also searched their home from top to bottom, because though it was new, they'd outfitted it with items from storage—including from Montgomery's hoard of precious things.

The butler had been delighted to have an entire home in which to showcase his treasures. Elena kept finding new artworks and gems every other week—but he wasn't filling the house. No, he loved rotating items so each got its time in the sun, before he returned it to his Aladdin's cave of a warehouse until its turn came again.

He hadn't minded at all when they'd asked to search the warehouse for a special item, though he hadn't understood when they'd told him he couldn't assist them by leading them to it—because Montgomery knew every piece in his hoard. Their search had been fruitless. While Montgomery possessed many unique and lovely items, he had nothing even close to the strange bladelike object Raphael had described seeing in Alexander's hand.

Raphael had even flown to Jason and Mahiya's home to check if it might've ended up in the safekeeping of his spymaster—for surely the power that allowed the objects to home in on an archangel would also understand that every member of his Seven could be trusted with the item.

"There's nowhere left," she muttered under her breath.

"Left for what?" her father murmured, lifting his eyelashes.

"An old relic," she said, helping him sit up and only then realizing that she'd been sitting there wracking her brain for over twenty minutes. "We're having trouble finding it."

Jeffrey drank from the bottle of juice Maynard must've brought for him; it still had condensation on the sides. "Have you tried the garden building?"

"The garden—oh, you mean the Legion's home?"

"Yes. They liked to collect things. I saw one of them in Central Park once. The being had found what looked like a broken metal bracelet, appeared fascinated with it."

Elena sat back, her heart a staccato beat.

What if it wasn't about an *old* place, but *old beings*?

She jolted to her feet. "Sorry, Dad. I have to go now. I'll come back later."

Jeffrey's smile was faint. "You're welcome for the idea."

Grinning past her nervous excitement, she shot back a "Thank you!" as she made her way out of the hospital. *Archangel?*

His mental voice was breathless when he responded. *A moment,* hbeebti. *Dmitri is in a bad mood.*

She withdrew; she'd seen those two spar and they treated it like a blood sport. Of course Dmitri could never beat Raphael if Raphael used his archangelic powers, but he never did in these sessions. That was the whole point. It put them on equal footing. And equally deadly to each other.

She was close to the Legion building when he got back to her.

We have come to a détente, Guild Hunter.

Don't even tell me the damage. She'd watched one of their no-holds-barred sessions and decided she didn't need to watch any more. Seeing Raphael in battle was quite different from watching him go head-to-head with his best friend, both out for blood—with feral smiles on their faces.

It had been obvious that they were having a ridiculous amount of fun, but she'd almost given in to the urge to shoot Dmitri with a crossbow bolt or five anyway. It hadn't mattered that Raphael was doing equal damage—Raphael was *hers*.

As Dmitri was Honor's.

Elena's friend and fellow hunter would not appreciate Elena skewering her man.

So Elena stayed away—as did Honor—while the two of them went at it.

There's no real damage.

Elena snorted. *Meet me at the Legion building. I'm almost there.*

Your wish. My command.

At least the blood sport had put him in a better mood, she thought with a twitch of her lips . . . just as the Hudson surged with an underwater quake. She knew it was a quake because the fucking bridge was moving, too. *Shit.*

The bridge settled a moment later, cars that had skidded to a halt as it buckled now speeding up to race off. Aware the city's emergency corps of engineers and other responders would already be en route to check the integrity of the structure, Elena left the bridge and carried on to land on the grass in front of the Legion building.

She didn't have to wait for Raphael—he didn't fly down but walked out of the Tower building, no doubt having left the receptionist, Suhani, wondering if she was having a fever dream. Because Raphael did not use the elevator to the ground floor. Ever.

Except today, apparently.

He was still dressed in the simple black sweatpants he'd been wearing to spar with Dmitri . . . and nothing else. No shoes, no T-shirt. All wings of a massive span, tumbled hair, and that naked muscle just gleaming with sweat—while a cut yet scarred his cheek and bruises bloomed down one side of his chest.

"No real damage?" she said archly.

A wicked grin. "He looks worse. And it's already healing."

The cut *was* sealing right in front of her eyes, but the fact it hadn't already done so was a sign of how bad it must've been to start with. Gripping his chin, she turned his head this way and that. "Hmm. If he does look worse, then keep a wide berth from Honor."

The grin widened before he leaned in to kiss her cheek. He looked young and wild and beautiful and she had to stop herself from hauling his sweat-slick body closer and licking him all over.

Later, she promised herself. "We need to search the Legion building."

It took him the merest second to make the connection. "They didn't bring anything with them out of their rest in the ocean." But he was moving toward the building with her as he said that.

"But they did collect interesting items once awake." Small things, lost things, like the bracelet her father had seen one of them pick up. "Maybe they found the Compass subcomponent and it's been sitting here all this time—same reason as with Hannah."

"Because it knew it was accessible to me at any time." Raphael shoved a hand through his hair. "When I think of the kind of beings that created artifacts that hold power through an endless span of time . . ."

"Fucking scary, right? Good thing they put themselves in permanent deep freeze."

"A cold truth indeed, hunter-mine." Gaze grim, he pushed open the door hidden behind a wave of falling vines, and they entered the lush and humid atmosphere inside the building.

52

The Legion had designed their home well—the external greenery died back in winter and rejuvenated itself in the spring, but inside, plants thrived all the seasons of the year. Certain things might slow in growth in the colder months, lose their leaves, or go dormant, but other trees and plants and bushes came alive in the cold, the Legion's garden a wonderland throughout the year.

Small birds twittered a bright welcome to them, Elena and Raphael so familiar to the smaller creatures that called the building home that they'd come to their hands if invited.

The bigger birds circled above, below the open roof.

When they closed the roof in the winter, they left open a small hatch protected by a secondary "roof"—because many of these birds were permanent residents, and not all had worked out how to get in and out through the "doors" on the upper levels that were nothing but sheets of thick, insulating plastic.

Elena exhaled, her soul opening up at the caress of green.

Raphael's mark came alive at the same instant, wildfire racing through each line.

He rubbed absently at it. "I'll go up," he said, sounding distracted.

"Go." Elena wondered if now he was close to it, he could feel the call of the ancient object.

She watched him take off, his body carved with the muscle of a warrior archangel. The large birds cleared a path for him, but didn't startle or scare. To them, angels were simply bigger birds.

As he ascended through the core of the building, the deliberately broken floors and ceilings creating a spiraling wonder of dense, dark green peppered with unexpected bursts of color, Elena decided she'd look on the ground level. The Legion had often put their finds in an old iron chest they'd salvaged from the ocean.

She hadn't touched it since the loss of the Legion. Neither had anyone else; everyone knew this was the Legion's place and these were the Legion's things. She might've taken charge of it, but the entire Tower watched over it. So it was no surprise to find the chest undisturbed.

Covered by vines, with grass and tiny pansies sprouting around it, it appeared an object lost in time. A grasshopper sat on top, its spindly legs carrying a body that was all but weightless.

"Sorry, buddy," she murmured, and reached down to lift the lid.

Skittering away at her telegraphed movement, the grasshopper nonetheless didn't go far. Instead, it perched on a glossy green leaf of the ornamental shrub next to the trunk, watching as she examined the items the Legion had considered treasures.

Her heart ached.

Right at the top lay an old throwing blade she'd discarded after the tip broke. Next to it sat the fragment of a gauntlet that she recognized as being part of a set Raphael used to own. She couldn't remember when it had been damaged—perhaps even in the battle that had brought the Legion to them?

Eyes hot and throat raw, she touched her fingers gently to the items before taking them out with care and placing them on the grass one by one.

Raphael spiraled up through the internal forest the Legion had birthed. It was no longer he and his hunter alone who came to admire this green jewel—many in the Tower had asked permission to visit, and Elena had given that permission with generous warmth. The only rules were that visitors were to cause no damage, and that they had to add a plant to either the inside or the outside.

Many of the Tower staff and residents had gone far beyond that, with some spending hours a week tending to the gift the Legion had left in their wake. He was sure he'd seen Holly and Venom walk inside with a pomegranate tree a few years ago, and today, he flew past a tree planted on what had been the eighth floor, its branches heavy with the distinctive purplish-red fruit.

He felt the urge to pick one of the fruits, tear it in half, and feed the luscious seeds to Elena. But something else drove him farther onward, higher and higher, until he thought he'd exit into the sky . . . but then he found himself slowing until he halted about three floors from the top.

To his left grew a tree that had rooted itself to the remnants of a lower floor and had then been further attached to the wall by vines that entwined around its trunk. It arched one strong branch over his head, the light that fell through the leaves a lace filigree on his skin.

He turned his hand under it, entranced.

Archangel? Did you find something?

Spell broken, he looked down and spotted the white fire of his consort's hair. *No. Have you had more success?*

No. Her mental voice held a thickness of emotion. *Just pieces of them.*

He almost dropped, went to her, but he *had* to go left, to the tree that grew in the middle of a high-rise in Manhattan. Landing on the jagged outcropping that was just barely big enough for the tree and the ferns around it, he looked for that which wasn't natural.

But his eye kept going to a knot of vines.

Power that ripples through time, he reminded himself, and didn't fight the urge. Instead, he knelt by the knot and reached out to separate the strands. The Legion mark sparked so bright a fire that he caught the light on the edge of his vision. *Elena. Fly to me.*

Her wings sounded behind him even as he tugged the vines apart without causing fatal damage. "There." The metal glowed obsidian-blue, and when he retrieved it, it pulsed with a gentle warmth.

The hum he'd first heard when Alexander showed them his piece of the Compass started again, louder and deeper. "Another gift, *hbeebti*, for which we must thank the Legion."

His consort's eyes were wide as she took in the object. Holding her hover because there wasn't enough room for her to land beside him, she said, "I see what you meant when you said it might look like a blade, but it's not."

"It comes from another time," he murmured. "A time that had to end before ours could begin."

Rising, he stepped off the ledge and handed the subcomponent to Elena as they both hovered with the leaves rustling overhead and birds circling to the sky. He wasn't the least surprised to see an owl with feathers as white as snow perched on a small orange tree opposite them, its eyes a pure and shining gold.

Thank you, Lady Cassandra, he said, knowing she'd

hear him no matter if she was falling deeper into her Sleep—her owl would carry his words to her. *For this interference that might save our very world.*

Her answer was distant and tired but clear. *It's not yet time for you to become the Ancestors. Not for eons yet.*

Elena's eyes glowed when she met his, the power in them as wild and alive as her. "I can hear it singing." A whisper. "A song inside my head."

"I hear a hum. Is that what you hear?"

But she shook her head. "No, it's a delicate melody . . . but it's slightly out of tune." She frowned. "Almost but not quite right."

"Suyin."

Elena's eyes flicked up from the object on her palm. "The last piece. The discordant note. She hasn't found it yet."

"Hers has always been the most difficult task. There is no way she can search the vastness of her territory in the time given."

Elena handed the living piece of their origins back to him. "The music's stopped. I must have to hold it to hear the song."

"The hum's constant for me now, but not intrusive. Like . . . having a pet purring in the corner."

They both looked down at the seemingly innocuous object.

"Oh yeah," Elena muttered, "that's no blade. And, to reiterate, I *never* want to meet the Ancestors. Just putting that out into the universe. Meeting their grandson or great-grandson Marduk is more than enough."

"In that we are in agreement. Come, Elena, I must inform the others," he said, and they flew upward instead of down to the ground.

Rather than making a call, he sent a simple message using the same system the Cadre used to talk: *Found.* He'd just finished the task when Elena picked up the object again, and he saw the "metal" begin to pulse with life as it had when he'd taken it.

Archangelic cells.

Just a few.

They shouldn't have been enough for this, especially when she showed no other sign of archangelic power. But, then, Elena had always been a being unique, an angel-Made. Ambrosia had changed her, and that ambrosia had come from him.

The obsidian-blue of the strange metal reflected in the silver clarity of her eyes as she turned it this way and that in open fascination—only to smile with joy sudden. "The melody just came into tune."

Suyin made the call a mere three minutes later. "We now have a complete set." She held up an artifact identical to the one in Elena's hands; Raphael's consort stood beside him for this meeting.

The others all held up their own finds, Zanaya looking askance at the glowing metal. "I can hear the hum you mentioned, Raphael. It took until I found mine to start."

The others confirmed they could hear it, too.

"Perhaps you heard it earlier because Alexander's and yours were in close proximity at the time?" his mother suggested.

"Perhaps." He blew out a breath. "We must meet in person again, to triangulate the position of the base into which these subcomponents must be placed."

"As soon as possible," Titus added, even his naturally warm expression tight today. "I've just had word of a volcanic eruption off the coast of New Zealand."

"Fuck." Raphael's imprecation wasn't the only one.

"Where do we meet?" Aegaeon said, and for once, he wasn't blustering. "The base could be anywhere, so we chance being too far from it no matter the location we choose."

All of them frowned, because he was right.

Elena, who never spoke at Cadre meetings if she could help it, said, "How loud is the hum you hear?"

Suyin was the first to answer. "Subtle. And I only hear that when I'm holding the object."

"I can hear it when it's in the room," Aegaeon said. "No farther."

The others said much the same, except for Alexander, who could hear it across the desert closest to his home. "But no farther. Perhaps an hour's flight on the wing."

That left Caliane. "It is irritating to the nth degree." His mother scowled. "Akin to a whispering courtier who will *not* be quiet. No matter if I fly to the mountains or across the ocean, I get no peace."

Her eyes zeroed in on Elena. "Yes, you are right," she said, though Elena hadn't spoken again. "If the hum is so loud for me, and louder for my closest neighbor than for any other of the Cadre, then we should meet here. Per Marduk, the Ancestors didn't intend for this to be a test except of cooperation."

Zanaya nodded. "Yes, it makes sense that the location would be provided once all the subcomponents were active. All we had to do was talk to each other to work it out."

"We fly now," Raphael said. "We can't risk waiting, and there's no point in coordinating a single arrival time, because it might be that the more pieces in proximity, the louder the signal—but all of us need to be contactable so that we can change route midflight if needed."

The agreement was total.

"Where is Marduk?" Elijah asked with impatience unusual for the Archangel of South America. "He should be there. We might need the entire current Cadre even if he doesn't believe so."

"I'll bring him with me," Raphael promised. "Fly safe." Words he'd never before said to the Cadre at large, but these were uncertain times.

"Remember the storm cells that have been forming over

the oceans," Suyin added. "A storm might not kill us, but it can break our bones and crumple our wings—and speed, as Raphael has pointed out, is of the essence."

Sober nods before the others signed off.

"Go, get changed into your flight leathers." Elena thrust the relic into his hand. "I'll find Marduk."

They separated without further words, their ability to work as a unit a thing that had grown until it was seamless. All the while, the subcomponent of the Compass hummed like a contented cat in the back of his mind. As the Legion had once murmured, their presence there but unobtrusive.

A clatter of sound, a loud crack.

He shot a look to the window . . . and saw his sunset-kissed city under assault from a squall of hail the size of small stones.

53

Elena stared at the round balls of ice at her feet. She'd been forced to drop and take cover under a rooftop restaurant's hard plastic awning when the storm hit. Thankfully, it had passed as fast as it had arrived, the melting ice the only evidence it had ever been there.

"I'll stay for a drink next time," she promised the vampiric proprietor before she flew off the building.

That was when she saw the cracked windows and shattered glass on the street. Hail had hit strong. No wonder Raphael had reached out to her with his mind after it started.

Her jaw tightening, she pushed up her flight speed to maximum. Because the situation would only get worse if the Cadre couldn't reset the Compass.

In good news, she didn't have to hunt long for Marduk. She located him crouched atop a building that overlooked Times Square and the surrounding area. It remained one of his favorite places to sit and watch the city—and it offered no cover. "The hail," she said, her breath coming short and fast. "Were you hurt?"

He gave her the strangest look before saying, "No," and turning his body in a way so only his scaled skin was exposed, his wings wrapped around him.

Elena whistled. "You carry your own protective shield."

Unfolding from the crouch, he smiled that Marduk smile that wasn't quite human in any sense of the word. And waited. Because he was Marduk and didn't appear to understand the concept of putting others at ease.

"We have eight pieces of the Compass," she said. "There is a hum. Loud for two of the Cadre, faint for others. We're assuming the Cadre has to fly to the loudest sound."

Marduk's eyes turned slitted and of a great reptile. His wings were slightly spread, and for the first time she realized that they weren't black at all but a shimmering hue akin to a black pearl. No color, and yet endless colors hidden within.

"That," he said in his gravelly voice, "is the one thing that is unpredictable. The old ones were powers, but even they couldn't divine how the Compass would respond to the people of each future time. When first created, the triangulation occurred through beams of light shot up into the sky, to merge into a pinpoint above the base."

Elena's eyes flared. "Wow." She could imagine it, scythes of light strong enough to be seen around the world. "The object glowed with Raphael and me, but that's it. No beam of light."

"Then we listen to the sound." He rose with a final look at the streets below. "This city of yours flows and breathes like blood in the veins or air in the lungs."

"There are other cities in the world that their folks might say are the same," Elena acknowledged, "but for me, it will only ever be New York." She powered up into the air, aware of Marduk coming up beside her.

When they landed on the Tower roof as the last light of

the sun's rays faded from the sky, he shrugged off the need
to change for the flight. "I am already in leathers."

She didn't comment that those leathers were sleeveless
and open halfway down his chest. His pants had laces up
the side that exposed skin and scales. But from what she
could tell, his scales might as well be armor. Apparently
that side made up for any heat loss from his more "ordinary" skin.

Raphael walked onto the roof just then, the Compass
subcomponent worn in a secure arm sheath on his left biceps, and his leathers an old and worn-in black. "Marduk,"
he said in greeting, before turning to Elena. "Take care of
our city, *hbeebti*."

"Always, Archangel." She leaned in to kiss him goodbye, and in the instant that their skin touched, she heard the
song of the relic on his arm, a hauntingly lovely melody
that made her vibrate from within.

Your eyes are aglow the shade of the object, Raphael
said into her mind before he drew back.

Marduk's chest rumbled with a sound that wasn't a
word. "You must come with us." An order directed at
Elena. "The subcomponent is reacting to you—there's a
risk that you may be needed at the end to complete the
Compass."

Elena thought of the song in her head, the way the relic
felt in her palm. *I guess, Archangel*, she said privately to
Raphael, *the old ones set it to resonate to archangelic cells,
never figuring an archangel would one day literally give
away a piece of his heart.*

Raphael nodded. "Then we'll have to go via the plane,"
he said, then pointed up when Marduk frowned. "The
metal machines that fly in the air."

Elena didn't argue; she knew her strength and level of
endurance in the air, and there was no way she could make
the long flight without several extended rest breaks.
But—"You don't know that I'll be needed," she pointed out.

"I might not be. You two fly ahead, and I'll follow. If it turns out you do need me, I'll already be on the way, and if I'm not, you can solve the issue while I'm still in the air."

A short discussion later and they'd all agreed on the plan.

The melody rang out in her head once more when Raphael cupped the side of her face, touched his lips to hers. A heartbeat later, all she heard was the susurration of his wings as they unfurled for flight.

Walking to stand on the edge of the roof, she watched as he and Marduk took flight into a sky that had begun to transition to night, two archangels, one the oldest living being in current existence, the other the youngest archangel ever made.

A shiver rippled over her when they disappeared into the clouds, taking a high flight path through thinner air. The music had stopped, the emptiness as haunting as when the Legion had stopped speaking to her.

But she had no time for melancholy.

Flying down to the balcony outside their suite, she made the call to the airport to let their pilot, Duncan, know that she needed to be in the air as fast as possible. Then, because—unlike the Cadre—she wasn't all but invulnerable to harsh weather conditions, she grabbed her specially designed daypack and quickly packed clothing that would protect her against snow and ice if they ended up in that type of environment.

Daypack snug between her wings, she took off toward the airport only minutes after Raphael's departure. When she called Dmitri, he said, "Raphael told me."

They hung up without further words, the city safe under his watch. She made her final call once she was on the plane, as Duncan began to taxi to the runway.

"Bethie," she said when her sister answered, "I have to head out of town for a few days." With no indication of how long this might take, the generic period seemed appropriate. "Will you tell Dad?"

After agreeing, Beth said, "Will you be safe in whatever you're doing?"

Elena squeezed the phone. "Yes. I'll see you all when I get back."

After hanging up, she stared out the window and thought of how a happy family of six had become a shattered grouping of three.

Drip.

Drip.

Drip.

The sound of blood dripping to the floor as it fell off her dead sister's broken fingers—it had haunted her for years, still did at times. Today, however, what haunted her was the memory of Beth's hand gripping hers, her little face white and pinched as her child's brain struggled to comprehend the horror.

First Belle and Ari, then Marguerite. Gone forever.

"I miss you," she said aloud as the plane took to the sky. "I'll always miss you." Some wounds didn't ever vanish; they just faded with time, until you could look at them without bleeding and breaking.

Another shiver rocked her.

Knowing it had nothing to do with her memories and everything to do with exhaustion, she got up and grabbed a blanket, then settled in for a rest. There was no knowing what the day would hold—she might as well sleep when she could.

It was the scent of gardenias that told her she was dreaming.

But she didn't look away from her mother's smiling face as they sat across from each other on the kitchen floor. Marguerite, so ethereal and beautiful, had thrown a woven rug over the tile, and they sat shelling peas from the big basket she'd picked from the gardens.

"*Chérie*? Why such a look on your face?" Marguerite's eyes held love unbound, the paleness of her hair aglow in the sunlight that poured in behind her.

The same sunlight caressed the dark gold of her skin.

Glancing down at her own hands, the hue of her skin part of Marguerite's legacy, Elena saw that they were the hands of an adult, not of the child she would've been were this a memory. "I'm scared I won't see you again after we say a proper goodbye."

Marguerite snapped a pea pod while smiling indulgently. "Ah, *azeeztee*. I will always be here." She placed her hand over the panicked beat of Elena's heart. "Your *maman* will never leave you." She reached for another pod. "It is impossible for a *maman* to leave her babies."

Elena wanted to tell Marguerite that she *had* left her once before, had left Beth, too. But she knew that would wipe away her mother's smile and cause a cloud to eclipse the sun, so she just snapped peas, ate a few, and spoke with the mother she'd never again see, no matter how long she lived.

54

Raphael and Marduk weren't the first to arrive at Caliane's home.

His mother hadn't moved into the magnificent Archangel Fort when she took over Neha's lands, had instead settled on an ancient oceanside palace that had gone from white to cream with time, and where the music of the water was a constant.

He found it . . . a thing to consider, that she'd chosen the ocean, when it was the ocean she'd used to commit the most terrible crimes against the people of two once-thriving cities. Perhaps one day he'd ask her why she did it—to punish herself? Or to ensure she never forgot what she'd done, the ocean a silent and relentless witness?

One thing he did understand was her choice to continue using the Archangel of Amanat as her formal title, rather than switching to the Archangel of India. "I will always rule Amanat, in all my lifetimes," she'd once said of the city so beloved that she'd taken it into Sleep with her. "Other titles will come and go but Amanat is forever."

The hum in Raphael's head had only grown louder as he neared his mother's palace. Once in proximity to the others who'd already arrived, it intensified into an irritation. They were in the right place. But even when the full eight of them stood with their hands out, the pieces of the Compass overlapping and touching, all they got was an angry hum. Adding Marduk to the mix made no change.

The archangel out of time shrugged when they looked at him. "Attempt it again after Raphael's consort joins us."

Alexander scowled. "Why does the hunter need to be present?"

Raphael didn't stir in insult—because from Alexander, referring to Elena's track record in the Guild *wasn't* an insult. Alexander respected warriors, and he'd come to accept Elena as one in her field. He more often called her a hunter or warrior than he did consort.

"My relic reacted to her," Raphael said, unwilling to share the painful reason why Elena carried within her a little bit of an archangel. His heart twisted in agony each time he thought back to that moment when he'd come so close to losing her forever.

"Raphael, you know I like Elena a great deal"—Caliane was as irritable as the rest of them—"but this doesn't make sense. It is a thing of the Cadre."

The others nodded.

Unexpected, but it was Zanaya who took the wind out of everyone's sails. "Actually, this is a thing of the Ancestors. Who knows what they built into it." She glared down at her own piece of the Compass. "For all we know, we need her because she was transformed with ambrosia and that's the magic last ingredient."

The group stared at Marduk.

Who shrugged again. "I was nothing to their power

when they chose to Sleep an endless Sleep. All I know of the Compass, I've shared with you."

The man was lying. Raphael knew that with every bone in his body. But *why* he was lying was the real question.

"Is the base apt to be buried or otherwise obscured?" he asked in an effort to work around Marduk's indirect recalcitrance. "Should we prepare to dig it up out of a volcano or smash through a mountain?"

Marduk's expression altered. "Do any of that and you will kill the base before the gift of their blood resets the Compass and the world."

"Kill?" Suyin asked, her pitch high and tone jagged. "Are you saying it is sentient?"

"A person." Caliane's face was white. "Dear Havens. The 'base' is a *person.*"

Marduk looked at her and bowed. "Wisdom lives in you, Lady Caliane." Sorrow in every line of his body. "Most specifically, a person who holds the trust of every single member of the Cadre."

"Such is impossible." Elijah rubbed his chin, his brow furrowed. "We are too varied a group."

"There is always one," Marduk insisted. "And now you will ask me why I did not mention this to you prior to this moment. As you did not yet have the subcomponents, it was a pointless discussion—and would have hindered you by weighing down your conscience. In ordinary times, archangels have countless millennia to come to terms with the knowledge."

Raphael looked down at the object shaped like a dagger in his hand. Not as sharp as a true weapon . . . but sharp enough to rend and tear and cut all the same.

His fingers were chilled, his skin tight.

When he lifted his gaze, he found himself accidentally locking eyes with Suyin.

Horror roiled across the delicate bones of her face.

"How are we meant to 'slot' these objects into place in a *person*?"

"A blood sacrifice?" Aegaeon cried out. "No! This is not our way, has *never* been our way." He made as if to throw his piece of the Compass down to the ground . . . only it stayed in his hand.

This time, the silence was deafening.

"Fuck!" Titus's booming voice. "I just tried it, too, and . . ." He held up the object.

Frowning, Raphael tried to put his blade back into the sheath on his upper arm. He was able to do so without problem. Seeing this, Elijah attempted to put his own into his thigh sheath. Again, a success.

"We aren't permitted to lose these things once found," Zanaya said, having already slid hers into a sheath visible below the shimmering green of the dress that hit her high on the thighs. "I did say they were cursed."

Teeth gritted, Aegaeon shoved his into an arm gauntlet. "The hum is making my head vibrate to bursting. I'm going to fly if we're to wait for the mortal you call consort, Raphael."

His heart a booming echo in his ears, Raphael said nothing to Illium's useless father. He spoke instead to another angel. *Is it Elena?* he asked Marduk. *The base? Is that why she reacted to it?* Because if it was Elena, then Raphael was ready to war with the entire Cadre and let the world crumble.

No one would be sacrificing his hunter.

Marduk's eyes weren't of an angel when he looked over, his mental voice as inhuman as his physical. *No, the base never has a response to the subcomponents until the end, when they are all together in front of the base. Also, I do not believe Aegaeon has a bond of trust with your consort.*

Relief and confusion crashed in a war inside Raphael. He'd been so quick to vow that he'd permit no one to touch Elena . . . but what about this unknown individual with no archangel in their corner?

He would not be a hypocrite, would not sacrifice a stranger but save his heart.

"What happens to the base?" he said out loud, halting the scattering of the Cadre.

Aegaeon was already gone, but the others froze in place.

"Do they die?" Raphael demanded, his wings pulsing with power. "Was Aegaeon right? Are we to purchase the safety of our world with the blood of an innocent?"

"I have been awake only once when the Compass had to be reset." Marduk's voice was a weight of crushed stone. "Then, it was a friend akin to me." He gestured to the side of his body that bore the shimmering scales. "He lived to see another day."

"But did he bleed?" Streaks of red on Elijah's cheekbones, this general who had always, *always* valued honor. "Did he hurt?"

"Yes. He was glad to do so to save not just our people, but our world itself." Marduk's slitted eyes, from another time, of another being, held each of theirs in turn. "The choice cannot be yours. The choice must be theirs."

Titus shook his head even as Raphael did the same. "Any being with honor will agree to it! That is no true choice!"

"Would you then strip their honor from them?"

The grim question silenced them all.

Icy winds ripped at Raphael's hair and bit at his skin as he stood waiting for Elena by the only suitable landing strip near Caliane's home—a thirty-minute flight on the wing. He was sick to his stomach in a way he couldn't ever remember being. Because never before had he contemplated the deliberate harming of a being who'd done *nothing* to him or his.

He enfolded his consort in his arms the second she stepped off the plane.

"Raphael? What's the matter?" Her hands stroking his back, her knuckles brushing the underside of his wings.

"I will tell you in the air." It came out rough. "There's no time to waste. The Mantle is mere meters from total failure and Marduk says there's no coming back from that, no halting annihilation once it begins. We must reset the Compass before it fails."

The wind made it difficult to get aloft, but once in the sky, it seemed to push them to move faster.

There was no more room to delay; he told Elena all of it.

His consort was quiet for long minutes before saying, *I'd do it. So would you. Marduk's right—we can't try to protect a person who may not want to be protected. They'll have family, friends, possibly even children they'd die to save. It has to be their choice.*

Raphael forced himself to release fists he'd clenched without noticing. *To buy the safety of the world by spilling blood? What barbarism is this?*

Marduk calls them the old ones. Angelkind calls them the Ancestors. And if Marduk's only a faint echo of what they were . . .

Yes. Whoever and whatever the Ancestors had been, their ways were not those of modern civilization. *They foresaw so much, but didn't foresee that we wouldn't wish to sacrifice one to protect the majority.*

Elena rode a wind gust that brought her just below and to his left. *Maybe they had no choice? Per Marduk, archangelic energies will always eventually destabilize the world.*

Everything we know is per Marduk, Raphael muttered. *How do we know he speaks the truth?*

Cassandra, Elena said simply.

Despite his anger at the shattering importance of the information Marduk had withheld, Raphael couldn't argue with Elena on that point. Because the Seer of Seers had made it clear that she wanted only the best for them. Half of him almost expected to hear her voice once again, but he saw no owls, felt no aged voice in his head.

It seemed she Slept at last, had found a fleeting peace.

"Wow." Elena came to a hovering stop above Caliane's palace. "I can see why your mother chose this as her home base in India."

The gentle sprawl of the palace gleamed a warm cream in the dull light of the cloudy day, the sand below a pale gold kissed by the frothy white caps of the waves rolling in to shore from an ocean azure blue even in this light.

"I want to ask her why the ocean." Raphael shoved a hand through his hair. "Never did I expect this."

Lightning burst out of the clouds before Elena could reply.

"Drop!" he yelled even as she did the same. They both collapsed their wings to accelerate the fall—but Raphael stayed above her, in the path of any bolt to come.

He'd survive a hit. She wouldn't, not even with his cells in her body.

She landed hard on the sand. Lightning was still hitting the water and the sand in strikes that burned the air when he joined her. Throwing an archangelic shield around them both, he ran with her to the shelter provided by the house.

The lightning might damage the structure, but at least it wouldn't be a direct strike on their heads. He'd seen several other angels fall from the sky at the first sign of the lightning storm and wasn't surprised when the Cadre ended up gathered on the wide covered balcony.

Aggravation at the headache-inducing hum or not, no one had gone far.

"We do it now," Titus said without preamble. "We have to know if it'll work."

No verbal replies. The eight of them just placed their relics and hands one on top of the other. Elena waited till the end, then looked at him.

* * *

Now, hbeebti.

Elena felt as if every cell in her body was vibrating in time with the energy that boiled the air. The entire living Cadre—and Marduk; so much power that it eclipsed the lightning that lit up the world in deadly flashes.

She didn't want to touch that stack of hands that glowed obsidian-blue, but she had no real choice. As the "base" would have no real choice. Because if that person held the trust of the entire Cadre, then they were a person with a good heart.

Here goes nothing, Archangel.

Glad that Raphael's hand was at the very top, she reached out and placed her own over his.

55

Nothing happened.

Even the lightning stopped.

A pulse later and their hands vanished in flames of obsidian-blue, and she could hear the melody in her head, perfect and piercing . . . and emanating from one specific direction. She turned, looked that way, and knew. "The Refuge!" Her throat felt as if she was screaming, and only then did she realize that the world was thunder, rain crashing around them with a force she'd never before experienced.

"Are you certain?" Caliane demanded, her face obscured by the obsidian-blue fire that held no warmth.

Elena made herself concentrate, even as an unknown force pushed her body to lean in that direction. "That way!" Gritting her teeth against the pressure, she pointed a finger on the exact bearing. "Either the Refuge or on the path to it!"

She tore her hand away from the others.

Breathless, she leaned over with her palms on her thighs, Raphael beside her. "I can still hear it," she said through her heaving breaths. "The melody. It hasn't lost any of its strength. I can feel the direction in my bones." A literal vibration, as if she was a tuning fork.

"Can you fly in this heaviness of rain?" Alexander demanded, his hands on his hips.

"Yes." To Raphael, she said, *Archangel, I have no idea if I can or not, but I have to try.* We *have to try.*

"We fly above Elena in a line." Raphael's voice was a command. "Shield her."

Not even Aegaeon protested. Elena didn't say anything, either. Because this wasn't about her pride. This was about Sam and Zoe and Maggie and Laurent and countless other children who'd hurt and scream and die if the world spiraled into a chaos of destruction.

Already dressed in the streamlined cold-weather leather jacket she'd brought along, she zipped it up to her throat, her small pack abandoned on the balcony. "Ready, Archangel."

Two seconds later, the entire Cadre was aloft.

Elena's heart caught at the sheer power of the sight, at the magnificence of these beings through whose veins ran energies so violent they could destroy the world itself. But she had only a breath or two to admire them before they settled into formation.

Taking a deep breath, she rose up through the driving rain, protected from the pounding only by the wings that created a living shield above her. The pressure eased at some point, and when she looked up, she saw that the archangels had stacked themselves in rows of three, creating a carpet of wings.

It was a carpet permeable, however; rain got through. But the protection still made it far easier for her to fly than if she were directly exposed. All the while, she thought about why she was the one to hear the melody. Yes, she had a piece of Raphael's heart inside her, but if it was about that, *he* should've heard the song, too. And it should've been far louder for him.

Cassandra, she said in an effort to reach the Ancient.

But there was no response today.

Her heart drummed a violent beat, struggling with what she was doing—leading death to a person who had no idea it was coming. "Fuck, fuck, fuck!" She kept hoping the melody would stop, the choice taken out of her hands, but it only grew stronger with each wingbeat.

Until by the time she had to stop for a rest, her muscles quivering with exhaustion, it was all she could hear, an opera rising toward crescendo inside a sealed theater. When Raphael told her he'd carry her, she just nodded. Because she'd seen areas flooding beneath them, homes being swept away, mountains crumbling in slides of mud and stone, and the landscape blurring as the earth shook again and again.

The world was falling.

So she kept on indicating the necessary direction, and though she'd much rather have flown on the wing, she stayed in Raphael's arms once she realized how much faster the entire group was with him carrying her.

Darkness fell. The rain halted, but no stars emerged.

Elena tried not to see that as an omen.

They came to a point where even the archangels had to stop to take a breath and refuel their bodies using the dried meats and nuts that Caliane's people had thrust into their hands prior to flight.

Their landing spot was an isolated grassland exposed to the wind and the fine spits of rain that had started up in the last hour.

Elena strode across cold and dark emptiness, both to stretch her legs and in an effort to outrun the certainty growing in the back of her brain. She'd come up with only two possibles—and one outlier—for people trusted by the entire Cadre. It had to be someone who had enough contact with archangels to build that bond. A senior person, then, and since this was a matter of the angelic race, most likely an angel.

Raphael walked to join her. "Your face tells me you're thinking along the same lines as I am." A glance back at where the others either spoke to each other or had walked off to stand by themselves. "There's a high chance we all have the same short list."

When Elena forced herself to name the people on her list, he nodded. "I can't think of anyone else. Not if it is to be an individual trusted by us, one and all."

"I wish it was me," Elena blurted out. "It'd be easier than basically going to a person—a *good, kind* person—to ask them to sacrifice themselves." Her breath accelerated, her shoulders rigid. "I know what I said before, but now the time's here . . . I don't know if I can do this."

The earth gave a violent shudder at her feet, cracking in a vicious line that put them on opposite sides. As if the world was sending her a warning, telling her this wasn't a choice. Not for her—and not for the person at the end of this flight.

Her face flushed, a scream tearing out of her. "I *hate* this!"

Raphael's face was cold in the way it got when he was holding back violent emotion. "This is what it means to lead, *hbeebti*. Some decisions carve out a piece of your heart."

Eyes burning, she flew across the new gorge and into his arms. He wrapped both his wings and his arms around her, a moment of warmth and love before they had to do a thing terrible.

56

Vivek hadn't slept for twenty-four hours straight, kept up by the pain in his leg and by the catastrophic natural events smashing through the planet.

It was as if the entire world had gone mad—and he knew something *big* was going on. Not only because of the information to which he'd been given access, but because every single archangel in the world was, at present, in Caliane's territory.

No one had told him that. He'd put it together after picking up multiple disparate pieces of information—and liaising with Jason. Part of both their jobs was to watch the other archangels, and when Vivek saw a photograph that a young vampire had excitedly posted of Aegaeon over Northern India, then Jason caught news of Suyin leaving China, followed by word from their spies that Alexander, Titus, and Zanaya had all left their territories, they'd realized the Cadre was on the move.

Dmitri had soon clued them both in: "Raphael's gone to an emergency meeting of the Cadre. Elena's with him." That's all he'd said within Vivek's hearing, but Vivek didn't need chapter and verse.

He was good at what he did because he could think for himself.

"Vivek." Dmitri's voice in his ear.

"I'm here." He kept on working, directing information where it would do the most good.

"Status of the Mantle?"

Vivek flicked over to that image and hissed out a breath. "Hours from failure. At the current rate, I'd estimate less than three."

Mind whirling after Dmitri hung up, he shot off a quick message to one of their people stationed with the angelic children, that communication part of his assigned tasks: *Is your location secure?*

Negative, came the devastating answer. *Severe quakes have damaged the foundations. We're evacuating the children to the secondary safe house.*

"Shit." He immediately disseminated the plan to the entire senior team.

The secondary location was aboveground, in a remote area of the Amazon jungle, and he knew the angels must have a way to get the children there without being spotted, but they'd still be traveling through violent weather.

He sent another message even as he brought up the weather systems en route: *Do you have assistance in avoiding weather?*

Yes. Hannah, consort to Archangel Elijah, and Mimata out of Southern Africa.

Of course Vivek recognized both names. *Listen to them. Both have experience with the weather along your flight path.* Mimata, for one, was a high-level courier; not one of the young kids, as most couriers were, but a senior angel who was called on to safely transport treasures—such as angelic children. *I'll also continuously forward you satellite updates so you can avoid storm cells.*

Thanks, Vivek.

Leaving the angel to get on with the transfer, he continued to put out as many fires as he could while shooting answers at questions asked by his people. He didn't realize he was gritting his teeth against the pain in his leg until a spasm locked it up in a knot so painful that it brought him to a screeching halt.

"Damn it," he said under his breath, reaching down to massage his calf.

His personal line rang at the same instant, Katrina's name on the screen.

He answered because he couldn't not answer when it was her. "Hi."

"What's wrong?" came the sharp response.

"Oh, nothing." He grimaced as sweat broke out along his spine. "Just one of those times I'm not sure being able to feel sensation is a good thing."

"You're in pain."

"Muscle spasm in my leg." Using his fingerprint to key open a drawer, he grabbed a blister packet of pills from the stash of medications in there. "A sec." He popped out five, chewed them down—his vampiric metabolism meant most mortal medications had no impact until he took a serious overdose.

Forcing himself upright because he'd learned through painful experience that being seated just made the whole thing go on longer, he continued to talk to Katrina using his earpiece. "Is your place still standing?"

"It has solid bones," was the clipped answer. "How bad is the pain?"

He thought about lying, knew she was too smart to accept bullshit. "Feels like someone's twisting my balls."

"Crude, but descriptive," was the cool response. "Can you come down to me when you stop for a rest?"

"No," he said, wishing it was otherwise. "I can't leave the Tower." Not given the current situation.

"This is who I am," he found himself adding, to this woman he barely knew . . . and wanted to know so much better. "It's important to me that I be here, do what I can."

"I know that," she replied, and once again, he had no idea how to read her tone. "Return to your work."

The call ended.

Exhaling, he wondered if her response meant he'd pissed her off. He couldn't tell, didn't know her well enough yet. But there was nothing he could do about it, so after walking off enough of the cramp that it wasn't debilitating—though he knew the affected muscles would continue to ache like a bitch for hours—he got back to juggling a hundred urgent balls at once.

When Izak walked in with a package half an hour later, he nodded at the young angel to leave it on a clear section of his circular desk. "Thanks," he muttered absently.

"Um, Lady Katrina was very firm that it was to be hand-delivered to you, and that I had to stay here until you opened it and confirmed it had arrived safely."

Fire under his skin, Vivek spun around in his seat. "Why is she commanding you like a courier?"

Blushing, Izak lifted his shoulders in a shrug, the arches of his wings a rich cream that Vivek knew was speckled with deep blue lower down. "I mean, she's not the kind of lady you say no to—she waved me down outside her establishment, and, well . . . here I am."

Jeez, the kid was green. "Don't even think about going into that establishment," Vivek ordered as he grabbed what he realized wasn't a box at all, but a discreet gray insulated cooler.

"I can't anyway." Izak moped. "She has an entry age of three hundred for angels."

Vivek grinned. "Right, of course she does." Katrina wouldn't want to be in the business of rescuing baby angels.

"It's not fair when she doesn't have any limit for vampires who've completed their century of service." A glare. "Hey! Why do you know her or anything about her place when you're nowhere near a hundred?"

"Vampires are already adults when they're Made—and I'm a unicorn."

"Ugh." Izak rolled his eyes.

Vivek opened the cooler but kept his eyes on Izzy. "I've opened it. No damage."

"What did she send?" Izak tried to arch his neck to look over the side of the desk.

"None of your damn business, baby angel." He pointed to the door. "Out, or I'll volunteer you to Nisia for infirmary duty."

Shuddering, Izak hotfooted it out of there. It wasn't that he lacked kindness or empathy. It was that the kid had spent way too long in the infirmary when he'd lost his legs and broken nearly all of the remaining bones in his body. Vivek got the aversion—and was the reason why Izzy *never* ended up doing infirmary duty even though most young angels pulled time there.

Nisia, the senior healer, was well aware of the reason behind Izzy's conspicuous absence—and she'd made sure to give Izzy the field first aid lessons he needed away from the place he so hated.

"I wouldn't normally countenance this kind of avoidance," she'd said to Vivek one day when he'd been in there for various tests, "but he's too young to have spent the amount of time he has in the infirmary. It has left scars."

"Trust me," Vivek had gritted out as he flexed his bad leg in the way she'd asked him to so she could measure his progress, "I understand the kid."

The healer hadn't made one of her trademark sardonic comments; instead, she'd said, "Izzy is lucky to have a friend like you. Many in angelkind have no true understanding of what it is not to have your body behave as you wish it to behave.

"It doesn't matter that they are often those with soft lives—not lives that put them in danger of losing limbs or wings, or even their very existence. Their talk can nonetheless cause harm to a vulnerable young heart."

She'd allowed him to relax his leg and, while he'd massaged it in the aftermath, had added, "He's safe in the Tower because he is the youngest of the angels, and treated much as a younger sibling by the vast majority of people. You do the same." A faint smile. "But you're also an example of a strong, powerful member of an archangel's innermost team who shares his aversion. The knowledge is a shield for him against less tolerant members of angelic society."

Now, smiling at the thought of Katrina imperiously waving Izzy down like he wasn't an angel assigned to the Tower, he looked into the cooler to find a small bottle of blood, an enormous pack of the small chewable sweets that he could still ingest even with his vampiric anatomy, and a bottle of salve on which was taped a note that read: *Put this on to ease your leg. The old ways are ofttimes yet the best.*

Rolling up his pant leg, he did as ordered. The scent that came from the salve was a rich, bright green. But the cool of it soon bloomed into a warmth that felt like heaven. He gave himself a moment to appreciate it before putting the salve safely back in the cooler, and quickly taking a drink from the bottle of blood.

Dark orchids and musk and secrets.

She hit him like a drug, dangerous feminine power and a luscious sensuality.

His cock went rock hard, his pulse racing.

Shuddering and kicking himself for that first gulp that had emptied a third of her gift, he put the bottle by the side of his desk in a safe spot and promised himself a sip every ten minutes. He'd make it last as long as he could.

Before returning to his work, he gave himself ten seconds to craft a message to her: *You are intoxicating. I am honored by the gift.* What little he knew of Katrina told him a formal acknowledgment would be appreciated; whoever she was, she'd come from another time, held to different mores.

No response, but he hadn't expected any. She'd said what she had to say in the form of the gift she'd sent him—the rest, they'd speak about when they were together. Turning back to his work, he rubbed the throbbing pulse on one wrist, the power of her blood fueling him as nothing else could have.

But the pleasure of tasting her went out the window forty-five minutes later, when he saw the current status of the Mantle. "Shit." He zoomed in, hoping he was wrong, that things hadn't accelerated this badly.

He wasn't.

They had ten minutes, if that, before the Mantle failed. "If you're planning something, Cadre," Vivek said aloud, "you better do it soon or it's game over."

57

Elena was on the wing again by the time they reached the edge of the Refuge. They'd passed the last mortal settlement some time back, and the knot in her stomach had grown into a stone lump in the intervening time.

There was no hope of a reprieve.

The song inside her head hovered a breath from a true crescendo as dawn began to light up the angelic homeland, the leading edge afire while the rest remained in shadow. Swallowing hard, she flew on—and wasn't the least surprised at her flight path.

The Medica and the Library both lie on this path, Raphael said inside her mind, putting her fear into words.

When she glanced at him, it was to see a face of wild, dangerous beauty set in austere lines. *There were only ever three choices.*

Jessamy, their teacher and Librarian. She might love one of Raphael's Seven, but no one in angelkind had ever even intimated that she wasn't neutral when it came to providing and recording information in her duties as the Librarian. She had assisted each of the archangels in the current Cadre at some point in time—and she had held their confidences.

Keir, angelkind's senior healer. At a few hundred past three millennia in age, he wasn't old in the grand scheme of immortal life, but he had a wisdom to him that was timeless, ageless. He also didn't discriminate when it came to treating those who were hurt or wounded. In a war, Keir would treat all combatants with equal care. He *had* done so in the war past, patching up any number of Lijuan's people.

Elena's third choice had been Andromeda, Jessamy's second in command. But Andi had been an outlier for the simple reason that she was much younger and therefore not taken as seriously by the Cadre.

She'd also learned en route that Andi wasn't currently in the Refuge; she'd gone to join the children nearly a week ago, taking charge of their education in this evacuation that had gone on far longer than anyone had predicted.

Jessamy and Keir.

It had to be one of them.

Her friends.

Inhaling a sobbing breath, she wished she could stop hearing this horrible music that was leading her to bring certain pain—and likely death—to one of the two most incredible people in the angelic race. Caught up in the horror of it, she wasn't ready for the crescendo to hit a shrill high note that stopped her in her tracks.

She looked down.

The low white buildings of the Medica glowed in the early morning light, its new skylight still covered by the night's dew. So high up, it took her a moment to spot him. Keir, his wings held tight to his back as he raised a hand in a wave just outside the building. *It's Keir*, she said to Raphael, then dropped as fast as possible to land in front of the healer.

She made it before any of the others. "I'm so sorry,

Keir." Words that didn't make anything better, but that she had to say.

Keir's full lips curved in a wise smile, the gentle brown of his eyes tired. "Ah, Ellie. You bring the Cadre to my door." A glance up to take in all the wings bearing down to land. "Will whatever this is stop the world from breaking?"

It didn't startle her in the least that he'd understood without any explanation; she didn't know if angels believed in reincarnation, but she'd always had the feeling that Keir was far more ancient than his immortal age. As if he'd lived an entire eons-long life, then been reborn into this youthful body with features delicate and wings of golden brown.

"Marduk says it will."

Gusts of wind around her, wings closing in snaps of sound, a churning maelstrom of power so vivid that it was a pulse against her body.

Keir greeted the Cadre with a mild incline of his head, his status as the senior healer of angelkind putting him on equal footing with them when it came to angelic etiquette. "It appears you have need of me."

Raphael was the one who stepped forward, the blue-black of his hair tumbled by the wind and his wings kissed orange by the sun. "You, Keir," he said, his voice thick with emotion writ large on his face, "are to be the world's shield against obliteration." He recapped the situation in under a minute, all of them conscious of the rapidly failing Mantle.

Keir stood in silence for less than five seconds in the aftermath. "I am a healer," he said when he spoke. "It makes the purest sense that this duty should fall on me." His smile was calm. "If the world itself is sick and I can heal it, then let us do it this very moment."

Shrugging off his robe to reveal a sleeveless tunic belted at the waist with a fabric belt that bore intricate embroidery, and matching brown pants, he went to drop the robe to the side, but Elena stepped forward to take it.

His fingers brushed hers, the energy in them a warmth she'd felt from no other angel—not even Raphael would compare his own Cascade-born healing gift to Keir's.

Her archangel's respect for the healer was as profound as Elena's.

Keir was the one who'd watched over her as she lay in a coma after Raphael kissed ambrosia into her mouth. Keir was the one who'd healed a devastated and broken Aodhan once upon a time. Keir was the one who had vowed to cherish and protect an archangel's orphaned child after she fell in battle to injuries so grave that she might never again rise.

And that was only a drop in the ocean of all he'd done.

"Cadre," he said right then, "I have a child under my care. The babe adores Jessamy. Ask her, this beloved friend of mine, to take care of him in my absence."

"It will be done." Caliane's beautiful, pained voice. "He will know no lack in life, this we promise."

Tears blocked Elena's throat, burned her eyes, even as Keir turned to Marduk. "Am I apt to explode or otherwise make a violent show of things? If so, we should step away from the Medica."

Marduk looked at Keir with eyes in their dragon phase, the pupils long slits. "I do not know if all reactions are the same," he said, and there was something akin to respect in that hard-to-read face. "But the Compass as a whole was created to balance the power streams of the world, so there is a risk."

"Very well. We move."

It was surreal, the eleven of them rising into the air as a group to make a short flight to the edge of the Refuge—but an area that remained under the Mantle. Should an explosion in fact occur, no one in the outside world would see it.

The sunlight hadn't reached their chosen location yet, the area cold with shadows.

Elena bit down hard on the inside of her cheek as she

landed, Keir's robe cradled in her arms. He smiled at her and she knew what he was thinking: he wouldn't need that robe if this ended as they thought it would.

Setting her jaw, she held the cloth closer, the gentle, comforting scent of Keir in every thread of the weft and weave.

"We don't have any more time." Caliane's voice held raw anguish. "The state of the Mantle is perilous at best."

Keir nodded. "My staff will deal with the Medica until you appoint a successor."

None of the Cadre moved. Not even that ass, Aegaeon.

"No," Zanaya spit out. "This is wrong. I will not spill a healer's blood. This is *not our way*."

Keir shook his head. "It must be done, Queen of the Nile. It seems we are born of a bloodthirsty people. It makes sense, if you think of it. We create vampires, after all—that thirst for blood stems from somewhere."

"How can you be so calm?" Aegaeon demanded, looking a touch green about the gills.

It made Elena like him far better, that he couldn't make himself do this horrific act.

"As I said, I am a healer, and the world is wounded, close to death. If my blood will cure that, so be it."

Frowning, Elena thrust Keir's robe into the hands of the archangel closest to her. It happened to be Alexander. Who stared at her, speechless. Ignoring the Archangel of Persia, she took the subcomponent from Raphael and strode over to Keir. *Archangel, I need you with me.*

Of course, Guild Hunter. But what are we doing?

I have an idea. All this talk of blood. Put your hand over mine. Halting in front of Keir, she placed the blade flat against the skin of his upper arm and saw the ripple of glowing obsidian-blue arc through his veins. "I need something to tie or tape this to him."

"Here." A strip of fabric that held a faint sparkle being handed to her.

A piece of Zanaya's dress.

"Is she decent?" she whispered to Keir *sotto voce* as she tied the blade to him while Raphael held it in place—she ensured she kept contact with his skin while making the tie. "That dress was short to start with."

Keir's cheeks creased in a smile deep and intense and rare on the healer, even his aged eyes warm with it. "Only just. If you need more strips, better to tear apart my tunic. The others are all in leathers."

Job done, she stepped back and pointed to Keir's arm—where a network of veins pulsed obsidian-blue on his upper arm. "What if we don't need to stab him?"

"The instruction is for a gift of blood," Marduk reminded them. "The subcomponents must become one with the base to create the Compass and initiate the reset."

She held his gaze, not flinching from the primal power of him. "A gift of blood doesn't mean a *gush* of blood. There's no harm in trying my way before we have to stab Keir—we have enough minutes if we're quick."

The rush of agreement from the Cadre made her like the whole lot of them more.

Elena cut away Keir's tunic on that, Raphael tore it into strips as fast as possible, and each of the archangels tied their parts of the Compass to Keir. Three more on his arms. Two strapped to his torso. The final two slid between the waistband of his pants and his skin.

Every single piece was flush with his skin . . . and Keir looked like he'd drunk radioactive mead, each vein and artery glowing and his eyes an eerie obsidian-blue. It was similar to how Illium had looked when power overwhelmed him . . . but not identical. Where Illium had screamed and burned as if being invaded by an alien force, Keir *glowed*, as if every cell in his body was its own stand-alone bulb.

He turned his hand palm up, then down, his wonder open as he said, "How very lovely."

The earth trembled.

Riding the wave, he looked at Elena with sorrow profound in his expression. "It hasn't worked, Ellie. I think—"

"Blood." Elena folded her arms, once again holding the robe Alexander hadn't actually dropped after all. "Prick yourself on one of those quasi blades."

His sorrow didn't fade, but he reached out with one finger and ran it across the sharp edge of a subcomponent. The dark "metal" that *was* probably made of the blood of the Ancestors morphed to glow as obsidian-blue as his veins.

"Well," Keir murmured, and then, without hesitation, began to "blood" each of the other artifacts. He used a different finger each time, and both his hands bled with small cuts by the time he reached the last one.

He met her gaze, took a deep breath, and made the final cut.

58

Elena cried out, throwing an arm over her eyes as Keir exploded in a burst of obsidian-blue light that erased the world from sight.

She couldn't see, couldn't hear, her eardrums buzzing.

59

Illium and Aodhan were in the process of rescuing passengers trapped inside a derailed train when every vein in Illium's body blazed gold. Fear was a metallic taste on his tongue, a silent scream on Aodhan's face.

A flash of light that set fire to existence itself.

60

"Keir!" Elena screamed, but all she heard was her own voice. *Archangel?*

No response, but it didn't feel like he was gone from inside her head—just as if he'd been muffled.

Blinking rapidly, she felt around with her arms, a sightless woman trying to understand her surroundings. And there he was, his fingers brushing hers. She'd know him anywhere, even in a place with so much light that it blinded.

He held on tight to her, but even when they were close enough that they *should've* been able to see each other's faces, all she saw was a buzz of white. Panic tried to beat its shrill drums, but she focused on the feel of his hand, the anchor that told her this was real—as did the ground under her boots.

Whoosh!

The sensation was like that of a storm being abruptly sucked into the earth. Or how she imagined that might feel.

A funnel of soundlessness that turned into a sudden piercing tone. Then . . . nothing.

She didn't open her eyes, didn't look at where Keir had stood.

"*Hbeebti*." Raphael's voice was still too quiet to her stunned hearing, but she grasped the wonder in it.

Raising her head, she sucked in a breath, her eyes widening.

Keir was . . . aflame. Consumed by a searing white fire that outshone the beams of the dawnlight that now fell on him. He was smiling, his head thrown back as he bathed in the inferno.

When the flames winked out without warning, he swayed from side to side as if drunk, then touched his hand to the skin of his forearm. "That was extraordinary."

At which point, he collapsed.

Thankfully, Titus was close enough to catch him, so he didn't crack his head on the rocks. "He's alive!" the Archangel of Southern Africa called out. "His heart is beating, and there, his chest rises and falls."

"Where are the subcomponents?" Suyin whispered, her attention on Keir.

Marduk hunkered down beside the healer. "Gone until they're needed again."

Raphael's phone rang at the same time.

Taking it out, he looked at the screen. "Vivek," he told Elena before putting the phone to his ear.

"The Mantle is regenerating at rapid speed," he announced within seconds.

"But the records exist now," Elijah murmured. "Of how the mountains of our homeland truly appear."

"It should not matter," Caliane pointed out. "Remember, part of the function of the Mantle is to discourage curiosity. And since our Ancestors were powerful enough to make the Compass, I do not think such modern things as photographs taken by eyes in the sky will defeat them. Mortals will forget they were ever interested in looking at these mountains, and soon the images will fade into obscurity."

Elijah spread, then closed his wings. "I can only hope you're right, Lady Caliane."

61

Illium woke flat on his back on the ground—to a sense of lightness he hadn't felt since before the Cascade. "I think, Sparkle, I'm normal again."

Aodhan continued to frantically pat him down in a search for injuries, the beauty of him a shower of light that was Illium's eternity. "What?"

Illium ran his fingers through Aodhan's hair, the strands so soft and fine for all that they appeared to be coated in crushed diamonds. "Whatever the Cascade shoved inside me, it's gone."

Finally satisfied that Illium was unharmed, Aodhan took Illium's face in his hands, said, "Explain."

"I'm in no danger of ascending." Relief was a drug that bled into his veins, his entire self euphoric. "Whatever was out of whack in me has been put right. Balanced."

"You're sure?"

"Beyond any doubt. I could . . . sense power on the horizon that was too big for me before. I can't even see a glimmer of it today."

Aodhan's hands trembled. "I'm going to sleep much easier now that I know you're in no danger of being torn apart by a premature ascension, but how do you feel about the loss?"

Illium closed his fingers on the glittering beauty of Aodhan's hair. "I'm happy that I have time to grow with you now, time to walk my own path, time to be part of Raphael's Seven. Because I'm not done there yet and won't be for a while. I plan to be his first general—he needs one, like all respectable archangels."

Aodhan's smile was affectionate and of the person who knew him best in all the world. "Of course you have to be first." Laughter that ended in a kiss, their wings and legs entangled.

"You know it'll still happen one day?" Aodhan murmured gently against his lips, the blue of Illium's wings reflected in the crystalline shards of his eyes. "You're the son of an archangel and Lady Sharine. There is a reason the Cascade chose you."

"Yes. But it'll be on my own natural timeline." He had hundreds of years to be a lover, a friend, a loyal warrior to his liege before he ever had to worry about the Cadre and politics.

Thank. Fucking. Havens.

62

Six months later, and the world hadn't suffered a natural disaster since the instant of the reset, the calm so pristine that it had been scary at first. Once they got over that, however, they'd put their backs into the cleanup.

Caliane had also been proved right. Articles about the "newly discovered" mountains had begun to proliferate when the Mantle started to drop. Those articles vanished overnight. They were still *physically* there if you searched for them, but the pages had no traffic.

People just weren't interested.

It freaked Elena out that there existed power that could effectively control people's minds from the other end of time. "Your Ancestors are flat-out terrifying," she said to Raphael that morning as she pulled on her clothes. "Just in case you forgot."

Raphael, already dressed, leaned against the vanity, watching her. "I don't think I am in danger of ever forgetting. It has come as quite the shock to realize that archangels are not the most powerful beings in existence."

"Well, the Ancestors seem to be happy Sleeping forever, so I wouldn't worry too much about becoming dragon food." The quip fell flat because her heart wasn't in it.

"I can't believe this is actually happening." She ran a shaky hand down her simple gown. Of a pale and delicate green, it was held up by pretty diamond clasps at her shoulders, the waist encircled by a fine diamond chain.

It wasn't her style . . . but it would've been her mother's. And today was about her mother and her sisters. Which was also why she wore butterflies of sparkling silver in her hair and would carry a basket of daisies to throw into the ocean.

The butterflies for Belle, the daisies for Ari.

Raphael stroked his hand over the surface of her wings even as he spread his own to close them around her. "You are ready, *hbeebti*."

Elena nodded, taking deep breath after deep breath. "The ceremony at the funeral home after the exhumations didn't feel like the real thing, you know?" It had been solemn and quiet, and nothing like any of them. "Today, I say goodbye to them the way it should've always been—as a celebration of their lives."

Raphael tucked a strand of her hair behind her ear. "You will do them proud." His belief in her was a sea storm inside her mind, crashing waves that went on forever.

It carried her on the flight to the remote ocean promontory where they were all to meet. Jeffrey had arrived first, stood on the cliff edge leaning on a cane. His health had improved vastly, but he still tired easier than he had before the heart attack, and the cane helped ameliorate that.

She'd half expected him to turn up in somber black despite what they'd talked about, but her father wore beige linen pants and a loose white linen shirt.

Around his wrist was a bracelet created of multihued threads.

Elena's throat threatened to close. She hadn't known

he'd kept any of Belle's bracelets. Neither had she known that he'd kept the shirt that Marguerite had hand-stitched. Ari was there, too—in the small leather-bound book he had tucked into the pocket of his shirt. The last gift Ari had ever given him.

When he reached out a hand, she didn't hesitate to take it.

Gwendolyn, who'd gone to her and Jeffrey's car to fetch more flowers, came over to kiss Elena on the cheek and greet Raphael. She still wasn't comfortable with the enormous pressure of his power, her eyes never quite meeting his, but she was genuine in her warmth.

As for Jeffrey and Raphael, they gave each other polite nods. Raphael loved her too much to forgive Jeffrey for the hurts he'd caused her, but her archangel had also accepted that Elena needed to heal the fractures between her and her father.

"If you wish me to welcome him to the Tower one day," he'd told her, "I'll do it without hesitation. As you welcome my mother, no matter if you worry that she will hurt me once more. He is your father. And unlike my mother, he is mortal."

Her archangel understood what that meant, had witnessed her anguish at the racing clock firsthand.

"There comes Beth with your grandparents." Jeffrey nodded down the track.

A dusty people mover stopped beside Jeffrey and Gwendolyn's equally dusty BMW sedan. Getting out, Harry jogged around to open Beth's door—who emerged with the urn held carefully in her arms. That urn carried the remains of Marguerite and her two daughters. They'd made the decision that this was about family. None of the three would wish to be separated.

Majda, as petite as the daughter she'd birthed but never got to watch grow into adulthood, her skin a darker gold than Elena's, emerged from the back seat after Jean-

Baptiste. Marguerite's father had eyes of silver-blue, and those eyes were trained on Majda as he took her hand with quiet words no one else could hear.

Their faces were worn, their grief a thing they'd carry forever.

But instead of walking over, Majda held out a hand and two younger figures emerged to join the group.

Maggie and Laurent.

"Hi, Auntie Ellie," Maggie said after running over for a hug.

Elena's nephew was right behind her.

"Hi, sweetie." Elena kissed the top of her head, then did the same for Laurent—who was already almost the same height as his older sister. "What are you two doing here?"

"We wanted to be here," Maggie said. "For Mama and for my grandma and aunts we never knew."

"Mama told us about them," Laurent said. "She says I remind her of Belle. She was a rebel like me." He grinned.

His innocent joy paired with Maggie's sweet empathy, it made this day a touch easier. "I'm glad you came."

A motorcycle sounded in the distance, followed by another vehicle.

She wasn't surprised when Eve swung off that motorcycle after parking it, or when Amy emerged from the vehicle. They were family. Even if they hadn't known Marguerite, Belle, or Ari, they knew Elena and Beth and Jeffrey.

It was for them that they'd come.

The person who'd driven in behind Amy, however, had come only for Elena: Sara. Deacon got out with her.

And Zoe, unfolding those long legs from the back seat.

Her best friend gave her a hug, as did Zoe and Deacon, then they stepped back to stand beside Gwendolyn, Eve, Amy, Maggie, Laurent, Harry, and Raphael. Elena wasn't surprised to see Zoe lean a little into Raphael after ending up next to him.

Her archangel put his arm around her goddaughter, his

eyes, that pure, painful blue, meeting Elena's over Zoe's curls. *You can do this,* hbeebti. His love surrounded her, phantom wings enclosing her in silken warmth.

Elena swallowed, took a deep breath, then squeezed her father's hand. "It's time, Papa."

The two of them, Beth, and their grandparents walked to the lip of the cliff. Elena had already checked the wind direction and speed, ensured it would carry the ashes out into the ocean, and from there, to whatever wild vistas existed around the world.

Now, Jeffrey took the urn from Beth, while she took charge of his cane.

"Bye, Mama," Beth murmured. "Bye, Big Sis One and Big Sis Two." Her voice hitched, but she carried on. "I wish I'd had longer with you—but I'll never forget you. I've told my son and daughter all about you.

"Maggie's like you, Mama, loves to sew and bake. One day, I think she'll be the heart of a happy family, as you were. As for my sweet Laurent, he's a handful, and that's putting it lightly. I can see you laughing with me over his shenanigans."

Elena gripped her sister's hand as Beth's words whispered off into sobs. Then she spoke her own. "I've been so angry with you for so long, Mama," she whispered. "But today, I'm letting that go even as I hold the memory of your love in my heart.

"Thank you for loving us with gentleness and warmth, for drenching our childhood in sunshine. I hope that you fly on the wings of freedom now, no longer caught in the grief of the past." Her rib cage pressed inward, her heart too big for her chest. "There's no pain anymore, Mama, not for you. I will always love you."

Jeffrey put his hand on her lower back, supporting her as her voice thickened, and inside her mind, the waves of Raphael caressed her in comfort. Her grandparents flanked them, Majda to Beth's left, Jean-Baptiste to Jeffrey's right.

"Belle," she said, "my wild and beautiful big sister, I miss you. I'll always miss you, but you taught me how to be a big sister with the way you always found time for me—even when I was at my most annoying." She laughed and it was a sound wet and rough. "Thank you for trying to teach my two left feet to dance, and for showing me how to punch out that kid in school who was trying to bully me."

Tears rolled down her face and she didn't stop them. "Ari, I miss you so much. I can imagine the wise counsel you'd have given me over the years, and all the tight, warm hugs in which you'd have enfolded me.

"I was so lucky to have you as a big sister. You taught me that love keeps no ledger, and that loyalty among sisters is forever. Thank you for my first ever secret diary with its own lock, and for never telling anyone about my first crush."

Taking a shuddering breath as Beth cried next to her, she said, "I hope I've done you both proud in stepping in as a big sister."

Marguerite's parents were the next to speak, their words in the language of the place where Marguerite had been born, flowing and lyrical. They sobbed as they said their goodbyes to their treasured child and to the granddaughters they'd never met. Both touched their fingers to the urn, couldn't seem to let go.

No one rushed them.

Then, it was time for Jeffrey to say what he would. Urn in his arms, he stared out at the water for a long time, his lashes blinking rapidly. But the tears still fell, still streaked that thin patrician face. When he spoke, it was in French. Words of love for his Marguerite, the wife who had left him broken.

Elena didn't attempt to translate; these were private thoughts from a husband to a wife—and they were also a kindness to the wife who stood with him today. Elena loved her father all the more for being respectful of Gwendolyn even as he said goodbye to the love of his life.

To his daughters, he said, "I've never forgotten you, my baby girls. Not for a single day. My guilt at not being able to save you, at not being there that day, turned me into a papa you wouldn't have recognized. It made me angry and hard and mean, and it almost destroyed my relationship with your Ellie.

"I'm so sorry for that. You would've been ashamed of me, and of what I became. I promise that I'll never again use your loss as an excuse to be a bad father. Ellie and Beth will know the papa they used to know—and so will Amy and Eve, these two sisters whose lives could never cross paths with yours."

His voice grew hoarse, torn. "I loved you from the day the nurses put you into my arms, my rebellious, funny Mirabelle who dragged me to dance in the rain. I know you would've always held me to account as you grew. You'd have chosen your own path, no matter what I said, and I'd have been so proud of you for always being you."

Elena leaned into her father, telling him without words that he wasn't alone, all of them connected by love and grief.

"My Ariel, my calm in the storm. You were such a sweet baby who grew into the sweetest little girl. You could always make me take stock, make me realize that nothing was as important as how much I loved you and your sisters and your mother.

"I know you'd have been my heir, the stable CEO who would have taken over the empire I built for my family. I would've never worried with you at the helm. I would've been so proud to have you there."

His shoulders shook with his tears. "I don't want to say goodbye," he managed to get out. "But I have to set you free."

Elena put down the basket of daisies, and then all five of them put their hands on the urn.

The ashes drifted to land gently on the ocean, becoming

part of the flow of life once more. The daisies every person there threw after the ashes were bobbing bits of brightness that they watched until they became too small to see, the last pieces of Marguerite, Belle, and Ari drifting off into a new existence.

63

Raphael had been ready to hold a devastated Elena after the ceremony, but though she was quiet in the aftermath, her gaze was free of torment. And that night, as they sat with their legs hanging over the edge of the Tower roof, their wings overlapping, she wove her fingers into his and said, "I feel lighter inside. As if I've let go of a weight that I've carried around since the day it all went wrong."

Lifting their twined hands, he pressed a kiss to her knuckles. "I'm glad of that, Elena-mine." He hoped that meant an easing of the nightmares that haunted her to this day. He hated waking to her pain. Even worse, he hated knowing that she had to deal with them on her own when he was away on Cadre business.

She echoed his caress, brushing her lips over his knuckles. "How are you feeling? About the whole 'blood of Marduk's line' business?"

He rolled his eyes like some insolent young buck. "I do

believe arrogance has a face and it looks suspiciously like Marduk's."

Elena's laughter wrapped around him, a welcome sound in the glittering dark of their city.

Smiling, he moved his wing affectionately over hers. "I suppose I'm grateful in a sense—not many angels ever get to see that far back into their lineage. There's also no doubting the connection, not with the mark so alive in general, and ablaze when I'm near him."

The Legion symbol shimmered at that moment, lit by an inner glow.

"Marduk is a bit much," Elena said, "but he's given me hope for the Legion's return, and for that, I can put up with him." She kicked her legs. "Do you think the Ancestors were all dragonish?"

"No. If that were so, Marduk would have more difficulty pinpointing those of his line. I have the feeling the Ancestors were as varied as we are today."

"Our world would've been more primeval then, too," Elena murmured. "I see what he means, that they were of their time."

"Yes, and they were wise enough to understand that." Raphael looked out at the sprawl of their city, so vivid and alive—and so peaceful. "This time, this world is ours. The Mantle is stable, and there have been no further unexpected natural events since the day you halted us from stabbing Keir without reason."

"Stop being annoyed at yourself for not thinking of it." She nudged his shoulder with her own. "I only thought of it because I'm still mortal in my head—the idea of a reset key that relies on stabbing a critically important person just felt 'off.' It seemed to me that your Ancestors wouldn't want to usher in a stable world by making you participate in a group murder."

"Never lose that mortal heart and mind, *hbeebti*. I'm not so sure our ancestors weren't exactly that pitiless."

"No chance on the mortal part." She put her head on his shoulder, and he wrapped his arm around her. "Are we at peace now?"

"Yes. A peace unlike any other." He frowned, tried to put what he sensed into words. "I understand now, about the power flows of the world.

"I ascended when it was already turbulent. I've never known true peace, but now I *feel* it. As if I was riding the rapids the entire time, only to emerge onto a glass-calm lake."

Elena nodded slowly, but didn't interrupt.

"This is also the first time since my ascension," he added, "that I know beyond question that no one wishes to launch a war, is going mad, or covets anything else held by others of the Cadre."

"I've only been around a droplet of time immortal-wise, but yeah, I can see it." Elena held up both hands, with one pinky down. "You and me, we're it forever and just want to be left alone to get on with making kissy faces and looking after our people."

His lips twitched, and he kissed her impertinent mouth with a hot, wet passion that had her wings stirring.

"I'm not done yet." Breathless, she broke the kiss to fold down another finger. "Titus only ever wanted Southern Africa and is probably the least warlike of anyone in the Cadre. Even you, my archangel."

"Agreed." The African archangel was good-natured to the core. "My theory is that it's because he has so many siblings—he grew a big voice to be heard over all his strong-minded sisters, but he also grew up learning to share."

"You know, I think you're right. Too many only children on the Cadre." A mock scowl. "Then there's Lady Sharine. He's more interested in building a life with her than in conquest.

"Alexander," Elena continued, "has definitely mellowed

since Zanaya came out of Sleep. They also seem focused on building up and strengthening both their territories rather looking to expand—and of course, in making kissy faces of their own."

"I do believe I will dare you to say that last to Alexander's face."

"Dare taken. Please save me when he tries the old smiting." She drew his laughing face down to her own, nibbled on his lower lip.

"What about Aegaeon?" he said afterward, in no hurry to rush this slow, mutual seduction.

"Hah! You think you've got me!" Settling back against his side, she elbowed him playfully. "But I did a bit of research thanks to Jessamy, and it looks like he never makes war unless he has a partner in archangelic crime.

"By himself, Aegaeon's a lush—yeah, he rules and he keeps a good territory. But the rest of the time, he's all booze, babes, and building monuments to himself. You know what that says about the size of a man's, er . . . assets."

Raphael ran his fingers along the sensitive arch of her wings, had the pleasure of feeling her shiver. "I forgot to tell you he's just begun construction on a grand palace, across the Danube from Michaela's old palace. Word is, that one wasn't grand enough for him."

"So that takes care of Aegaeon." She folded down another finger. "Your mother is self-explanatory."

Raphael nodded as she folded that finger. In this waking, Caliane had never wanted to rule anything but Amanat. But she'd stepped into the breach when necessary and would help India heal from the trauma left by the reborn that had infested it during the war.

"I've heard Eli was aggressive in his younger years," Raphael said, "but he is akin to a calm big brother these days. Since the day of my ascension, he has always been one of the cooler heads on the Cadre."

"And Suyin," Elena said, "has eons of work ahead of her

to get China back to the thriving civilization it once was. She literally has no time for any type of archangelic pissing contest."

"That leaves Marduk."

"Do you get the impression he's just . . . *amused* by us all?" Elena bristled. "I honestly want to smack him sometimes."

Raphael threw back his head and laughed before turning to kiss his Elena's scowling mouth. *That, hbeebti, is how you ended up consort to an archangel.* No fear, no regrets, that was his Elena.

She was smiling when they broke the kiss, her eyes silvery light. "Best decision of my life." She traced the outline of his lips with a fingertip. "Getting back to your irritating ancestor, did you notice he never says he was an *actual* child during the time of the Ancestors? He only mentions his age in comparison to theirs—which is a whole different kettle of dragon scales."

"Yes. But I have a feeling Marduk isn't going to give us a straight answer there."

Elena's lips turned down. "No, I guess not. Seems like he's mostly marking time until he can go back to Sleep with his consort. Who I'd love to meet—she sounds like a badass."

Exactly like the woman by his side, Raphael thought. "He might be marking time, but he's not like Qin. He has given the Cadre his solemn oath that he will stand with us until another archangel rises to take his place, whether that is in one hundred years or in a millennium.

"Though he has also warned us that if it goes much beyond five hundred years, his consort will likely wake—and in a bad temper, so let us hope that it doesn't come to that."

"How's Astaad's territory doing with Marduk in charge? Any news?"

"Andreas called while you were with Sara and your sisters. I have the strong feeling we're not going to get him back. He has the kind of mettle to deal with Marduk, and Marduk appreciates that."

Raphael would be sorry to lose the powerful angel to another court, but he accepted that the opportunity would allow Andreas to stretch his wings. "I think Marduk will ask Andreas to be his second."

Elena whistled. "I can see it."

"But Andreas is still mine as of now, and so he has reported back—in his words, the population of powerful vampires are 'shit-scared' of Marduk. Andreas has no idea what Marduk said or did to their leadership, but they've turned as 'meek and mild as neutered dogs,' so it appears even if Marduk is marking time, he's doing his job as an archangel."

Elena put down the last of the nine fingers she'd initially raised. "There you have it. Peace. Everyone too busy with their own business and uninterested in inciting chaos."

Raphael threw up a small shower of archangelic power, golden sparks in the night. "I will be Cassandra tonight and say I foresee a future of great prosperity, advancement, and beauty. One that will be known in later times as a Golden Age full of balls, fascinating discourse, and of course, wild block parties thrown by the legendary hostess Elena Deveraux, Consort and Guild Hunter."

Elena's shoulders shook. "You know what? I think I can deal with throwing a few parties if it means the world isn't falling to pieces around us." She looked out at the city. "We've taken a few knocks together, haven't we, Archangel?"

"More than our share."

"Peace will be good." She sighed. "Can you see those white owls?"

"Oh yes." They circled gently, not far from them. "She Sleeps, but her owls watch for her."

"I hope they don't feel any need to disturb her rest for a long time. Cassandra has earned her rest—and her Qin."

She spread her fingers on his thigh. "I talked to Keir just before. He's still saying he feels no different except perhaps more centered and grounded."

"I asked Marduk if, while awake, Keir would always be the base part of the Compass, and he shrugged and told me the old ones didn't share their plans with a 'wet behind the ears' angel."

Elena snorted, then stirred, a molten heat in her blood. "You want to dance, Archangel?"

"With you, *hbeebti*? Always."

"*Knhebek*, Raphael."

"*Knhebek*, Elena."

Dropping off the roof edge with whoops as carefree as that of the children in the Refuge, they spread their wings halfway down and swept out and over the glittering heart of their city.

ABOUT GOLLANCZ

Gollancz is the oldest SF publishing imprint in the world. Since being founded in 1927 Gollancz has continued to publish a focused selection of bestselling and award-winning authors. The front-list includes **Ben Aaronovitch**, **Joe Abercrombie**, **Charlaine Harris**, **Joanne Harris**, **Joe Hill**, **Alastair Reynolds**, **Patrick Rothfuss**, **Nalini Singh** and **Brandon Sanderson**.

As one of the largest Science Fiction and Fantasy imprints in the UK it is no surprise we have one of the most extensive backlists in the world. Find high-quality SF on Gateway written by such authors as **Philip K. Dick**, **Ursula Le Guin**, **Connie Willis**, **Sir Arthur C. Clarke**, **Pat Cadigan**, **Michael Moorcock** and **George R.R. Martin**.

We also have a strand of publishing in translation, which includes French, Polish and Russian authors. Gollancz is home to more award-winning authors than any other imprint, with names including **Aliette de Bodard**, **M. John Harrison**, **Paul McAuley**, **Sarah Pinborough**, **Pierre Pevel**, **Justina Robson** and many more.

The SF Gateway
More than 3,000 classic, rare and previously out-of-print SF novels at your fingertips.
www.sfgateway.com

The Gollancz Blog
Bringing you news from our worlds to yours. Stories, interviews, articles and exclusive extracts just for you!
www.gollancz.co.uk

GOLLANCZ
LONDON